Invasion of the Chosen

Tournament of the Gods Book #3

By Timothy L. Cerepaka

An Annulus Publishing Book

Annulus Publishing, Cherokee, Texas, 2016

Published by Annulus Publishing

Formatting by Timothy L. Cerepaka

Contact: timothy@timothylcerepaka.com

Cover design by Elaina Lee of For the Muse Design
(http://www.forthemusedesign.com/)

ISBN-13: 978-0692669532

ISBN-10: 0692669531

Acknowledgements

I would like to thank my uncle, James Wilhite, for helping me get this manuscript into publishable shape. I'd also like to thank the rest of my family for supporting me while I wrote this novel. You guys rock.

Chapter One

THERE WAS THAT darkness again, the darkness that had followed Braim Kotogs, a red-haired, former mage and current participant in the Tournament of the Gods, ever since he had returned to life not long ago. The despairing darkness that he had tried to ignore, that he had successfully ignored for a while, but which had suddenly returned full force a week ago.

Braim rubbed the back of his head, where he felt the darkness, but that did not make it go away. Of course getting rid of it would not be that simple. It never was. He wasn't exactly sure what had gotten rid of it before, but perhaps it had never really been gone at all and he had only been granted a brief reprieve from the darkness for reasons unknown to him.

Braim Kotogs currently stood in the streets of World's End, an island city also known as the Throne of the Gods, which was located on the very edge of Martir. All around him, the busy minor spirits who were the primary inhabitants of the island—known properly as 'katabans'—walked and talked among each other. Some glanced at the strange human being who stood on the sidewalk, but most ignored him, because katabans in general ignored humans unless necessary.

That was okay by Braim. While he was an adventurous man

who loved excitement, he didn't like being the center of attention, especially the center of attention of the katabans. Most katabans tended to treat Braim with respect due to his status as a godling, but he still found their ways strange and he was all right with having only the most minimal of contact with them.

Even so, Braim couldn't help but stop in the street when he felt the darkness clawing at the back of his head. It was like a very bad itch, except worse because there was no real way to get rid of it. He remembered what Diog, the God of the Grave, had once told him, that the darkness was a sign that Braim was an unnatural being who should not exist.

That guy was crazy, Braim thought, shaking his head as he stepped out of the way of a katabans couple coming down the street in the direction he was going. *Just not sure if he is crazier than the Ghostly God or not.*

"Braim!" said a familiar voice behind him, causing Braim to look over his shoulder to see who it was. "Glad to see you!"

It was Malya, a short, middle-aged woman who carried two swords sheathed at her waist. She seemed to be in high spirits today, because she was walking down the street toward him at an unusually fast pace, as if she had very important news to share with him. She was even smiling, which made her look nice and also made Braim wonder just how beautiful she might have been in her younger years.

"Hey, Malya," said Braim, turning to face her, though he tried not to wince when he felt the pain in his head from the darkness. "How'd you sleep last night?"

"Wonderfully," said Malya as she stopped in front of Braim. She looked up at the clear sky and sighed. "Doesn't this weather just look great? It reminds me of Friana, except even better. That makes sense, of course, because this island is the home of the gods and all."

Braim looked up at the snatches of sky visible between the tops of the massive buildings that made up the city. It was indeed very blue, without any clouds in sight. The sun was shining, but to Braim there was something about the sun that seemed a little darker than usual. He even thought he saw something dark slither across it, though he dismissed it as his eyes playing tricks on him.

Looking down at Malya, he said, "Yeah, it is. But what are you doing here? I thought you were already at the Stadium, what with you being in the next sub-bracket challenge and all."

"I almost overslept," Malya admitted. She looked quite sheepish, playing with the curls of her hair as she said that. "I was training so hard last night for today's sub-bracket challenge that when I went back to my apartment and laid down on my bed, I immediately fell to sleep. And I probably would have slept through the whole day if the owner of the building hadn't woken me up to let me know that breakfast was ready."

Braim had to smile at that. "And then Alira would have been pissed. As usual."

"Oh, I don't want to anger her," said Malya with a shudder. "She can be very bad when she gets angry. I'm just glad that I've never gotten on her bad side. I just remember how angry she got toward Carmaz last week."

Braim's smile vanished the instant Malya mentioned Carmaz's name. Instead, it was replaced with a scowl, one Braim didn't really intend to show, but it came out anyway and he didn't bother to hide it. Just the memory of that traitor was enough to make

Braim angrier than he ever had been in his life.

Malya, to her credit, seemed to notice, because she said, "Oh, I'm sorry, Braim. I almost forgot about how you feel about Carmaz. I'm just so used to talking about him like he's a friend, but then I remember that he's no longer in the Tournament, which I still find rather sad. He was a good man, or at least I thought he was, anyway."

Braim forced himself to stop scowling and instead put on a somewhat grudging smile, which was the best he could come up with at the moment. "It's all right. I understand. We all thought Carmaz was a friend. I mean, I did, for sure, but I guess that just goes to show that you can't trust everyone, huh?"

"It sure does," said Malya.

"Anyway," said Braim, glancing at the sky again, "why don't we head to the Stadium now? We're going to be late unless we hurry on quick."

"Oh, of course," said Malya, nodding. "Lead the way, Braim."

Braim nodded and soon the two were walking down the street again, though they both walked a bit more quickly than normal in order to ensure that they would make it to the Stadium on time.

As they walked, Braim could not help but think about Carmaz, despite doing his best to avoid thinking about his former friend since he was sent back to his home island a week ago. Braim had always been told that Ruwans were an untrustworthy bunch, but he had never actually believed that until Carmaz went and betrayed him.

He helped the Ghostly God kidnap and torture me, Braim thought. *No way am I ever going to forgive that. Not unless I completely lose my mind, anyway.*

But from what Braim could tell, most of the other godlings thought of Carmaz's betrayal the way Malya did. They were mostly shocked and unable to understand why he had done it. After all, Carmaz had had a reputation as a kind, heroic, and humble figure, one you could always trust in a tight situation. Braim had especially grown to trust Carmaz after Carmaz saved Alira and several others—including Malya—from the Void, which was not a mean feat by any stretch of the imagination.

Now, however, Braim wanted nothing to do with Carmaz. The last he'd seen of the guy, Carmaz had been escorted away by a couple of Soldiers of the Gods, who had been given orders to return him to Ruwa. And to Braim's knowledge, that was exactly where Carmaz had been taken, was exactly where Carmaz *should* be, given what he did.

Though if you ask me, he got off a little too easily for all of the crap he put me through, Braim thought. He tried not to scowl because he didn't want to make Malya feel uncomfortable. *Grinf should have punished him. I mean, that's a pretty blatant injustice right there if you ask me, helping a crazy god kidnap me for his own insane schemes.*

What made Carmaz's betrayal even worse was how it had resulted in Braim losing his magical powers. Braim had assumed that his powers would return to him at some point (despite having been told otherwise by the Ghostly God), but it had been a full week since he had lost his powers and he was still no closer to regaining them than when he had lost them. Every now and then he'd grab his wand and try to cast a spell, only for nothing to happen.

It was so bad that Braim didn't even carry his wand anymore.

It was currently back at his room in the inn he was staying at, locked safely within one of the drawers. He felt awkward without it, even though it would have been useless to carry at this point.

Braim had hoped that some of the gods might try to help him regain his magical powers, but so far not a single one of the gods who called World's End their home had approached him on the subject. He wondered why that was until it occurred to him that the gods were doing their best to stay out of the Tournament and that they didn't want to cross Alira, who would most likely get onto them if she thought that they were causing trouble. Or maybe the gods just thought that Braim could handle the Tournament on his own without magic.

Of course, Braim recalled the Ghostly God telling him that not even the gods could grant magical abilities back to mortals. Only the entity known as the Mysterious One—who didn't even exist on the mortal plane—could do that, and right now Braim had no way of contacting the Mysterious One at all. He had hoped that the Mysterious One would contact him, seeing as the Mysterious One had worked with Braim's old master the Arbiter in the past, but Braim had seen no sign of the Mysterious One recently. Braim supposed that the Mysterious One was likely still in the Spirit Lands overseeing things there, but that didn't make Braim feel any better about it.

Can't he just come by for a quick minute and give me my powers back? Braim thought, kicking aside a rock on the street as he and Malya walked past a merchant who was hawking some kind of fancy silverware that he didn't pay any attention to. *Would it really kill him to do that? If he's an Almighty One, surely he should be able to do that much, at least.*

Thinking about the loss of his magical powers also made Braim think about the Ghostly God, who was at least as responsible as Carmaz for Braim's current predicament. The Ghostly God might be even more responsible, considering it had been he who had come up with the plan to kidnap Braim in the first place.

Last Braim had heard, the Ghostly God had been banished from World's End by Alira for the duration of the Tournament. Alira obviously didn't want any of the gods causing any more trouble in the Tournament, which Braim appreciated, even though he was sure that the Ghostly God would come up with some way to get around his banishment. The deity still hadn't learned all of Braim's secrets, after all, so Braim figured that it was only a matter of time before the Ghostly God tried to kidnap him again.

Well, unless I become the God of Martir, that is, Braim thought. A genuine smile appeared on his face, though it was a crueler one than normal. *Then I could dissect* him. *Or at least threaten to do it to him if he doesn't leave me alone.*

That was really the only reason Braim was even bothering to participate in the Tournament at this point. He now understood just how much danger his life was in and how powerless he was to protect himself from others who would harm him. If he won the Tournament and became the God of Martir, then no one would ever be able to harm him again. Prior to the kidnapping, he had only participated in the Tournament because Alira had told him to, but now he was eager to take on whatever challenges showed themselves and win.

And he was willing to do whatever it took to win. This new determination to win actually surprised Braim a bit, but he found that he enjoyed it quite a bit.

"Have you visited Raya recently?" asked Malya, her question snapping Braim out of his thoughts as the two of them turned down a street.

Braim looked at Malya suddenly. "What? Oh, I haven't. Have you?"

"Every day," said Malya, nodding. "I know that the doctor working on her said that she's going to be fine and that her hand and arm are going to heal, but she just looked so awful when Keeper brought her out of the basement of Anwan's shop. I thought for sure that she would die."

"So she's doing well, then?" said Braim.

"Better than she was a week ago," said Malya. "I personally think that she still looks a little pale, but she's got her attitude back and is eating again. The only problem is her hand."

"The one the Void cut off?" Braim asked as he and Malya stopped briefly to allow two burly katabans hauling a cart between them to pass.

"The new one she got," said Malya as they resumed walking. "Have you seen it?"

"No," said Braim, shaking his head. "What's it made out of?"

"Some kind of magical substance that I don't know the name of," said Malya as they resumed walking. "The doctor told me its name, but it was completely unpronounceable so I didn't catch it. It's bluish-white, though, and quite pretty."

"You mean they couldn't just use advanced panamancy to reattach Raya's old hand?" asked Braim. "Granted, I'm no panamancer, but I'd think that would be a simple thing for the katabans to do."

"The doctor said that they would have if she had lost her hand in a normal way," said Malya. "But the fact that the Void removed it makes fixing it a lot more complicated. Injuries caused by the Void seem a lot more permanent than normal injuries. Even divine magic doesn't seem to work on them, so Raya is having to make do with the fake hand they've given her."

"How is she doing with it?" asked Braim as they turned down another corner and then went down a steep street. "Is she handling it well?"

"As well as you would expect her to," said Malya. "She thought it was strange and demanded at first that they remove it, even after they explained to her why they had to do it. But I think she will get used to it eventually."

"I hope so," said Braim. "Just a question, but how has Raya handled Carmaz's betrayal and disqualification from the Tournament?"

Malya scratched her chin. "She was extremely distraught, the poor girl. She cursed out Alira and seemed to think that Alira just did that because she doesn't like Carmaz. I tried to explain to Raya that Carmaz actually did break the rules and that his disqualification, while hard, was actually legitimate, but you can guess how she responded to that."

Braim nodded. "No surprise there. Do you think she'll be at the Stadium as well?"

"Maybe," said Malya. "I don't know for sure, though, because despite the magical healing she's received, she still seemed to be recovering the last time I saw her. I'm sure she'll be fine in the end, though. She's a lot stronger than she looks."

"If you say so," said Braim.

9

After a few more minutes of walking, the two reached the Stadium, where they found a handful of stragglers entering the Stadium. Among them were Yoji and Tashir, who stood outside of the Stadium arguing about something that Braim only got to hear the very end of, from the sound of it.

"... No, Limitlessness is *not* sustainable," said Yoji, who had his arms folded over his chest with an annoyed look on his face. "It is a fact established by centuries of magical research and tradition. Mortal bodies cannot handle Limitlessness for very long."

"That may be true for some, but there are just as many people who can handle Limitlessness better than others," said Tashir. "What about Darek Takren? He's supposed to be a Limitless and to my knowledge, he is doing well."

Braim was surprised to hear them talking about Darek. Darek was a friend of his, one of the few he had, but he had never believed that people outside of North Academy actually knew about him. Then again, Braim supposed it made sense, seeing as Darek was one of the few mages in the world who had achieved the state of Limitlessness, which meant that he had no limit to the amount of magical power he could use. Braim had heard that that was rather uncommon and believed impossible by most mages, though he didn't see what was so impossible about it if Darek could do it.

Of course, thinking about Darek's Limitlessness made him think about his own complete lack of magical ability again. That thought made the darkness in the back of his head even more insistent and painful, but he ignored it as best as he could as he and Malya approached the two arguing mages.

"Hey, guys, what's up?" said Braim as he and Malya stopped before them. "Has the sub-bracket challenge started yet?"

"Greetings, Braim, Malya," said Tashir, nodding at them both. "But no, the sub-bracket challenge hasn't. Yoji and I had simply gotten caught up in a discussion about Limitlessness."

"An argument that I am winning, by the way," said Yoji. "So far, Tashir hasn't made much of a good case against mine."

"Only because you refuse to look at the facts," Tashir said, rolling his eyes. He pointed at Braim. "Braim, you know Darek Takren, don't you? The Limitless Mage, right?"

"The Limitless Mage?" Braim repeated. "Is that what they're calling him now?"

"Among us aquarian mages, yes," said Tashir, nodding. "It was Archmage Yorak who began to call him that, actually. Why? Isn't he known for his Limitlessness among you humans?"

"Frankly, I couldn't say," said Braim with a shrug. "It's not like I've been back to life long enough to find out what other people call one of my friends."

"Ah," said Tashir. "Well, it doesn't matter, because the point is that Darek exists and that his existence proves that Limitlessness is indeed possible."

Yoji looked quite angry about Tashir's point, but rather than actually refute it, he just threw up his hands into the air and said, "Well, who cares, anyway? We need to go into the Stadium and get ready for the next challenge, anyway. At least Malya does."

Tashir smirked, but instead of pushing the point, he simply nodded and said, "I agree. I would rather not get on Alira's bad side today, though I have a feeling that she will be short with us anyway."

"Why?" asked Braim. "Is she in a bad mood today or something?"

"Yes," said Tashir. "Or rather, she's been in a bad mood all week. I was outside the city walls this morning, training with my sword, when I saw her walking along the beach grumbling under her breath about something."

"Huh," said Braim, scratching the side of his head. "Why was she out on the beach? She never struck me as the kind of woman who enjoys long walks on the beach."

Tashir shrugged. "I do not know. When she saw me, she told me to go train elsewhere because she wanted to be alone. I obeyed her because she seemed likely to kick me out of the Tournament if I refused."

"So you didn't find out anything about why she wanted you gone?" asked Braim. "Nothing at all?"

"Sadly, I did not," said Tashir with a sigh. "I tried to ask her, but she did not want to answer any of my questions. But one thing I did notice about her was how she seemed to be waiting for someone, because when I left she began pacing back and forth on the same few feet of sand, looking out to the ocean every now and then like she expected someone to rise out of it."

"Wonder who she was going to meet," said Braim. "You don't think she has a boyfriend, do you?"

"If so, then I think Samvan is going to be very disappointed," said Tashir. "But truly, no. It might have been one of the gods, perhaps Anke, the Goddess of the Sea, but I am not sure."

"Eh, it's probably not worth worrying about," said Braim, shaking his head. He gestured at the entrance to the Stadium. "Let's just go inside now, because I don't want to be late."

"All right," said Tashir. He frowned. "I forget, which challenge was it again? The Avian Goddess one or the Skimif one?"

"Avian Goddess," said Malya as the four of them started walking toward the entrance. "So that would be me, though I don't know what the challenge will be."

"No surprise there," said Braim as he pushed open the doors and stepped aside to allow the other three to enter after him. "Alira *never* tells anyone what the challenge will be ahead of time. Kind of annoying if you ask me."

"But it's worked out so far, hasn't it?" asked Tashir as he, Yoji, and Malya entered the lobby, which was full of the rest of the godlings, who were still talking among each other and did not seem to notice their entrance. "Though I agree that it would be a lot better if she at least gave us a clue ahead of time so we could properly prepare. The challenge I participated in had nothing to do with sword-fighting, so I did a lot of sword training for no reason."

Braim closed the doors behind them when they all entered and looked at the crowd of godlings standing in the lobby. The crowd was noticeably thinner in comparison to the first day of the Tournament, which Braim realized had to do with the fact that about thirty of the godlings had already been eliminated from the roster so far.

And once these next two challenges are finished, we'll be down to fifty, Braim thought. *And I'll hopefully be one of those fifty.*

Oddly enough, however, Braim did not see Alira anywhere, even when he looked above the heads of the other godlings at the platform where she usually stood over them. As far as Braim could tell, Alira was nowhere to be seen at all, which troubled him because Alira was never late or absent for any of the sub-bracket challenges.

"Wonder where Alira is," said Braim. "It's almost time for the next sub-bracket challenge to start, isn't it?"

"It is," said Malya, nodding. She rubbed her hands together anxiously. "Perhaps she is finalizing the details of the challenge."

At that moment, Samvan, with his black, shoulder-length hair and dark skin, walked by, causing Tashir to say, "Samvan! Where is Alira?"

Samvan stopped and looked at them and shrugged. "I don't know. That's actually what I've been trying to do is figure out why she isn't here yet. I thought she'd be here already, but I haven't seen her all day and no one else seems to know where she is, either."

Samvan did sound genuinely worried for Alira, but Braim was not surprised. He had learned that Samvan had a crush on the Judge of the Tournament, which seemed like a very strange thing to him. Sure, Alira was a beautiful woman, but her cold attitude and almost fanatical adherence to the Tournament's rules made her unattractive to Braim.

Different strokes for different folks, I guess, Braim thought.

"This isn't like Alira at all, to be late and to not let us know ahead of time that she will be," said Samvan. He rubbed the back of his neck and looked back toward the empty stone platform that Alira usually stood upon. "Something must have happened to her, but it can't have been anything serious because I walked past her living quarters on my way down here and I didn't see anything out of the ordinary when I passed."

"Where *does* Alira stay, anyway?" said Braim. "I don't remember her ever telling me."

"In the Temple of the Gods," said Samvan, looking back at Braim. "She wanted to sleep in the Stadium, but it was not built with a living quarters for individuals, so the gods allowed her to stay at the Temple instead."

"You sure seem to know a lot about her," Braim said. "Did she tell you that?"

Samvan looked a little sheepish as he scratched the back of his head. "Well, it's more that I learned that stuff through observation, really, rather than conversation with her."

Braim understood 'observation' to mean 'stalking' in this case, but before he could say anything, Malya grabbed his arm and said, "Do you feel that?"

Despite Malya's petite form, her hand gripped Braim almost too painfully. He tugged his arm out of her hand, but Malya still looked as serious as ever.

"Feel what?" said Braim. "What are you talking about?"

"Oh, of course you can't," said Malya, shaking her head. "What I mean is that spike of divine energy. You probably can't feel it because you lost your magical powers. Sorry about that."

Braim looked at Yoji and Tashir. The two of them also looked like they had sensed this 'spike of divine energy,' which Braim did not understand. He felt rather embarrassed that he couldn't feel it, as he was certain that he could have felt it if he had still had his magical powers.

"Yes, I felt it as well," said Tashir. "But that could only mean that one of the gods is—"

15

Tashir's words were interrupted by a sudden column of white-hot fire exploding into existence on the platform where Alira usually stood. The sudden appearance of the column of fire caused the crowd of godlings to look up at it in surprise. A handful of the jumpier ones started, including Samvan, who nearly fell on his behind when he landed, and Yoji, who dropped his wand onto the stone floor but hastily picked it up before anyone noticed.

Then the column of fire vanished, revealing that it was not Alira who stood on the platform. Instead, a large, muscular man in golden armor, wielding a massive burning hammer, stood on the platform. He had dark skin, like that of a Carnagian, and golden hair. His eyes were literally flame and he radiated so much heat that even Braim could feel it from all the way on the other side of the lobby.

The newcomer looked down upon them all with a harsh, judgmental frown, like that of a judge looking down at a criminal who was obviously guilty of committing a horrid crime. And despite being on his own, the newcomer looked like he could completely destroy them all if he wanted to.

"Who is that?" Braim asked Malya, though he asked it in a whisper because he didn't want the newcomer to hear him.

"That's Grinf," said Malya. Her voice was disbelieving. "The God of Justice, Metal, and Fire. And also the patron god of Carnag, if I am not mistaken."

"What's he doing here?" asked Braim. He gulped. "You don't think he's going to punish us for some law we broke a long time ago, do you?"

Malya shrugged. "I have no idea. Let's listen and find out

what he has to say. Maybe he will tell us what happened to Alira."

Braim nodded and looked back to the god. Braim had heard much about Grinf, as he was one of the more famous gods due to being considered the patron of one of the most powerful nations in the world, but this was the first time he'd seen Grinf in person. It was hard not to stare at the sheer power that Grinf radiated, power so obvious that even Braim could sense it.

Grinf raised his mighty gavel and said, in an authoritative voice that reminded Braim of the eruption of a volcano, "Godlings of Martir, my human name is Grinf, the God of Justice, Metal, and Fire, but my aquarian name is Druom. You may refer to me by either name. It makes no difference to me."

Braim blinked, but then recalled that humans and aquarians had different names for the gods. It seemed confusing to him, but he decided that it wasn't worth worrying about at the moment. He listened more closely to Grinf as the god continued to speak.

"Now, according to the schedule, the Avian Goddess Sub-Bracket Challenge is due to begin very soon," said Grinf, who glanced at a clock on the walls. "Therefore, I must ask all Avian Goddess Bracket challengers to—"

A hand shot up from the crowd of godlings, which Braim noticed was from Samvan. The former prison guard was holding up his hand as high as he could, even stepping on tiptoes in an attempt to make sure that Grinf saw his hand. It was rather embarrassing to Braim, but Samvan didn't seem to notice or care what Braim thought.

Grinf, however, did notice, though he didn't look happy about it. Still, he addressed Samvan, saying, "Godling, what do you have to say? I do not tolerate unnecessary interruptions, so your question had better be intelligent or I may not allow you to ask another."

"Yes, Lord Grinf, I understand," said Samvan, who still held up his hand. "My question is this: Where is Judge Alira? She is supposed to be the Judge of the Tournament, isn't she? So why isn't she here now? Why are you in her place? I mean no disrespect by this question, Lord Grinf, I just don't understand what is going on here."

The annoyance on Grinf's face vanished, though the god still didn't look happy. He just said, "That is a wise question. I was going to inform you all later, but I suppose there is no further point in delaying informing you all of what happened to her. Very well: Judge Alira is missing and, until she is found, I am to take her place as the Judge of the Tournament of the Gods."

Chapter Two

PRINCESS RAYA MANA, daughter of King Tojas Malock and Queen Hanarova, Princess of Carnag, did not like to look at her new hand. In fact, most of the time she pretended it wasn't even there. She sometimes liked to believe that she hadn't actually lost one of her hands, that it had all been a very scary dream, but every time that illusion would be shattered when she looked over at her hand or unconsciously attempted to grab or touch something with it.

Right now, Raya lay in her bed in her apartment, her right arm —and by extension, her new, artificial hand—underneath the blankets; her other hand was not. Instead, her left hand was holding open a book that the katabans doctor had given her. He had told her that by reading this book every day, it would help speed up the process of healing. He had said that it was an old katabans medical technique that was very popular and effective for healing these types of magical injuries.

But Raya didn't really understand what he meant by that. Raya couldn't even read the words in the book because they were written in another language entirely. The only parts of the book that she understood were the illustrations, but even they were strange, because the artist's style was very abstract, hardly straightforward or understandable, which was her preferred art style.

Still, Raya tried to read the book anyway because it distracted her from her hand. Though she didn't really think of it as *her* hand. It was more like a foreign appendage that had been forcibly attached to her arm due to the loss of her original hand.

Raya remembered well how the katabans doctor, who had introduced himself as Ilran, had attached her new hand to her arm. He had assured her that it would not be a painful process and had also made some weird quip about how her new hand might help her get out of a sticky situation one day, but when he placed her hand against the stump that was her arm, it had burned as hotly as if she had been set on fire and so she had screamed.

Granted, at the time Raya had just barely recovered from the Void's assault on her, which may have been part of the reason for the pain, but Raya still felt pain from her wrist every now and then. It was a sharp pain, too, and didn't seem to be getting better at all. If anything, Raya believed that the pain was getting worse, because it was getting harder and harder for her to ignore with each and every passing day.

Raya lowered her book just then and, against her will, pulled her artificial hand out from under her blankets. It gleamed silver in the candlelight from her bed and the fingers moved as naturally and easily as the fingers of her left hand. Even so, Raya loathed it and was tempted to rip it off, but she decided against trying it because she was pretty sure that it was stuck on as firmly as her original hand had been, if not more firmly, and besides she had already seen more than enough of her own blood to last a lifetime, so she was not in the mood to see any more ever again.

It is an unnatural abomination, Raya thought, lowering her artificial hand and averting her eyes from it. *It is awful. I cannot imagine ever using this voluntarily. I should have rejected the doctor's offer to attach it. Simply awful.*

Raya then looked around her room. She was all alone, but she knew that Keeper was somewhere nearby. He wasn't in her room with her, or in her apartment. He had instead returned to the ethereal, where he promised to watch her and keep her safe. He had also said that he was going to go to Carnag to tell her parents about what had happened to her, which both relieved and worried Raya. It relieved her because she believed that her parents would probably send her something nice—maybe a new dress—to make her feel better, but it worried her because she didn't want her parents worried about her well-being, especially when there was nothing they could do about it.

Though Raya *was* annoyed at how her parents had sent Keeper to protect her without first telling her that. She felt betrayed by their deceit, even though she knew that her parents had only had her best interests at heart. She wanted to go to Carnag and demand that both of them explain why they had refused to tell her about Keeper, but she supposed that she wouldn't get to do that anytime soon, as she doubted Alira would let her or any of the other godlings leave World's End for any reason until the Tournament was over.

Thus, Raya had nothing to do except lie in bed and wait until the doctor said that she was well enough to get up and leave. When that would be, she didn't know, which only added to her frustrations with the world right now.

So bored, Raya thought with a yawn. *I've been lying in bed all week. I wish I could have gone to the Stadium and watched the next sub-bracket challenge instead.*

But Ilran had told Raya that she needed to stay in her bed. He had said that she had suffered a very traumatic experience and that she needed plenty of bed rest before she could be allowed to walk around the city on her own again. Raya supposed he had a point, because even when she just thought about walking, it made her legs feel shaky and weak.

But my room is just so boring, Raya thought, looking around at her room again. *No one to talk to, not even any good men to look at. Just this stupid boring old book that I can't even read.*

Raya closed the book and put it back on the nightstand by her bed. She then slumped down in her pillows and blankets, wondering if the next sub-bracket challenge in the Tournament was about to begin or not.

It doesn't really matter, I guess, Raya thought with a sigh. *It's not like I am going to get to see it. I wish I could, because that would be infinitely more interesting than lying here in bed all by myself.*

Thinking about the Tournament caused Raya's mind to wander over to Carmaz. She scowled at the thought of him, her grip tightening on her blankets in frustration.

Raya didn't know why Carmaz had to go and break the rules like that. She had only learned about his disqualification from the Tournament after he was long gone. By then, it was impossible to argue with Alira and persuade her to change her mind. Not that Raya had tried, because she was still resting in bed and hadn't left her bed since she had been placed on it a week ago.

Even so, Raya knew just how stubborn Alira was. She could imagine the Judge telling her that it didn't matter what she, Raya, thought about her judgment. What mattered, Alira would most likely say, is that Carmaz broke the rules and thus must suffer the same consequences that all rule breakers do.

But Raya thought that Carmaz should have been pardoned for his rule-breaking. According to Malya, Carmaz had been the only member of the group that had attacked Anwan's shop to actually go down into the dark chamber where the Void was and try to save her from Anwan. He had gone down without bringing any of the others with him or even telling them where he had gone.

It was the most heroic thing that Raya had ever heard of anybody doing. Yet rather than be rewarded for it, as he should have been, Carmaz was punished for it by being kicked out of the Tournament.

And it is all *because of Braim Kotogs,* Raya thought. *Because he told Alira that Carmaz had helped the Ghostly God kidnap him. If Braim had kept that information to himself, then Carmaz would still be here with me.*

Raya had not seen Braim at all since the battle at Anwan's Tailoring. Braim had not even attempted to visit her, which she was sure was because he didn't want to face her wrath. He was probably feeling very full of himself at the moment, she thought, feeling very proud that he had exposed the actions of someone who had 'broken' the rules. And she hated him for it.

I wonder how Braim would feel if he was disqualified from the Tournament after doing something very heroic, Raya thought. *He'd probably be upset then, wouldn't be so proud and full of himself after that.*

Unfortunately, Raya was not sure how to get back at Braim for what he did to Carmaz. She considered framing him for breaking one of the rules, but that seemed too risky, because there was always the chance that she would be caught and then kicked out of the Tournament as well. And as much as she loved Carmaz, she wasn't quite ready to give up a chance at godhood just to be with him.

But it would be a lot of fun to do that, Raya thought. *I mean, I'm in the running to become the next Goddess of Deception, after all. Why not embrace that role by doing what any self-respecting Goddess of Deception would do in this situation?*

Just as Raya began to think about how she would achieve this (and she knew she would do this because she had to, if only for Carmaz's sake), she heard the door to her apartment open and close. The sound made her freeze, especially when she did not hear any footsteps following the opening and closing of the doors. She sat up in bed and listened hard, but did not hear anything else in her little apartment.

"Doctor Ilran?" Raya called, raising her voice to make sure that whoever was on the other side of the door could hear her. "Is that you?"

There was no response. That told Raya that she had either heard nothing at all or perhaps had heard the door to one of the apartments next door open instead. That was possible, seeing as Raya was not the only person in this apartment building, but the opening and closing of the door had sounded like it had come from just outside the door to her room.

There's no way that anyone could even get into my apartment anyway, Raya thought, glancing at the key lying on her nightstand. *Only three people on World's End have access to my room: Myself, the apartment owner, and Doctor Ilran. But if it was Ilran who just entered, then he would have announced his presence. He's not exactly the quiet, unassuming type, after all.*

The problem now was that Raya still didn't hear anything. That meant that either the person who entered the apartment was standing completely still or was simply moving very silently. Whatever the case, it made Raya feel very uncomfortable, knowing that there was a stranger in her apartment who she could do nothing about.

If this person is going to try and harm me, then I can't even defend myself, Raya thought with a gulp. *Keeper might be nearby, but he might also still be back at Carnag explaining to my parents what happened. I wish Carmaz was here to protect me, but I guess I'm on my own for now.*

Then Raya heard the sounds of light footsteps making their way to her door. She immediately grabbed the book on her nightstand, as it was the only 'weapon' she currently had access to, and held it close to her chest, ready to throw it as soon as the intruder, whoever he or she was, entered he room. Assuming the intruder was smart at all, throwing the book probably would only delay him a little. Still, it was better than nothing, in her opinion, so she readied her aim, holding her breath to make sure that she didn't make any unnecessary noises that would allow the intruder to hear her before she wanted him to.

Then the doorknob turned. As the door slowly pushed open, Raya lifted up her book, ready to throw it the minute the intruder showed his face in her apartment. She was not, however, prepared for what she saw.

Standing in the doorway was a person she had never seen before. The person was a blonde-haired, pale-skinned woman with violet eyes that pegged her as an Itrijan. She wore gray, ragged-looking mage's robes, with a wand in her right hand. She looked a little bit older than Raya herself, but not by much, although the age lines on her face and the few gray hairs scattered among her blonde hair made her look slightly older than she probably was.

"Ah," said the woman. Her voice was rather shrill and harsh. "Look what we have here. Princess Raya Mana, Princess of Carnag, I assume?"

Raya, who continued to hold her book up and ready to throw, blinked, but said, "Of course that's who I am. Who are you? You're not one of the godlings."

"Of course I'm not," said the woman, shaking her head. She made a face. "I would never want to become a goddess. Sure, that would boost my magical power to heights even I can't imagine, but then I'd be stuck with those divine idiots for the rest of my life. No, I'm much happier as a Limitless mortal, even though everyone and their dog wants me dead."

"You still haven't answered my question," Raya pointed out. "Who are you? Are you a heathen, perhaps?"

"You could describe me as such," said the woman. "Truthfully, though, I prefer to think of myself as a woman who rages against the gods. 'Heathen' implies I am part of some greater social movement to liberate humanity, but I really don't give a damn about liberating anything. I just want revenge, plain and simple."

"Revenge?" Raya repeated. "Revenge against who?"

"The gods," said the woman, gesturing at the ceiling. "The ones who have repeatedly treated me as less than because they don't need me anymore. And men, too. Most of the people in my life who've treated me badly are men, though I hate the gods more."

"What are you doing in my apartment?" asked Raya. "Are you going to harm me?"

"Actually, I'm not," said the woman, shaking her head. "Instead, I'm here to kidnap you."

"Kidnap me?" Raya repeated. "What makes you think that I would ever allow you—or anyone else—to kidnap me? I prefer not to be kidnapped, thank you very much."

"Because you are currently too weak from your recent encounter with the Void to put up too much of a fight," the woman said. She smiled. "Don't look so shocked. I've done my research. I know all about what's been going on in this little corner of the world now. Well, not everything, but enough to tell me that this is the perfect opportunity to get the revenge I so want."

"You still haven't told me your name," said Raya. "What is it?"

"Aorja Kitano," said the woman. "Recognize it?"

"No," said Raya, shaking her head. "Should I?"

"You should," said the woman. "But if you don't, it's not an issue. I don't care if my name is known by spoiled brats like you. All I care about doing is kidnapping you, which I can do even if you don't know who I am."

Raya didn't trust this Aorja woman one bit. Yet it was pretty clear that there was not much she could do to resist Aorja. After all, she really was rather tired and weak from the Void's attack on her. That meant she was in the perfect condition for a psychotic

27

woman like Aorja to kidnap her and do only the gods know what to her.

But then an idea occurred to Raya, an idea to save herself, and she said, "Oh, I wouldn't kidnap me if I were you, because I have a bodyguard who is very nasty."

"Bodyguard?" said Aorja. She looked around the room. "I don't see anyone else here, nor did I see anyone in the hallway outside your room."

"That's because he exists in the ethereal," Raya said. "He's a massive automaton, bigger than you and me combined, and more than willing to kill anyone who threatens my safety. He'll strike you down the moment you try to harm me and leave you a bloody pulp as a result."

Aorja almost looked worried for a second, but then she said, "Well, if that was the case, then why didn't he kill me as soon as I entered your room? Is he taking a nap?"

"Because he wanted to lull you into a false sense of security, of course," said Raya without missing a beat. "The minute you try to touch me, he'll pop out of the ethereal and shoot you dead. He'll shoot you so much that there won't be anything left of you to bury."

"That's a rather audacious claim," said Aorja. "But I think you're lying, because if this automaton bodyguard of yours actually existed, then I would be dead already. So no, I don't believe a word you said, but nice try."

Damn it, Raya thought. *She's too smart. Or maybe I need to come up with a better lie.*

"So," said Aorja, "because you are obviously incapable of defending yourself from me, I think I'll knock you out for a bit.

That will make you a lot easier to carry out of here."

"But where are you going to take me and why are you kidnapping me?" asked Raya. "What have I done to you?"

"Nothing," said Aorja. "Really, I honestly don't give a damn about you. I only need you for the rest of my plan. Otherwise, I wouldn't even look in your direction."

Raya felt more than a bit offended at the implication that Aorja didn't think she was very important. Of course Raya was important. She was the Princess of Carnag, after all, and on her way to becoming an actual goddess. She thought that that, at least, should be enough to make her important, but Aorja apparently disagreed.

"As for where I am going to take you, are you really that naïve?" said Aorja with a laugh. "That's generally not how kidnappings work. But you'll find out soon enough. So why don't you take a quick nap? I promise to wake you up as soon as we get to where I am taking you."

Before Raya could argue with Aorja, the mage raised her wand and jabbed it in Raya's direction.

Without warning, Raya suddenly found it impossible to stay awake. She tried to fight her sleepiness, but despite her best efforts, she soon lost all consciousness and drifted into a deep slumber.

Chapter Three

CARMAZ KORVA STOOD over the fire outside his hut, carefully stoking it every now and then to ensure that it would not go out. He glanced at the dead swamp rat skewered over it, which he had caught about an hour ago. It was going to be his lunch, but first he needed to get the fire to the right temperature in order to properly cook the rodent. He wanted to eat it right away, because it had been hours since his last meal and his stomach growled every now and then to remind him of that.

But even so, Carmaz didn't think he'd enjoy it even if it was cooked to perfection already (which he knew it wasn't). He'd eat it because he had nothing else to eat, but he still remembered the good food he used to eat on World's End. In particular, there was a kind of dark meat that he had been given, which the katabans had called *kalack*, which had tasted something like squid and butter. It had been his favorite meal there, but he doubted he'd ever have it again.

Standing up from his fire, Carmaz looked around the tiny camp he called home. Even calling it a 'camp' was too kind. He didn't even really have a tent. All he had was a thick, old piece of canvas that he had found washed up on the beach the day after he returned from World's End, plus the few belongings that the people of Conewood, his old hometown, had allowed him to take with him, such as the lock-pick that his grandfather had given him and an old pillow and blankets.

Conewood ... Carmaz shook his head. He should have expected the people to kick him out when he returned. He remembered how they had treated him when he and Saia had announced that they were going to World's End, and now that they knew that he had lost the Tournament (though he had not told them why, mostly because they had not asked), they had kicked him out of the village he had called home for all of his life. And rather violently, too. Carmaz felt the scar on the side of his face from where Barc had slashed at him with a knife, a scar he was sure he was going to carry for the rest of his life.

As a result, Carmaz had had to go deep into the wilderness, away from Conewood and the other villages, into the Swamp of Light, where he had found a tiny clearing that no one seemed to be using. Working hard every day, Carmaz had set up makeshift fences around the area, made mostly of brush and branches from the trees, in order to let any travelers know that it was his little piece of the island, and to keep out any animals that came nearby.

Not that I expect to get any travelers, Carmaz thought as he poked the fire with a stick he carried with him. *No doubt news of my failure has reached the other villages on the island. If anyone comes after me, it will probably be a pirate of some sort or maybe a wild animal.*

Carmaz didn't feel sorry for himself too much. He had had more than enough time to think about Alira's judgment. He realized that, regardless of his motives, he had broken the rules and that Alira had already warned him and the other godlings that breaking the rules was always grounds for instant disqualification, no questions asked. Carmaz always valued fair play, so he did not blame Alira for making that decision.

What did upset him—at least when he had a few minutes to think about it, which was rare due to how busy he had been over the past week—was the fact that Ruwa's fate was indeed sealed now. His participation in the Tournament of the Gods had been Ruwa's brightest and last hope in centuries, but with his loss, there was no one else in the Tournament to represent Ruwa. Whoever would become the next God of Humans would likely ignore Ruwa, just as the last God of Humans did, and then the next God of Martir would also neglect the Ruwans and leave them to squabble and fight over what scraps were left on their dead island.

Braim might become the next God of Martir, Carmaz thought. *And he's not going to treat Ruwa any differently than Skimif had. In fact, he will probably treat it even worse because he will remember how I helped the Ghostly God to kidnap him.*

All of this would have been bearable, perhaps, if the Ghostly God's research on Braim had actually bore any fruit. But as far as Carmaz knew, the Ghostly God's research had revealed nothing new about the resurrection process. Saia was dead and would stay dead.

And I betrayed his memory, Carmaz thought, feeling the growing heat of the fire over which he cooked his swamp rat. It was better than the cold rain that had been falling on the trees recently. *If Saia knew what I had done, I bet he would be back in Conewood now just like everyone else, disappointed in my sheer stupidity. What a pathetic man I am.*

Of course, it was impossible not to think about the Void when he thought about Saia. In particular, he kept seeing the Void's possession of Saia's body in his mind's eye, especially when he slept. It had been a grotesque insult to Saia's memory and had shaken Carmaz far more than anything else he had experienced on World's End. The black skin, the cruel green eyes, the distorted voice … it had all been perfectly calculated to destroy Carmaz's mental fortitude and make him doubt himself.

If the Void were here right now, I'd stab her in the face, Carmaz thought. *Even if she wore Saia's face … no, not his face. Maybe that was his body, but that wasn't him, not at all. It was a puppet, pure and simple.*

Carmaz had no idea what happened to Saia's body after Raya had banished it to the ethereal. He suspected that the katabans must have gotten rid of it, but he didn't know that for sure and he wasn't sure that he would ever find out.

Now the flames of the fire were starting to lick the underside of the skewered rat. Carmaz turned the spit over to get its back cooked as well and then realized that he was thirsty. He reached for his flask, which was tied to his waist by a string, only to discover that the flask was empty.

Looks like I'll need to refill it, Carmaz thought. *But that would mean leaving behind my swamp rat undefended. Something might crawl out of the bushes and steal it while I'm away.*

It was a difficult decision, but Carmaz was very thirsty and did not want to put it off any longer. So he grabbed the swamp rat's spit off the flame and carried it by his side. He would take it with him to the nearby pond with drinkable water in it. He would rather not, but Carmaz had learned the hard way that leaving out freshly-cooked food unprotected in the wilderness was the best way to attract hungry, wild beasts that only cared about their own survival and not the property of other beings.

So Carmaz climbed over the makeshift fence surrounding his territory, made his way down the very rough, muddy, and ill-defined path he had carved out since discovering this spot, and eventually arrived at the pond he used for drinking water. It was a very small, muddy pond, probably filled with all kinds of unhealthy things, but Carmaz did not have access to a well or anything else, so he just made do with what he had. He hadn't gotten sick so far, which either meant that Dranyx's luck was on him or the water wasn't as dirty as he thought.

Bending over the water, Carmaz dipped his flask into it. But then he paused. He sensed the presence of another being in the area. He hadn't heard or smelled or seen anything, but Carmaz had lived on Ruwa long enough to just know when he was alone and when he was not even without any evidence to support that feeling.

And right now, Carmaz was aware that he was not alone at all. He raised his head, still holding his flask in the pond, and did a cursory scan of the trees and bushes around him. He saw nothing, but his survival instincts still told him to get his water and leave quickly before the being he sensed found him.

So Carmaz hastily filled his flask up—no doubt also getting some mud and leaves in it, but he didn't care about that at the moment—and stood up just as a loud *crack*, like that of a tree limb being snapped off a tree, filled the air. He looked around in time to see a tree falling toward him at an alarming speed.

Carmaz jumped backwards out of the tree's path. Even so,

when the tree slammed into the ground, it splashed water and mud all over him. Carmaz furiously wiped the muddy water out of his eyes and looked to his left, in the direction that the tree had fallen from, in order to find out who or what had tried to squash him with that tree. He had expected to see a pirate, as pirates were sometimes known to come inland to chop down trees to get wood for their ships, but the thing standing behind the tree's stump was no human at all.

Yes, it was humanoid, certainly, but its skin was made out of stone and its eyes were nothing more than carved round holes from which purple lights glowed. The creature's hands were also stone, but instead of normal hands, it had a saw for its right hand and a sword for its left, which were also made out of stone. The stone giant was twice as tall as Carmaz but five times as thick. A smell of ancient stone somehow emanated from its body over the stink of the Swamp, which was amazing because the Swamp water's smell was powerful.

Carmaz had never seen anything like this creature in his life. It reminded him somewhat of the remains of the broken statues at Castle Ruwa, except unlike the statues, it looked nothing like a human being whatsoever. He didn't think it was a god or katabans, either, because he was pretty certain that there weren't any gods or katabans that looked like that.

The stone behemoth, whatever it was, raised its hands, which folded back to reveal two empty holes in its arms. Then two normal, five-fingered hands emerged from within its thick forearms and the stone behemoth grabbed the end of the tree and began to drag it away.

Surprised, Carmaz stepped back farther from the tree as the

35

stone behemoth dragged it through the mud. He had thought that the stone behemoth was going to attack him, but with the way it dragged the tree, it was almost like the stone behemoth didn't even notice him, as though he was nothing more than an insect.

"Hey!" Carmaz called as the stone behemoth dragged the tree away inch by inch. "Who are you? Where did you come from? Are you from Ruwa?"

The stone behemoth looked up at Carmaz for only a second before returning its attention to the tree. Then the stone behemoth suddenly stopped dragging the tree and paused where it stood. It might have been thinking, though about what, Carmaz couldn't tell because the stone behemoth's 'face,' if you could call it that, didn't show any expression that Carmaz recognized.

Then the stone behemoth walked, albeit slowly, around the tree, each loud footstep splashing water into the air. The stone behemoth did not seem bothered by the mud clinging to its legs and thighs. It simply made its way over to the middle of the tree, at which point Carmaz could now see that the stone behemoth was covered in markings that might have been a language, though it didn't look like any language that he knew of.

The stone behemoth then raised its right hand, which retracted to its forearm, at which point it was replaced by the saw from earlier. The stone behemoth then brought its saw hand back down on the tree's center.

Another loud *crack* and the tree split in two clean down the middle. The stone behemoth nodded, pleased with its progress, and then lifted up the lower half of the tree and placed it on its shoulders. Still not paying attention to Carmaz, it turned and began walking back into the swamp, somehow avoiding sinking into the muddy earth that it walked upon, even though it was probably very heavy.

Carmaz just stood there in surprise, uncertain what to do, watching the stone behemoth as it walked away. He considered ignoring the creature and going back to his camp and getting some rest, because he was pretty sure that this was nothing more than a hallucination brought on by the bad water he had been drinking since returning to Ruwa.

On the other hand, Carmaz didn't trust that stone behemoth at all. While Carmaz had never explored the entirety of Ruwa, he knew enough about his home island to be one hundred percent certain that there were no giant stone behemoths like that creature walking around the Swamp of Light. There were legends of strange and terrifying creatures, like the flesh-eating tree, living in the Swamp, but none of those legends had ever mentioned a stone behemoth like this.

Carmaz's instincts told him that he should follow the damn thing and figure out what it was and where it was going. It didn't seem very dangerous, despite its large size, because it had completely ignored him when it was cutting up that tree and perhaps couldn't even see him, because he was pretty sure it didn't have any eyes. As a matter of fact, Carmaz now figured that it hadn't chopped down that tree to kill him. It had probably not even noticed him standing there.

Even so, the fact was that this creature was titanic and monstrous. With its sword and saw, combined with its obviously massive strength, Carmaz knew that the behemoth could easily cause a lot of trouble if it wanted. It might even attack Conewood at some point, which made Carmaz shiver with dread, because

Conewood was his home and he did not want it destroyed, even though he was banished from it.

So Carmaz, as quietly as he could, walked after the stone behemoth, which was still visible through the trees of the swamp, hoping that he would be able to find out where it was going before nightfall, because it was never a wise thing to be out in the Swamp after dark.

The stone behemoth was easy to follow. Its heavy footsteps splashed loudly in the muddy ground, it walked through tree limbs and brush without effort, and moved at a slow but steady pace. It never looked to the side, never looked over its shoulder, and never stopped. It simply kept walking as if it had an important date that it could not miss.

Carmaz kept a good distance from it, however, because he didn't want it to notice him. Sure, it didn't seem to notice anything around it or even in its immediate path, but Carmaz had lived on Ruwa long enough to know that you did not underestimate the strange creatures that lived in the Swamp of Light. Once, he had seen one of the villagers from Conewood get swallowed whole by a wide-mouth, a rare giant plant found in certain parts of the Swamp that looked like a beautiful rose but was actually capable of swallowing living beings whole.

Speaking of a wide-mouth, Carmaz noticed that the stone behemoth was walking directly toward one. This wide-mouth was much larger than any wide-mouth that Carmaz had seen. In fact, it was almost as big as a tree and its rose-like scent was almost overwhelming even from a distance. It stood still, however, and showed no indication of its true nature until the stone behemoth was only a few feet away from it.

Then, faster than Carmaz's eyes could follow, the wide-mouth opened its petals to reveal a gaping maw full of sharp, barb-like teeth. It then latched over the stone behemoth's head, clamping down hard.

But then the wide-mouth made a weird growling sound and let go, pulling its head back quickly. Carmaz noticed that its teeth were cracked, probably as a result of trying to bite down on the stone behemoth's rock hard skin, but before the wide-mouth could do anything else, the stone behemoth raised its sword arm and slashed at it with astonishing speed.

The stone behemoth's sword cut through the wide-mouth's stem. The wide-mouth let out a last growl of shock before it fell over and crashed into the muddy water to its side, where it partially sank and stopped moving.

As if nothing had happened, the stone behemoth resumed its march to its unknown destination. When Carmaz passed the wide-mouth—very reluctantly, because he had heard stories that wide-mouths could still kill even if you cut off their heads from their bodies—he could not take his eyes off its corpse. That was the first time Carmaz had ever seen anyone defeat a wide-mouth so quickly and so easily.

But what truly struck him was how the stone behemoth had failed to hesitate to kill when faced with a dangerous enemy. It had simply raised its sword and cut the wide-mouth's head off with the same skill as a butcher chopping up a ham. He could just imagine it rampaging through Conewood, chopping the villagers in half and destroying huts wherever it went without any mercy or hesitation.

That was the last example of its might that Carmaz saw for the rest of the journey, however, because the stone behemoth faced no more enemies for the rest of the trip. It simply walked deeper and deeper into the Swamp, going into parts that even Carmaz had not known existed. Once the stone behemoth had to wade through a deep part of the water that went up to its thighs, yet that did not slow it down at all, not even with the tree half on its shoulders, though Carmaz had had to climb up and travel across the upper branches of a couple of trees to cross it without sinking himself.

The deeper they walked into the Swamp of Light, the darker it became. This was something that Carmaz had heard about, that the Swamp supposedly became darker the deeper you went in. Most of the Swamp's light was visible from outside it, but not from inside it. Why that was, Carmaz didn't know, though he wished that it wasn't true, because more than once he almost tripped over a root or sank into a patch of mud that was deceptively shallow, mostly due to the lack of light that made it difficult for him to determine how deep the mud actually was.

But still the stone behemoth walked, its pace as steady as ever. Of course, without any real eyes, there was no way that the stone behemoth could even be aware of the differences in lighting that Carmaz was.

It must be following a predetermined route, Carmaz thought, carefully stepping over a patch of mud that he figured looked deceptively shallow. *As if it came this way ... or someone told it to come this way.*

Another thing Carmaz noticed about this part of the Swamp was how many tree stumps there were. At first, he had seen only a few, but the deeper he and the stone behemoth traveled, the more of them he saw, until soon he saw almost as many tree stumps as trees themselves. And they all looked like they had been cut down recently by the stone behemoth, too, although Carmaz didn't know where the trees themselves had gone, although the gouges in the mud where they had obviously been dragged off gave him a clue.

After a couple of more minutes of walking through the ever-darkening Swamp, the massive stone behemoth stopped. So did Carmaz, although he stopped behind a bush in order to avoid being spotted. At first he thought that the behemoth might have finally noticed him and was going to do something about him, but then the stone behemoth raised above its head the tree it had been dragging along behind it for the last several minutes and slammed it into the mud in front of its feet.

The impact of the tree half smashing into the earth sent mud flying everywhere, splattering the stone behemoth and even sending a few drops falling onto Carmaz's head. The stone behemoth, as usual, did not even flinch. It simply took another step forward, but instead of walking into mud, it stepped onto what looked like a bridge made out of logs. The stone behemoth walked down the bridge, though Carmaz still couldn't see its ultimate destination.

Who built that bridge? Carmaz thought as he stepped out of the bushes and made his way over to the bridge while avoiding possible sinkholes in the earth. *I didn't think anyone even lived out here. Yet apparently someone not only lives out here, but has constructed a bridge, too.*

When Carmaz reached the spot where the stone behemoth had

thrown the tree half that it carried, he saw that most of the tree half was deeply submerged into the mud. It was like a post that had been driven into the ground. In fact, when Carmaz looked closer, he saw that there were more trees driven into the mud upon which the log bridge itself was built, which were clearly supporting it.

Maybe this stone monster built this bridge, Carmaz thought, looking up at the back of the stone behemoth as it walked farther and father away. *If so, then it is obviously smarter than it looks.*

Carmaz considered going back now and forgetting all about this, but only for a second. In the next, he climbed onto the wooden bridge, which was surprisingly steady under his feet, and resumed following the stone behemoth. He liked walking on this bridge better than walking through the muddy Swamp, because the bridge was solid under his feet and not nearly as muddy or wet as the Swamp itself.

It wasn't long before Carmaz finally saw the behemoth's destination. Between the gap in the stone behemoth's legs, Carmaz saw a massive cave mouth rising from the Swamp water. The bridge appeared to extend from the cave, like initial construction of the bridge had started there. The cave itself appeared to have been dug out of the Swamp itself, because it appeared to be constructed out of mud.

The stone behemoth did not hesitate to enter the massive cave mouth. Carmaz, however, hesitated just long enough for the stone behemoth to disappear within it. Carmaz was not sure that he wanted to follow it in, because, he had no idea what lived in that cave exactly.

All sorts of possibilities to explain the cave mouth and the stone behemoth came to mind. The most prominent was that this was some sort of strange nest for this kind of creature, like it was going home to rest after a long day of work. The stone behemoth might have even had children in there, though Carmaz doubted that it could even reproduce.

Maybe I should just go back now, Carmaz thought. *Just because it's building a bridge doesn't mean that it is doing anything wrong. Maybe it just got tired of wading through the muddy water and so built this bridge so it wouldn't get dirty anymore.*

But that thought didn't seem likely to Carmaz at all. He didn't know what this creature was, but if it was smart enough to chop down trees and build a bridge using them, then it was smart enough to be a threat to every person on Ruwa, including the people of Conewood. He decided to go into the cave and find out as much as he could about it so he could determine what kind of threat it was.

Then he would leave and return to his camp. And if he learned anything that could affect the rest of Ruwa, he would at least try to tell everyone else, whether they believed him or not.

Stepping into the dark tunnel, Carmaz heard the regular, dull footsteps of the stone behemoth not far ahead of him. Unlike before, however, the stone behemoth's pace had picked up a little, as if it was in a hurry to get to wherever it was going. That just made Carmaz all the more curious about its destination.

As for the cave itself, it was not a cave at all, but rather a tunnel that sloped downwards for an unknown length. It was wide-open and tall enough that Carmaz couldn't touch the ceiling even if he got on his tiptoes and reached as far as he could with both of his hands. The place smelled of dried mud and swamp water, but the earth beneath his feet was as solid as the log bridge back at its entrance, if not more so. It was, however, slightly muddy, probably due to the fact that the stone behemoth had been walking along it. Carmaz walked quietly in order to avoid attracting the stone behemoth's attention to him.

The tunnel was dark, much darker than anywhere Carmaz had been in his life, except for the Void, obviously. But that didn't seem to be much of a problem, because as far as Carmaz could tell, the tunnel had no traps or guards or anything dangerous in it. At least the stone behemoth did not hesitate to keep going forward. Even so, Carmaz kept his ears open in case there were any traps set for the uninvited intruder.

This trip seemed much shorter to Carmaz than the last, because it was only a couple of minutes later that a light shone up ahead, which appeared to be the end of the tunnel. The stone behemoth's black silhouette looked strange to Carmaz, but he again kept his head low and his steps quiet, because he had a feeling that the stone behemoth was not working alone and that whoever it worked for was probably on the other side of that light.

Then the stone behemoth walked into the light, but Carmaz did not follow it. He instead hid behind a small outcropping to the left side of the tunnel and peered around it to see where the stone behemoth had walked into.

The tunnel opened up into a massive stone chamber— reminding Carmaz somewhat of the Void chamber underneath Anwan's shop back on World's End, although much bigger and without any markings to indicate that it was the home of the Void's followers. The chamber had a ceiling that soared above his head, even above the head of the stone behemoth, but that was not what Carmaz focused on.

Instead, he saw that the stone behemoth was not, as he had speculated, a single individual. There were at least a hundred similar stone behemoths in the center of the room, but rather than standing tall, they were curled into balls on the floor. Each one looked like it had been inactive for a long time, because they were covered in thick dust. And beyond them was another tunnel that seemed to go deeper still into the earth, but it was too dark and far away for him to see what lay beyond it.

Who made those? Carmaz thought. *Where did they come from? And how come I've never even heard of these things until today?*

That was when Carmaz noticed two figures walking toward the stone behemoth. Like the behemoth, they were also clearly made out of stone, but unlike the behemoth, they were much closer to a normal human being in size. One of them was a male, with a sleek, black obsidian skin and two glowing green eyes. The other was female, with a brighter diamond skin and glowing blue eyes. Both were humanoid, although the male had a long stinger tail extending from his back over his head and the female had two wings protruding from her back.

From what Carmaz could tell, neither of those figures were human, aquarian, katabans, gods, or even half-gods. Still, he thought they looked dangerous anyway, so he kept silent as he watched the two of them approach the stone behemoth, who had stopped a few feet from the rest of his fellow stone behemoths and stood there looking ready to report to the two smaller stone figures.

Then the male spoke. His voice was rough and gravelly, but also had a commanding authority to it that told Carmaz that this was a being used to issuing orders to inferiors, like an army general. "Gol, what is the status of the log bridge?"

The stone behemoth—perhaps named 'Gol,' if the smaller stone figure was accurate—suddenly made grinding noises like two rocks being rubbed against each other. It was the most painful and annoying sound that Carmaz had heard in his life, but even he could tell that it was speaking in some kind of strange language, whatever it was. He only wondered why it did not speak Divina, but maybe it could not.

Then Gol stopped making the noise, prompting the male figure to say, "Ah, so it sounds like the bridge is coming along well. Thank you, Gol. Keep up the good work. You will be well-rewarded for your efforts when the invasion is complete."

Invasion? Carmaz thought. *Are these beings plotting to invade the surface?*

The male figure then looked at the female figure and smirked. "See, my lady? I told you we could depend on Gol here to make the bridge. By my estimation, it should not take him more than a week at most to finish the bridge. By then, everything should be in place and the stage set for the invasion itself."

"I admit that you do have a point, Stalac," said the female figure, who sounded reluctantly impressed. "I thought you had chosen a dumb spot to begin the invasion, since it is in the middle of a swamp, but I suppose the surface dwellers won't see it coming, because few surface dwellers actually live in the swamp

46

or keep an eye on it closely enough to notice anything out of the ordinary happening in it."

"Indeed, my lady," said the male figure, whose name was apparently Stalac. "But that's not the best news of the day. Gol, please show our lady what else we did while she rested."

Gol nodded and then walked over to one of the stone pillars supporting the chamber's ceiling. It then pushed in a button on the pillar's surface, causing a portion of it to slide away to reveal a set of thick metal bars that looked like they had been built just recently.

But it wasn't the bars themselves that had gotten Carmaz's attention. No, his attention instead was on the figure who lay on the floor of the cell behind the bars, like she was unconscious or perhaps resting. He recognized her.

Those glasses ... those silver robes ... Carmaz thought. *No way ... it can't be ...*

Then the figure raised her head to look at Gol and that was when Carmaz knew that it was indeed Alira, the Judge of the Tournament, and she was indeed trapped by these mysterious figures, whoever they were.

Chapter Four

THE NEWS OF Alira's disappearance spread like a shock wave through the crowd of godlings. Braim exchanged a look of surprise with Tashir, while Yoji and Malya just stared in disbelief, as if they weren't sure that they had heard Grinf correctly.

Samvan, who still had his hand up, was the only godling who seemed to have retained the ability to speak. "What do you mean that Alira is missing? Where is she? When did this happen? How come no one told us until today?"

With Samvan's words acting like a spell, the rest of the godlings started shouting their questions, too, but as far as Braim could tell their questions were exactly the same as Samvan's. The sound of so many godlings shouting at once was deafening in the lobby of the Stadium until Grinf shouted, "Silence!"

That one word was enough to quiet the entire crowd of godlings. But everyone still looked at Grinf like they expected him to answer all of their questions to their satisfaction.

"We do not know where Alira is," said Grinf, his voice commanding and authoritative despite the annoyance in it. "She was discovered missing from her quarters earlier this morning. The Soldiers of the Gods did a thorough sweep of the city, but could not find her anywhere. Some of the gods have left World's

End to search the rest of Martir for her location, though they have not yet reported any luck in actually finding her or even a clue as to where she vanished."

Now Braim didn't think of Alira as a friend, but he knew that her disappearance could not mean anything good. He suspected that she had probably been kidnapped by the Void, as she was the only entity he knew of who could kidnap a person from right under the noses of the gods themselves. Of course, Braim did not know that for sure, but it seemed highly likely to him.

He apparently was not alone in that theory, because Samvan shouted, "Was it the Void? Did the Void kidnap Alira in order to disrupt the Tournament?"

"We do not know at this time who or what kidnapped Alira or if she was kidnapped at all," said Grinf. "Regardless, her disappearance does not change the fact that the Tournament of the Gods must go on. I volunteered to take her place until we can locate her again. If I hear any news about the search for her, I will let you all know in due time."

Murmurs and mutterings spread throughout the crowd of godlings, but no one actually voiced any objections to Grinf taking the job.

"Now, with that out of the way, we must continue with the Tournament," said Grinf. "All of the participants in the Bird Goddess Bracket must line up on the left side of the lobby in front of the door to the Stadium field, where they will begin the challenge. The rest must go to the right side and up into the box where they will be able to view the challenge from the viewer bubbles, as usual."

Though the godlings obviously still had many questions, no

one dared to ask another, because Grinf did not seem likely to answer or even tolerate any more questions from them. Braim, Tashir, and Yoji wished Malya good luck and then went to join the large crowd of godlings going into the door on the right side of the lobby and up the tall staircase that led to the box.

As they walked up the staircase, Braim listened to the other godlings gossiping madly about Alira's disappearance. Most of them were speaking rather quietly, more like muttering, but in the confined space of the staircase, Braim could still hear their rampant speculation as clearly as if they were speaking normally:

"I still think the Void kidnapped her. It is only logical."

"Nonsense! It was probably the Void's followers, the Empty, I think they called themselves."

"Isn't that the same as saying the Void kidnapped her, though? Maybe the Void ordered her followers to kidnap Alira."

"I think the gods must have done away with her. We all know how much the gods dislike Alira."

"The gods, getting rid of Alira? That doesn't make sense, even if they do dislike her. I think it's more likely that she lost her sanity and ran away to some random corner of Martir. Mark my words, they're going to find her a babbling lunatic in the middle of some random spit of land in the southern seas soon enough and they'll have to spend the next several months fixing her."

All of these speculations and much more filled the confines of the staircase as the godlings climbed up higher and higher. Braim didn't partake in any of them, mostly because he didn't want to speculate about something that he knew so little about.

Still, as the godlings exited the staircase and entered the box (which had noticeably fewer seats than before), Braim looked at

Tashir and Yoji and asked, "What do you guys think happened to her?"

"It is not my place to say," said Tashir as he, Braim, and Yoji made their way to the seats in the back, where they usually sat when watching these events. "The only thing I sincerely doubt is that Alira simply left on her own. It seems likely to me that she was indeed kidnapped, though by who and for what reason, I don't know."

"I'm with everyone else," said Yoji as the three of them sat down on three of the seats in the back. "I think the Void is behind it. It's the only logical conclusion. The Void has been trying to cause us trouble for a long time now. It only makes sense that it would kidnap Alira, which it must have known would cause a lot of confusion and fear among us."

"But if the Void has her," said Braim, leaning back in his chair, "then can we be sure that she is even still alive?"

"I don't know," said Yoji, shaking his head. "Maybe the Void kidnapped her for a greater purpose. If so, she's probably still alive."

"What could that 'greater purpose' be?" asked Braim.

"Again, I don't know," said Yoji. "Probably just trying to psyche us out so that we let our guard down. I imagine she'll be trying to attack us again pretty soon with Alira gone and the gods searching for her."

"I hope not," said Tashir with a shudder. "We barely survived her first attack. If she attacked us again, then I do not even want to contemplate what she will do to us."

"Oh, I'm not concerned about that," said Yoji, waving off Tashir's concern. "I'm just concerned that the Tournament may not be judged fairly without Alira."

"Fairly?" Braim repeated. He looked down to the front, where Grinf was now standing, although the God of Justice was looking at the vision bubbles appearing in front of the seats. "Grinf is supposed to be the fairest god of them all."

"That's just what his supporters say," said Yoji, rolling his eyes. "But it is a well-known fact among Hollechians that Grinf hated Hollech. And since I am one of the people in the Hollech Bracket, I'm afraid he'll treat me and the other Hollech Bracket participants worse than the others."

"Now that is what I call an irrelevant concern," said Tashir. "I am no Grinfian myself, but even I know that Grinf is supposed to be an impartial judge in all matters relating to justice and fairness."

"Oh, I wouldn't be so sure if I were you," said Yoji, folding his arms over his chest and frowning. "There's an old story among us Hollechians about how those who followed Grinf were always given harsher judgments in the Heavenly Paradise than the followers of other gods, and never for good reason. I, for one, believe it."

Braim was about to tell Yoji that Grinf actually had no say in the fates of the deceased, but then thought better of it. He was in no mood to get into a protracted theological argument with Yoji, even though he was aware that he had experience on his side and Yoji didn't.

So Braim just shrugged and said, "Let's agree to disagree. Anyway, I wonder what this challenge will be. Any theories?"

"It will likely have something to do with birds," said Tashir. "Beyond that, I cannot say."

"Who cares?" said Yoji. "All I care about is Alira's disappearance. And Grinf judging us Hollechians unfairly."

Braim shrugged and reclined in his chair, folding his hands behind his head as he did so. He looked at the vision bubbles and saw Malya and her opponent—an elderly man who looked like a vulture—standing opposite each other, although it was impossible to tell at the moment what their challenge was supposed to be.

Then a voice to Braim's right said, "Has anyone taken this seat yet?"

Braim looked to his right and saw someone he had never seen before standing there. It was a young woman, probably close to him in age, wearing her black hair in a ponytail. She wore a green tunic, the same as the one worn by every godling, and she seemed rather small and mousy even though she was at least as tall as Braim.

"No, no one is," said Braim, gesturing at the seat next to him. "You can sit here, I don't mind."

The young woman smiled and said, "Oh, all right. I was just worried because I always see you sitting with someone and I just —"

"It's not an issue," said Braim, shaking his head. "Really, it isn't."

The young woman looked a little embarrassed by her own rambling, but then she nodded and sat down in the seat. She seemed very nervous about something. Maybe it was Alira's disappearance or the Tournament itself that was worrying her. That Braim could understand, because the Tournament was hugely stressful for himself as well.

"So what's your name?" asked Braim, looking away from the

53

vision bubbles to focus on the young woman. "Don't think I've ever seen you before."

"My name is Tamra Nason," said the young woman, though she stumbled across her own name briefly. "I know who you are already. Braim Kotogs, right?"

"Yep," said Braim. "But how did you know my name if we've never met before?"

"Because everyone knows your name," said Tamra. "You're the only mortal to come back to life. How can I *not* know your name?"

Braim nodded, because her explanation made sense. Still, it did feel a little weird to meet someone who already knew his name even before he introduced himself to her. He hadn't realized how famous he was.

"So what bracket are you in, then?" said Braim.

"The Skimif Bracket," said Tamra. "Just like you."

"Oh," said Braim. "That's cool. So we might be competing against each other in the sub-bracket challenge that's supposed to be later this evening, right?"

Tamra's eyes widened like she had never considered that before. "What? Oh, I mean, yes, I think so."

"I'm not going to ask you about what you think the challenge will be, by the way," said Braim as he turned his attention back to the vision bubbles, which showed the Avian Goddess Sub-Bracket challengers preparing to begin their challenge (although Braim still didn't quite know what the challenge was supposed to be about). "Mostly because I know that no one knows anything about the next challenges."

"Okay," said Tamra, though she sounded a little put off by

Braim's honesty. "I didn't really want to talk about it. It just makes me nervous, thinking about that upcoming challenge, and I don't like getting nervous."

"Same here," said Braim, nodding. "I just try to take things as they come, rather than worry about what may or may not happen in the future. Makes life a lot easier."

"I agree," said Tamra, though she said it a little too quickly in Braim's opinion, as if she had rushed to get it out. "I don't like getting nervous, either. I like to take things very nice and easy. Yes."

Braim found Tamra's way of speaking rather strange. Either she was socially awkward, which was possible, or there was some other reason for why she spoke and acted the way she did. But she seemed harmless, so Braim didn't worry too much about her odd behavior.

"What island are you from?" asked Braim, folding his hands behind his head and glancing at the vision bubbles to see if the challenge had started yet (it hadn't).

"I'm from Kikasa," said Tamra. "It's the westernmost island in the Northern Isles. What about you?"

Braim shrugged. "No idea. When I came back to life, I forgot about things like my home island and where I am from. I've been living in North Academy for the past few months, though, if that means anything."

"North Academy?" Tamra repeated. She leaned forward a little too close for Braim's liking. "You mean the most prestigious magical school in the entire Northern Isles? *That* North Academy?"

"The one and only," said Braim, leaning away from her as

much as he could without leaning into Tashir, who sat to his left. "You sure seem interested in it."

"Of course I am," said Tamra, pulling back and putting her hands on her cheeks in excitement. "I'm not much of a mage myself—can barely light a candle with pyromancy—but I love magic and I love mages and I love learning about the various different magical schools in the Northern Isles. Did you know that there are over one hundred magical schools in the Northern Isles, not counting the aquarian schools located in the Undersea?"

"No, I didn't know that," said Braim, returning to his original upright position, although it still felt like Tamra was leaning into his personal space. "That's, er, a lot of schools."

"It is," said Tamra, nodding. "But none of them come even close to producing as many magically-skilled students as North Academy does. I've always wanted to visit the school, but it's very hard to get there because it's located in the northern reaches of the Great Berg."

"Yeah," said Braim, nodding. "That's kind of the point. North Academy only allows students in who can prove that they are serious about learning magic. That's why it's located where it is and why it is so hard to get to it."

"I know," said Tamra. "But I wish that I could go there someday anyway. Just imagine all of the amazing things I could learn if I was there."

"Maybe I can take you there as a guest someday," said Braim. "Not anytime soon, but—"

Tamra gasped. "Really? You would let me come and visit? That's very generous of you. I'll have to take you up on that offer after the Tournament."

Braim nodded, but he wasn't so sure that he should have made that offer. Jenur, the Magical Superior of North Academy, did not usually permit guests and he wasn't sure he could convince her to let them in, even though Jenur trusted him.

Then again, if I become the God of Martir, I could take Tamra and anyone else anywhere I wanted and no one else could tell me not to, Braim thought.

Aloud, Braim said, "All right. Anyway, what kind of job did you do back on Kikasa?"

Without warning, Tamra looked away for a moment. It was a very brief moment, but Braim didn't miss it, even though Tamra seemed to think he did, because when she looked at him again, she had a rather apologetic smile on her face.

"Oh, my old job was nothing," said Tamra, waving off his question just like that. "It was boring and not at all as interesting as living in the most prestigious magical school in all of the Northern Isles."

Braim was no fool. He could tell when someone was trying to steer the conversation away from dangerous waters, although he didn't know exactly what was so dangerous about asking Tamra about her job. It couldn't be *that* bad, could it?

On the other hand, Braim didn't really care about her old job and had only asked the question just to be polite. Maybe later on he would ask Tamra more about it, but for now he decided to simply nod in understanding.

Then Braim looked at the vision bubbles again. It looked like the challenge was finally starting, because he saw Malya and her opponent both standing over a couple of small, brightly-colored birds that looked like they were injured. From what Braim could tell, it appeared that this challenge was about who could heal their injured bird the quickest, which seemed like a rather tame challenge in comparison to some of the past ones. Still, Braim didn't mind tame, because 'tame' was preferable to the constant stress and worry that he and the others had been under ever since the Tournament first started.

But 'tame' was not far from 'boring' and so in short order Braim found himself bored once again. He looked at Tamra again and said, "How long do you think that this challenge will go?"

"About as long as the other challenges, I expect," said Tamra. "Why?"

Braim shrugged, but now he found himself rather interested in learning about Tamra's old job. He had thought that he wasn't interested in it, but now decided that he was. At any rate, he was curious about why Tamra was avoiding the subject. He decided to see if he could get her to tell him at least a little bit about it, if nothing else.

"So," said Braim, glancing at the vision bubbles again just to keep an eye on what Malya was up to, "you said your job was boring."

Tamra looked rather defensive all of a sudden, but she said, in a friendly tone, "Why, yes, yes I did say that. Why do you ask?"

"I'm just trying to figure out why you thought it was boring," said Braim. "Was it just not challenging or exciting or something?"

Tamra looked like she was analyzing everything he said, which almost took Braim by surprise, because she had certainly not seemed that smart to him.

But then her analyzing expression faded and was replaced by

her usual meek face. "It just wasn't very challenging is all. Simple work, didn't require a whole lot of thought or time or effort. Often, I'd be done with my work halfway through my shift and so would have lots of time to do the things that I wanted to do, like study the different magical schools and the ways in which they differed."

Very vague non-answer there, Braim thought. *And it probably isn't even an accurate non-answer. She's hiding something. Of that, I have no doubt.*

Aloud, Braim said, "Yeah, those are the best kinds of jobs, aren't they? Always give you plenty of free time. At least, I'd think those kinds of jobs are good. I haven't held a job since I came back from the dead, so I don't really remember if I ever had a job like that before."

"Regardless, I'd say that your description of that kind of job is spot on," said Tamra. "But assuming I win the Tournament, then I won't have to worry about going back to that old job or to any job at all. I am so looking forward to that."

Tamra sounded very much like she disliked her old job, but Braim had a feeling that she was only saying this in order to change the subject. He decided to play along with her for a little while, just to make her lower her guard, and then once he knew that she was sufficiently relaxed, he'd ask her about her old job and trick her into giving him more details.

"I'm looking forward to it as well," said Braim. He stretched his arms and legs. "After all, I'm sure that being the God of Martir comes with all sorts of perks that other normal jobs lack."

"Oh, right," said Tamra, folding her hands over her lap. "I forgot. You are also in the Skimif Bracket, right?"

"Yeah," said Braim. "So that means that we'll probably have to compete against each other. After all, there can be only one winner in each bracket."

"Yeah, you're right about that," said Tamra. "But that still doesn't mean we can't be friends, right?"

"Sure," said Braim, nodding. "Although I think you're jumping the gun a bit by calling us 'friends,' seeing as we just met today."

"Oh, you're absolutely right," said Tamra with a laugh that Braim could quite clearly tell was forced. "I just got ahead of myself is all. You know what I meant."

"Of course," said Braim. "Anyway, what do you think about Alira's disappearance? Do you have any theories about what might have happened to her or where she might have gone?"

"Oh, I don't know," said Tamra with a shrug. "She could be anywhere. It is a little bit disconcerting, because I'd never imagine that Alira would disappear like this, but at the same time I'm not too worried because the gods are looking for her and I'm sure they will find her in due time."

Tamra seemed a little too carefree about Alira's disappearance. Then again, he could tell that Tamra didn't like Alira much, a feeling he understood, because while Alira may have been fair and just, she could also be very mean.

"Yeah, but to have her vanish like that, without any explanation at all ..." Braim shuddered. "Just freaks me out. Especially since none of us even knew about it until earlier, when Grinf told us about it."

"I know," said Tamra. "But—"

Tamra did not get to finish her sentence, because at that

moment, a figure in crystalline armor dashed into the box. It was one of the Soldiers of the Gods. In fact, it was Captain Garvan, the leader of the Soldiers, who looked like he had run a mile, because when he stopped, he put his hands on his knees and panted heavily.

"Lord Grinf!" said Captain Garvan, holding up one hand to catch the god's attention. "I have terrible news to share with you and the godlings."

"What is so terrible about this news?" asked Grinf in annoyance. "Was Alira found dead in an alley somewhere in the city?"

"No, sir, Judge Alira is still missing," said Garvan. "But there has been another disappearance. No, excuse me. A kidnapping."

"A kidnapping?" Grinf repeated. "Who?"

Wiping the sweat off his forehead, Garvan said, "Princess Raya Mana, one of the godlings. She is missing from her apartment, where she was recovering from the Void's attack last week. And no one knows where she is or if she is even still alive."

Chapter Five

WHEN RAYA AWOKE, she tried to convince herself that she had not actually been kidnapped by Aorja, but rather that it had all been a very strange dream that she had experienced due to her body still adjusting to the loss of her original hand. She almost believed it, too, before she heard Aorja's harsh voice say, "Oh, looks like the pretty princess is awake."

Raya looked to the right, where Aorja's voice had come from. Aorja was sitting on a rickety old wooden chair, her arms folded over her chest, like she had been watching Raya for a while now. The air in the room was hot and uncomfortable, while the room itself was tiny and dark, with only a single window to the right of Aorja's head, which was currently closed, although light peeked through the cracks.

Blinking, Raya tried to sit up, but she found that her body was bound by thick ropes that were tied far too tightly to her body for her comfort. She struggled against it, but quickly gave up.

"What happened?" Raya asked. "Where am I? How do I get out of here?"

Aorja laughed. "You think I'm just going to tell you how to escape? I knew you royals can be a bit thick sometimes, but honestly I didn't know that you guys could be *that* dumb."

"Well, then let me go," Raya said. "As Princess of Carnag, I demand that you free me and that you do so right away. I could call my parents and ask them to bring down the full might of the Carnagian Navy upon your wretched little head."

"And how, silver spoon, do you expect to contact your parents when you are bound and far from them?" asked Aorja. "And I know you can't use magic, either, because you do not own a wand and don't radiate even the slightest bit of magical energy. You're just bluffing, and not even bluffing very well at that."

Raya scowled, but did not admit that Aorja had a point. Instead, she said, "Then can you at least tell me where we are? Are we still on World's End?"

"World's End? Nope," said Aorja, shaking her head. "We're on a tiny, rather obscure island called Ruwa. Ever heard of it?"

Raya's eyes widened. "That's Carmaz's home island."

"Who?" said Aorja with a frown.

"Carmaz Korva," Raya repeated. She sighed. "He was one of my fellow participants in the Tournament, but was unjustly kicked out because he 'broke' a rule. He was the handsomest man in the world."

"Ugh," said Aorja. She made a vomiting gesture. "I don't like men anymore. Can't trust any of them. This just confirms my belief that you're an idiot."

"Carmaz is not untrustworthy," Raya said. She struggled to sit up, but even her legs were bound by the ropes. "He is kinder and braver than you."

"Uh huh," said Aorja. "Well, I don't really care. You're not going to get to see your favorite guy anyway. I just wanted to let you know where you are because this island has been my home base ever since Jakuuth Grinfborn's army was defeated. And it's worked pretty well, considering how none of the gods have managed to find me yet."

Aorja sounded pleased with herself, but Raya was not. She tried to sit up again, but failed, so she just resigned herself to lying on the uncomfortable, bumpy mattress underneath her.

"All right," said Raya, looking at Aorja with defiance. "You have me. What are you going to do to me now? Torture me?"

Aorja shook her head. "Nah. Not unless you act uppity. I mean, I'd sooner kill you than torture you. I just need you in one piece for my plan. You're nothing more than a bargaining chip to me."

"How rude," said Raya with a loud *humph*. "I am more than a mere 'chip.' I am a bargaining diamond, which is far more valuable than a chip."

"You're missing the point," said Aorja. "But it really doesn't matter if you missed it or not. The point is that I have you now and that you are going to be very useful for getting what I want."

Raya felt rather offended at Aorja's implication that she was not very intelligent, but she decided that Aorja was not going to apologize. So she would ask her about something else.

"And what, exactly, *do* you want?" asked Raya. "Money? Power?"

"That would be great," said Aorja with a sigh. "But really, my desires are a bit more unconventional. You see, I want the gods to grovel at my feet. I am tired of being on the run from them. That's why I kidnapped you."

"I'm afraid I don't follow," said Raya. "How does kidnapping me lead to the gods groveling at your feet? It makes no sense to

64

me."

"Because you're one of the participants in the Tournament of the Gods, obviously," said Aorja. "That makes you valuable. I mean, I could have kidnapped any godling, but I picked you specifically because you were alone and unable to fight back."

"You said you were going to use me as a bargaining chip earlier," Raya said. "Does that mean you are going to barter me in exchange for something from the gods?"

"Exactly," said Aorja, nodding. "Finally, you're catching on. I guess you're not as dumb as I thought you were."

"Dumb?" Raya repeated. "Of course I'm not *dumb*. I'm the Princess of Carnag. I have received first class education in the matters of Carnagian history, reason, law, and many, many other subjects. I dare say I've had far more education than you."

"Guess it must have all been a gigantic waste of money, considering how dull you are," said Aorja, shaking her head. "I imagine that there are peasant children on Carnag who are brighter than you."

That was almost enough to make Raya rolled off her bed toward Aorja, but the ropes were heavy as well as tight and so all Raya succeeded in doing was move around awkwardly. She glared at Aorja instead, hoping that her sheer disapproval would be enough to make Aorja apologize, although the mage didn't appear at all apologetic about anything she just said.

"Now," said Aorja, resting her chin on her hands, a wicked grin on her face. "Are you smart enough to figure out exactly what I want the gods to give me in exchange for you? Or do I have to spell it out for you?"

Raya bit her lower lip, thinking about it for a moment, and

65

then said, "You said you wanted the gods to grovel at your feet and to leave you alone. I assume that you want the gods to pardon you for your crimes in exchange for my return."

Aorja chuckled. "Close, but not quite there. Yes, I'd like it if the gods would leave me alone and tell everyone else to, but we all know that the gods would *never* honor such a promise to anyone. Even as a Limitless, I don't have the power to defend myself from the gods if they decided to break that promise. No, what I want is much larger than that."

Aorja sat up straight, her violet eyes gleaming with insanity. "I want to become a goddess."

Raya's eyes widened. "You want to become a goddess?"

"Yes," said Aorja. "More specifically, the Goddess of Martir. In exchange for your safety, I am going to demand that the gods ascend me to godhood. I know they can do it, so this isn't an unrealistic thing to ask for."

"How foolish," said Raya, shaking her head. "The gods would never give someone like *you* that much power. You realize that, don't you?"

"I do, but that's why I went to all of the trouble of kidnapping you," said Aorja. "After all, they need you to participate in the Tournament and attempt to win. Without you, the Tournament cannot go on. Therefore, they will have to come to me at some point and accept my offer or continue to exist incomplete, as they have already."

"What if the gods just take me away from you?" asked Raya. "Did it ever occur to you that if the gods are as powerful as you think they are, that they could easily crush you and take me back to World's End on their own?"

"Of course I am aware of that," said Aorja. She sounded rather offended. "That is why I have come up with contingencies. If the gods try that, then I will kill you right here and now so it will be for naught. Besides, I've hidden my location from the gods using a neat spell I learned recently, so they can't find us even if they tried."

Raya had no doubt that Aorja would indeed kill her if she had to. Aorja seemed insane enough to do that and much worse if she felt that she was cornered and without any options. Especially in light of the threats that Aorja had already made to her earlier, which made Raya almost scared enough to shut up and go along with whatever Aorja asked.

But Raya still wanted to escape, so she said, "At what point will you tell the gods that you have me?"

"When I feel that they have become sufficiently afraid enough to agree to whatever demands I make of them," said Aorja simply. "So, in a few hours, give or take. Until then, you should take it easy and relax, because you aren't going anywhere for a long—"

Aorja was interrupted by a loud crash outside, followed by the roar of a monster that Raya had never heard in her life. Aorja looked to the door and sighed. "I'll be back. It sounds like Zeeree broke something. Better make sure it wasn't anything important."

Aorja stood up and was out of the hut instantly, closing the door behind her as she left. She actually slammed the door behind her, causing the old hut to sway rather dangerously for a brief moment.

When Aorja left, Raya immediately struggled against her ropes again. Of course, she gave up just as quickly, because she wasn't a very physically strong person and the ropes were too thick for her to break.

Still, Raya was not going to just lie here and let Aorja use her like a bargaining chip. She wished that she had some way of contacting Keeper and calling for his help, but unfortunately Keeper had not given her any method with which to contact him. He was still at Carnag, as far as she knew, and likely wouldn't even know about her disappearance until well into the evening, at which point it would be too late for him to save her.

That means I will have to save myself, Raya thought. She grimaced at the thought. *I guess this is what Father meant when he told me that royalty needs to be self-sufficient.*

Raya considered her escape options. She was not strong enough to snap the ropes, nor did she have a knife or anything else sharp enough to cut through the ropes. She didn't have any magical powers that she could use to break herself free, either, which made her wish that she had accepted the magical lessons that Father had offered to pay for her back when she was sixteen.

Raya almost despaired that she might not be able to escape at all when it occurred to her that she could simply open a portal to the ethereal and escape. She would be extremely safe there, even if she was still bound in ropes, because there was no way for Aorja to enter it. All Raya would have to do after that was find a katabans who could take her back to World's End.

But the thought of opening another portal like that made Raya feel a deep sense of dread. Yes, Raya could indeed open portals like that. She had already opened portals to the ethereal three times already. It wasn't an impossible task for her, per se.

The problem was that Raya just wasn't very good at it. It often took a good deal of her strength just to open a portal. While Raya was not terribly weak at the moment, she still felt rather tired at the mere thought of opening a portal. Besides, Raya had never tried to open an ethereal portal while she was bound. She had always associated portal opening with the act of raising her hand, but she could not raise either of her hands at the moment.

It's worth a shot, though, isn't it? Raya thought as she forced herself to get over her fear of the exhaustion and pain she was about to feel while opening the portal. *Better to try and fail than to never try at all, or so Father always says.*

Raya concentrated hard on opening a portal just to the side of the bed. She would open the portal and then roll into it. After that, she'd figure out her next step.

But unfortunately, no matter how hard Raya focused, no portal opened up beside her bed. The ground was as solid and dirty as ever, making Raya feel hopeless again.

There must be some way for me to escape, Raya thought, glancing down at the ropes and scowling at them, even though she knew that the ropes didn't pay her any attention. *But how?*

In desperation, Raya looked around the room in which she lay, her eyes darting about for anything, anything at all, that she could use to escape from this place.

There was Aorja's chair, but it was not sharp or close enough for her to use as an escape tool. The walls were made of a thin, grimy wood and had nothing on them that she could use to escape. They were very bare, which made her wonder if Aorja rarely used this hut.

Actually, the walls were not totally bare. Leaning against the wall opposite Raya was a very old, rusty-looking rake. It was leaning against the wall with its head, with the handle on the dirt floor. It seemed like an odd way to stand a rake to Raya, but then, she was not a farmer or laborer, so she didn't really know for sure if that was the normal way a rake was stored when it wasn't in use.

It was the rake's teeth that most interested Raya, because they looked sharp enough to cut through her ropes. The only problem, of course, was getting those teeth in contact with her ropes. Raya could not simply stand up and walk over to the rake, but she didn't just want to lie here and wait for Aorja to return and do who-knows-what to her, either.

There must be some way I can get that rake's teeth to cut my ropes, Raya thought, thinking hard. *But how?*

Then Raya remembered how the old hut had swayed rather dangerously when Aorja slammed the door shut earlier. Perhaps, if Raya somehow managed to make the hut sway, then she might be able to cause the rake to fall forward onto her ropes and maybe even cut them open entirely. It was worth a shot.

Raya's bed was placed right next to the wall, so she figured that all she needed to do was roll into the wall hard enough to cause the rake to fall forward onto her ropes. Then she could rub her ropes against it until they snapped and she would be free at last.

The idea seemed brilliant in her head. Unfortunately, Raya had a hard time with the rolling part. Whatever these ropes were made of, they deeply restricted her movement. It was very much like being held in the hands of a giant that did not want to let her go.

Still, Raya kept trying to roll, putting as much effort into this as she had put into anything else in her life, if not more so, considering the consequences of failure. She finally succeeded in rolling over onto her belly. Unfortunately, that only brought her a couple of inches closer to the wall and certainly had not given her the momentum she needed to move.

But Raya did not give up just yet. She put in more of her strength again, and this time succeeding in rolling once more. She hit the wall, but the momentum of her blow was so weak that the hut did not even shudder under her blow. It was enough to make her depressed, but then Raya shook her head and decided to try again and again until she finally got it.

So, bracing herself for impact, Raya rolled again and again into the wall, but unfortunately her rolls did nothing to help her. Each one was even weaker than the last, largely because Raya was getting tired and had less and less energy to expend with each roll.

Eventually, Raya gave up and lay on her back on the bed again, panting hard. She looked at the rake, which stood against the wall as innocently as ever, but to her it was her greatest foe at the moment. Or maybe the hut was her greatest foe. In any case, Raya figured that someone was her greatest foe and that she would have to figure out who so she could figure out who she was supposed to be angry at.

I just want to be angry at everyone and everything, Raya thought. She wanted to kick out at something, but the ropes kept her from doing even that much. *Ugh.*

Then Raya looked down at her hands. She looked at her right hand in particular, which was shining a blue-and-white light that made her feel a little ill. In the rush of her current circumstances,

Raya had forgotten how much she hated her new hand.

Stupid useless new hand, Raya thought. *I think I'll be angry at* you *today, because you are the worst part of all of this. Can't even bend your fingers all that well. What a joke.*

Raya wanted to take off her artificial hand and throw it away, but then she remembered that she couldn't move and that her new hand was as attached to her as her other hand was, for good or ill. She would just have to be content with what she had, but that thought just made her angrier and more frustrated than ever.

But then the words of Doctor Ilran returned to mind, about how her new hand might help her get out of a sticky situation someday. Her current situation was certainly sticky enough, but that still didn't help her figure out exactly *how* it was supposed to help her.

Maybe it has some super secret powers that I don't know about, Raya thought. *But even if it does, how am I supposed to access those powers? Just hope that they decide to activate on their own?*

No. Raya decided that there had to be some way she could use her new hand to escape. She focused on it, hoping to feel some sort of connection in it that would allow her to escape. She was ready for something, anything, to happen, but the longer she focused on her hand, the longer nothing happened, and the more she began to believe that Doctor Ilran's earlier quip had been nothing but a dumb joke just to make her feel better about her awful situation.

Just as Raya was about to give up all hope, her hand started to glow. Before Raya's startled eyes, the fingers of the hand elongated longer and longer, until soon she was staring at long, serpentine versions of her fingers that she had not expected to see.

Then the long, serpentine fingers made their way over to the ropes binding Raya's ropes to her body. They then became as sharp as knives and cut through the ropes, causing them to fall silently off Raya's body.

Raya immediately sat up. As soon as she did, the fingers of her artificial hand returned to their original length and the hand itself ceased glowing. Raya held her hand up to her face, looking at it in amazement.

I was too harsh to this new hand, I think, Raya thought. *Maybe it isn't so stupid after all.*

Raya kissed her hand, but then stopped and listened for any movement from the outside. She didn't hear Aorja or this mysterious Zeeree fellow coming, but for all she knew they could both still be standing outside the door. Nonetheless, Raya swung her legs over the side of the bed and made her way to the shuttered window. She cracked the shutters open just enough for her to peek through.

Through the crack in the shutters, Raya saw tall trees surrounding the area around the hut. She did not see Aorja or Zeeree anywhere, but that did not mean that they were not nearby and would not try to capture her again if they saw her.

But I still have to escape, Raya thought. *Maybe I should try opening another ethereal portal, now that I am free.*

Stepping away from the shuttered window, Raya turned around and held up her hand. She concentrated hard, as hard as she could, expecting to feel that same surge of energy she always felt whenever she opened an ethereal portal.

But Raya felt nothing at all. She waved her hand up and

down, side to side, and all around, but no portal opened and she could not feel any surge of energy flow through her body. She looked at her bluish white hand, wondering what the problem was.

Maybe I'm just too tired to do it, Raya thought. *I do feel rather worn out from everything that's happened to me today so far. Maybe I just need to rest and I will get enough energy to escape.*

Of course, Raya had no time to rest and wait. If Aorja walked back in on her now and saw that she was free, then that would probably just make Aorja kill her then and there. Or at least hurt her badly enough to make it impossible for Raya to escape on her own.

I need to escape this hut and figure out where I should go from here, Raya thought. *Aorja said that it's impossible for the gods to locate us, but maybe if I go far enough, I'll eventually step outside of the boundaries of Aorja's spell and the gods will be able to locate me. At the very least, if I can get far away quickly enough, then I might be able to find some place to rest and then use the ethereal to escape once I feel better.*

So Raya made her way over to the door of the hut. She cracked the door open just wide enough for her to peer through, but as before, she did not see Aorja or Zeeree anywhere. Of course, she didn't really know what Zeeree even looked like, but considering how she saw no one at all outside, she believed he probably wasn't there unless he could turn invisible or something like that.

But Raya did hesitate. After all, Aorja and Zeeree should have been right out there, but she didn't see them anywhere. It was like they had vanished. That seemed unusual to her, because Aorja would undoubtedly wish to keep a close eye on Raya so she could not escape without her knowing.

Then Raya heard the loud footfalls of some massive being nearby and a green-skinned giant, with mechanical legs, stepped into view. It was the ugliest creature that Raya had ever laid eyes on. It had crooked teeth and small, dull gray eyes. Its body was scarred horribly, as if it had fought in a lot of battles and had barely survived. It looked big enough to eat Raya whole if it wanted to or simply sit on her and squish her underneath its immense weight. A strong smell of swamp water and wet metal followed the creature, which almost made Raya gag.

At the creature's side was Aorja, who was explaining something to it. She was speaking loudly enough for Raya to hear her from where she stood, which made Raya go even quieter than usual in order to not miss whatever Aorja was telling the creature.

"All right, Zeeree," said Aorja, gesturing at Raya's hut, though she wasn't actually looking at the hut. "You make sure that the prisoner in there doesn't escape. I'm going to Deeproots to get you a nice treat, so I won't be far and I will be back very quickly, all right?"

The creature, which must have been Zeeree, grunted in understanding. Aorja smiled.

"All right," said Aorja. "See you later."

With that, Aorja raised her wand, spun it twice, and vanished into thin air.

Raya immediately closed the door and stood very still, listening as Zeeree made his way over to Raya's hut. A second later, Zeeree's massive footfalls stopped and then she heard him sit down. She cracked open the door again, but even narrower this time.

Zeeree was sitting in front of the hut with his large back to the door. He seemed to be chewing the nails of his fingers, but Raya didn't dare try to sneak out with him so close.

Once more, Raya closed the door and then stepped back. She wasn't sure how she was going to get out of this situation at all now.

Zeeree doesn't seem very intelligent to me, but he doesn't need to be in order to hear me escaping, Raya thought. *If he hears me trying to escape, who knows what he'll do to me? I need to find another way out.*

Raya looked around the hut again for another possible exit or escape route, but unfortunately she didn't see any other doors to open. There was a window, but it was too small for her to climb out of, even though she was fairly small and thin herself.

Looks like I only have one way out now, Raya thought, looking at the door again. *Great.*

Then it hit her. A distraction. That was what Raya needed more than anything. She needed some way to distract Zeeree from the door long enough for her to slip out and escape into the wilderness. That was easier said than done, however, because Raya didn't know *how* to distract him.

Raya looked around at the interior of the hut, searching for anything that she could use as a distraction. There was the rake, still standing against the wall, and the ropes on her mattress, but none of that seemed like it would work as a distraction to her until an idea occurred to her that seemed likely to work.

Walking over to the rake, Raya grabbed its rough handle and

removed its head. She then walked over to the window, which she opened silently, and then aimed the rake's head. She didn't have a particular target in mind for the rake head, so she threw it as hard as she could with all of her might as far away from the hut as she could.

The rake head flew out of the open window and landed with a dull *thunk* on the earth dozens of feet away from the hut. Raya was surprised at how far she had thrown it because she didn't think she was strong enough to throw anything that far.

But that didn't matter to her at the moment. What mattered was that she heard Zeeree grunt in surprise, stand up rather noisily, and then start walking over to the rake head in order to see what it was.

As soon as Raya heard Zeeree get up, she dashed from the window to the door, which she cracked open to peer through. Zeeree was no longer there, although there was a rather disgusting and large puddle of some kind of green goop where he had been sitting moments before.

Bracing herself, Raya opened the door just wide enough for her to slip through, which she did. When she closed the door, she looked to the right just in time to see Zeeree bend over the rake head and pick it up with one of his massive hands. He then turned it over in his hands, staring at it as if he had never seen anything like it before.

But Raya didn't stick around long enough to see if Zeeree was going to return to his post. She turned and ran as fast as she could toward the tall trees surrounding them on every side. She tried not to make any noise, but it was hard to be quiet because her every instinct was telling her to run as fast as she could, regardless of how much noise she made in the process.

Indeed, Raya probably would have made it to the jungle around them had she not slipped on a patch of mud and fell on her behind. The sudden fall caused a small yelp to escape her lips. And as soon as she yelped, she heard Zeeree grunt again.

Looking over her shoulder, Raya saw that Zeeree, still holding the rake head in his hands, was staring at her like she had spooked him.

Their eyes met for a brief instant before Zeeree grunted in anger again and started walking toward her. His small, dull eyes shone with murderous anger far worse than anything Raya had ever seen in her life. She doubted that Zeeree would kill her, but she still did not want to end up in his hands just the same.

Scrambling back to her feet, Raya made a break for the jungle, not even bothering to be quiet now. She heard Zeeree pick up the pace behind her and heard his every step bring him closer and closer to her, his long legs allowing him to close the distance between them quickly.

Raya figured that if she could just make it to the swamp, then she would be fine. She just had to run fast, keep it up, even though she was exhausted and drained from everything else that had happened recently.

A quick glance over her shoulder showed her that Zeeree was indeed rapidly gaining on her. His skin was glistening that same foul-smelling green goop she had seen before and there was no reason in his eyes at all. Instead, they had just a dogged determination to catch and put Raya back to where his mistress had kept her before her escape.

That just spurred Raya to run as fast as she could, but even at her fastest, Zeeree still kept up with her. He reached for her with his massive hands and Raya was almost certain that he was going to capture her despite her best efforts.

Then an idea occurred to Raya and, without warning, she turned and ran to the left. Her sudden change of pace must have taken Zeeree by surprise, because he also tried to come to a stop. But he was running too fast and thus ended up tripping over his own feet and falling face-first into the muddy ground hard enough to shake the ground.

Raya, however, didn't even smile when she saw her plan worked. She just continued to run to the swamp, never looking back, never slowing down, until she passed through the tree line into the bushes. She had to slow down her progress here, because the bushes and vines and tree limbs got in her way. Even so, Raya was now convinced that she was home free and that all she needed to do now was find a quiet, safe place to rest and then she would figure out her next course of action.

That was when Raya stepped into a deep patch of mud and suddenly fell forward. Like Zeeree, she landed face-first onto the mud, but tried to break her fall by holding out her arms. It helped somewhat, but she still fell into it and got mud all over her clothes, body, face, and hair.

The impact jarred her, but Raya tried to get up anyway. Unfortunately, she found that the mud was too soft for her to gain any footing. She pushed against it, but the more she pushed, the deeper she sank in.

Panicked and dirty, Raya struggled against the mud, but no matter how hard she tried, the mud clung to her ever more strongly and she could not rise out of it.

Then Raya heard crashing through the trees and bushes behind her and looked over her shoulder. Zeeree was tearing through the trees and bushes, an angry expression on his now-muddy face. He now looked less like he wanted to capture Raya and more like he wanted to kill her in cold blood.

And worse, there was no way for Raya to fight back and defend herself.

Chapter Six

WHEN ALIRA WAS revealed by the stone behemoth's actions, it was impossible for Carmaz not to stare at her from his position behind the rock. He wondered what she was doing here and how she had gotten captured at all. She was the Judge of the Tournament of the Gods. She should have been back on World's End presiding over the current Tournament. How did she end up here?

As Carmaz watched, Alira opened her eyes and looked up at the stone behemoth. The other two stone beings, the one named Stalac and his female companion, walked over to the caged Judge. Stalac looked quite pleased with himself, while the female looked at Alira skeptically. Alira, for her part, glared at the two of them, mostly because the bars in her cell kept her from doing anything else.

"See, my lady?" said Stalac, gesturing at Alira. "That is indeed Judge Alira, the Judge of the Tournament of the Gods. She has been kidnapped, as per your request."

"That truly is her?" asked the female, who sounded very skeptical. "Are you certain that she isn't simply some human woman who *looks* like her?"

"I am no human woman, golem," Alira said. She sat up, glaring at the stone people the entire time. "I am the one and only

Judge of the Tournament. There is no one else like me in the whole of Martir. If you are going to insult me, then at least have the decency to come up with far more accurate ones."

"That's her," said the female in a deadpan voice. She looked at Stalac. "How did you kidnap her anyway? I thought that the gods were keeping a strict eye on her."

"It was extremely simple, my lady," said Stalac. "We have formed an alliance with a human mage on the surface who agreed to kidnap her in exchange for us helping her achieve her own goals. The human mage arranged to meet Alira in an obscure part of World's End, where she knocked her out and brought her directly here."

The female, however, didn't look at all pleased with Stalac's story. She said, "You mean that a human knows about us?"

"Just one," said Stalac, folding his arms over his chest. "She promised not to tell anyone about our existence, so do not fret or worry, because the invasion will still begin without anyone being the wiser. I don't think the human even knows about what we're planning to do. She just knows that we are going to strike against the gods."

"You should have consulted with me about this, Stalac," said the female. "I have given you much freedom because I am aware of your power and authority, but I do not want you to abuse that freedom by jeopardizing our long term goals."

"My lady, I would never jeopardize our long term goals for anything," said Stalac. He tapped the side of his head. "I am always thinking long term. Indeed, I can barely think short term. I ask that you trust me on this, as you have in the past."

"Very well," said the female. "I suppose it is too late for us to take this back. Still, next time you involve a Martirian in one of our plans, please consult with me first. I do not want any of our plans needlessly jeopardized by those who we cannot perfectly trust. Understood?"

"Absolutely, my lady," said Stalac.

"Let me out," said Alira, grabbing the bars and shaking them. "I demand freedom. It is my duty to return to World's End and judge the Tournament. No one else is fit for the job except for me. Do you understand?"

"Make all the demands you like, Judge, but we are not going to be letting you free any time soon," said Stalac. "We need you out of the way because you were the largest obstacle between us and the invasion. Without you, the gods are divided and scared, which will make the invasion that much easier."

"You golems are foolish," said Alira. "Foolish and evil. By what right do you have to kidnap me and hold me down here in a cell like a common criminal?"

"We have every right to do as we please," said the female. "You don't understand that we are at war with the surface dwellers. In war, you do whatever will bring you closer to victory, always without the permission of your enemy."

"You have no right," said Alira. "I am the Judge of the Tournament. I have more authority in this world than you do."

"Over your fellow Martirians, perhaps, but not over us," said the female. "But please, keep repeating your meaningless title over and over again like any of us actually care. You could be one of the Powers themselves and I still wouldn't give a damn about you."

Alira looked around at the cell she was in. "Why can't I use my magic to escape?"

"We blocked it, of course," said Stalac. "We have been studying Martirian magic for some time now. Though you still have the magical power within, you cannot access it. Wouldn't want you leaving so early without our permission, after all."

Alira punched the bars, but that didn't do anything to them. She then swore in some language Carmaz didn't understand, although he caught her meaning well enough.

"Are you going to kill me?" asked Alira.

"No," said Stalac, shaking his head. "Not right away, anyway. We just need you out of the way long enough for the invasion to begin. It's quite simple."

"Of course, a lot of people are going to die in the coming invasion, but not you," said the female. "Not yet. We need you here, alive, but once you outlive your usefulness, we'll consider taking your life."

For the first time in Carmaz's memory, Alira actually looked frightened. She let go of the bars and slumped against the back wall of her cell, looking rather defeated.

"Now," said Stalac, turning to the female, "let's go and discuss our next course of action. With Alira in our grasp, I don't believe that there is much else to stand in our way."

"Agreed," said the female. "Still, I did not know that we had Alira until now, so I believe we should review the plan again and make any necessary revisions."

"Of course," said Stalac.

The two stone people—golems, Alira had called them—walked away to a doorway behind Alira's cell that appeared to lead into a separate room. When they stepped into it, the door closed shut.

Then the stone behemoth from before walked over to its other comrades and curled up next to them. Thus, the only awake figures in the chamber were Alira, who looked like she didn't know what to do, and Carmaz, who was not quite sure what he had just seen or what any of this meant.

Maybe I should just leave, Carmaz thought, glancing over his shoulder at the tunnel behind him. *Not like there's anything I can do about this. I don't even like Alira all that much.*

But Carmaz dismissed those thoughts quickly. While many of the details of the situation were foggy to him, one thing was clear. These golems, whatever they were, were planning to invade his world and kill a lot of innocent people, probably including many of his fellow Ruwans.

If Carmaz could get Alira out of here, then they might be able to warn the inhabitants of the surface about the coming invasion. Carmaz still didn't care for Alira much, but if rescuing her was what it took to save Martir, then he would do it.

Standing up from his hiding place, Carmaz made his way into the open chamber as stealthily as he could. He feared that the stone behemoth might hear him, but the behemoth did not move at all from its curled up position by its friends. It appeared to be asleep, which was good for Carmaz if true, but he didn't want to take any chances, so he moved as silently as he could.

Alira had lain down, as if to go back to sleep, but when she saw Carmaz approaching, she sat up again and stared at him in sheer disbelief.

"Carmaz Korva?" Alira said, though she spoke in a whisper, probably because she understood what would happen if she didn't.

85

"What are you doing here?"

Carmaz just shook his head to indicate to Alira that she should keep her mouth shut. He reached her cell soon enough and started looking for a lock to pick, which he soon found a couple of feet to his right. It was a very large, odd-looking lock, closely resembling a slab of stone, but Carmaz figured he could pick it quite easily with the lock-pick that his grandfather had given him a long time ago.

Pulling the pick out of his pocket, Carmaz stuck it into the lock and fiddled with it for a couple of tense seconds before he heard that familiar *click* that meant he had succeeded. Carmaz then carefully removed the lock from the cell door and gently laid it on the ground without making a sound.

After depositing the lock on the ground, Carmaz pulled open the cage door, which opened silently. As soon as the door was open, Alira jumped out of the cell and landed on the ground. She then straightened up and looked at Carmaz with a mixture of confusion and gratitude, as if she was not sure which emotion to express first.

Alira opened her mouth to speak, probably to thank Carmaz, but he put a hand over her mouth and shook his head. He nodded at the sleeping stone behemoths, none of which had stirred through all of this.

Alira, thankfully, seemed to get it, because she did not utter another word at all. She just nodded in understanding, causing Carmaz to remove his hand from her lips. He then nodded toward the chamber's exit, indicating their escape route, and thankfully Alira again seemed to understand, because she nodded again.

So Carmaz turned and started walking as quickly and silently to the exit as he could, Alira following closely behind. Even so, the tension in the air made every step feel like it took forever, as if Carmaz and Alira were walking on the ocean floor. Carmaz kept looking around everywhere as they walked, but he didn't see anyone who could possibly see the two of them escaping.

If someone sees us ... Carmaz didn't finish that thought.

The two of them were about halfway across the chamber when Carmaz heard the movement of stone behind him. He stopped, as did Alira, but she said, in a low whisper, "What are you doing? We have no time to waste standing around here. Let us go immediately."

Carmaz nodded, but then looked over his shoulder. The stone behemoth from before, the one that had gone to rest beside its companions, was stirring again. Then the stone behemoth raised its head and looked at both Carmaz and Alira with its featureless eyes.

Without warning, the stone behemoth let out a long, loud roar that made Carmaz and Alira freeze. The roar caused the rest of its brethren to stir, while the door to the room that Stalac and the female had entered opened and the two golems stepped out with puzzled expressions on their faces.

"What the hell is going on—" Stalac ceased speaking the second he laid eyes on Carmaz and Alira, who had still not moved from where they had froze. "Who is that?"

"It doesn't matter who it is," said the female in anger. She pointed at Carmaz and Alira. "Men, arise and capture them both! Don't let them escape."

Carmaz snapped out of his paralysis and, grabbing Alira's arm, ran to the exit as fast as he could, dragging Alira along.

Alira, however, wrenched her arm out of his hand, but followed him anyway, running so fast that she was soon running at his side and was almost overtaking him. Carmaz could hear the grinding of stone limbs as the other behemoths came to life at the female's words, but he didn't look back at all. He just kept his eyes on the tunnel exit, hoping against hope they could escape in time.

"You won't get away from us!" shouted Stalac behind him.

A stone hand burst from the floor and reached for Carmaz and Alira. The two separated, causing the stone hand to grab empty air, but then the entrance to the tunnel began to descend downwards. It would only be a few minutes before the tunnel completely closed itself off, and if it did, then Carmaz and Alira would be completely trapped down here for good.

So the two picked up speed, but then more stone hands burst from the floor and reached for them again. The presence of so many grabbing stone hands slowed their progress considerably, but neither Carmaz nor Alira stopped. They just dodged or jumped over the grabbing hands as best as they could, but it became increasingly more difficult because more and more hands rose from the earth with every step they took. Carmaz didn't let himself despair, however. He just kept going, keeping his eyes on the exit the entire time, knowing that he and Alira would get there as long as they kept going.

One of the hands almost succeeded in grabbing Carmaz's ankle. He felt its stoney fingers brush against his ankle, but thankfully its fingers were not long enough to actually catch him.

The tunnel entrance was about halfway down now, and rapidly closing, causing Carmaz and Alira to pick up a burst of speed. The two of them jumped and rolled underneath the tunnel entrance that was more than halfway down. Carmaz rolled back to his feet quickly, but Alira apparently didn't have much experience in the matter, because she ended up falling flat on her stomach, her glasses falling off her face. Nonetheless, she grabbed her glasses and jammed them back on her face as she stood up and dashed up the tunnel to freedom. Carmaz joined her.

As they ran, Carmaz heard the muted shouts of anger and curses behind the now-closed tunnel door. He didn't bother to look backwards, however, because then he would have to slow down and he didn't want to do that at all.

Fifteen minutes later, Carmaz and Alira stood together in a small clearing not far from the tunnel, although it was hidden by the trees standing around them. They would have run much farther, but Alira had clearly been out of breath and Carmaz was not in much better shape, so the two had agreed to resting in a relatively safe space until they felt ready to resume their escape. Besides, it didn't seem like the golems were chasing them right away, although Carmaz kept his ears open anyway just in case their pursuers tried to sneak up on them.

Alira sat down on a log, brushing strands of hair from her eyes. Her glasses were slightly muddy, so she removed them and began wiping them off with her robes. Her eyes looked rather small without her glasses, though she still looked like the kind of woman you wouldn't want to mess with if you valued your life.

Carmaz leaned against a tree and slid down until he was sitting on the muddy ground. He looked at Alira, but did not see any injuries on her. Still, she had such an unfriendly demeanor about herself that he wasn't sure what to say at first.

Then Alira said, without looking at him, "Thank you, Carmaz, for rescuing me. I believe this is the second time you've done so."

Carmaz blinked. "Second time?"

Alira finished wiping off her glasses. She held them up to the light radiating off the trees and then put them back on her face. "Yes. How could you forget the Void's first attack on World's End? It was you who awoke me, which allowed me to save us all from her darkness."

"Well, I didn't do that on my own," said Carmaz. "Tashir, Malya, and ... and Saia were also there."

"Yes, but I must thank you anyway," said Alira. She looked at Carmaz now, although her expression was as hard to read as ever. "I was certain I was going to be killed back there. The golems are a vicious people and they will do whatever it takes to achieve their goals."

"Just who are these golems anyway?" asked Carmaz. He glanced to the right, but did not see or hear anything sneaking up on them. "Where did they come from? I have never heard of them before."

Alira rubbed her forehead. She looked absolutely exhausted. "I am not surprised. Few have. Only the gods were aware of their existence, but the gods never thought much about them because, for much of their lives, the golems slept."

Carmaz looked at Alira in confusion. "Slept?"

"Rested, I think, is the more accurate word," said Alira. She leaned back on the log, putting her hands behind her for support. She then pointed at the ground under their feet. "Do you know what exists underneath Martir? Have you ever wondered about it?"

Carmaz shook his head. "No. I've been more concerned with my life here on the surface than on whatever exists underground."

"I suspected as much," said Alira with a sigh. "You see, Carmaz, deep beneath Martir's surface—even beneath the Mican layer—is a race of stone creatures that the gods have dubbed the resting golems. There are thousands, maybe even millions of them, and they have been down there for as long as the gods have known about them, which is to say, for thousands of years at least."

"Millions of those creatures?" Carmaz repeated. He tried to imagine millions of stone behemoths like the one he had followed all rampaging through the Swamp, which was enough to make him shudder. "Impossible. There can't be *that* many below."

"There are," said Alira. "I was told about them by the God of Language, who you know as Ranama. He explained to me that the resting golems were discovered by Mica, the Goddess of Ink and Stone, but that the gods didn't know what they were. They are not even sure that these resting golems are creations of the Powers."

"You mean that they might have been created by someone else?" asked Carmaz. "Like who?"

"No one knows," said Alira, shaking her head. "Anyway, the gods have largely ignored their existence because the resting golems have never awoken, nor have they ever reacted to any of the gods' many attempts to awaken them and find out what they were."

"But now they *are* awake?" said Carmaz.

"Some of them," said Alira. "The vast majority still rest, but a handful are trying to awaken their brothers and invade the surface. They are doing so discreetly in order to avoid attracting

91

the attention of the gods, who would stop them if they knew about their plot. You no doubt heard them speak of the invasion."

"Yeah, I did," said Carmaz, nodding. "But why Ruwa? Why are they going to start the invasion here? Why do they even want to invade Martir at all?"

"I cannot say for certain why a race of naturally heavy beings chose an island that is largely swamp and jungle as the starting point of their invasion," said Alira, "but if I had to guess, I would say that they believe that no one else would expect their invasion to stop here, either, and that they have magic to help them get around the problems their weight present. I believe they are also building that bridge from the tunnel mouth to the rest of the island to make it easier for them to invade."

"And Ruwa would be a very easy island for them to conquer," said Carmaz in realization. "We have no real united army to fend off invaders. The only reason other nations haven't tried to take Ruwa yet is because everyone else thinks this island is either cursed or just plain useless. Even the gods barely acknowledge our existence."

"Indeed," said Alira. "Now I do not know exactly why they want to invade, but I can only assume that Martir must have been built on top of their world and that they want to destroy us because of it. But I don't know for sure, and I don't need to, either, because whatever their motivation, they are all dangerous and must be stopped."

"I agree, but who are their leaders?" asked Carmaz. "What are their names?"

"The male is Stalac, while the female is called Lady Dia," said Alira. "I do not know either of them well enough to guess at their origins and motivations, but it seems to me that Lady Dia is golem royalty while Stalac is the general of her army. They tend to bicker a lot, though they seem united on the core issues of their invasion plan."

"We need to figure out how to stop them," said Carmaz. He stood up and listened again, although the Swamp was quiet at the moment. "Any ideas?"

"We must first find the gods and then return to World's End," said Alira. "It is of utmost importance that I return so that I can return to judging the Tournament. The gods can deal with the golems."

"How do we contact the gods?" asked Carmaz. "Didn't the golems say that they had blocked your magic back there?"

Alira folded her arms over her chest and looked away. "Yes, they did. And I am not sure how to unblock my magic. Golem magic seems different from Martirian magic, far too different for me to understand, and therefore too different for me to counteract."

Then Alira looked at Carmaz again and said, "Do any gods dwell on Ruwa? Such as the God of the Swamp?"

"I don't think there *is* a God of the Swamp," said Carmaz, shaking his head. "At least, no one has ever mentioned one to me. Nor are there any other gods. As I said, the gods tend to ignore Ruwa, so we don't have one."

Alira swore. "But what about mages? Mages are known as the People of the Gods, after all. If we can find a mage—any mage—then we should be able to contact the gods."

"There aren't too many mages on Ruwa," said Carmaz. He stroked his chin. "But now that I think about it ... there is a hermit living somewhere in the Swamp who is said to be a practitioner of magic. I think he is somewhere near here, in fact."

"Why did you not tell me about him sooner?" said Alira. She stood up and looked in every direction, all of her exhaustion seeming to have vanished completely now. "Where is he?"

Carmaz scratched the back of his head. "I'm not sure you want to meet him."

Alira looked at Carmaz with confusion. "Why? If he is a mage, as you said, then that means he can contact the gods. And if we can contact the gods, then we can inform them of the invasion and they can put a stop to it before it even begins."

"He's supposed to be … crazy," said Carmaz. "Very, very, *very* crazy."

"Crazy? How?" asked Alira.

"Well, I have never actually met him, of course, because he never visited Conewood," said Carmaz, "but the stories I always heard about him described him as a mad mage who sucked the blood out of tiny animals and wore their skins as his clothing. He'd use a kind of dark magic that no one understood to do all sorts of horrible things to animals and people alike, which is partly why he lives alone, because no one wants to be around his dark magic."

Alira raised an eyebrow. "Dark magic? Is that supposed to frighten me? I think not. You will take me to this hermit and you will do so without hesitation."

Carmaz frowned as he stood up. "You're not my leader. So why don't you try a nicer tone?"

"Nicer tone?" Alira repeated. She walked up to him until their faces were inches apart, actually causing Carmaz to step back slightly to get some space. "Why should I treat *you* nicely when the entire world is about to be invaded by a race of unstoppable golems? Besides, I don't see the point in treating rule-breakers like yourself with any respect."

Alira said 'rule-breakers' like it was the harshest slur she knew. And Carmaz actually did feel somewhat offended by it at first, at least until he shook his head and said, "Well, if we're going to be working together to stop this invasion, then I thought we could actually treat each other a little bit more kindly. You don't even have your magic anymore, which puts you on the same level as me if you think about it."

Alira humphed and turned away from Carmaz. "Fine. I don't need the help of a rule-breaker like you. I will go and find this hermit myself."

"The Swamp is a pretty big place," Carmaz said. "There are lots of stories of people getting lost. Sometimes they get sucked into the mud, sometimes they get eaten by monsters and wild animals, and sometimes their souls get stolen by ghosts and their corpses wander the Swamp all by themselves ready to capture anyone else unlucky enough to get lost in here."

Alira looked over her shoulder at Carmaz, a look of disbelief on her features. "Do you honestly believe that there are ghosts in here that steal people's souls?"

Carmaz shrugged. "I've never seen any, though Saia once told me that he saw the ghost of this little boy who died in the Swamp when we were kids. Just saying that even us Ruwans sometimes have a hard time navigating and surviving the Swamp on our own, so if you just walk off on your own like this, you'll probably be dead within the hour."

Alira bit her lip and looked away. Carmaz could tell, however, that she was thinking about what he had just said. Part of Carmaz secretly hoped that she would decide to go off on her own anyway, seeing as he would have enjoyed seeing her arrogant self get taken down a notch by the Swamp's harsh environment.

But then Alira turned back around. She was still frowning, but she said, in a very reluctant voice, "Very well, Carmaz. We will work as … equals, at least until we find the hermit you speak of and return to World's End."

Alira sounded like she was forcing herself to say every word. Carmaz enjoyed hearing the strain in her voice, mostly because he liked knowing that she had to rely upon him now.

Aloud, however, Carmaz said, "All right, then. We need to head east from here, but be careful, because the Swamp is full of dangerous things that will kill you the moment you let your guard down."

Chapter Seven

ACCORDING TO CAPTAIN Garvan, the disappearance of Princess Raya Mana was discovered by Doctor Ilran, who had come up to her apartment to administer her daily medicines and to check on her progress. The doctor had entered her room only to discover that Raya was not in her bed and he performed a thorough check of the entire apartment before concluding that she had indeed vanished, had likely been kidnapped based on the available evidence.

All of that Braim learned from what Garvan had told Grinf after making the dramatic announcement. Grinf ordered Garvan to have every Soldier of the Gods in the city search everywhere for her and to also put out a notice to the rest of the katabans and gods to keep an eye out for Raya or her kidnapper, whose identity was unknown according to the Captain.

When Garvan left to do as Grinf commanded, Grinf informed the rest of the godlings that the Avian Goddess Sub-Bracket Challenge was still to continue and that all of the godlings were not allowed to leave the Stadium until it was over. Not that Braim wanted to leave, because if Raya had been kidnapped like that, then there was a high likelihood that the security of the other godlings was in danger as well.

That didn't stop the rest of the godlings from talking about the kidnapping, however. Even as the first of the vision bubbles started to fade away with each victory (except for Malya's, which showed that both Malya and her opponent were having more trouble with their birds than the other participants were), most of the attention was now on Raya's kidnapping and the identity of her kidnapper.

"Okay, this is really weird," said Tamra, rubbing her hands together anxiously. "*Two* disappearances in one day? First Judge Alira, now Princess Raya. This has got to be the Void's doing."

"I agree," said Braim, nodding. "Only the Void would have any interest in kidnapping Alira and Raya. The only question is, what is the Void trying to accomplish by kidnapping them both like this?"

"I do not know," said Tashir, shaking his head. He folded his arms across his chest, a disturbed expression crossing his shark-like features. "But I wonder if there are going to be any more kidnappings before the day is out."

"Maybe you'll be next, Braim," said Yoji, folding his hands behind his head and propping his feat on the back of the seat before him. He seemed remarkably relaxed about this recent turn of events. "After all, you're as special as Alira and Raya, what with having come back to life recently and everything."

Braim looked down at the floor under his feet to see if there was any movement in the shadows. He saw none, but that hardly comforted him because he knew exactly how sly the Void could be.

"Let's not focus on such awful thoughts," said Tashir, looking at Yoji in annoyance. "And why are you taking this so easily? Raya is also a participant in the Hollech Bracket, same as yourself."

Yoji shrugged. "What do *I* have to be afraid of? If the Void is behind this, she probably wants us too scared to fight back. Being a prodigy, I have no reason to be afraid of anything that the Void does. I can handle it like a champ."

Yoji punched the air when he said that. His arrogance seemed unwarranted to Braim, but he decided not to mention that at the moment.

Braim looked at Grinf. The god was entirely fixated on the vision bubbles and the challenges displayed on them, but somehow Braim could tell that Grinf was not nearly as interested in those challenges as he seemed. Likely Grinf was thinking about the recent kidnappings and what they meant and how to deal with them.

"I wish there was something we could do to help," said Tamra with a sigh. "I never knew Raya very well, but I feel awful not knowing where she is. She might be dying even as we speak."

"Let's focus on some more positive things, shall we?" said Tashir. "I mean, of course Raya's death is always a possibility, but I have always believed that negative thoughts in a negative situation can make said situation more negative than it already is. I believe we must hope that Raya is well and that we will save her, and we will."

"Or that the Soldiers and gods will, anyway," said Yoji. "Or heck, maybe it was one of the gods who kidnapped Raya. I mean, Braim was kidnapped by two different gods already, right?"

"Yeah, but why would any god kidnap Raya and Alira?" asked Braim. He shook his head. "It's way more likely that the Void did it, and I think I even know why: it was Raya who stopped the Void during her second attack on World's End, so she probably wants vengeance on Raya for what she did to her."

"Then she is definitely dead by now," said Yoji, nodding. He shrugged. "Oh well. Nice knowing her while she lasted. She was kind of hot."

Tashir slapped Yoji in the back of the head, causing Yoji to yelp and rub the spot where Tashir had slapped him. Lowering his legs back onto the floor, Yoji glared at Tashir and asked, "What was that for?"

"For saying such negative thoughts aloud like that," said Tashir. "Were you not listening to what I said about negativity affecting a situation?"

"Whatever," said Yoji. He yawned, but then glanced at Tashir as if he expected the makhimancer to hit him again. "I didn't do anything wrong. I'm just saying that if the Void *really* wants to get revenge on Raya, then she probably is already dead."

That caused Tashir to start arguing with Yoji. Braim tried to stop them, but the two mages completely ignored all of Braim's attempts to get them to stop fighting until Grinf barked an order at the two to shut up and watch the challenge. As a result, they did stop arguing and begin focusing on the vision bubbles, though they ignored each other and treated the other as if he did not exist.

The sub-bracket challenge went on for a little while after that, but eventually Malya defeated her opponent and the other challengers followed suit until all of the vision bubbles vanished. After that, Grinf told the rest of the godlings that the next and final sub-bracket challenge—the Skimif Sub-Bracket Challenge —was to take place later in the afternoon. For now, the rest of the godlings were allowed to leave and do what they pleased as long as they returned to the Stadium when the next sub-bracket challenge was about to start.

So Braim went down with everyone else to the Stadium lobby to congratulate the five winners. Or he would have gone to congratulate Malya, but when he and the others entered the lobby, he saw a large figure who he had not expected to see again standing there.

The figure was tall, bulky, and metallic, with a skull-like head that made him look a lot scarier than he actually was. He was speaking with Malya, who didn't seem very disturbed by the large figure's appearance, though the other winners stood a good distance from the two of them, like they did not trust the armored figure at all.

"Who is that?" Tamra asked Braim in a whisper as they and the other godlings stopped to watch. "A god?"

"No," said Braim, shaking his head. "An automaton. Raya's bodyguard. Think it's name is Keeper."

"Keeper?" Tamra repeated. Then realization flashed in her eyes. "Oh, I remember hearing about him, though this is the first time I've seen him. What's he doing here?"

"No clue," said Braim. "I thought he'd be out searching for Raya."

Then Keeper looked over to the crowd of godlings and his eyes focused on Braim. He then pointed at Braim and said, "Braim Kotogs, I would like to speak with you in private for a moment."

Braim didn't like being singled out like this, especially by a figure as large and hulking as Keeper, but he nodded and separated from the rest of the crowd. Keeper said something in a low voice to Malya, who nodded and gave him a grateful smile.

Then Keeper walked over to Braim, while the rest of the godlings made their way around Keeper to congratulate the winners. Most of them looked at the large automaton in awe and curiosity as they passed him, which made sense, because automatons were not very common in the Northern Isles, even among the very rich.

Keeper and Braim stood in a corner of the lobby while everyone else congratulated the winners. While the general atmosphere of the lobby was rather cheerful because of the congratulations going around, Keeper approached Braim with a very somber mood, evident even though Keeper's face was incapable of making any facial expressions.

"Braim Kotogs," said Keeper. He held out one massive hand to Braim. "I believe this is the first time we've met, though I have seen you before."

Braim took Keeper's hand, which swallowed his hand whole, and shook it. He was surprised to find out just how gentle Keeper's shake was, although it still felt strong to him nonetheless.

"Yeah, same here," said Braim. He removed his hand from Keeper's and looked up at him. "So I guess you heard the news?"

Keeper nodded. "Yes. Her Majesty Princess Raya is missing and no one knows where she is. I only just came back from Carnag ten minutes ago. I have been asking around for anyone who might know anything, but so far I have received no clues for me to follow. It is very frustrating, which I believe is the word you humans would use to describe this situation."

"Well, she *was* just discovered missing not even an hour ago," Braim pointed out. "Given time, I bet the Soldiers will find more evidence to help us locate her."

"You don't understand," said Keeper. "When I left Carnag, I told His Majesty King Malock and Her Majesty Queen Hana that their daughter was safe and recovering from the Void's attack. If they were to discover that I had failed in my duty to save her *again* ... oh, I do not even want to think about it. It is therefore of utmost importance that I find out where she is and rescue her, without delay."

Braim shrugged. "I'm sorry, but I can't help you there. I don't even know where she is. I just learned about it maybe half an hour ago myself."

"I was about to ask you because you are one of Raya's friends," said Keeper. "But you truly do not know who might have kidnapped her?"

Braim raised an eyebrow. "Friend? When did I ever say I was one of Raya's friends?"

Keeper tilted his large head to the side. "I thought you and Carmaz Korva were her closest friends. You mean to say you aren't?"

"Don't get me wrong, I don't hate her anything," said Braim, holding up his hands defensively. "I was just never really that close to her. That's all."

"I see," said Keeper. "Human relationships confuse me. I will have to make note of this so I do not make that erroneous assumption again."

"All right," said Braim. "But if you want my theory, the other godlings and I think it was the Void that kidnapped her. She and the Void don't get along very well, so we think the Void might have kidnapped her in order to get revenge on her for all of the times that she's foiled the Void's plans."

"That is a possibility I have not considered before," said Keeper, stroking his large chin. "But I do not believe I can go into the Void, otherwise I'd be destroyed. Literally, because automatons react to the Void's corrosive force even worse than mortals do."

"Like I said, it's just a theory and might not be correct, but it's all we have at the moment," said Braim. "Sorry I couldn't be of more help. I'd love to help, but this all just happened recently and no one really knows anything yet."

"Very true," said Keeper. "Still, I must not give up. Tell me, where is Carmaz Korva? It is my understanding that Princess Raya fancied him, so perhaps he might be able to help me locate her."

You can say that *again,* Braim thought, but aloud he said, "He was kicked out of the Tournament for breaking the rules. He's probably back on his home island of Ruwa, so he most likely has no idea Raya is even missing."

"A logical deduction," said Keeper. "That means that asking him if he knows anything would be a waste of time. I shall instead search the city for her. It is all that I know to do right now, at least until more facts and clues are uncovered."

"Sounds like a plan," said Braim, nodding. "Again, wish I could help, but I'm just as ignorant as you are in this situation. If I find out anything, though, I'll let you know."

"Thank you," said Keeper. "You are a true friend … er, acquaintance, of Princess Raya, I mean."

With that, an ethereal portal opened behind Keeper and he stepped into it backwards. A second later, the portal closed, leaving Braim standing all alone in the corner of the Stadium lobby while the others continued to congratulate the winners.

Braim was about to join them, but he found himself thinking about Carmaz. He knew that if Carmaz was here, he'd be the first to go looking for Raya, because despite constantly rejecting Raya's advances, Carmaz had always seemed to care about her anyway.

But not about me, I guess, Braim thought, shaking his head. *It's better that he's not here. We don't need that kind of person anywhere near us.*

So Braim went over to congratulate Malya on her victory, pushing all thoughts of Carmaz out of his mind. He decided that he didn't need to think about his former friend, not anymore, and perhaps never again if he could help it.

A little later on, Braim returned to his room in the inn. The innkeeper had left him a plate of chicken and rice on his dresser for his lunch, which Braim ate, although katabans chicken tasted awful and the rice was even blander than usual. But Braim ate it anyway because he was hungry and wasn't in the mood to go and find a restaurant to eat.

As Braim sat in the wooden chair by his dresser, munching on the chicken in his hands, he wondered what the Skimif Sub-Bracket Challenge was going to be. Grinf seemed to be taking a leaf from Alira's book because he did not tell Braim or anyone else what the challenge was going to entail. Braim just hoped that it didn't require any magic, because with his magical abilities still lost, he would be at a complete disadvantage and would probably lose within the first five minutes of the start of the challenge.

I can't *lose,* Braim thought. *Not yet. Not when losing means being at the mercy of whichever god happens to want to experiment upon or kill me me.*

Braim finished his chicken and rice quickly, but now didn't know what else to do. He considered taking a nap, but he was not feeling particularly tired at the moment, even with a full belly. He also considered visiting some of the other godlings, but the idea of getting up and walking around the large city to meet the others made him feel exhausted just thinking about it.

I think I do *need a nap,* Braim decided. *Just rest for a couple of minutes and then figure out what to do from there.*

So Braim stood up and placed his plate on the dresser before he heard something outside his window. He looked at the window, but did not see anything outside it except for the buildings and streets of World's End. Still, he knew he'd heard something, so he was going to investigate it before taking his nap.

Walking over to the window, Braim pulled aside the shutters and poked his head outside to see if he could spot what had made that noise. The streets outside of the inn were empty at the moment, with not even a squirrel in sight. There was, however, a strong wind blowing through at the moment, which was probably the source of the thing he had heard outside his window.

Pulling his head back into the room, Braim pulled the shutters closed just as he heard movement behind himself. Braim whirled around in time to see a sharp, black blade fly at his face.

Without thinking, Braim jumped to the side, causing the blade to miss him. But the blade was not by itself. It was actually held by a woman in dead gray robes, her head hidden by a hood and a balaclava that completely obscured her whole face. Even her eyes were covered by a bandanna that was the same color as the mask she wore. She was slipping something into her pocket, though what it was, Braim couldn't see.

Staggering backwards, Braim said, "Who the hell are you?"

The woman did not answer. She just turned to face Braim and started advancing on him, her black knife reminding Braim far too much of the Void. It even seemed to move like the Void, unless Braim's eyes were playing tricks on him. Whether they were or weren't, the woman's intent was easy to tell, so Braim would have to fight back as best as he could.

Braim reached for his wand before remembering, just as he grabbed it, that he did not have any magical power at all and that his wand was therefore little more than a useless piece of finely-carved wood. That realization almost distracted him from the woman, who chose that moment to lunge toward him again with frightening speed.

This time, Braim dodged the blow easily, but took advantage of the opening she left to punch her. The woman, however, moved out of the range of Braim's fist without moving her legs. At least, Braim didn't see her legs move, but the entire fight was happening so quickly that he just dismissed it as his eyes not keeping up with what was going on around him.

The woman twirled her knife in her hand before hurling it at Braim. Again, Braim dodged, but was surprised to see that the knife was attached to a thin steel chain that allowed the woman to jerk the knife back. It flew back into her hand and the woman jumped toward Braim, jumping far higher and longer than a normal human woman should have been able to do.

Braim rolled forward underneath her as she passed. Rising to his feet, Braim grabbed his plate off the top of his dresser and turned around and hurled it at her. The woman had landed with her back to Braim, but she immediately whirled around in time to catch the plate and carefully place it on the floor at her feet.

That took Braim by surprise, because he had expected her to knock the plate out of the air and smash it to bits. He was so surprised that he almost forgot he was still fighting her, but he remembered quickly when the woman ran at him again, this time moving even faster than before.

By the time Braim had registered that, however, the woman was already within stabbing range, so close that Braim could see the markings on the handle of her knife. She threw her knife at him again, but as before, Braim dodged by jumping to the side.

Only this time, the woman seemed to have expected that, because she followed his movement and turned to face him. Rather than stab him in the face, however, she pulled out her chain and wrapped it around his neck.

Braim tried to yelp in pain, because the chain was a lot sharper than it looked and so bit his neck harshly. But one tug from the woman choked off his yelp before he could even let it out, and soon he stopped feeling air flowing into his lungs and his vision became watery due to the tears in his eyes from the pain.

In desperation, Braim lashed out with his fist, actually punching the woman in the face. She let go of his neck immediately, causing Braim to gasp for fresh air and to feel his neck, which was bleeding slightly from where her chain had cut into it, but it did not feel fatal or deep at least.

Lowering his hands, Braim looked up to see the woman staggering backwards, her hand over her masked face. Braim hadn't thought he'd punched her *that* hard, but he guessed that he was stronger than he thought. In any case, he knew he couldn't beat this woman on his own, so he'd have to call for help.

"Innkeeper!" Braim shouted, his voice somewhat hoarse from having been choked. "Someone is trying to kill me! Call for help!"

Braim didn't know if the innkeeper heard his calls for help or not, but the woman assassin apparently believed that he did, because she looked up in alarm and, without another word, dashed toward the window. She jumped through the open window, but Braim ran after her to see where she was going.

When he reached the window, Braim saw the woman land in the streets with ease and then make off to the north. He tried to follow her progress from his window, but the woman soon became lost among the buildings of the city. She was gone.

A second later, the door to his room burst open and the innkeeper—a portly male katabans with bright red hair—staggered in. He looked like he had just awoken from a nap.

"Eh?" said the innkeeper. "What be the—"

The innkeeper noticed Braim's bloody neck and gasped. "How that happen to you?"

Braim looked down at his neck, which was still quite bloody from where the woman's chain had bit, and said, "I was attacked just a few minutes ago by a woman I've never seen before. Call the Soldiers."

The innkeeper nodded quickly, saying in his normal somewhat broken Divina, "Yes, yes, yes, I shall. And doctor. Will get doctor as well for neck."

The innkeeper then turned and ran, leaving Braim alone in his room, wondering just who that woman was and why she had just tried to kill him. He had a feeling that that would not be the last time he'd see her again.

Chapter Eight

ZEEREE RAISED HIS massive fists above his head. Raya struggled against the thick mud that she had fallen into, but it sucked her in and clung to her hands, clothes, and body like a second skin. She kept looking over her shoulder at Zeeree's massive form, even though there was nothing she could do to stop him. She prayed to Grinf and to the gods in general to save her, despite not being at all sure that any of them were actually listening to her at all.

Then, through the bushes ahead, Raya caught a glimpse of blue. She at first thought that it was nothing or maybe some kind of swamp beast, before a spear, painted as blue as the sky, flew out of nowhere over her head. Raya watched, surprised, as the spear landed directly in Zeeree's chest.

The half-god let out a bellow of pain and staggered backward from the blow. He began trying to remove the spear from his chest, gold blood leaking out of the wound. It pleased Raya to see Zeere in such pain, especially when she noticed how much difficulty that Zeeree was having in removing the spear.

Then she heard a voice say, "Grab on!" causing her to look in time to see a rope land on the mud just within her reach. It came from within the bushes, meaning that Raya couldn't see who had thrown it, but she could see two blue eyes in the bushes that looked human.

"What are you waiting for?" the eyes asked. They had a masculine voice, with a slightly wild tinge to it, but Raya didn't analyze it too much.

Raya just grabbed the rope, and as soon as she did, she was jerked out of the mud. The mud clung to her body, but it was no match for the strength of the person who had thrown the rope, who hauled her out of the mud as easily as if she had not had any mud on her at all.

Now Raya was on much more solid ground than before and she let out a sigh of relief as her savior stepped out of the bushes. He was a tall man with a bushy brown beard, which made him look older than he actually was. He wore a simple green shirt, which looked old and worn and faded, with several pockets on the front that bulged with things that Raya could not see. His skin was quite dark and dirty, like he had been rolling in the dirt all day, but his arms were muscular and he looked like he could wrestle a baba raga in a fight and win.

"Are you okay?" asked the man as he looked down at Raya with concern. "Did the monster harm you?"

Raya shook her head, but cringed when she looked at her own muddy clothing. "No, but that monster hurt my fashion by making me run into that mud like that. Gross."

The man looked relieved that she was okay, but he didn't ask her any other questions. He just grabbed her by the collar of her shirt and hauled her to her feet, which she would have protested as absolutely boorish and unacceptable behavior under normal circumstances but which she today said nothing about because she was grateful that he had saved her.

Then the man grabbed her artificial hand—which he didn't even seem to notice wasn't normal—and said, "We must go quickly, before the monster recovers."

Raya looked over her shoulder at Zeeree. The half-god was still trying to remove the spear from his chest, but he seemed to be having little success, which made Raya wonder how deeply the spear had penetrated his chest.

Then she looked at the man again and said, "While I agree that we should go, can you give me a name—?"

"Herune," the man said simply. "You?"

"Raya," said Raya. "Princess Raya, Princess of—"

"I don't care," Herune cut her off. He then turned and said, "Now we must go, before the witch returns."

Herune suddenly took off through the bushes. Raya, who had not expected him to move so fast, was almost thrown off her feet by his speed, but she just barely managed to keep her balance as she ran with him. She heard Zeeree continue to roar in pain after them, but she did not dare look back anymore, because if she did, she wasn't sure she'd be able to keep running.

Then Herune looked to the right and gasped. "Duck!"

He immediately fell to the ground, pulling Raya with him. Raya fell rather awkwardly on her stomach, which she would have complained about if a burning fire bolt hadn't flown past her head and struck one of the nearby trees, causing it to burst into flame. Raya looked in time to see Aorja standing in the direction where the fire bolt had come from, aiming her wand directly at them with a murderous expression on her face.

"Where do you two think you're going?" asked Aorja. Her eye twitched. "Do you really think that you can escape *me*? Because if you do, that's rather amusing. Unfortunately for you, however, amusing me will not be enough to save your lives."

Aorja waved her wand again, this time causing vines to shoot down from the trees toward Raya and Herune. Raya screamed, but Herune drew a wand from his pocket and waved it at the vines.

The vines suddenly became entangled in each other, stopping halfway to Raya and Herune. Aorja gasped in surprise, but then Herune pointed his own wand at Aorja and the tree next to her suddenly lashed out with one of its branches and struck her in the face.

The blow knocked Aorja flat onto her back. Like when she saw Zeeree get stabbed, Raya felt a certain sense of satisfaction at seeing Aorja get knocked down like that, but it was not a feeling that she got to dwell on for long, because Herune jumped to his feet and hauled her up again, saying, "Come on! We don't have a whole lot of time to waste."

Raya agreed, so she let Herune take her hand again and pull her through the branches and bushes of the Swamp. As they ran, Raya heard Zeeree roaring again, except this time he no longer sounded like he was in pain. Instead, his roars sounded angry and were followed by the loud crunching of tree branches and bushes and the sloshing of large feet making their way through the muddy earth, causing Raya to look over her shoulder.

Zeeree was following them now. He had a huge gap in his chest, bloody and hideous, where Herune's spear had pierced his chest. Raya even thought that she saw Zeeree's heart, although she didn't know for sure because she was too busy staring at Herune's blood spear, which Zeeree now held in his hands like a murder weapon.

There was no grace to Zeeree's rampage at all. He was just tearing through the swamp, knocking down small trees, sending mud clods flying everywhere, batting aside any birds unfortunate enough to get in his way, and even pushing aside any trees too big for him to knock down. Even worse, he was making rapid progress and Raya figured it wouldn't be long before the half-god caught up to them. His chest wound didn't seem to slow him down at all. If anything, it seemed to be the driving motivation behind his rage, keeping him going after them no matter what.

Raya looked at Herune and shouted, "Zeeree's gonna kill us! What's the plan?"

Herune didn't even look over his shoulder. He just shouted, "Keep running! We'll be safe. Just trust me."

Raya wasn't sure she could 'just trust' Herune, even though he had saved her. Still, she decided she could do that at least until they got away from Zeeree.

Speaking of the half-god, Zeeree was gaining on them and seemed ever more likely to catch up with them. Now Raya did not know exactly what Zeeree was going to do if he caught them, but she sincerely doubted that all he wanted to do was give them a big hug.

Then Herune waved his wand under their feet and above their head so quickly that Raya at first thought it was just a trick of the eyes. Especially when nothing magical happened as they ran, making her think that Herune had done nothing until she heard Zeeree roar again, except this time there was a hint of confusion combined with his anger, followed by the sound of something heavy sinking into the mud.

Looking over her shoulder, Raya saw that that particular bit of swamp floor had essentially become a sinkhole. Zeeree had sunk up to his waist and was sinking further even as he struggled to pull himself out of it. A dozen vines shoot down from the trees and wrapped themselves around his arms, but when Zeeree pulled down on the vines in an effort to use the stationary trees as leverage to get out of the sinkhole, the trees fell directly on top of him, because the ground around them was also little more than a sinkhole. Zeeree roared in frustration, but that did him no good because there was no one to get him out of there.

Nonetheless, Zeeree somehow managed to hurl Herune's blue spear after them. Both Raya and Herune ducked in time to avoid the flying projectile, which landed in the center of another tree. Herune just waved his wand at the spear and it flew after them, hovering beside the two runners like some kind of strange bird.

Zeeree's roars behind them were as audible as always, but they no longer seemed as scary as before because he was incapable of actually chasing them. Indeed, Raya believed that they were home-free at this point, because with both Zeeree and Aorja down, there didn't seem to be any other obstacles in their path.

Of course, just as Raya thought that, a massive hand made of mud rose from the earth in front of them, completely blocking their path. Raya and Herune skid to a halt just as the massive hand came down on them with the force of a thousand pounds of dirt.

But Herune raised his wand and forced the giant mud hand to go to the side. It slammed into the earth to their left, covering both Raya and Herune in even more mud (some of which got in Raya"s mouth), but Herune continued to run as if they had not just been about to be squashed underneath the force of that hand. Raya

116

looked around as they ran, trying to spot Aorja, but didn't see her until she caught a glimpse of blonde in the trees above.

Raya tried to warn Herune, but before she could, Aorja jumped down from the trees and landed in their path. Again, Raya and Herune came to a stop as Aorja aimed her wand at them.

"All right, swamp freak, I'm going to give you a couple of options because I'm a reasonable woman," said Aorja. "Either give me Raya back and I will let you go crawl back onto whatever tree you fell from or I will step over your body to get her."

Herune didn't look very afraid of Aorja, even though he must have been able to sense her power due to his obvious status as a mage. His grip around Raya's hand was as strong as ever, which told Raya all she needed to know about his choice.

"You'll kill me no matter what I do, witch," said Herune, shaking his head. "That's just in your nature. You kill and kill and kill, even if you don't need to. I know how you have used your power to terrorize the lives of the innocent people of Ruwa."

Aorja actually smirked. "Well, I admit that I do enjoy killing, but only if it's someone I absolutely hate. Or if they get in the way of my amazing plans, like you."

"Say what you wish, but I am no fool and neither is this woman," said Herune, gesturing at Raya behind him with his wand. "But I am afraid I cannot say the same for you."

"Call me what you like, but I'm still the Limitless one around here and you're just an average mage of average strength," said Aorja. "If I wanted, I could destroy this entire swamp in the blink of an eye. How would you like that?"

"Would not be very convenient for me, I must admit," said Herune, "for the jungle is my home and I would have nowhere to go if it was destroyed."

"Then give me Raya," said Aorja. "Now."

Raya gulped, but then she noticed movement in the treetops above her. It looked like a snake was slithering through the trees, but she didn't pay too much attention because she didn't like snakes and because she was sure that Aorja would use any distraction she could to attack them both if given the chance.

"No," said Herune. He held up his wand before him like a sword. "I'd sooner slit my own throat than let you take this innocent woman and use her for your own vile purposes, whatever those may be."

"Very well, then," said Aorja. The tip of her wand started to glow and crackle with energy. "Guess you can say good bye to your precious, stinky—"

Aorja was interrupted when another vine shot down through the treetops and wrapped around her wand arm. Aorja had only a split second to look at it in confusion before the vine jerked her upwards out of sight. Then Raya heard her scream, but it sounded like it was getting fainter and fainter, as if Aorja was going farther and farther away. A second later, Raya could hear Aorja's screams no more.

Without explanation or comment, Herune started running again. Raya followed, but she still looked up at the treetops, trying to catch a glimpse of Aorja, but she saw no sign of the mad mage anywhere among the thick branches and leaves above.

Looking back at Herune, Raya asked, "What happened to Aorja? Where did she go?"

"I threw her," Herune answered, still without looking at her. He did, however, gesture in an easterly direction with his wand.

118

"Somewhere east as far from us as possible."

"Threw her?" Raya repeated in alarm. "How?"

"Using that vine, obviously," said Herune as their feet splattered across the muddy ground. "Like a catapult."

"Is she dead?" Raya said, unsure if she should say that with hope or horror.

"Highly unlikely," said Herune. "Maybe broke her legs, possibly paralyzed for life depending on where she landed, but she's too mean and nasty to die like that. But she'll probably be unable to come after us again for a while."

Raya wished that Herune had actually killed Aorja, but she supposed that you couldn't have everything you wanted in life. Nonetheless, she was thankful for Herune's rescue, so she simply kept her thoughts to herself as she followed him through the jungle, doing her best to ignore the angry roars of Zeeree, who sounded like he was still stuck in the sinkhole that Herune had trapped him in. She just hoped that wherever Herune was taking her, that she would be safe and be able to find her way back to World's End at some point.

Chapter Nine

WHAT IS THE name of the hermit we are looking for?" asked Alira as she and Carmaz walked through the thick undergrowth of the Swamp. She was walking a little bit behind him because Carmaz had told her that he knew the Swamp better than her and so was better equipped to handle any dangers that might lie in their path.

"Herune, I think," said Carmaz, ducked under an overhanging branch before walking upright again. "Most of the time, we just call him the Swamp Hermit."

"How long has he lived out here in the Swamp?" asked Alira as she stepped over a fallen tree that was partway sunk in the mud.

"No idea," said Carmaz, shaking his head. "I've heard stories about him all my life, so at least thirty years, but maybe longer. Saia, when he was alive, once told me that the Hermit was there when Ruwa fell a thousand years ago and is immortal, but I'm not sure about that because Saia told me a lot of things that weren't true when we were children." Then Carmaz looked at Alira. "Why do you want to know?"

"Because I dislike ignorance," said Alira. "I prefer to have complete knowledge of my situation, whatever it may be, so that when I go into it I know what I am getting into. Anyway, is he friendly?"

Carmaz shrugged. "Some say that he protects the lives of innocent people who get lost in the Swamp, especially young children who don't have any parents. Others say he's a cannibal who lures lost people into the Swamp and then kills them when they least expect it, especially young children."

Alira frowned. "You humans certainly place a lot of emphasis on your young, it seems."

Carmaz thought of Frissa, the young girl from Conewood, when she said that, but aloud he said, "Of course we do. Our children are our future. It only makes sense that we would value them."

"I see," said Alira. "Well, it's nothing I would understand. I cannot procreate, but I have no need to. So long as I continue to judge the Tournament, I will be happy and content."

Carmaz nodded and then swatted an annoying insect that had been buzzing in his ear. "All right. But have you ever thought about what you'd do *after* the Tournament is over?"

For the first time since Carmaz had known her, Alira looked genuinely confused. She tilted her head to the side and adjusted her glasses. "What?"

"After the Tournament is finished," Carmaz repeated. "What will you do then?"

Alira was silent for a couple of seconds as they walked. Then she said, "How did Ruwa fall?"

The change in subject was abrupt. Carmaz was tempted to return the conversation to the original subject, but then he heard in Alira's tone a clear sign that she was not interested in discussing her future plans with him. Carmaz hadn't really been interested anyway, seeing as he and Alira were not that close. He had merely asked out of idle curiosity, though a part of him did wonder if Alira had any plans for a life post-Tournament of the Gods.

So Carmaz said, "I don't know the exact details, but the story I was always told is that about one thousand years ago, Ruwa was a great island nation and its inhabitants were very rich. Even the poorest of Ruwans never had to worry about food or water or clothing. All of that came to an end, however, when the king of Ruwa caused a magical disaster to sweep over the island that completely destroyed its economy and crops, killing thousands and injuring many more."

"That is awful," said Alira. "What happened after that?"

Carmaz shrugged. "The people recovered, but not to the same extent as they once did. The royal family was dead and the population had shrunk to perhaps a third of its original size. The people cried out to the gods for aid, but the gods ignored them. Other nations stopped trading with and visiting us, except for pirates and other criminals like them. Ever since then, Ruwa has lacked both a government and a united people, with the majority of its inhabitants living in scattered, independent villages all across the island."

"You sound bitter," said Alira. She pushed aside a branch in her path.

"You think?" said Carmaz. He shook his head. "Of course I'm bitter. Everyone on Ruwa is bitter. The gods—who we believed cared for our long-term well-being—abandoned us when we needed them most and we are hated and feared by everyone else because they think the gods cursed us. That's not even counting my own personal issues, which I think you are aware of."

"If you are going to demand that I allow you to participate in the Tournament again—" Alira began.

Carmaz cut her off. "No. I'm not asking that. I know I broke the rules and that breaking the rules has consequences. I'm just saying that Ruwa is not a happy place and I am not a happy person because of our shortsighted gods. I don't expect any sympathy from you or anyone else."

Again, Alira fell into silence. He found it hard to tell if she was impressed or not, but he didn't care. He had lived his whole life, after all, not giving a damn if the gods or anyone else cared about him, and he would live the rest of his life, however short, in the same way.

Then Alira said, "The gods are very shortsighted. That much I agree with you. I have not lived on Martir as long as you, but the gods do seem to lack wisdom and foresight, despite their age. It is frustrating to work with them because they do not seem to learn no matter what happens to them."

Carmaz looked at Alira in surprise. "I didn't think you'd feel that way about them."

"I'm not interested in befriending the gods," said Alira. "They have shown themselves to not be very intelligent or wise. Back when I was on World's End, I limited my interaction with them rather severely, because I did not want to let their attitudes cloud my judgment."

"How would you describe their current attitudes?" asked Carmaz as he stepped over a mud puddle that looked very slippery.

"Scared," said Alira. "They are getting along well enough

without a God of Martir to lead them, but they are still afraid. They fear that the Void will destroy us all unless we get the new gods created right away. They do not believe they can stop it by themselves, not anymore at least."

Carmaz frowned when he thought of the Void. He had not seen any sign of it since returning to Ruwa, which made sense, seeing as the Void was all the way on the other end of the world. Still, he knew just how powerful it was and how it could easily destroy all of Martir if it was allowed to. He hadn't thought that the gods would be afraid of it, however.

"But without you there, how can the Tournament continue?" asked Carmaz. "Who is going to judge it?"

"In all likelihood, one of the gods will take up the mantle of judge," said Alira. "Who, I don't know, but one of them will. Even so, I must return to World's End as quickly as I can, because it is still my duty to judge the Tournament, a duty given to me by the Powers themselves."

Carmaz nodded, but then looked ahead and stopped. "Wait. I think we're at the Hermit's house."

Alira stopped and looked in the same direction as Carmaz. She briefly removed her glasses, cleaned them of some of the mud that had gotten on them, and then put them back on her face, probably so she could see the Hermit's house better.

The Hermit's house was much larger than any other building on Ruwa, at least that Carmaz had seen. It looked more like a compound, with large stone walls covered in mud and plants surrounding it. A simple stone path, partially covered in mud, led from their current position all the way up to the front gates, which were somewhat stylized to resemble tiger heads. The place looked abandoned and they saw no one on the outside.

"That is a large house for a hermit," Alira said.

"Agreed," said Carmaz, "but I was told that he lives in a fortress with tiger head gates. This is the first time I've been to it, but I'm confident that this is his home."

"Then where is he?" said Alira, looking around the area with an impatient expression on her face.

"Not sure," said Carmaz. "Depending on which story you believe, he could be either helping an innocent lost person find their way back home or eating them. Or maybe he's taking a nap."

Alira punched Carmaz in the arm. Despite being thinner than Carmaz, her punch actually hurt quite a bit, causing Carmaz to rub his arm and say, "What was that for?"

Alira rolled her eyes like Carmaz had just missed a self-evident revelation. She did open her mouth to speak, but before she could utter even so much as one word, something started to rise from the muddy, swampy water between them and the Hermit's house.

The thing that rose was vaguely humanoid and completely made of mud. It towered over both of them, mud dripping off its body, a strong stink of swamp water and mud wafting off its form and into Carmaz's nostrils. It was tall enough to reach the treetops above, the top of its head brushing against the leaves and upper branches. Its face was vaguely humanoid, with a simple set of eyes, a nose, and a mouth, but it had no fingers at the end of its long appendages, which Carmaz could not think of as arms because they barely resembled them.

Alira stepped back, clinging to Carmaz's arm, but Carmaz didn't move. He just watched as the creature looked down upon

125

them with its large eyes, blinking every now and then, but still saying nothing.

"What is it?" Alira asked in a low voice. "Have you ever seen a creature like that before?"

"No," said Carmaz, shaking his head. "I've never even heard of it. But it's probably the guardian of the Hermit's house. Some tales do say he has one, though they never describe it or explain what it is."

Then the mud giant suddenly spoke. Its voice was deep but mushy, if that made sense, though it was quite clear despite the fact that it appeared to lack teeth and a tongue. "State your names and your business, intruders, or prepare to rest underneath the Swamp forever."

"I am Carmaz Korva," said Carmaz. "A native of Ruwa. And this is Alira, the Judge of the Tournament of the Gods. We come here because we need to speak with your master, Herune the Swamp Hermit, whose aid we need in order to contact the gods and warn them of an impending invasion by a force beneath Martir."

"Invasion?" said the mud giant. The figure leaned forward a little, causing its stink to become even more pronounced. "Who is invading Martir? The aquarians?"

"No," said Carmaz, shaking his head. "A new race called the golems. They are going to use the Swamp of Light as their entryway into Martir. The gods don't know about this yet, so we must contact them at once and tell them about it so they can stop the invasion before it begins. Again, we must speak with your master about this."

The mud giant stood upright again, knocking a couple of

upper branches off the trees and sending them splashing into the waters below. Then it looked to the right, almost as if lost in thought, before looking back at Carmaz and Alira again.

"You wish to speak with my master?" asked the mud giant.

Carmaz nodded impatiently. "Yes, we do."

"But you already are," said the mud giant. It gestured at itself. "I am Herune the Hermit. This is not my true form, but a puppet I use to defend my home and communicate with the outside world."

"Oh," said Carmaz. He sighed in relief. "Well, that's good. I —"

"But I do not find your claims to be very credible," said Herune. "Where is your proof of this invasion, of these golems? How do I know that you two are not merely thieves who want to steal from me, or even worse, murder me?"

"We have no actual proof of this invasion," Carmaz admitted. "But if you go west of here, you will eventually find an artificial tunnel and down that tunnel you will find an entire army of golems waiting to invade. One of the golems has even been cutting down trees and using them to build a solid bridge for the rest of his brethren to walk upon so they don't sink into the mud of the Swamp."

"I have heard rumors of a mysterious giant of stone appearing in our Swamp, chopping down trees and taking them away to whereabouts unknown," said Herune. "It sounds to me like this giant of stone may be the same as your golem."

"It probably is," said Carmaz. "So I hope you understand how serious the situation is."

"I do," said Herune. Then his giant form shrugged. "But I do

127

not care."

"What?" said Alira. She let go of Carmaz's arm and stepped forward. She seemed to have forgotten her fear, because she was now glaring at Herune as if he had just broken a rule in the Tournament. "What do you mean, you don't care?"

"About the outside world," said Herune. "What do I care if these 'golems' you speak of invade the world? As long as they do not intrude upon my domain, how does it concern me?"

"The golems aren't going to leave you alone if they invade," Alira said. She pointed behind her. "They want to conquer everything. And we're not even asking you to fight them off. Just help us contact the gods so they can deal with it."

"That's another thing," said Herune. "I cannot communicate with the gods."

Both Alira and Carmaz shared a surprised look when they heard that, but Alira recovered from the surprise quickly and said, "Hold on. As I understand it, mages need to have faith in the gods in order to use magic. Are you not a mage?"

"I suppose I am," said Herune. "But I am a cursed mage, forsaken by the gods like the rest of Ruwa. I can still use magic, but the gods have ceased speaking with me and do not wish to speak with me again, so I cannot contact them even if I wanted to."

Carmaz ran his hand through his hair. "Damn it. What are we supposed to do now?"

Herune shrugged. "I don't know. My time in this world is getting shorter and shorter every day. I might even die before the invasion starts. In any case, there is nothing I can do about it, so there is nothing I can do to help."

"Can you at least let us into your home?" asked Alira, putting her hands together in supplication. "Carmaz and I have been traveling on foot for a long time now. We need food and water. If you can give us that, then we will leave and never bother you again."

Herune's giant turned restlessly. It seemed to Carmaz like the mage was having an inner battle with himself, his desire for solitude clashing with his desire to help others.

Finally, Herune said, "Very well. The gates are unlocked. You may enter and get as much food and water as you need. But once you are finished, you must leave and never return."

"Thank you," said Alira. "I will remember your aid after we leave."

Herune's giant shrugged. A moment later, it sank back into the mud, until soon it was gone completely. Alira immediately made her way down the path, while Carmaz followed her. He stayed close to her, because despite Herune's promise, he didn't trust the Hermit at all.

A couple of minutes later, Carmaz and Alira stood in the courtyard—which was thankfully made of dried, solid earth under their feet—of Herune's home. It was fairly wide open, despite the tall walls surrounding it. Ahead of them was the home itself, a large building with wide double doors that were currently closed. A balcony stretched out above the doors, but there was no one on it, although there were some glass doors that seemed to lead into a room. Herune himself was still nowhere to be seen.

Then the double doors opened and Herune's voice came from it. "Please enter. I have some food and water set out for you two already."

Carmaz and Alira exchanged looks, but then Carmaz's stomach rumbled, so he shrugged and walked ahead of her. The two walked up the massive front steps and into the hall of the building itself.

The air in here was oppressively hot and humid, causing Carmaz to sweat even more than he already was. Alira also looked humid, rolling up the sleeves of her robes, though Carmaz wasn't sure what good that did because of the humidity.

It was also rather dark, save for the light streaming in from the windows to his left. The light revealed a startling variety of weapons on the wall opposite: Swords, axes, knives, darts, arrows, and many others. Most of those weapons did not look like they had been used in years, especially the ones with what was obviously dried blood on their blades. Next to the weapons was a rack that was empty, though what could have been on the rack, Carmaz didn't know. It looked like it might have held some hats at one point, but he wasn't sure.

There, in the middle of the room, set on a table, was a very simple-looking meal. Two bowls of swamp soup—recognizable thanks to its brown-and-green coloration, as well as the way it smelled like olives—and two cups of clear water stood on top of a small table. There were two chairs on either side, old and rickety by the looks of them, which Carmaz assumed was where they were supposed to sit.

But Herune himself was still nowhere to be seen. That made Carmaz wonder just how much Herune valued his privacy, that he would not even appear to welcome them to the meal he had somehow prepared for them in his own home.

"Please sit," said Herune's voice, which now sounded like it was coming from the building itself. "Eat quickly. I dislike entertaining guests, so I do not want you to stay longer than necessary."

"You mean you aren't even going to show your face?" asked Alira, who sounded quite incredulous. "Even though we are your guests?"

"It is my home and it is my decision whether to show you my face," said Herune, his tone turning sharp. "I can also throw both of you out of here if you'd like. There's a mother swordtooth nearby that is looking for food to feed her newly-hatched babies. Perhaps she would like to feed them human flesh."

Carmaz gulped and said, "Oh, that won't be necessary. We'll eat and leave and won't bother you again. Just as we promised."

"Good," said Herune. "And do not ask me any questions. I'm not in the mood to answer them."

With that, Herune stopped speaking. Carmaz and Alira walked over to the table and sat down. As soon as they did, Carmaz picked up his spoon and started eating. It felt good to have some swamp soup. It had been a long time since he had last had this food, because it was very hard to make on one's own and often took too long to be practical.

Alira, on the other hand, looked at the soup as if it was some kind of poison. She poked it with her own spoon, but otherwise did not touch it.

"What's the matter, Alira?" asked Carmaz, taking a break from slurping down the soup to look up at her. "Eat up. This stuff's great."

"I'm not very hungry," said Alira. "I don't need to eat because

I am not a human like you."

Carmaz shrugged. "Suit yourself. It's still really good, though. You're missing out." Then he lowered his voice. "Though I think you should still eat anyway. Don't want to offend our host."

Alira looked up at the ceiling, as if she thought that Herune was watching her from there. Then she looked down at her soup bowl, sighed, and started to eat, albeit far more slowly than Carmaz.

As they ate and drank, Herune did not utter so much as one word to either of them. He was obviously still there, watching and listening to them, but Carmaz did not know what the Hermit was thinking. He decided that it didn't really matter, because they were lucky enough that Herune was letting them stay here and eat. Having grown up his whole life hearing stories about the Hermit and yet never actually meeting him, Carmaz found it hard to focus on his food.

If only Saia was still alive, Carmaz thought, *then he could be here with us, too. He always liked learning about the Hermit. What would he do if he had the opportunity to actually* be *in the Hermit's home?*

Of course, Carmaz couldn't get too excited, because Herune's presence hung over them like a heavy rain cloud. Still, a part of him wished he could stay here a little while longer, if only to confirm some of the wilder stories that he had heard, such as the story that claimed that Herune could change gender at will or that he was actually a human manifestation of the Swamp itself.

Alira, on the other hand, seemed torn between reluctance to eat her food and a desire to get out of here as fast as possible. She would eat several spoonfuls of the soup in rapid succession, only to stop with a sick expression on her face. For whatever reason, the Swamp soup did not seem to settle well with her. It occurred to Carmaz that he didn't even know what kind of food Alira did like, although if she really didn't need to eat at all, then she probably didn't have any favorites whatsoever.

Still, by the time Carmaz finished his soup, Alira had finished hers. The two then finished their glasses of water and stood up, though Alira stood up first.

She then looked at the ceiling and said, "Thank you, Herune the Hermit, for allowing us to dine in your home. I promise to repay you for your kindness when I return to World's End."

"You know where the door is," said Herune's voice again, just as sharp as ever. "Now leave."

Carmaz and Alira nodded and made their way to the double doors, which had closed by themselves after they entered. They were just about to open the doors themselves when the doors began to open on their own again.

Carmaz first thought that it was Herune getting the doors for them like before, but then he heard Herune's voice say, "Oh no. Another visitor."

Another visitor? Carmaz thought, exchanging puzzled looks with Alira as the doors slowly opened inwards, forcing them both to step back to avoid being hit. *Who could he be talking about?*

When the doors opened all the way, Carmaz looked and saw two people standing on the front steps of the entrance. One was a young, bearded man and the other a blonde-haired, dark-skinned woman, but he did not recognize the man.

The woman, however, he *did* recognize, especially when she said, "Carmaz? Alira? What are you two doing here?"

Carmaz and Alira stared at the woman in shock, but Carmaz managed to say, "Raya?"

Chapter Ten

BRAIM STOOD ON the sand of Last Beach, the beach on the back of World's End right before the sea. He looked at the sword in his hand, which felt heavy yet comfortable. It had a long, thin blade and, according to Tashir, was supposed to be easy to handle for newbie swordsmen like himself. He slashed it through the air a couple of times to test it and found that he quite liked how it handled, although it wasn't quite as natural or graceful as it could have been just yet. But that would come in time, once Braim got more experience.

Tashir stood opposite Braim, his own sword drawn. He looked a little concerned about Braim, even seemed to cringe when Braim swung his sword. No doubt that was because Braim didn't know how to use a sword well yet and didn't want Braim to harm himself or anyone else, even though there weren't many people on the beach today.

As a cool breeze blew in from the ocean, Tashir said, "Braim, are you certain that you would like to learn how to use a sword? While I am by no means against anyone learning self-defense, I think you are moving too quickly and should perhaps take a moment to think this through before you do anything else."

Braim looked at Tashir in annoyance. "Tashir, I was nearly killed in my room by some assassin lady I've never even seen.

And I can't use magic anymore, so I need some way to defend myself."

Tashir looked up the beach. Three Soldiers of the Gods stood near the scattered trees just outside the walls of the city, looking quite stoic as a group. One of them was leaning against the tree, while another sat in the grass, and yet another was polishing his own blade.

Nonetheless, Braim knew that all three of them were very carefully watching Braim and Tashir, as they had been assigned to protect Braim after this most recent assassin attack. The identity of the assassin was still unknown, but Braim had been informed that the Soldiers were investigating the attack and looking for any clues that could help them find her, whoever she was. So far, the Soldiers had only discovered that the Soul Collector, which Braim had kept in his dresser, was missing, which meant that the assassin had likely stolen it, though why, Braim didn't know. All he knew was that he didn't like the idea of an assassin like that woman having access to such a powerful weapon, even if he knew from experience that the Soul Collector did nothing against him. He just hoped that the Soldiers found the assassin before she used the Soul Collector on anyone else.

In the meantime, however, Braim had asked Tashir to teach him how to use a sword so he could better defend himself.

"Yes, but learning how to use a sword takes time," said Tashir. "It is not quite so simple as stabbing your enemy. You must study under a true master, try out many different sword types and techniques to discover which work best for your body, and learn the necessary discipline to turn your blade into an extension of your own body before you can use a sword with any skill."

"Can't I do all of that in a few hours?" asked Braim, glancing at the sun overhead, which was quite hot here on the beach.

"No, you cannot," said Tashir. He rolled his eyes. "The best you can learn in a few hours is basic self-defense techniques. Even then, they will be very crude and difficult to do well. You will not have the wits to react accordingly in an actual do-or-die situation outside of this training."

"Tash, I've been in a lot of different do-or-die situations recently and have come out of them alive, so I think I know what it takes to survive," said Braim. "Anyway, you agreed to teach me what you know, so let's go and do it."

Tashir looked like he wanted to turn and walk away, but then he shook his head and said, "Fine. I will teach you, as quickly as I can, how to use your sword, but be warned that you will probably not be very good even at the end of this session."

"I just need to be good enough to learn how to defend myself," said Braim. He raised his sword. "What are we waiting for? Let's get started."

"Very well," said Tashir in a reluctant tone. He raised his own sword, holding it before him with the blade crossing his body. "First, you must learn the proper sword-holding techniques. Do you see how I grasp the hilt?"

Braim looked. Tashir gripped the hilt with both hands, with the right hand above the left, and the thumb of the right hand on the sword's crest. "Yeah, I do."

"All right," said Tashir. "Now copy how I did it. This is important because how you hold your sword will determine how well you can use it to defend yourself against a foe. There are many different ways to do it, but this is the way that works best for this particular type of sword."

"What if I want to learn how to fight with one hand?" asked Braim, though he copied Tashir's grip on the sword anyway.

"It only makes sense to learn how to fight with one hand if you either use two swords or have a shield in your other hand," said Tashir. "If not, then you must learn how to fight with both hands. It is actually much easier to learn how to fight with two hands than one, because it gives you much greater focus and much less weight to deal with."

"Maybe I should go to Malya after this and ask her to teach me how to use two swords," said Braim.

Tashir frowned. "Are you going to keep complaining about my teaching style or are you actually going to try to learn?"

"I'm learning, I'm learning," said Braim, double-checking his grip to make sure that he was copying Tashir's method exactly, which he was. "Anyway, what's next?"

"If you are holding your sword correctly, then the next thing we do is learn how to slash," said Tashir. He held his sword high above his head. "Watch and learn."

Braim nodded, his eyes on Tashir's blade. Tashir closed his own eyes, as if deep in thought, and then, without warning, brought his sword down far faster than even Braim's eyes could follow.

Tashir's sword struck the sand, sending up a small cloud of sand into the air. Tashir then opened his eyes and brought his sword up, which he then pointed at Braim as a way to silently tell him to do the same thing.

That slash hadn't looked very difficult to Braim. Making

certain that he was holding the sword correctly, Braim raised it above his head, copying the motion similarly to how Tashir had, but before he brought it down, a chill went down his spine and he looked to the south.

All the way across the sea, on the very edge of Martir, was the massive black wall of shadow known as the Void. Braim had almost forgotten that it was there, having been so caught up in the recent happenings that he hadn't been paying attention to much else. But now that he was looking at it again, he found it impossible to ignore, because he was remembering the Void's recent attacks on World's End and how it was likely behind the disappearances of Raya and Alira.

The Void was currently not doing anything to harm him or anyone else, but he still didn't want to look away from it, now that he saw it. He kept staring at its endless darkness until Tashir's voice, harsher than normal, said, "Braim?"

Braim shook his head and looked at Tashir. The makhimancer was looking at Braim with a concerned expression on his shark-like features. The nearby Soldiers of the Gods did not seem to be paying them attention, but Braim knew that the Soldiers were a lot more observant and intelligent than they let on.

"Sorry," said Braim, shaking his head and lowering his sword. He rubbed the back of his head, still feeling the darkness in there. "I just got distracted."

Tashir nodded. His eyes darted over to the Void before he looked at Braim again. "Yes. The Void can be quite distracting, can't it?"

Braim nodded, too, and said, "Then why don't we go train somewhere in the city or on the other side of the island, at least? I

139

don't trust it."

"Because Last Beach is the perfect private place to practice," said Tashir. "The northern tip of the island is where the katabans fishermen dock their boats and there are no private training facilities anywhere on World's End. Trust me, I checked thoroughly and could not find one, except for the private training grounds of the Soldiers, who do not allow anyone outside of their group to use for any reason whatsoever."

Braim sighed, but then said, "All right. Where was I?"

"You were going to mimic my slashing movement with your sword," Tashir said, gesturing at Braim's sword. "In case you forgot, hold it like so and then bring it down like this."

Tashir repeated the motion. Braim saw him do it, but for some reason it was like he wasn't watching Tashir do it at all. He blinked, but the memory of Tashir slashing his sword evaporated from his mind instantly and that gnawing darkness from before clawed the back of his mind, causing him to rub the back of his head in irritation.

"Now, do as I just did," said Tashir. "Sword up and then down. A very simple motion. Don't over-think it."

"No one's ever accused me of over-thinking anything," said Braim as he raised his sword above his head. "Anyway, I prefer to act rather than to think."

Then Braim froze and looked up at his sword. It gleamed slightly in the light of the sun overhead, but that was not what he was looking at. He seemed to have forgotten what he was supposed to do next, but that was odd because Tashir just told him. Yet the memory was not there for some reason.

Shaking his head, Braim told himself, *It's easy. Just slash ...*

up? Right? Left? No, down, I think.

So Braim brought his sword down onto the sand in front of him. The blade hit the sand with a dulled *thump*, causing Braim to pull his sword out of the sand and look it over just to make sure it was okay. It didn't look damaged to him, so he looked up at Tashir and gave him the thumbs up.

"Did I do well?" asked Braim, lowering his hand and waiting for Tashir's judgment.

Tashir nodded. "Yes, although I would say you were far too hesitant about bringing the sword down. You should have brought it down swiftly and without hesitation, because in a life-or-death situation, you often do not have the luxury to hesitate and think about your next course of action."

Braim felt a twinge of annoyance at Tashir's words. *Luxury? There's nothing luxurious about forgetting the thing you just heard five seconds ago.*

But Braim did not say that aloud, mostly because he wanted to get on with the training, but also because he didn't want to bring up his apparent memory issues with Tashir. He dismissed the issue as nothing more than a temporary failure of his memory, which happened to everyone at some point or another.

"So what's the next step?" asked Braim.

"Do the slash again," said Tashir. "I want you to be able to do it as quickly and easily as cutting a loaf of bread. As the Prophet once said, 'Practice is to mortals as worship is to the gods.'"

Braim had no idea who this 'Prophet' was, but he nodded anyway, even though he really wanted to move onto the next lesson.

So he raised his sword above his head again, but as before,

Braim found himself confused. He looked at his sword, which now looked like a foreign object to him that he had never seen before. He almost threw it away before he remembered that it was his sword and that he needed it if he was going to learn how to defend himself.

Okay, but what was I actually going to do *with it?* Braim thought, still staring blankly at his sword. *I need to train with it, but that doesn't tell me what technique exactly I am practicing.*

Then that darkness in the back of his mind started gnawing at him again, only this time it was so bad that Braim dropped his sword onto the sand at his feet and put both hands on the back of his head. The pain was intense, far more intense than any pain he had ever experienced before, even worse than the pain he had felt when the Ghostly God had tried to rip his soul from his body.

"Braim?" said Tashir in a concerned voice. "What is the matter? Braim?"

Braim looked up at Tashir. His friend was looking at him with even more concern than usual, but Braim didn't want him to worry, so he said, "It's nothing, Tash. It's just a really bad headache is all."

"Are you certain of that?" asked Tashir. "Perhaps we should return to the city and let you rest for a bit before we continue with our training."

Braim shook his head and lowered his hands, even though the pain in the back of his head was worse than ever before. "Nah, I'm fine. It'll go away. We have more important things to do than worry about that. Let's keep practicing."

To prove that he was fine, Braim bent over and snatched the sword off the sand. He then held it above his head, just as Tashir had done, and brought it down hard on the sand before him.

Just as Braim's sword made contact with the sand, a terrible, stabbing pain struck the back of his head like a mallet. Crying out in pain, Braim let go of his sword once more and staggered backwards. He fell flat on his back, both hands on the back of his head, as Tashir cried out, "Braim!"

Braim heard the armored feet of the Soldiers of the Gods running to him across the sand, but pretty soon he heard nothing at all, because he completely lost consciousness.

Chapter Eleven

FTER SEVERAL MORE minutes of running, Herune indicated that it was safe for them to slow to a walk. He told Raya that his home was not far from their current position now and that they didn't need to run anymore. He also told her that walking was a lot quieter than running and left less marks for others to follow, so it would be harder for Aorja and Zeeree to track them down.

That was fine by Raya, because all of the running and excitement of the last hour had left her exhausted. She normally was not this active, because as Princess of Carnag she was not expected to be active and athletic. Nonetheless, she put some effort into walking by Herune's side, because she didn't trust this stinky, murky Swamp at all and didn't want to get killed or eaten by anything that might be lurking nearby hidden from view.

Despite her exhaustion, however, Raya had a lot of questions for Herune. Because they were no longer running for their lives, she decided to ask them, starting with the most pertinent one on her mind at the moment.

Ducking to avoid a low overhanging branch, Raya said, "So, Herune, why did you save me? Not that I don't appreciate it, but we've never even met."

"Because I hate witches like Aorja," said Herune. He waved

his wand before them, causing the ground to become dry under their feet, although Raya noticed that the ground returned to mud as soon as they walked over it. "She has been terrorizing the people of Ruwa for several months now. This is the first time I've directly fought against her, even though I've been meaning to save innocent lives from her as soon as I learned of her existence."

"So I'm the first person you have saved from her?" said Raya. "Why haven't you saved anyone else?"

"Because I'm not *supposed* to save anyone else," said Herune. "I'm not even *supposed* to be interacting with other people. But sometimes, you just have to do the right thing even if you are not supposed to do it."

"Why aren't you supposed to save anyone?" asked Raya. "Who told you that you weren't allowed?"

A fierce scowl appeared on Herune's face, visible through his bushy beard, before he shook his head and said, "What is your name?"

That was not exactly a subtle change of subject, causing Raya to say, "Why are you changing the subject?"

Herune glared at her, the first time he'd done so since saving her. "Because I don't feel quite comfortable telling you all of my secrets, even if I did save your life. You're still a stranger to me, you know."

"Fair point, although you're just as strange to me as I am to you," said Raya. She brushed back her hair and said, "Nonetheless, you may call me Princess Raya Mana, Princess of Carnag. I'm surprised you didn't recognize me."

Herune looked at her with a blank look on his face before saying, "Why would I recognize someone I have never even heard of before?"

Herune did not say that in a cruel tone of voice. Nonetheless, Raya was more than a bit offended at his ignorance, prompting her to say, "How could you not recognize the daughter of King Malock and Queen Hana, the rulers of the most powerful nation in the Northern Isles?"

"I've heard of Carnag," Herune said. "And King Malock, but I didn't know he had a daughter. How did you even get out here?"

"Aorja kidnapped me," said Raya, folding her arms across her chest to show her displeasure. Then she looked at him expectantly.

"What?" said Herune. "Is there something you need?"

"I expect you to apologize for your ignorance," said Raya.

Herune looked at her like she was crazy. "What do I have to apologize for? Is ignorance a crime on Carnag or something?"

"No, but it is rude," said Raya. "So? Are you going to apologize or not?"

Herune now looked like he was considering sending Raya back to Aorja, but then he shook his head and laughed. He slapped her on the shoulder, causing Raya to say, "Hey! What's so funny?"

"Your joke," said Herune. He had to stifle another laugh. "Acting like I have to apologize to you just because I've never even heard of you ... my, you Carnagians sure have a strange sense of humor, I'll give you that much."

"Humor? Ignorance of royalty is no joke," said Raya.

"Sure, sure," said Herune, nodding rather condescendingly. "I'm sure you'll make a great Queen yourself someday with that kind of humor, though I suppose I wouldn't know, considering how Ruwa has no king or queen to rule us."

Raya felt so offended that she almost turned and walked away before remembering that she was in the middle of a great big Swamp that she knew nothing of.

Instead, seeing that she was probably not going to convince Herune to apologize, Raya said, "Very well then, Mr. Herune, where exactly are you taking me again? Your, er, 'house'?"

Raya said 'house' because she doubted that Herune—who as far as she could tell was just a simple swamp-dweller, his obvious magical prowess notwithstanding—lived in anything much better than a shack, if even that.

"Pretty much," said Herune. He gestured ahead of them with his wand. "Don't worry about Aorja finding us, either. It's magically hidden from other mages, so there's no way she or her ugly monster pet could ever find it even if they searched for it all day every day for a year."

"So it's safe?" said Raya. She breathed a sigh of relief. "Good. I was worried that Aorja and Zeeree might come after us again."

"They will, but they won't be able to find us," said Herune. "Anyway, you still haven't explained why Aorja kidnapped you. Did Aorja kidnap you in order to blackmail your parents?"

Raya shook her head and then explained to Herune about the events leading up to her kidnapping. She didn't tell him everything, of course, because she didn't quite trust him completely. Sure, he had saved her life, but he was still a stranger to her and so might not be completely trustworthy.

When she finished, Herune looked quite disturbed. He scratched his chin through his beard and said, "Well, I can't say that doesn't surprise me. Aorja always seemed like she hated the gods. Really, though, I don't see how she could have possibly hoped for that plan of hers to work, considering how powerful the gods are."

"I know," said Raya. "But she was quite serious about killing me if she had to. She is the most psychotic individual I have ever had the displeasure of knowing in my life."

"Sure sounds like it," said Herune as he stepped over a fallen tree limb in their path. "So it looks like you need to get back to World's End, then, for the Tournament."

"Exactly," said Raya, nodding. "I must return at once. Can you teleport me back there?"

Herune shook his head. "Nope. Sorry. Teleportation has always been my weak point. The magic I learned is mostly botamancy, with some biomancy thrown in for good measure. Telemancy has always been hard for me because I'm not a very cerebral guy, although I can do very basic things like use telekinesis to move small objects and the like."

Raya's shoulders slumped. "Then how am I supposed to get to World's End? Can't you contact the gods, at least?"

"Nope," said Herune, far more quickly than he should have. "Never talk with the gods."

"Never?" said Raya. "But don't you mages draw your magical power from the gods?"

"We do, but that doesn't necessarily mean we like them," said Herune. He looked ahead with a displeased expression on his face. "Why talk with the gods when they refuse to speak with us? They have neglected Ruwa for years, so I don't see any reason to talk with them."

"I don't care," said Raya. "All I care about is getting back to

World's End. Is there at least a port nearby with a ship that could take me to Carnag?"

Herune laughed. This was a harsher laugh than his previous one, so harsh and loud that it almost sounded like the bark of a dog. "Another good joke. But no, there are no functioning ports on Ruwa. No one ever comes or leaves, except for the pirates, and even they don't always come here on a regular basis. You might be able to build a raft to take you away, but then you'd have to get past the storms and sea monsters."

"Sea monsters?" Raya repeated. "What kind of sea monsters?"

"The kind that you don't want to even think about," said Herune. "In any case, it looks like you're stuck here with me for now, Princess. But maybe once we get to my home we can come up with an idea about how to get you back to where you belong."

"I sincerely hope so," said Raya. She looked at the mud and smelly swamp water around them with a disgusted look on her face. "Because this Swamp is disgusting."

"Only if you refuse to see the beauty in it," said Herune. Then he looked ahead. "Oh, it looks like we're almost home. Just a little farther now."

Raya also looked ahead, but she didn't see anything to suggest that they were nearing any 'home.' She just saw more swamp and trees and mud and water, which made her wonder if Herune knew something she didn't.

Raya looked at Herune again and said, "Do you live on your own out here?"

Herune suddenly frowned, like Raya had brought up a sore subject. "Why do you want to know that?"

"Because I want to know how you learned magic on your

149

own," said Raya. "I've always heard that Ruwa is an island without mages, yet here you are, a mage who is as magical as any. Did you teach yourself?"

Herune seemed to be resolutely avoiding looking at her face. "No, I did not."

"Who taught you, then?" said Raya.

"You'll see," said Herune. "Not long now before we get home."

Raya noticed that Herune was suddenly becoming a lot less talkative after she asked him that question. She suspected it was something he did not like to talk about, though why, she didn't know.

But before she could ask him more about it, Herune pointed at her artificial hand and said, "What's wrong with your hand? Never seen anything like it."

Raya looked down at her artificial hand. She had almost completely forgotten about it in the recent excitement and stress. She flexed her fingers before looking back at Herune, who was now eying her hand with the same caution that she had used to view it with.

"I lost my hand recently and had the katabans of World's End give me this artificial one to replace it," said Raya. "It's nothing to be alarmed about. It actually is what helped me escape from Aorja and Zeeree before you came along."

"Is it magic?" said Herune. He waved his wand at it and frowned. "If it is, I've never felt anything like it."

"It is katabans magic," said Raya. "Unfortunately, I can't tell you much about how they made it or the full extent of its powers and abilities because they didn't explain that to me."

"Okay," said Herune, turning his eyes back to the path they walked upon. "Maybe I should go to World's End sometime and ask those katabans how they did it. I think knowing how to conjure a replacement hand via magic could be very useful."

Raya looked at Herune's hands, which looked pretty normal to her, causing her to say, "Why would you think that? Your hands look whole to me."

"I've got my reasons," said Herune as the two of them stepped through a gap in the trees. Then he suddenly pointed and said, "Here it is. My home."

Raya looked ahead again. She had expected to see nothing more than a tiny little one-room hut, maybe with a thatched roof and a cute little chimney, but nothing more than that.

What she saw instead was a building that she could best describe as a small fortress. Four walls surrounded the main building, with twin gates that resembled tiger heads for some reason. The walls were covered with mud and growing plants, making the entire place look quite abandoned. Indeed, if Herune had not identified the building for his home, Raya might have simply assumed it was the abandoned ruins of the Ruwan military from ages past. A simple dirt path led from their position to the gates, though it was surrounded on both sides by deep puddles of swamp water that were too murky to see through.

Raya looked at Herune. "Did you build this yourself?"

Herune shook his head. "No. It was originally built and controlled by an assassin's guild known as the Dark Tigers. Ever heard of 'em?"

Raya shook her head. "No, I have not."

"The Dark Tigers were the most famous assassin's guild in the

151

entire Northern Isles about thirty years ago," said Herune. "They were hired out by powerful politicians in nations like Shika and Itrija to assassinate political rivals or enemies. But the organization ended when their leader, Nijok Wirm, was killed on a mission in the Great Berg. And without Wirm to keep the group together, the Dark Tigers had a very bloody falling out, which resulted in most of the Tigers killing each other off. The survivors abandoned their base for greener pastures."

"Oh," said Raya. "So you took it over because no one else lives there, then."

"Pretty much," said Herune. "It's not so bad, really, aside from the bloodstains on the walls and floors that even magic can't scrub out. Lots of room and plenty of weapons for defense. Anyway, let's keep going. Not much farther now."

Herune walked down the dirt path to the small fortress, with Raya following somewhat closely behind. She wasn't much of a superstitious person—her parents had always taught her that there was usually a reason for everything in the universe—but seeing that abandoned hideout of the most notorious and deadly assassin's guild in the entire Northern Isles made her suddenly feel very ill, far more so than the stink of the Swamp did. Raya now started to wonder if the ghosts of the Dark Tigers' enemies haunted the place before reminding herself that ghosts did not exist and, if they did, certainly would not haunt places in the middle of nowhere like this.

When they approached the gates, Herune waved his wand and caused the gates to open on their own. The two of them passed through the gates into the courtyard of the abandoned hideout, where Raya could now see the double doors and wide front steps of the main building. There was a balcony above the entrance, with a light flickering through the shattered glass doors, which meant that someone was here.

Raya looked at Herune again as they walked to the front steps. She pointed at the balcony above. "Who lives in the upper floor? I thought you lived by yourself."

Herune grimaced, as if he had hoped that she would not notice the light and would therefore not ask who was up there. "I don't live by myself. I live with someone else. My teacher."

"Your teacher?" said Raya.

Herune's shoulders slumped, but as they approached the doors, he said, "He's more than my teacher. He's also my—"

He was interrupted by the doors to the main building opening inwards all by themselves. At least Raya did not see Herune wave his wand to open them, though she supposed it could have been possible that Herune had used his magic too discreetly for her to notice.

In any event, Raya looked into the main building, curious to see what the inside was like. As the doors opened, allowing the light from the Swamp to spill in and illuminate the interior, she saw two people standing on the other side of the threshold. At first, the darkness of the interior made it impossible to tell who those two people were, but when the doors were opened all the way and the light was illuminating the inside, she recognized the man and woman instantly.

"Carmaz? Alira?" said Raya in surprise, unable to believe her own eyes. "What are you two doing here?"

Both Carmaz and Alira looked almost too shocked to speak, but then Carmaz managed to stammer out, "R-Raya?"

153

Herune looked between Raya and Carmaz and Alira and frowned again. "Do you three know each other?"

But Raya got over her own shock quickly. Spreading her arms wide, she said, "Carmaz! How I've missed you so!" and dashed over to hug him.

Although Carmaz was clearly surprised, he stepped out of the way to avoid her hug. Raya—who had not been expecting that—staggered and almost tripped. Luckily, she caught herself before she fell and then turned to face Carmaz, although she didn't try to hug him again because she was pretty sure that he would just dodge her like always.

So Raya put her hands together and said, "What are you doing here, Carmaz? You're looking as fine as always, if a little grungier, but that really does add to your look."

"I was about to ask you the same question," said Carmaz, who looked like he was ready to run the minute Raya became too friendly for his tastes. "I thought you were back on World's End. How did you end up all the way up here?"

"Very long story," said Raya. She then noticed Alira, who was watching the both of them with a puzzled expression on her face. "I think the real question is what Alira is doing here."

Alira removed her glasses and wiped them off briefly before returning them to her face. "It's a story that I believe is probably as long as yours, Raya, though I won't go into it right now."

Carmaz then gestured at Herune. "And who is this guy?"

"I'm Herune," said Herune, folding his arms over his chest. "Where did you two come from and what are you doing in my house?"

"I invited them in," said a deep, elderly-sounding voice that seemed to come from everywhere at once, causing Raya to start. "I did not expect you to bring back a girl, however. I thought you loathed them."

Carmaz looked between the ceiling and Herune, a puzzled expression on his face. He pointed at Herune and then at the ceiling, saying, "Hold on. You said your name is Herune, but that can't be right, because Alira and I were invited inside by a man named Herune. There can't be two Herunes, can there?"

Raya was just as confused as Carmaz until Herune sighed and said, "The truth is, the Herune you know is my father and I am his son. I was named after him, which I know is confusing, but my old man has always been very vain and self-centered, which is why he named me after himself."

"Says the petulant child who brings back women without my permission," said the voice of the older Herune, which still sounded like it was coming from everywhere at once. "You think only of yourself and nothing more."

Herune the younger glared at the ceiling. "Why don't you come and say that to my face, old man? Have you even shown yourself to these people or are you just going to pretend to be a disembodied voice?"

"Son, you know how weak and elderly I am," said Herune the elder. "I require rest, but very well. I believe that I need to teach you a lesson in respect, anyway."

A second later, an old man appeared near a small but nice-looking table in the center of the room. He must have teleported, because Raya had not seen him walk there at all.

The old man looked just like Herune the younger, except older and with a much longer beard that was entirely gray. He leaned on a wooden staff that was tipped with a jagged knife and he was leaning over almost constantly, yet he gave off an aura of power that even Raya could feel. He wore old brown, stained robes that made him look like a ghost.

Herune the elder looked at the others with only the barest interest. "What? You three look like you've never seen an old man before in your life."

Carmaz shook his head and said, "No, it's just that I've grown up hearing the stories about you, so actually seeing you in person is—"

"Bah," said Herune the elder, interrupting Carmaz like he hadn't spoken at all. "All those tall tales and legends the Ruwans came up with about me are about as truthful as a Hollechian. I admit, however, that it has been very fun, encouraging these rumors and adding some of my own juicy details to them whenever possible to confuse the matter further. It certainly is amusing, at any rate."

Before anyone else could ask another question, Herune the younger stepped forward and said, "All right, Father, you said you were going to teach me a lesson in respect. Would you like to do it here or outside?"

"Outside, of course," said Herune the elder. He rolled his shoulders, which made a cringe-inducing cracking sound that made Raya wince. "I'd rather not mess up the interior, which I've spent so much time making look nice."

But before either of the Herunes could do anything, Carmaz stepped in between them and said, "Hold on. What the heck is going on here? Herune, er, the elder, why didn't you tell me and Alira that you had a son? And why is Raya here?"

156

"I did not tell you about my son because I did not see a need," said Herune the elder, his tone calm. "Now, Carmaz, why don't you stay out of this little family feud? It is none of your business."

"But I didn't even know that the legendary Herune the Hermit even had a son," said Carmaz, looking between the two Herunes with confusion on his face. "I was always taught that there was just one Herune."

"I was alone for a while, but then I had a son—if you even want to call him that—and did not bother to invite anyone to his birth," said Herune the elder with a snort. "It isn't like his birth was anything special, considering how thousands of babies are born all around the world every day."

Raya was shocked at how harsh Herune the elder's words were to his own son. She looked at Herune the younger, but he didn't look offended so much as annoyed.

"Well, what should we call you two, then?" said Carmaz, putting his hands on his hips. "We can't call both of you Herune. That would be too confusing."

"You do not need to call us anything special because you three are not going to be staying here long enough to need to do that," Herune the elder replied. "But if you must, you can call me the Hermit and my son by his given name. I couldn't care less either way."

Herune the younger stepped forward, his wand out and held like a knight's sword. "Now that we have that all figured out, get out of the way, stranger. You have nothing to do with this, so don't get involved. This is between us and us only."

"I'm getting involved because right now is not the ideal time for us to fight among ourselves," said Carmaz. He didn't looked at

157

all intimidated by the glares from Herune and the Hermit, which just made Raya love him more than ever. "If we fight each other, we'll distract ourselves from the *real* enemy, who is mobilizing their forces to invade Martir even as we speak."

"You mean those imaginary golems you spoke of earlier?" asked the Hermit. He chuckled. "Again, I couldn't care less. Now unless you'd like to spend the rest of your life as a blind frog, I would suggest that you step aside and allow the two of us to settle our differences the way we've always done."

But Carmaz didn't move at all. He just said, "No. I want some answers and I want them now. If I have to beat some sense into both of you to do it, then I will."

Raya could not help but love Carmaz's strength. Even though both the younger and the elder were obviously powerful mages, Carmaz showed no fear at all when he spoke to them. That might not have exactly translated to actual fighting prowess— considering their power, Carmaz would probably end up getting defeated pretty easily if he tried to fight them—but Raya admired him for it anyway.

The two Herunes glared at Carmaz, making Raya think they were going to put aside their spat long enough to beat up Carmaz instead.

Then the Hermit shook his head and said, "Very well. I'd rather not embarrass my son in front of strangers, anyway. Family matters ought always to be conducted in private."

"You're only saying that because you know you'd lose if you tried to take me on here and now," Herune said.

A flash of anger crossed the Hermit's features and he took a step forward, but then Carmaz said, "Hermit, don't."

The Hermit rolled his eyes, but said, "Fine. I was just trying to intimidate my son a little is all. Is that such a bad thing?"

"Typically, fathers don't intimidate their grown sons whenever they're angry with them," said Carmaz. Then he looked over his shoulder at Herune. "And sons don't pick fights with their old men, either."

Herune looked angry enough to hit Carmaz with a spell anyway, but he must have had great self-control, because he just took a deep breath and said, in a forced calm voice, "All right, what do you want to know? And who are you, anyway?"

"I'm Carmaz Korva, a native of Ruwa and a former participant in the Tournament of the Gods," said Carmaz, gesturing at himself. Then he pointed at Alira. "And she is Alira, the Judge of the Tournament of the Gods."

"Never heard of either of you two before," said Herune. He then stopped in thought. "Wait ... Carmaz Korva. I think I've heard that name before. You were the Ruwan chosen to participate in the Tournament of the Gods. I overheard a couple of people talking about you a while back."

"Yes, that's what I just said," said Carmaz, nodding. "And I was ... well, I got kicked out because I broke the rules."

Carmaz sounded quite ashamed of that, even though Raya didn't want him to be ashamed. Alira, on the other hand, looked pleased that Carmaz was ashamed of his rule-breaking. Raya absolutely hated the smug look of satisfaction on Alira's face, which she wanted to tear off.

"Explain what you are doing here, then," said Herune. "I'm listening."

So Carmaz broke into the strangest story that Raya had yet

159

heard today, though Raya hung on his every word regardless. Alira occasionally chimed in with details that Carmaz either had forgotten about or had not been present to witness, while Herune and the Hermit listened as well. Herune's expression became increasingly somber the more Carmaz spoke, while the Hermit just shook his head, rolled his eyes, and muttered about how this was all just one big waste of time. Nonetheless, the Hermit never interrupted or told them to stop.

When Carmaz finished, Raya then told him and Alira about how she had ended up in Ruwa. The Hermit listened to her story with far less skepticism than he had listened to Carmaz's story with. In fact, he actually looked alarmed when she mentioned how Herune had gotten rid of Aorja, and by the time she finished, the Hermit was tugging at his beard and looking out the windows worriedly.

"It sounds like all of us have been through a lot today," said Carmaz, stroking his chin in thought. "You haven't been able to contact the gods at all?"

"Nope," said Raya, shaking her head. "And Herune, can't, either. But what about—"

"Don't ask me," the Hermit said. "The gods don't listen to me much, either. Not that I care, because I could live the rest of my days without hearing from any of those fools."

"An army of golems just beneath the island's surface ..." Herune said. He was looking at the floor with a lost expression on his face. "How come we've never heard of them before?"

"Because they have done a very good job of remaining hidden from everyone, of course," said Alira, leaning against one of the building's support beams with her arms folded. "They intend for their attack to be a complete surprise, to conquer as much of Martir as they can before the gods or anyone else even realizes what is happening."

"But it can't be all that bad, can it?" said Herune. He rubbed his hands together anxiously. "I mean, even if they do attack, won't the gods be able to defeat them anyway?"

"I cannot say for certain," said Alira, "but the golems seemed very confident about their ability to win. I suspect they must know some magic—not Martirian magic, of course—that they will use to negate the gods' own power or at least fight back with. They managed to take away my own abilities, after all, so I don't think it is far-fetched to assume that they might be able to do something similar to the gods."

Raya rubbed the back of her neck nervously. She hadn't realized that there could be such a powerful enemy lying just beneath the surface. It made her all the more anxious to get back to World's End and let the gods deal with it.

The Hermit, on the other hand, just shook his head and said, "Even if these golems exist, I am not going to fight them unless they decide to intrude upon my domain. I am much more worried about Aorja coming and finding us. She is a wrathful woman, full of violent impulses, and if she discovers us, then she will not hesitate to kill us all."

"Father, Aorja cannot find us no matter what she does," said Herune. "Remember? The spell you cast on our location makes it impossible for someone like her to find us."

"Then how did Aorja and I find this place?" asked Carmaz. "Neither of us have any magical powers we could use to get past your spells, after all."

"It may have to do with the fact that you are a godling, which may mean that you are affected by magic differently than a normal mortal would be," said the Hermit. "Or possibly the spell is growing weaker. If so, then we are even less secure than I thought."

"The spell is as strong as always, father," said Herune. "I just checked. It's not worth worrying about."

"On the contrary, I'd say that it is very much worth worrying about," said the Hermit. "This spell is what has kept us hidden from the rest of Ruwa for years. If it is failing, then that is an ominous sign indeed."

"Only because you're starting to get senile in your old age," said Herune. He shook his head. "Never mind. The point is, the spell is working now and we are currently safe from all outside threats, whether they're Aorja or those golems that Carmaz told us about."

"But we won't be safe forever," Carmaz said. "The golems are going to invade very soon. If we're going to end this attack before it begins, then we need to contact the gods and tell them about it. Even just a handful of gods should be able to stop them."

"But the gods don't listen to us," said Herune. He rubbed his forehead in exasperation. "They ignore us because we are from Ruwa. Or have you forgotten that already, Carmaz? As a native of Ruwa yourself, I'd think that you would already know that."

Carmaz folded his arms across his chest. "Just because I know that doesn't change the truth, which is that we cannot stop this all on our own. As much as I hate to admit it, we need the gods."

"We need some way to contact them, though," said Alira. She adjusted her glasses and looked at the Hermit. "Are you certain that you don't have any way of contacting them? No way at all?"

"I could possibly send them a gray ghost," said the Hermit, stroking his beard. "But I do not believe it is possible to send a gray ghost to a god. The gods communicate with humans differently than we humans communicate with each other. Any gray ghost sent to the gods would likely be ignored, considering how the gods tend to ignore most human attempts at communicating with them."

"If only we could send someone in person to World's End," said Herune. "But neither I nor my father can teleport that far due to our own limits. Even if we did island-to-island teleportation, it would still take us weeks if not months to reach World's End. And by then, it would likely be too late to stop the invasion."

Everyone now looked quite disappointed by Herune's words. Raya was also disappointed, but then an idea occurred to her that she thought might work.

Holding up a hand, Raya said, "I think I know how we can get someone to World's End."

The others all looked at her in surprise, which told Raya that none of them had expected her to come up with an idea. She felt insulted by that implication, but on the other hand she didn't want to get into an argument with everyone about how they shouldn't be so shocked that she is capable of coming up with good ideas at the moment.

"What is it?" asked Alira.

"As a half katabans, I can open portals to the ethereal, which is the primary method that katabans use to travel quickly across the world," Raya said. "Sometimes the gods use it, too, but in any case, I could open a portal and then travel along the ethereal until

I get to World's End or find a katabans who would be willing to take me there."

"That would actually work?" said Herune in surprise. He was now looking at Raya with more interest than before. "But isn't World's End still thousands of miles to the south of Ruwa?"

"Time and space in the ethereal don't work exactly the same as they do here," said Raya, shaking her head. "I could probably reach World's End within a day if I tried. I could do it even quicker if I find another katabans on the ethereal, which should be easy because katabans travel on it almost all the time."

"In that case, then I don't see why you shouldn't do it," said Herune. He looked at the others. "Anyone else have any objections to this plan?"

Carmaz folded his arms over his chest. "No, but I have to admit that it seems a little too easy. Raya, are you sure there aren't any downsides to your plan?"

Raya folded her hands behind her back, trying to look as innocent as she could. "Well … opening an ethereal portal is not exactly easy for me, I hope you understand. I've only done it a few times and each time has taken an enormous amount of effort and energy on my part. The first time I did it, I actually blacked out completely."

"That's not good," said Carmaz.

"And I have to admit that I have not actually traveled that far on the ethereal before, either," Raya continued. "I'm not at all sure that I could find World's End on the ethereal. It would be very difficult for me to do, but that's why I plan to find a katabans who could take me there. I needn't do it on my own, you know."

"I don't like the idea of you blacking out upon entering the

164

ethereal," said Carmaz. "If that happens—"

"What choice do we have, Carmaz?" Alira interrupted. She nodded at Raya. "Raya is our only chance of alerting the gods of the coming invasion. I say we should take whatever option is available to us, no matter the risk involved."

"I agree with Alira," said Herune. "If this is our best shot at saving Martir, then I see no reason why we shouldn't do it."

Raya looked at the Hermit. He seemed to have lost all interest in the conversation at hand, because he was now staring out the window like he was looking at something far more interesting. Raya wanted to make him listen, but she supposed that it didn't really matter whether or not he was, because she could open the ethereal and escape no matter what he thought of this situation or their options.

"All right, then," said Carmaz, although he sounded very hesitant about it just the same. "Raya, I'm on board with your plan."

"Excellent," said Raya, smiling. She raised her artificial hand. "I'll see you all soon, hopefully."

Alira pushed herself off the support beam and said, "Wait. I want to come with you."

Raya froze and looked at Alira. "Why?"

"Because I'm useless here," said Alira, gesturing at herself. "And, as the Judge of the Tournament, it is my duty to return and judge the Tournament, to put it redundantly. I would be better served back on World's End, where I am supposed to be, than here on Ruwa, where I do not need to be. Here I am a liability, as I am unable to defend myself or do much more than stand around and worry with everyone else."

165

"Makes sense," said Carmaz. "Anyway, I'd imagine that the gods would be more likely to take you seriously than they would Raya, especially because you know where the golems' point of invasion is located and so can show them where it is."

"Carmaz, you can come with me, too, if you want," said Raya. "I'd love it if you—"

"No," Alira said, shaking her head. She pointed at Carmaz. "He broke the rules. He cannot come back to World's End and participate in the Tournament. I do not believe in second chances. He must stay here."

Raya looked at Alira in surprise and anger. "What? But Carmaz saved your life. Doesn't that mean anything?"

"Just because he saved my life does not mean that he should be exempt from the rules," said Alira. "Not that I expect you to understand, seeing as your feelings for him are clearly clouding your ability to think rationally, but that is just the way it is."

Raya lowered her hand and glared at Alira. "I can think very rationally, thank you very much. And I'd say that Carmaz *does* deserve to return to the Tournament as a reward for helping you."

"That is not your place to decide," said Alira. She gestured at herself. "But it is mine, and I say he must stay here, where he belongs."

"Raya, it's fine," said Carmaz, before Raya could argue the point further. "I'm in agreement with Alira. I broke the rules and therefore should have to suffer the consequences for my actions, like anyone else. Please don't waste time fighting over me, especially in such an urgent situation."

Raya was tempted to ignore Carmaz and keep arguing, but she always respected his opinion, so she nodded and said, "All right,

Carmaz. If you're happy, then I'm happy."

Carmaz sighed in relief, while the Hermit suddenly spoke up and said, "Oh, and here I was looking forward to a very nice cat fight between two good-looking girls. That would have been the only good thing to come out of this entire visit."

"Father," said Herune, "you *do* realize just how serious this situation is, yes?"

"Certainly," said the Hermit. "But that doesn't mean I have to *take* it seriously."

With the way Herune groaned, Raya was under the impression that the Hermit usually behaved this way. She felt disgusted at the Hermit's desire to see her and Alira fight, if only because it meant that he was a dirty old man.

But then Alira walked over to Raya and said, "Regardless, we must leave right away. We don't know how much time we have before the invasion begins, so the faster we leave, the faster we can ensure it doesn't even start."

"All right, then," said Raya. "Let me open the portal so we can leave right away."

So Raya once again raised her hand and concentrated hard on opening an ethereal portal. The others all stepped back, as if they sensed what she was about to do, which was good because Raya did not want to harm any of the others by accidentally opening a portal on them.

Just as Raya did that, however, a loud *crack* and *boom* echoed through the air. In fact, there were several *cracks* and *booms*, which Raya soon realized was the sound of trees being knocked over outside.

"What's going on?" said Herune, looking around in alarm. "Is

167

there something in the Swamp?"

The Hermit walked over to the nearest window and peered out. He then pulled his head back in and, looking over his shoulder, said, "There's a gigantic humanoid stone creature making its way through the Swamp toward us. Never seen anything like it."

"The golems," said Carmaz with a gulp. "I didn't think they'd track us down and actually come after us."

"It's just one?" said Alira, who now looked far more worried than she had a moment before.

"As far as I can tell, yes," said the Hermit. He then glared at Herune. "Didn't I tell you that the cloaking spell was failing? Now we must deal with this golem."

Herune rolled his eyes. "It shouldn't be that big of an issue, Father. If it's just one, we can use our magic to stop it."

"Perhaps you are correct," said the Hermit, although he sounded annoyed just the same. "It is heavy, so all we need to do is—"

The Hermit was interrupted by an explosion that sent bits and pieces of rock flying through the window on the opposite side of the room, followed by the roar of a monster that was too familiar for Raya's tastes.

Herune dashed over to the second window and looked out it just like his father. Then he ducked as a lightning bolt flew inside and struck the opposite wall, leaving a smoking crater where it hit.

"By the gods," said the Hermit, staring at the crater in the wall of his home in shock. "What was that?"

Stepping aside so he would not be visible from the window,

Herune looked at the others and said, "Aorja and Zeeree. They're making their way here from the opposite side of the Swamp. And they looked angry, to put it lightly."

The Hermit shook his head. "I cannot believe this. A golem, a half-god, and a crazed Limitless. All on *my* property. The gods must hate me."

"If they're both here—" said Raya, but Carmaz interrupted her.

"You two need to get out of here right away," said Carmaz, gesturing at her and Alira. "We'll hold off the golem and those other two. We'll be fine."

"We will?" said the Hermit in disbelief.

Carmaz rolled his eyes, while Alira said, "I agree with Carmaz. There isn't much either of us can do to fight against the golem and Aorja and Zeeree. We would simply get in the way."

"But I don't want to leave Carmaz behind like this," said Raya. "I know how vicious Aorja can be. She won't spare any of you once she finds out I'm gone."

"It doesn't matter," said Carmaz. "I mean, none of us are even in the Tournament of the Gods anyway, while you two are. You have to leave now."

Alira grabbed Raya's arm, causing Raya to look at her. The Judge had a serious look in her eyes, as she always did, though she also looked a little gentle, too.

"Please, Raya, listen to Carmaz," said Alira. "I understand your desire for him to be safe, but you are not doing him or anyone else any favor by arguing about this. We need to enter the ethereal now, before either the golem or Aorja and Zeeree get here. If we're quick, we might even be able to save Carmaz and

169

the others even if they cannot fight off the incoming attackers."

Raya didn't want to go, but she understood Alira's logic. So she looked at Carmaz one last time and said, "Please don't get yourself killed, okay?"

Carmaz, much to her relief, nodded and said, "Not planning on it. And you stay safe, too."

That made Raya smile and gave her enough confidence to open a portal. She focused on opening an ethereal portal again and succeeded, although as usual it drained her of a lot of her energy. Still, when the portal popped open, she walked in quickly, with Alira by her side, and once they were on the other side, the portal closed immediately. Raya caught one last glimpse of Carmaz before the portal closed and it was seeing him talking with Herune and the Hermit, likely about how they were going to deal with the golem, Aorja, and Zeeree.

"He's so brave, isn't he?" said Raya, looking at Alira. "Carmaz, that is."

Much to Raya's surprise, Alira nodded. "Indeed he is. It almost makes me regret kicking him out of the Tournament. Nonetheless, rules are rules, as you know."

"I know," said Raya, nodding. "I just—oh, never mind. Which way should we go from here?"

Alira pointed to the south. "If the ethereal does mirror Martir, then World's End is that way. Now let us hurry, because we have no time to lose."

Chapter Twelve

A S SOON AS Raya and Alira disappeared through the portal, Carmaz looked to Herune and the Hermit and asked, "What's the plan?"

"Plan?" the Hermit laughed. "There *is* no plan, son. Hard to come up with a plan if you didn't even expect to need one."

"So are you just going to let the golem and Aorja and Zeeree destroy this place?" asked Carmaz, gesturing at the building they stood in.

"Of course not," said the Hermit, shaking his head. He held his staff in both hands, a look of determination in his eyes. "This is my home, the only place I know. And if those idiots think they will be able to destroy it without a fight, then they have another thing coming."

"I'll fight as well," said Herune, raising his wand. "But what about you, Carmaz? You don't even have a wand. How can you help?"

"I'll figure something out," said Carmaz. "Anyway, I think we need to split up. Herune, you can fight Aorja and Zeeree, and Hermit, you can fight the golem."

"Why should I listen to you?" said the Hermit. "I don't even know you, yet you are acting like you can tell us what to do. Besides, that's an awful plan, because if we are divided, we will be much weaker than if we worked together."

"Well, then what do you suggest we do?" asked Carmaz, rubbing the back of his head in frustration. "Any better ideas or just criticism of mine?"

The Hermit looked thoughtful for a moment, but then a wicked smile appeared on his face. "I have a brilliant plan, actually, one that should go off without a hitch, assuming it works."

"Then give us the details," said Carmaz. "We're listening."

"All right," said the Hermit. He gestured for Carmaz and Herune to come closer. "Listen carefully now, because it will require all three of us to know our parts in order to pull it off without a hitch. But if it works, it will not only get rid of those three outside, but also entertain us greatly."

A few minutes later, Carmaz exited the Hermit's home through a back door that Herune showed him. This back entrance took him directly into the swamp itself and was hidden by foliage and trees, meaning that Carmaz could sneak out without being spotted by either the golem or Aorja and Zeeree. Herune exited through another way, but that was fine because the two of them needed to go different ways in order for the plan to work.

When Carmaz exited the building, he immediately made his way to the west side, where the golem had been spotted approaching. As he walked, he thought over the Hermit's simple yet brilliant plan, just to have it at the front of his mind so he would not forget it.

The plan was very simple. Carmaz and Herune would attempt to lure their respective enemies to the gates. Then they would manipulate the golem and Zeeree into fighting each other and the two monsters to tear each other apart, while Aorja would be too distracted trying to stop the fight to stop the Hermit from attacking and defeating her. The Hermit believed that the golem would be willing to fight Zeeree because it would see Zeeree as just another Martirian who was getting in the way of its mission, while Zeeree would fight the stone golem because it was a reactionary monster that attacked first and asked questions later.

If this works, we might at least be able to live long enough for the gods to arrive and save us, Carmaz thought. He then grinned grimly at the thought. *Funny how a bunch of heathens—that is, us—are putting all of our faith into the gods, although my faith is really in Raya and Alira.*

Not that that was much better. Raya was such a silly girl that Carmaz feared that she would somehow mess up her very simple role in this entire thing. Granted, she had Alira, who was a lot less silly and far more focused, but Carmaz had the nagging feeling that *something* was going to go wrong and Raya and Alira would get into trouble. He wasn't sure what, though, and so he decided not to worry about it at the moment and instead focus on the present.

Carmaz looked into the jungle. The stone golem—which was the same giant one from before—was already at the tree line. It hacked through the branches of the trees before it, causing the branches and leaves to fall with a splash into the muddy water below. The stone golem then stepped out of the tree line, its eyeless face focused on the home of the Hermit. Its hands were the buzz saw and the sword, which made it look even more dangerous than it normally did.

But Carmaz knew he didn't have to fight it, so he didn't feel as anxious about its weapons as he might have before. He just waved his hands at it and shouted, "Hey, rocks for brains! Remember me?"

The golem looked in his direction when he shouted. It stared at him for a moment, perhaps trying to make sure that he was actually who he appeared to be, and then started stomping toward him. Again, the golem could seemingly walk on the water, because its feet did not sink into the mud and its pace wasn't even slowed down.

Carmaz could still move much more quickly than it, however. He dashed over to the front gate of the Hermit's mini fortress, where he stopped. He then turned to see the giant golem picking up its pace, going from a slow walk to a slow but steady jog. By Carmaz's estimate, the golem would be upon him in less than a minute.

Another loud explosion caused him to look over his shoulder in time to see Herune run up to him. The swamp mage's beard flew to the side as he ran, the edges of which were blackened and smoking.

"Aorja coming after you?" asked Carmaz.

Herune nodded when he reached Carmaz. He gestured behind himself with his head. "I didn't even have to say anything. Just appeared and she tried to blow me up. Almost got my beard."

Carmaz was about to respond, but then Aorja and Zeeree appeared from around the corner of the building. This was the first time Carmaz had seen either of them. Aorja was a pale-skinned woman with blonde hair, although her hair was muddy and had leaves in it and she looked like she had hastily healed her wounds with magic. She rode on Zeeree's shoulders like a toddler on the shoulders of an adult, one hand grasping the half-god's large head, the other holding her wand, which was glowing rather dangerously.

Zeeree himself was almost completely covered in mud and he smelled like it, too. He was at least as tall as the golem, though even bulkier, and looked more than willing to crush both Herune and Carmaz under his fists. A low growl emitted from his throat as he and Aorja approached them, while the golem came from the other side, now moving even faster than before.

Carmaz and Herune stood back to back, watching as their enemies closed in on them. Oddly, neither the stone golem nor Aorja and Zeeree seemed to notice the other just yet, but that was probably because they were so caught up in their desire to kill both Carmaz and Herune that they didn't really notice anything else.

"I see you, Herune," Aorja said, her voice shrill and deranged. "I don't know who your friend is, but I'm going to kill him, too, because he's standing next to you and I don't care about him. Zeeree, faster!"

Zeeree picked up speed, now running much faster than a being of its size ought to have been able to, sending tons of mud flying everywhere with every stomp of its massive feet. The stone golem also started running faster, almost matching Zeeree in speed now.

Carmaz then looked at Herune suddenly. "Hey, did your father say how we're supposed to avoid getting crushed between them?"

Herune grabbed Carmaz's arm and said, "Wait for it."

"Wait for it?" said Carmaz. He looked at Zeeree and then at

the golem, both of whom were getting closer and closer with every step. "Wait for what?"

Herune held up his wand to silence Carmaz. "Just wait for the right moment."

Again, Carmaz looked at the two monsters. Zeeree held his fists up, while the stone golem looked ready to slice and dice Carmaz and Herune into pieces. Both were so close now that Carmaz could practically taste their collective stink, causing him to say, "Herune ..."

"Now!" Herune shouted.

Without warning, two vines shot down from the walls and yanked them both off the ground. Carmaz almost panicked because he couldn't feel the ground beneath his feet, but then he landed on the wall next to Herune. The vines let go of them and returned to their original positions on the wall, but before Carmaz could tell Herune to warn him next time he did something like that, Zeeree and the golem collided.

Zeeree brought both of his massive fists onto the golem's head, creating an audible *crack* that echoed through the entire Swamp. The golem, on the other hand, swung both of its blades at Zeeree's body, hitting it with so much force that Aorja flew off of Zeeree's head and landed into one of the mud puddles on in front of the fortress with a yelp and a splash.

The golem's blades cut into Zeeree's skin, prompting Zeeree to howl in pain before it smashed its fist into the side of the golem's face. The golem staggered back from the blow, but then retaliated by slashing at Zeeree's face. The flat of its blade slammed into Zeeree's face, but the half-god did not stagger. It merely grabbed the golem's sword and snapped it off the golem's arm before throwing the weapon away, where it landed tip first into the mud.

But the golem was not dissuaded by that. It swung its buzz saw at Zeeree, the sharp blade cutting through his chest and causing Zeeree to howl again. Golden blood leaked from the wound in Zeeree's chest, yet that wound didn't seem to slow him down at all. Zeeree grabbed the golem and the two started to wrestle right there in front of the gates, each one attempting to dominate the other but neither one seeing any real success.

As for Aorja, she sat up in the muddle puddle, which was waist deep, and shook her head. She looked confused for a moment before seeing Zeeree's battle with the golem, which was now getting so vicious that even Carmaz was starting to rethink the wisdom of the plan.

"Zeeree, what are you doing?" Aorja said in annoyance. "That thing's not Herune or Raya. Just kill the damn thing already so we can—"

Aorja was interrupted when a massive hand made out of mud rose from the mud behind her and slammed down on her. And she was gone from view, although Zeeree and the golem were still fighting each other to the death.

"Got her," said the Hermit's voice to Carmaz's right.

Immediately, the Hermit appeared next to Carmaz, a look of satisfaction on his elderly features. "I think we aren't going to be seeing her again, unless she happens to have the ability to breathe in mud, anyway."

Carmaz nodded and then looked down at Zeeree and the golem. "What do we do about them?"

"Watch and learn," said the Hermit.

He waved his staff at the other mud puddle and the mud giant from before rose from the earth. Once it rose to its full height, the mud giant stomped over to the wrestling Zeeree and the golem, mud dripping off its massive frame as it walked. This time, it was even bigger than before, towering over even Zeeree and the golem, the top of its head brushing against the upper branches of the trees that covered the area.

Neither Zeeree nor the golem, however, seemed to notice the mud giant until it slammed them both on the head with its huge hands. The resulting collision sent tons of mud flying onto the wall and onto Carmaz, Herune, and the Hermit. The Hermit and Herune used their magic to deflect the mud, but Carmaz was hit full on in the chest and face with it, causing him to stagger backwards and almost fall off the wall, although Herune grabbed his arm and pulled him back before he did.

As for Zeeree and the golem, Zeeree seemed to have forgotten all about his fight with the golem now. He turned and rammed headfirst into the mud giant, sending the giant staggering backwards from the blow, but the mud giant then grabbed Zeeree and slammed him into the earth. The golem, on the other hand, walked over to Zeeree and brought its buzz saw blade down on his back.

Zeeree let out a howl of pain as the golem's blade cut into his back. But then he lashed out with a kick, striking the golem in the knees and causing it to fall down on its hands and knees. Then Zeeree jumped up and punched the mud giant in the face, sending a large chunk of the mud giant's face flying away.

But more mud from the giant's head returned to the spot where it had been hit, reforming its damaged face instantly, and then it slammed its fist into Zeeree's open mouth. Zeeree choked and gasped, but was unable to stop the mud giant from funneling an almost-endless amount of mud into Zeeree's system, which Carmaz thought had to be enough to put down Zeeree for at least a little while.

Then the Hermit frowned, like his worst fears had just come true. "Uh oh."

Before Carmaz could ask him what he meant, the mud giant exploded. Large clods of mud flew everywhere, causing Carmaz, the Hermit, and Herune to duck to avoid the worst it, while Zeeree fell to his hands and feet and started throwing up mud. The golem had also ducked to avoid most of the mud, though now it was rising to its feet again with clear intent to resume its battle with the half-god.

"Why did you blow up your mud giant?" asked Carmaz, looking at the Hermit in surprise.

The Hermit, however, shook his head and pointed to the mud puddles beyond the walls. "I didn't. She did."

Carmaz looked and his heart failed him when he saw Aorja standing up in the mud, her wand out and aimed at the spot where the mud giant had been moments before. She was completely covered in mud, ruining her clothes and her blonde hair, but she looked more murderously angry than disgusted at the moment. Her chest heaving up and down, she shouted, "I'm going to kill all you bastards! Kill you with so much pain you won't even remember what it was like to live without it!"

Carmaz looked between Herune and the Hermit. "What do we do now?"

"It's obvious, isn't it?" said the Hermit. "Run."

With that, both Herune and the Hermit vanished into thin air.

Carmaz looked around wildly, but did not see either of them anywhere.

"Oh, come on!" Carmaz shouted, even though there was no one to hear him except for Aorja, Zeeree, and the golem. "Are you guys *really* abandoning me like this? You really *are* bastards, you know that?"

Of course, Carmaz got no response, but he didn't expect to. He turned to find a way off the walls, but then Aorja appeared right in front of him out of nowhere. Up close, she looked even worse than he thought, with mud clinging to her body like a second skin. She jabbed her wand at his chest, but before she could cast a spell, Carmaz grabbed her arm and yanked it upwards.

A loud *boom* emitted from the wand and then a huge burst of flame shot into the air where it harmed no one. Aorja looked surprised that Carmaz had managed to stop her, but she got over her surprise quickly and lashed out with her leg, striking him in the side with surprising force.

The blow was enough to send Carmaz staggering to the side. He reached the edge of the wall and tried to catch his balance, but then he fell and landed hard on the dried ground in the mini fortress's courtyard. The fall wasn't far, but the impact was still jarring, enough to stun him for a few seconds.

Then Aorja reappeared next to him and pointed her wand at his face. Carmaz, however, grabbed Aorja's ankles and pulled, causing her to fall down on her back with a surprised yelp.

Rather than stand up, however, Carmaz reached for her wand, which she had dropped. He wrapped his hand around it at the same time that she did, causing the two to struggle over the wand on the ground.

But it was only for a brief moment, because Carmaz's superior physical strength allowed him to wrench the wand out of her hands. He then scrambled to his feet while Aorja got back up to hers, the two of them standing opposite each other like dueling swordsmen.

Panting, ignoring the pain in his head and back from the fall, Carmaz held up the wand and said, with a triumphant smile on his face, "Got your wand. Now you can't do anything against me."

To Carmaz's surprise, however, Aorja laughed. "Oh, you pitiful, poor swamp rat, thinking that I *need* a wand to cast a spell. What a funny joke."

Aorja held out her hands and unleashed a lightning bolt that zigzagged through the air toward Carmaz. Carmaz, who had not been expecting that, tried to dodge it, but the bolt struck him in the chest, the blow enough to cause him to let go of the wand, which flew through the air toward Aorja.

But Carmaz didn't pay attention to where the wand went because he fell to the ground flat on his back. The lightning bolt had literally shocked him. His whole body felt stunned, making it almost impossible for him to move. His hair was burnt to a crisp around the edges and his entire body spasmed involuntarily every now and then. He gasped for air, but even that was painful, causing a striking pain in his lungs that made him regret having done that.

But then Carmaz started to rise from the ground. It was not of his own free will, however. Instead, he seemed to be floating upright for no reason, like he was a puppet being held up by its strings.

Then he noticed Aorja pointing her wand at him. Her eyes

were glowing with anger, which made him realize that Aorja was using her magic to lift him up.

"I really shouldn't be wasting my time with you, seeing as I don't even know your name, but when you stole my wand, that was the last straw," said Aorja. "Time to die.'"

Aorja twisted her wand and suddenly Carmaz could no longer breathe. It felt like someone had wrapped their fingers around his neck and was trying to squeeze the air out of him. He gasped, but there was nothing he could do because he was still stunned from the lightning bolt that had hit him. He could only watch Aorja's twisted grin, which was the last thing he'd ever see.

Just then, however, Aorja looked down at her legs suddenly. Carmaz followed her gaze and saw that her legs had become as rigid as stone, which seemed to be because of the mud on them drying into a solid casting.

"What the hell?" said Aorja. She looked around. "Who—?"

Herune suddenly appeared behind Aorja and stabbed her in the back with his wand. At least, that's what it looked like to Carmaz, although he didn't see how Herune could possibly do that when his wand wasn't sharpened like a knife.

Regardless, Aorja let out a yelp of pain and fell to her knees. As soon as she did, Carmaz felt the pressure disappear off his neck and he fell to the ground. He could not break his landing due to how stunned he was, so he ended up falling flat on his back. But that wasn't so bad, because he could now breathe clearly again.

Then Carmaz heard someone appear next to him and he managed to look up and see Herune standing above him. "Herune? What—"

"No time to explain," said Herune. He bent over and grabbed Carmaz by the collar of his shirt. "We have to get out of here. I only paralyzed Aorja for a moment. Hang on. I'm not very good at teleportation."

With that, Herune tugged at Carmaz's shirt collar and the courtyard of the Hermit's fortress vanished around them. The last thing Carmaz saw before they left was Aorja on her hands and knees, aiming her wand at them, but not in time to stop them from vanishing from her sight.

Chapter Thirteen

BRAIM DID NOT know where he was. He found himself walking alone through a misty, ghostly place, which was devoid of everything. There was a white road under his feet, but the place was as silent as a graveyard. It didn't even have any smells.

The place looked familiar to him, even though Braim was not sure where he might have seen it before. He rubbed the back of his head, looking for any landmarks that might indicate where he was, but no matter where he looked, he saw nothing to jog his memory. This place might as well have not existed, and he wasn't even sure that it did, being as it did not look anything at all like a real place. Perhaps it was just a hallucination.

"Hello, Braim," said a familiar rattling voice somewhere to his right. "Long time, no see."

Out of the mist came a tall skeleton wearing auburn robes and wielding a crystal and gold wand. The skeleton had glowing green eyes as well, eyes that Braim recognized very well.

"The Mysterious One?" said Braim, not stopping or slowing his pace as the skeleton walked beside him. "What are you doing here? Where am I?"

"This is your dream, more or less," said the Mysterious One, gesturing at the area with his wand. "Your subconscious has pulled your memories of the Spirit Lands up from the dredges of your mind and is using them to construct this dream. It's good because I thought that you might have forgotten the Spirit Lands, but I see that you have not."

Braim blinked. The Spirit Lands were a realm that existed beyond Martir, where all who died went. Most spirits just passed through the place onto the actual afterlife, whatever it was, but when Braim had first arrived there prior to his resurrection, he had been chosen to act as a protector and guide to these spirits in order to keep them safe from a malevolent spirit. Even so, that did not mean that Braim knew what was going on right now or why the Mysterious One was here.

"So this is a dream, then," said Braim. He looked down the misty road, but still saw nothing ahead of them. "Last thing I remember was falling unconscious on Last Beach while I was training with Tashir. Not sure why it happened, though."

The Mysterious One nodded. "Yes. I am aware that that is how you fell into your current mental state. Right now, everyone is trying to make sure you are okay and some think you might not even be able to participate in the Tournament."

Braim looked at the Mysterious One with a start. "Wait, are you saying that I'm in a coma?"

"Not exactly," said the Mysterious One, shaking his head. "At least, not the kind of coma you mortals normally suffer from. If that were the case, awakening you would be very easy."

"You mean it won't be easy?" said Braim. "You sure sound like you know a lot about me, even though you haven't been anywhere near me since you brought Alira to Martir."

"The Dark Lady has grown ever more dangerous and

185

persistent since you left," said the Mysterious One. "Without the Arbiter to help me, I've had to use all of my wits and cunning and power to keep her at bay. I only managed to get enough time to visit you through sheer luck, and even then, I will have to return to the Spirit Lands soon."

Braim shuddered. "Right. How could I forget your, er, 'sister'? I take it she still hasn't gotten over Uron's death."

"By no means," said the Mysterious One. "But in any case, that is not what matters. What does matter is that I have been keeping an eye on you since you returned to life, mostly because I, too, was interested in finding out how the universe would treat you."

"Buddy, you're not the only ultra-powerful being who has wanted to know more about me," said Braim. "Diog and the Ghostly God beat you to it. Well, okay, Diog just wanted to kill me outright, but that wasn't too different from what the Ghostly God tried to do to me, to be honest."

The Mysterious One chuckled. "Oh, I'm not as sadistic as they. The gods tend to be very blunt, particularly when dealing with mortals who refuse to give them what they want. Anyway, as an Almighty One myself, I have a more unique view of life and death, but even in my beginning-less existence, I have never seen anything quite like you before."

"You make that sound like a good thing," Braim said. He rubbed the back of his head, which ached. "Being unique isn't all its cracked up to be. Constant headaches and a terrible feeling like nothing about me is even right. Sometimes I think that Diog was right when he said I was an unnatural abomination that needed to be destroyed."

The Mysterious One tapped his chin with one bony finger. "To a certain extent, I'd say that Diog was not entirely wrong. Your nature truly is unnatural. And while I don't have all of the answers, I do believe I know why you feel the way you do."

"You do?" said Braim, looking at the Mysterious One in surprise. "What is it? Is it really because I'm not supposed to exist?"

"Not exactly," said the Mysterious One. "Do you remember Uron's true nature?"

Braim nodded. "Darek explained it to me. Uron was once a mortal, but then he and the Great Snake, your brother, ended up merging. That allowed him to exist as a spirit trapped on Martir until he got my body, but then I got my body back and he doesn't even exist anymore. Why? Is it relevant to your theory?"

The Mysterious One nodded. "Glad you remembered all of that. At the time, I had assumed that Uron's erasure from the universe was due to his unnatural state of being. There wasn't—and still isn't—an entity like Uron, a strange merging of mortal and higher spirit that caused so much grief for everyone on Martir. I had believed that his unique nature clashed so terribly with the Spirit Lands because there had literally never been anyone quite like him before and likely never will be again, which was why it erased him from existence when you forced his spirit out of your body."

"But it wasn't, was it?" said Braim. "There was another reason he didn't just end up as another bodiless spirit after I got my body back, wasn't there?"

"I believe so," said the Mysterious One. He looked at Braim, although his skull face showed no emotion. "My belief is that

187

Uron's erasure from existence was in fact a natural part of the universe. It is how the universe treats those who died and came back to life and then die again. Rather than go on to become normal spirits like most, they do not get a second chance at death. They simply cease to exist entirely."

Braim's eyes widened and he actually stopped. "Hold on. Are you telling me that if I die, then my spirit will literally cease to exist? I won't just go on to the Spirit Lands and then beyond the Gates like every other spirit?"

The Mysterious One stopped as well and looked down at him, his expression still unreadable. "Yes."

"Then how does this tie into the constant feeling of wrongness I suffer from?" asked Braim, rubbing the back of his head again. "What does it mean?"

"It means that you were never supposed to come back to life at all," said the Mysterious One. "And your body is simply reacting the way any body would in such a situation. It isn't trying to kill you, exactly, but it isn't trying to save you, either."

Braim felt sweat on his forehead, which he wiped away with one of his sleeves. "But why? Why does the universe do this to people like me and ... and Uron? Why does it erase our very spirits from existence?"

"I do not know," said the Mysterious One. "That would require understanding the universe itself, which I am afraid to say that I don't, owing to the fact that it existed well before even I did. My guess is that the universe does not want anyone returning from the dead. To the universe, the person who comes back to life is like a criminal who knowingly breaks the same law twice. At that point, there is no excusing ignorance, and thus more extreme

—and permanent—measures are to be taken to deal with the lawbreaker."

Even though it was just a dream, Braim found it hard to breathe. He put his hands on his chest, which now felt tight.

"In any case," said the Mysterious One, "there is nothing I can do about it, as far as I can tell. My only advice is that you should probably avoid dying, but you already know that."

"You mean I'm still going to die of old age anyway, even if I avoid illness and getting killed by someone else?" asked Braim.

"I see no reason why you shouldn't," said the Mysterious One. "Uron was immortal, but that was due to the influence of my brother on his spirit. You, on the other hand, are just a regular mortal who came back to life. So you will probably live as long as any regular mortal, barring any anti-aging spells you might cast on yourself, anyway."

Braim gulped. Death hadn't scared him quite so much as it did now, mostly because he had thought he already knew what lay in the beyond. Yet if the Mysterious One was right, then there was nothing—literally *nothing*—that awaited him on the other side.

But then a question occurred to him and he asked the Mysterious One, "What about Darek and Aorja? Their spirits went to the Spirit Lands and returned. Are they also going to cease to exist after death?"

"No," said the Mysterious One. "They technically didn't actually die. They simply used a spell to cross over to the other side for a little while. Once they die, their spirits will probably go on to the Spirit Lands, like everyone else's."

"What about my magical powers?" said Braim. He pulled out his wand from his belt and held it up for the Mysterious One to

189

see. "The Ghostly God took mine away. Can you give it back to me? You gave Darek back his when he lost his power to the same device, didn't you?"

The Mysterious One nodded, albeit too slowly for Braim's liking. "That I did, but there is something about your existence that bars me from granting you your powers back. I believe it is due to your unnatural existence, which even I barely understand. Therefore, I cannot help you there, though I wish could."

Braim's spirits fell, even though he hadn't thought they could fall any further than they already had. His grip on his wand tightened so much that he almost snapped it.

"What am I supposed to do, then?" said Braim. He scowled. "Just wait until the day of my death? Is that it?"

"Braim, there's no need to get angry at me," said the Mysterious One, folding his arms across his chest. "I am merely telling you the truth, which is that you are different and will thus be treated differently upon your death."

"I don't *want* to be different," said Braim. He pointed his wand at the Mysterious One, even though it was a useless gesture. "I want to be like everyone else. Just a normal guy who doesn't suffer from a blank memory and a body that doesn't even want to exist."

"I can't help you there, unless you'd like for me to put you out of your misery already," said the Mysterious One. His calmness in the face of Braim's anger only succeeded in angering Braim more. "Though now that I think about that, that would cause you more harm than good."

"Of course it would," Braim snapped. "I would literally cease to exist. Ask Uron how that's working out for him."

"Good point," said the Mysterious One. "But I don't think this news is all bad. There is a silver lining that I think you haven't noticed."

"And what, pray tell, is that silver living?" said Braim. "If you're just going to say that my death will mean one less soul for you to judge—"

"You can avoid nonexistence by simply not dying," said the Mysterious One. "Think about it. By winning the Tournament of the Gods, you will become the God of Martir, which means you will be immortal and invincible."

"That worked out real well for Skimif," Braim said.

"Only because my brother existed and had the God-killer," said the Mysterious One. "But with both my brother and the God-killer no longer in existence, you will have literally no equal in Martir if you win the Tournament. Then you will never have to worry about nonexistence ever again."

Braim considered the Mysterious One's words. It made sense, when he thought about it. After all, the God of Martir truly was without equal on Martir. Even the other gods were not capable of defeating whoever the current God of Martir was. In fact, the gods in general were incapable of being killed by anything less than a god, though even that was forbidden by the Treaty written up by the Powers ages ago.

But then Braim thought of a possible threat to the God of Martir and said, "What about the Void? Couldn't she kill me if she wanted to, even if I became the God of Martir?"

The Mysterious One shrugged. "I doubt it. The Void could not kill Skimif when he was alive, though she did contain him and the rest of the gods for a while. But you and the other gods will be able to keep her presence from expanding and covering all of Martir at the very least."

"I guess you're right," said Braim. "But I will still have to actually survive that long. And considering how I was almost killed a little over an hour ago, if even that, I might not."

"I believe you will," said the Mysterious One. "Due to circumstances outside of my control, there isn't much I can do to help you, but I trust that you have the knowledge and cunning to make it. You were a great protector of the spirits, after all, and the one who defeated Uron in the end."

Braim nodded, but deep down, he wasn't so sure that he believed the Mysterious One. The Mysterious One may have been wise and powerful, but that did not mean that he was right about everything.

But Braim did not share his doubts with the Mysterious One, so he merely said, "Thanks for the vote of confidence, Mysterious One. I'll try to keep it in mind when I participate in the next challenge later this afternoon."

"You are most welcome, Braim," said the Mysterious One.

"By the way, do you happen to know what happened to Raya and Alira?" asked Braim. "They both disappeared and no one, not even the gods, know where they are."

"I am sorry to say that I do not," said the Mysterious One, shaking his head. "The most I can say is that I think they are probably both still alive, but again, I don't know where exactly because I don't pay very much attention to either of them."

"Okay," said Braim. His shoulders slumped. "Well, thanks for letting me know, anyway, even though that doesn't really help me."

"I may be an Almighty One, but that does not make me an all-knowing one," said the Mysterious One with a shrug. "Anyway, I must leave now. I sense that the Dark Lady is going to launch yet another assault and I must return so I can deal with her before she gets away with too much."

"All right," said Braim. "See you later. Next time, try to show up in person, all right?"

"Of course," said the Mysterious One. "Now good bye, Braim. I hope that my theory about your soul is wrong, because if it isn't … well, I just hope that you win the Tournament."

With that, the Mysterious One melted into the mist. Braim watched him go, but then he realized that the entire area he stood in was starting to melt away, too, leaving only an empty blackness that he could not see in.

And then, without warning, Braim woke up. He gasped for air and heard a familiar voice to his right say, "Braim?"

Panting and sweating, Braim looked down and saw that he was lying on his bed in his room. He then looked to his right and saw Tashir sitting in a chair by his bed. Malya stood by him, the two looking very concerned about him. There was no one else in the room with them, but Braim thought he heard people outside his room talking, although who it was and what they were talking about, he didn't know.

"Malya? Tashir?" said Braim, blinking. He yawned. "What are you two doing here? How did I get here?"

"Your bodyguards took you here after you collapsed on the beach," said Tashir. "They let us stay with you because we wanted to make sure you were okay."

Braim felt sand in his hair, which he brushed out with a sweep

193

of his hand. The back of his head also continued to throb, reminding him immediately of the Mysterious One's warning, a thought which filled him with pure dread just thinking it.

"How do you feel, Braim?" asked Malya. She rubbed her hands together anxiously. "Sick? Well? Can you stand?"

"I think so," said Braim as he moved his legs, which were a little stiff but otherwise unharmed. "How long have I been out?"

"Half an hour," said Tashir. "We were worried that you might not awake up in time to participate in the sub-bracket challenge, but it looks like you will get a chance to do that after all."

Braim sat up and shuddered, even though it wasn't cold. "Right. So there's still plenty of time for me to go and get ready."

"You should probably continue to rest," Malya suggested. "You look awful. Pale skin, bags under your eyes … almost like a corpse."

Braim almost asked for a mirror so he could see what Malya was talking about, but when he thought about it, he decided that he could live a little while longer without seeing the negative effects that that dream had had on him. He rubbed his eyes, however, because they felt tired and worn out.

"What happened?" said Tashir. "Why did you fall unconscious like that? Was the proximity to the Void too much for your body to handle?"

"I don't know," said Braim with a shrug. "It's nothing worth worrying about, in my opinion. Nothing bad happened and I feel fine. I'll probably feel even better by the time that the next sub-bracket challenge starts."

Both Malya and Tashir looked relieved that Braim was fine, but Braim was, of course, lying. He remembered the Mysterious

One's theory about the nature of his own death. He didn't want to mention it to either of them, however, because he didn't want to worry his two friends with a theory that was probably not right, although an unsettling feeling in the pit of his stomach told him that there was more truth to it than he cared to admit.

Instead, Braim said, "Tashir, I still want to learn how to use a sword. I'm not going to go around unarmed ever again."

"Are you certain that you feel up to it, Braim?" asked Tashir. "You look rather awful and tired."

"It doesn't matter how I look," said Braim, shaking his head. He put one hand on his chest. "I need to learn how to defend myself and that's all that matters. I'll push my body to the limit if I have to."

"Don't you want to rest up for the challenge?" asked Malya. "I mean, none of us know what the challenge will be, of course, but it might be physically taxing, so—"

"Thanks for the concern, Malya, but I'll be fine," said Braim. "You just worry about that assassin who tried to kill me earlier. She's the biggest threat to me at the moment."

"All right," said Malya, although she didn't look pleased at Braim brushing off her concern. "Still, just don't push yourself too much, okay? You aren't a god yet."

"I know," said Braim. He swung his legs over the side of his bed and said to Tashir, "Now let's get started. Teach me as much as you can in the time we have so that when the challenge starts, I'll be ready, no matter what it is."

Chapter Fourteen

THIS WAS THE first time that Raya had ever spent so much time in the ethereal. Of the few times that she had opened ethereal portals, she had always been in the ethereal briefly, often for less than a minute, so she didn't get to quite experience the full thing that so many katabans depended upon for their daily traveling needs.

The ethereal was a wide, long white road that stretched for as far as the eye could see. Bright stars in a variety of colors dotted the dark sky above and below the road, but there was no wind blowing through and the temperature was even and nice. The road was soft under Raya's feet, almost spongy, although it was far sturdier than any sponge and felt extremely old, which made sense, because as far as Raya knew the ethereal had been created at the same time with the rest of Martir. There were no side roads or buildings, although Raya did see portals that seemed to lead to other parts of Martir, but neither she nor Alira stopped long enough to look into any of them except to confirm that these portals did not lead anywhere.

Alira walked by Raya with a lot less interest in the ethereal than she did. The Judge seemed to treat the ethereal as nothing more than an annoying and unnecessary detour on their way to their actual destination, because she kept her face facing firmly ahead at all times, like she thought she could somehow speed up their progress if she kept looking the way they were going.

The two hadn't spoken much since leaving Ruwa. Alira had made it clear that she wasn't interested in even the smallest of small talk with Raya, which was fine by her, because Raya wasn't interested in talking with Alira very much either. The Judge had always struck her as being very distant and difficult to approach, so Raya was perfectly fine with not talking with her. She didn't really think of Alira as a friend anyway; she was barely even an acquaintance.

So Raya thought about Carmaz instead. She wished that he was still with her and wondered how well he, Herune, and the Hermit were doing. She had confidence that Carmaz was going to be all right, but deep down she just wasn't sure if Carmaz could survive against an enemy as powerful as Aorja. Granted, Carmaz had two mages to help, but even then, Aorja was a sadistic and unyielding foe. And that wasn't even counting Zeeree, who was a force of nature all by himself.

Carmaz will be all right, Raya told herself. *He's strong and brave and smart. I just need to focus on getting to World's End and informing the gods of the invasion. Then they'll rescue him and all will be well again.*

"Raya?" said Alira, snapping Raya out of her thoughts and causing her to look at her. "Do you know why the ethereal is so … quiet?"

"Quiet?" Raya repeated. "What do you mean?"

"I mean, we are observably alone," said Alira, gesturing around the ethereal. "I see no other katabans here at all, even though this is supposed to be the road that all katabans use to

197

travel across Martir. Have you noticed?"

Raya looked around and noticed that Alira was right. The entire ethereal was completely empty, aside from the two of them. Raya looked forward and backward, even squinted, but saw no one else no matter how hard or in what direction she looked.

"That is weird," said Raya. She rubbed her wrist. "Maybe they're down the line somewhere. The ethereal is a big place, after all, so maybe it's big enough that you can find entire stretches that are completely empty like this."

"That is a possibility, but I consider it rather unlikely," said Alira. "When I first came to Martir, Nimiko, the God of Light, told me that katabans can be found traveling on the ethereal at all times of day and night. He said that on high traffic days, the ethereal can be so packed that it is almost impossible to walk upon."

"Maybe this is just a slow day," said Raya.

Alira again shook her head. "No. I think the ethereal ought to be full of katabans right now. Do you know why?"

Raya shook her head.

"Because of us," said Alira. She gestured at them both when she said that. "You and me. We were both kidnapped, remember? I consider it likely that the gods have sent out katabans to find us. Logically, we should have already run into one of those katabans by now, who should have then taken us back to World's End as per the gods' likely orders."

"Well, if that's the case, then why do you think that no one has found us yet?" asked Raya. "Where do you think they all are?"

"That is a question I do not have the answer to," said Alira. "I might be over-thinking this, but I think it is just as likely that I am not. There is a reason we are alone in the ethereal, even if we do not yet know that reason."

"Then we should walk even faster," Raya said. "How much longer until we reach World's End, do you think?"

"I cannot say," said Alira. "I only visited the ethereal once, shortly after my arrival on Martir when the gods were showing me around. I was told that time and space in the ethereal works differently from the rest of Martir, so we could be five minutes or five hours away from World's End right now."

"Oh, come on," said Raya. "Do you really think Carmaz will be able to survive five hours against Aorja?"

"It doesn't matter what I think about that if that's the truth," said Alira. "What matters is that we should not let our guard down in this place. Because if the katabans are not here, then that means that something else likely—"

Six ethereal portals burst into existence around them. Before either Raya or Alira could react, gray-cloaked figures jumped out of the portals and surrounded the two of them on either side. The figures drew swords and spears out from their robes, pointing them at Raya and Alira and cutting off all avenues of escape in the process.

"What the hell?" said Raya, looking around as she and Alira drew closer, trying to see all of their assailants at once. "Where did these guys come from? And who are they?"

"Empty followers," said Alira. She adjusted her glasses as she looked around at them. "Followers of the Void, in other words."

Raya nodded. Now she understood why those gray cloaks looked familiar. They were the cloaks worn by members of the cult known as the Empty, which was comprised of katabans that followed the Void. The only Empty follower Raya had known on a personal level was Anwan, but her negative experience with him had been enough to make Raya wary of the entire cult and all of its members therein.

"How do we defeat them?" asked Raya, trying to keep an eye on all of the cloaked figures at once but failing.

"Not sure," said Alira. She glanced at Raya. "Do you have any weapons on you?"

"No," said Raya, shaking her head. "You?"

"Of course not," said Alira. "And my magical powers still have not returned. It appears that we are entirely defenseless, then."

"Defenseless?" said one of the Empty followers. He took a step forward, green eyes peering out from his dark hood. He was taller and skinnier than the others and seemed to be the leader. "Oh, goody. That will make it so much easier for us to avenge our mistress."

"How did you find us?" asked Alira. "Not even the gods know where we are."

"The Void told us," said the lead Empty follower simply. "She has been very angry ever since Raya ruined all of Brother Anwan's hard work a week ago. She has kept an eye on the princess ever since then, waiting for the perfect opportunity to send us, and so when you two entered the ethereal, alone and unarmed, she saw the perfect opportunity to have us kill you both in cold blood."

Raya noticed that the chest area of this follower's robes looked like it had been hastily sewn back together. It was even faintly red, like blood, which made Raya wonder who had harmed this katabans and why they hadn't been able to just kill him.

"So why haven't you killed us already?" asked Alira. "It's not like there is anything to stop you. Neither of us are particularly good fighters, after all."

"We wanted to see the absolute terror and hopelessness in your eyes before we killed you," said the Empty follower. Raya could just imagine that he was smiling like a mad man, even though she had no idea what his face looked like exactly. He then drew a completely black sword out of the folds of his robes, which looked as black as the Void's darkness. "Now, seeing as we did not come to have a conversation with you, let's move onto the killing. Don't worry; we'll be quite quick and thorough about it."

The Empty follower gestured at his fellow followers. "My brothers and sisters of Emptiness, kill Princess Raya and Judge Alira. Show them what happens to those who defy the Void and show them the fate that awaits all who stand against her plans."

The Empty followers said nothing in response. They simply raised their weapons and moved in as silently as spirits. Indeed, Raya didn't even see their feet move, though that may have been because their robes went down to their feet and thus hid them from view.

Raya and Alira drew closer together. Raya looked at Alira and asked, in a whisper of a voice, "Any escape plans?"

"Still thinking," said Alira, "although it is starting to look to me like this will be the end."

"Not very encouraging, are you?" said Raya in an angry whisper, almost a hiss. "You're supposed to be smart enough to figure out how to get us out of this situation alive."

"Where did you ever get the idea that I am a competent

201

thinker in combat?" asked Alira, glancing at Raya in confusion. "I'm afraid that there isn't much I can do in these sorts of situations."

Raya scowled, but had no time to respond, because now the Empty followers were practically upon them. In desperation, Raya looked down at her whitish-blue hand, but right now it seemed as useless as a bucket of paint in this situation. Nonetheless, she raised it and her other hand above her head in order to protect it, although it was more out of instinct on her part than anything.

Then the Empty followers, still silent, brought their blades down upon Raya and Alira's heads. Raya, having never been hit like this before, wasn't sure exactly what to expect, but she expected it to be extremely bloody. She prayed a quick prayer to the gods to keep Carmaz safe.

A microsecond after Raya prayed that prayer, however, a burst of energy emerged from her whitish-blue hand. The energy formed a large barrier, same color as her hand, over her and Alira, which blocked the weapons of the Empty followers, causing many of them to curse in surprise. The lead Empty follower even shouted, "What is this? Where did this barrier come from?"

Raya was too surprised to do anything else, but Alira apparently wasn't, because she grabbed Raya's arm and pulled her along behind her. The barrier came with them, allowing the two women to break through the Empty followers surrounding them, knocking over most and causing the lead Empty follower to shout, "Go after them! Do not let them escape!"

That was when Raya got over her shock and started running with Alira, doing her best to keep up. She kept looking over her shoulder, however, and saw that the Empty followers were running after her and Alira with their weapons raised. They looked like an angry mob that wanted to tear her and Alira apart, which wasn't too far from the truth when Raya thought about it.

But Raya didn't focus on them for long. She turned her attention back to the road ahead of them, even though she wasn't sure where they were going or if they would be able to outrun the Empty followers at all. Raya was still rather worn out from the events of the day and already felt her limbs becoming sluggish and heavy. Her lungs started to burn and every step seemed to jolt her spine. And considering how weakly Alira was starting to run, it was clear that the Judge was also starting to lose her strength.

"I don't think we're going to make it," Raya said as they ran. She looked around. "Don't see any portals to World's End anywhere."

"Keep running and stop talking," said Alira without looking at Raya. "We have to keep running and keep moving. We cannot stop or slow down at all. The fate of the world depends on us."

Raya nodded, but then without warning tripped and fell. She landed on her hands and knees, which was not a large impact by any means, but her fatigue finally caught up with her and she found it impossible to get up. Alira came to a stop a few feet ahead and looked back at her with a disbelieving expression on her face.

"Did you just trip?" said Alira. "Now?"

"Yes, I tripped," Raya snapped. She tried to stand up, but failed. "Can you help me get up or are you just going to stand there and judge me like that?"

Alira sighed in annoyance, but then dashed back to Raya and

helped her back to her feet. Raya, however, found it hard to stand up and she would have fallen right back down had Alira not held her upright.

"I'm sorry, Alira, but I just can't stand on my own," said Raya. Her voice sounded weaker than usual even to herself. "Too tired. Need rest."

"It's fine," said Alira, although her annoyed tone suggested that it was not. "We'll survive. We'll just keep going no matter what."

Unfortunately, their movement was much slower now, because Raya could barely take even one step forward on her own. Alira had to slow down her pace to match Raya's, at which point it became blindingly obvious to Raya that they were not going to survive. She tried to raise her hand again and create another barrier, but she was too weak to do even that much.

The Empty followers were closing in as quickly as ever. Raya was now certain that she and Alira could not survive together.

So Raya said to Alira, "Alira, we're not going to make it. Not when we're moving this slowly."

"You don't know that for sure," said Alira, shaking her head. She glanced over her shoulder at the Empty followers, but didn't slow down her pace at all. "Don't let despair win. We must keep going no matter what."

But Raya knew that was false. She also knew that only one of them could survive and she knew who it had to be.

"Alira, you have to go on without me," said Raya. She tried to push herself away from the Judge. "The Tournament needs you more than it needs me. If you leave me, you might be able to survive on your own."

204

Alira looked at Raya like she had lost her mind. "Are you sure that you understand what you are saying? This can't be the same self-centered Princess Raya that I've known for the past month and a half, is it?"

"Shut up," Raya snapped. She gestured behind them at the Empty followers, who were now closer than ever, and gaining still. "It's either you or me, and it has to be you. I can't even walk by myself I'm that pathetic. But you can, so you have to go and do it."

Again, Alira shook her head. "No, I don't. I'm getting us both to World's End alive, whether you like it or not."

"Then you're dooming us both to certain death," said Raya. She looked again over her shoulder at the Empty followers and then back to Alira. "I just wish that I had lived long enough to give Carmaz a proper good bye."

Alira seemed to be struggling to say something. She also looked at the incoming Empty followers, and then back at Raya. There was a look in her eyes that Raya had never seen before, a look that she could not identify.

"If this truly is our end, then I have one last thing I'd like to say to you before we die," said Alira.

Raya, confused, said, "What?"

Alira took a deep breath, but before she could utter another word, the sound of gunfire overhead caused both of them to immediately duck. They hit the ground as bullets sailed overhead, but the bullets were not aimed at either of them. Instead, the bullets flew toward the Empty followers, striking a few while causing the rest to immediately scatter and flee. They opened ethereal portals and vanished to who-knows-where, although they did not leave behind the bodies of their wounded brethren, who they helped drag with them to safety.

Raya had no idea where those bullets had come from until she looked in the direction they shot from and saw a familiar automaton standing dozens of feet ahead of them, one hand with gun fingers aiming in their direction. Smoke rose from the automaton's gun barrel fingers as it lowered its hand after all of the Empty followers had fled.

"Keeper?" said Raya in surprise, looking at the automaton in astonishment. "Where did you come from?"

Keeper walked over to them immediately, crossing several feet with every step. "Princess! I have been searching for you all over World's End. I am so glad that you are alive and unharmed. Your parents will also be relieved to know this once I tell them, even though they don't yet know that you are missing at all."

Raya and Alira stood up again, but they both looked around just to make sure that the Empty followers were indeed gone. Neither of them saw anything, so they walked over to Keeper as quickly as they could, meeting the massive automaton about halfway. The automaton smelled of gun powder and metal, but it was the best scent that Raya had smelled in a long time.

That was when Keeper noticed Alira, who he pointed at and said, "Is that Judge Alira? Why is she with you?"

"It's a long story," said Alira. She sounded a lot weaker than she had before, which made Raya think that Alira must have been pretending to be strong prior to Keeper's appearance. "But how did you find us? Not even the gods know where we are."

"Truthfully, I found you through pure luck," said Keeper. "I searched World's End for you and spoke with many katabans and godlings and gods about you, but all of the evidence seemed to point to the conclusion that you were no longer there. I decided that you must have been taken off the island, though to where, I didn't know."

"Did anyone even come with you?" asked Raya. "Or are you by yourself?"

"No one seemed to believe me when I said you were not on World's End, so I decided to test the theory by myself," said Keeper. "I decided to go to the Northern Isles in order to ask your parents for aid from the royal mages in order to find you, but along the way I ran into you two here and you know the rest."

Raya had never been happier to see Keeper in her life, but she was too tired to express that happiness properly right now. She just nodded at him to show her approval and said, "Well, I am happy to see you anyway, Keeper. I thought I would never see you or anyone else ever again."

"Why would you think that?" asked Keeper, who sounded worried now. "And just where have you and Alira been all this time? Everyone on World's End has been worried sick about your disappearances."

"It's a long story," said Alira. "Can you take us back to World's End? We'll fill you in on the details on the way there. All you need to know is that all of Martir is threatened by a new foe that even the gods do not know of but which must be stopped immediately."

"Of course," said Keeper, nodding. "I will be more than happy to transport you to World's End. Especially if if there is a new threat that we must do something about."

So Keeper scooped up Raya and Alira in his massive arms,

turned, and ran back the way he came, moving fast for a being his size. Raya didn't say anything as they ran, mostly because she had now given into the exhaustion that had threatened to make every breath her last since she and Alira had left Ruwa.

Thus, Raya decided to take this moment to nap, as she didn't think they were going to be attacked again on their way there. Before she closed her eyes, however, she looked at Alira, who must have had the same idea as her because the Judge was also asleep now, her arms folded comfortably over her chest and her head down.

Raya briefly wondered what it was that Alira had wanted to confess to her earlier, but she was so tired now that she didn't feel like waking Alira up and asking her about it. She made a mental note to bring it up later, after all of this madness was over and she was feeling better.

So Raya, yawning, closed her eyes and quickly drifted off to sleep, feeling secure in Keeper's arms. Her very last thought before she fell asleep was that she hoped that Carmaz was still alive.

Chapter Fifteen

ONE MOMENT, CARMAZ was looking at Aorja, who was aiming her wand at him. The next, everything around him became as black as night, but only for the briefest of moments, because a second later, Carmaz was back in the Swamp, breathing in the thick, humid air, his hands digging into the wet mud underneath him.

Immediately, Carmaz coughed and hacked. His throat and lungs ached immensely from where Aorja's magic had applied pressure to them. While his throat and lungs would undoubtedly heal in time, the fact was that every breath was painful and he wasn't even sure he could speak.

Carmaz also felt Herune's hand on his collar and heard the bearded mage's voice above him saying, "Carmaz, are you all right?"

Still coughing, Carmaz looked up at Herune. The young mage was looking down at Carmaz with genuine concern on his features, which puzzled Carmaz because he didn't know Herune well enough for Herune to care about his well-being.

In any case, Carmaz shook his head and said, in a hoarser voice, "N-No," before suddenly coughing and hacking again.

"I'm sorry, but I can't really heal you," said Herune. "I'm not much of a panamancer, so there's nothing I can really do to help. I can heal small scratches and broken bones, but healing the pressure that Aorja applied to your throat is beyond my training."

Carmaz rubbed his throat. He didn't speak because he was in too much pain to do so. If he could speak, he would have said that his throat was probably going to heal on its own and that it just needed time and space in which to do so.

"You saved the stranger?" said the Hermit's voice to Carmaz's right. "You truly are a foolish son. Aorja will be after him and us now. We will never know another peaceful moment in our lives from now on, thanks to you."

Carmaz looked to his right. The Hermit sat not far away on a stump. His shoe-less feet were deep in the mud, which seemed like a dumb move to Carmaz, as that would make it harder to escape in a hurry, but he said nothing about it due to his throat still aching and hurting as badly as it was.

"I saved him because I didn't want to give Aorja the satisfaction of killing one of her enemies," said Herune in annoyance. "And it was the right thing to do. Not that you would understand, since your idea of 'morality' basically boils down to 'stay away from me and I won't kill you.'"

"My son, my morality is far more nuanced than that," said the Hermit with a huff. "It can be more accurately boiled down to 'don't poke the sleeping dragon.' Of course, you never grasped the finer points of my teachings, so it's no surprise to me that you don't even understand my morality."

Carmaz groaned. He didn't like getting caught in familial disputes like this. He would have told the two of them to cut out this nonsensical snipping, especially with the invasion of the golems so near, but again he could not gather the vocal strength to do that. He just shook his head in disapproval, although neither son nor father seemed to notice. Or if they did, they did not care.

While the Hermit and Herune bickered with each other, Carmaz looked around at their surroundings to get an idea of where they were. They were still in the Swamp, but it was not a part that he was familiar with. Long red vines that he recognized as belonging to trees called soldier's blood hung around them, while a heavy silence hung in the air like a blanket. As far as Carmaz could tell, they were not anywhere near any of the villages or settlements on the outskirts of the Swamp.

Carmaz still had a lot of questions, however, so he sat up and said, forcing himself to speak despite the pain, "Where … are we?"

The Hermit and Herune stopped bickering and looked at him. The Hermit said, "This is a place I occasionally like to retreat to when I feel that my home is not sufficiently isolated from the rest of the world. It has no real name, although I like to think of it as my silent sanctuary, as this is the quietest part of the Swamp."

"What if Aorja uses her magic to find us?" asked Carmaz, painfully aware of his hoarse voice, though he was determined to speak anyway.

"Impossible," said the Hermit. He gestured at the blood red vines hanging around them like the veil on a bride. "A little known fact about the vines of soldier's blood trees is that they have the ability to block topomancy; that is, the magical discipline that allows a mage to locate anyone anywhere in the world. As a matter of fact, I might even be the only one to know this, as I discovered its odd properties when I was a much younger man and have never heard any other mage speak of or write about it before."

"That's convenient," said Carmaz. He tried to stand up, but found that took too much effort on his part, so he stayed where he was on the muddy ground. "Are we far from your home, then?"

"Far enough that neither Aorja nor her freakish overgrown deformed baby could accidentally stumble upon us anytime soon," said the Hermit. "But don't for a moment believe that we will be safe here forever. There is no food or water here, at least not enough to sustain us long term. If we do not wish to turn our sanctuary into a mausoleum, then we will need to move on at some point."

Carmaz frowned. "You mean you aren't going to try to go back and get your home back?"

The Hermit shook his head. "And risk getting killed by Aorja? While I will mourn the loss of my home, I prefer my life over any nicely stacked pile of brick and wood."

"Live to fight another day?" said Carmaz.

The Hermit gave a harsh laugh that was almost like a croak. "Live to flee and live in peace. While I am a powerful mage with decades of experience, even I am no match for a Limitless like her, even if she were not an insane woman whose grasp on morality is even more questionable than the gods'. She is mad."

"I could fight her," said Herune. He looked to the west, even though there was nothing to see except for the heavy curtain of red vines hanging around them. "And beat her. I'm strong. I can do this."

"Son, that is pure foolishness and you know it," said the Hermit. He coughed. "You have far less experience than me. In fact, you've never even beaten me in a proper magical duel. The only reason you survived against Aorja when you saved that princess girl from her was because Aorja was not prepared for your tricks."

Herune looked at the Hermit in annoyance. "Tricks? They're not tricks. They're proper magical techniques, no different from your ability to make your voice sound like it's coming from everywhere at once."

"Be that as it may, neither of us have what it takes to defeat her," said the Hermit. "Better for us to flee and get as far away from her as possible than to fight and risk dying a painful death. If we move quickly, we might be able to catch a pirate ship leaving Ruwa."

Carmaz looked at the Hermit in surprise. "Leave Ruwa? But what about the invasion?"

The Hermit shook his head. "I do not care. Haven't I said that enough times already? You are certainly a thick-headed one."

"But …" Carmaz had to stop for a moment to let his throat rest, and then he continued when it wasn't hurting as badly. "But Ruwa is our home. Are we just going to let Aorja, Zeeree, and the golems take it?"

"Raya and Alira are going back to World's End, are they not?" said the Hermit. "When they return, they will tell the gods, who will then take care of it for themselves. I believe that we have done our job here, no matter how you look at it. And, while I hate saying this, it's time we put the security of Ruwa in the hands of the gods."

Carmaz's hands balled into fists. "Like we've done for the past several centuries? Tell me, Hermit, how has that worked out for us?"

"Who cares?" said the Hermit. He brushed some dirt out of his long, gray beard. "If you want to go and get yourself killed, be my guest. I'm not a hero. Never have been, never will be. I believe heroes are foolish, but I also believe people should do what they want, so go and get yourself killed. Doesn't bother me one bit."

"Then I will go with him," said Herune, putting one hand on Carmaz's shoulder and causing Carmaz to look up at him in surprise. "We have no idea when the gods will arrive—or if Raya and Alira will even reach them at all—so if we can do anything to slow down the golems' invasion, I think we should do it."

The Hermit did not immediately respond, even though he clearly had some choice words for Herune's declaration. He looked a little disturbed, as if he was caught in a terrible dilemma that he had not expected to find himself in. He grunted, but didn't say anything.

Then the Hermit said, "If that is what you will do ... then I suppose I can't stop you."

That seemed like an oddly level thing for the Hermit to say, especially after the heated exchange between the two mages just moments before. That told Carmaz that there was something strange going on here that he wasn't aware of, but which he knew that he needed to know.

So Carmaz said, his voice slightly stronger than before but not by much, "Why do you two even stay with each other if you can't stand each other? Sorry if that's butting into your business, but it just doesn't make any sense to me right now."

Herune and the Hermit exchanged a look that made it clear that they were silently trying to decide whether to answer

214

Carmaz. Carmaz didn't see why they shouldn't, but then, he was essentially still a stranger toward them, after all, so it wouldn't make sense for them to tell him anything about their personal business if they didn't want to.

Then the Hermit nodded, causing Herune to look at Carmaz.

"All right, Carmaz, I'll tell you," said Herune. "We've decided that we can trust you with this knowledge, but don't tell anyone, because it's too sensitive for the rest of the world to know. All right?"

Carmaz nodded. "Of course. Go on."

Herune took a deep breath and said, "Have you noticed anything unusual about my father?"

Carmaz shook his head. He then looked at the Hermit. "No, I haven't. But I take it that there is."

"Correct," said Herune. He pointed at his father. "You see, Carmaz, my father is cursed. You can't see it right now, but he has the Cursed Mark on his chest. Have you seen it before?"

"No," said Carmaz. "I have not. What is it?"

"Let me show you," said the Hermit.

He grabbed his shirt and lowered it, exposing his thin and hairy chest to Carmaz. Underneath the Hermit's chest hair was a black 'x,' which almost looked like paint, although when Carmaz looked more closely he realized that it was not merely painted on the elderly man's skin, but *inside* his skin, as if someone had colored in his body.

The Hermit raised his shirt to cover it again as Carmaz said, "That looked painful. How did you get it?"

"The gods," said the Hermit. He winced when he covered the Cursed Mark again. "It was thirty years ago, before Herune's birth. I was once a member of the assassin's guild known as the Dark Tigers. Have you heard of them?"

Carmaz thought about that for a moment. "Yes ... I think so. I remember being told stories about their leader, Nijok Wirm, or the Tiger Man as the stories always called him. I was told that his spirit still haunts the Swamp. Is that true?"

"I've never seen his spirit anywhere," said the Hermit, "though it wouldn't surprise me if the bastard is still around here somewhere. He was never the kind of person to give up, a trait which eventually led to his downfall, although to this day I still don't know the full details of his death."

"Anyway," said Herune, who seemed to be continuing his father's story, "when the Guild fell apart after Wirm's death, father met my mother. They married and soon my mother became pregnant with me."

"What happened to your mother?" asked Carmaz.

The Hermit lowered his head, as if ashamed of something he had done. "We were not married long, but while we were, it was the happiest days of my life. You see, the gods were not happy with the crimes I committed as a Dark Tiger. So they sent Grinf, the God of Justice, to punish me for what I did."

"How did he punish you?" asked Carmaz.

The Hermit gestured at his chest. "Grinf branded me with a Cursed Mark. It is not merely a mark of my own crimes, but a poison. It has slowly been killing me and draining me of strength over the three decades since Grinf gave it to me. But that wasn't the worst part of my punishment."

Then the Hermit looked up at Carmaz with pain in his eyes. "The worst part was what he did to my wife. She was an innocent and kind woman, much better than a man like me deserved, and heroic. When she saw Grinf punishing me, she tried to stop him, but then Grinf turned and ..."

The Hermit's voice broke. He looked down again, seemingly unable to continue. Tears leaked from his eyes and trailed down his cheeks onto his beard and then onto the muddy ground of the sanctuary, but he did not sob or cry at all.

It was Herune who finished the story, although with the way his voice choked, it was clear that he was affected by his mother's death as much as his father was. "Grinf killed her. He burned her to death with his just flames. Right in front of my father's eyes. It was after I was born, although I was only a year old. I can't really remember it, except I have a strong aversion to fire now."

"That's awful," said Carmaz. "I'm sorry to hear that."

The Hermit looked up again, except this time with harshness in his eyes. "I don't need your sympathy, boy. I have lived for thirty years on my own with that memory, without any sympathy from my fellow Ruwans, who branded me a freak and shunned me from their society. I returned to the Tigers' hideout and made it my home."

Carmaz rubbed his throat, which didn't hurt as much now as it did before, although it wasn't back to normal yet either. "So are you two together because of your wife's death?"

"The story is not over yet," said the Hermit. He nodded at Herune. "Grinf did not only give me a Cursed Mark when he poisoned me. He tied my life force to that of my son. I will die of the Cursed Mark no matter what, but my son's connection to me has kept its spread to a crawl. As long as Herune and I stay together, the Cursed Mark will not kill me, but if we should go our separate ways, I will die immediately."

"Wow," said Carmaz. "I've always known that Grinf is a harsh god, but I didn't know he was that harsh."

"He believed it was the best punishment for me," said the Hermit with a chuckle. "Grinf explained to me that I had spent a good portion of my youth traveling to islands all around the world and killing innocent people. Therefore, my life would be tied to an innocent—my at the time one-year-old son—and made it difficult if not impossible to leave."

"That's crazy," said Carmaz. "Is there any way to get rid of the Cursed Mark?"

"Only a god can take it away," said the Hermit. "And none of the other gods care enough about me to heal me, anyway. I've accepted that I will probably die by the poison spreading from the Mark. It no longer bothers me anymore."

"Believe me, I've searched for a cure, but there aren't any other mages on Ruwa and the few books we have on magic don't address the problem," said Herune with a shrug. "Nothing we can do about it."

"That, Carmaz, is why I don't care much for the gods or for the golem or anything else," said the Hermit. "I care for myself and my son, in that order. The gods have already shown that they have nothing but contempt for me, as have the Ruwans. I have no reason to risk my safety for them or anyone else."

The Hermit's tone was even more bitter than usual. It was like all of his anger and frustration toward everyone was now unleashed, like he was not bothering to hide it anymore. He looked just about ready to walk away and never look back.

Even so, Carmaz said, "I understand now, but we still need to stop the invasion. Maybe you don't care, but I do. My people need me. The gods might or might not help us, but in any case, we must do something about it. Even if we can only delay the invasion for a little while, that would be better than not stopping it at all."

"I happen to agree," said Herune. "Father, you can stay out of the fighting if you want, which might be wise considering your condition, but I want to help Carmaz. You saw the power of that golem that attacked our home. If there is an army of beings like that, then we won't stand a chance if they awake and go on to kill everyone else."

"Didn't I already say you could go with him if you want?" said the Hermit. He shook his head. "You are an adult. You can do whatever you want whenever you want. You don't need your old man's approval, even if I'd rather you stay with me. I just don't want you to die and take me with you."

"I probably won't, since we likely won't actually fight them," said Herune. "We can slow them down, which doesn't have to involve any direct combat at all."

"I agree," said Carmaz. He rose to his feet, because the strength in his legs had returned and he was starting to feel better. "I even have an idea about how we could do that."

"Maybe you will delay them, but why?" said the Hermit. He looked directly at Carmaz when he said that. "From what I understand, Carmaz, you were rejected by your fellow villagers for breaking the rules of the Tournament in World's End. Why do you feel the need to save Ruwa when your own people hate you?"

Carmaz thought about that for a moment. He thought about Saia, who he had promised to protect Ruwa; he thought about

219

Frissa, the young girl who had given him the old Ruwan coin in his pocket; and he thought about his own parents, who, if they were still alive, would have expected nothing less from him in this situation.

So Carmaz said, "I'm doing this for an old friend. He's no longer with us, but if he was, he'd want me to do this. I promised to him that I'd save our people. I originally meant I'd win the Tournament and use my new powers as a god to help Ruwa, but now I know that I need to defend Ruwa no matter whether I am mortal or divine. That's why."

The Hermit stroked his beard. He looked rather impressed by Carmaz's short speech, as if he had never heard such eloquent reasoning before in his life. "Well, I suppose I understand you now, Carmaz Korva. I thought you were just another brainless wannabe hero who only did things because they are the 'right' thing to do, but your motivations are far more understandable than that. Still, I see no reason to aid the very people who have rejected you."

"You don't need to," said Carmaz, shaking his head. He looked at Herune. "Ready to go?"

"Yes," said Herune, nodding. "We don't know how much time we have left before the golems begin their invasion, after all. We should head out as soon as possible."

"Agreed," said Carmaz. He rubbed his throat. "But first, I need to rest for a little while. My throat is still in pain. After that, however, we can head out and put my plan into action and save Ruwa and the world."

Chapter Sixteen

BRAIM STOOD IN line with the ten other godlings participating in the Skimif Sub-Bracket Challenge. He looked to the right, watching the rest of the godlings— those who were going to watch—as they disappeared into the staircase that led to the box where they could watch the challenge. He saw Malya wave at him in encouragement as she went inside the staircase, while Tashir merely nodded.

Braim gave them the thumbs up, but he said nothing because he was busy trying to figure out what the challenge was going to be. Grinf stood to the right of the entrance to the Stadium's field, gesturing for them to enter. The God of Fire, Metal, and Justice had reassured Braim that he would be safe in here from any assassins and that the gods had taken special precautions to ensure that no one who wasn't supposed to be inside the Stadium could get in. Braim wondered if that included the Void, although considering how quiet the Void had been since her last attack, he dismissed her as being a non-threat at the moment.

Ever since Braim had awoken from his dream, he had not seen any sign of that assassin lady who had attacked him in his room. The Soldiers of the Gods were still searching the city for her, but to his knowledge, they had not found any clue as to her identity or whereabouts. It was like she was a ghost who vanished into thin air.

To say that that made Braim uneasy was an understatement. He still remembered the Mysterious One's theory about what might happen to him if he died. That he had somehow managed to survive was a victory in itself, but now he was aware of just what would have happened to him if the assassin had successfully killed him. He would have literally ceased to exist.

But hey, Grinf is probably right, Braim thought as he followed the godlings ahead of him into the entryway to the field. *There's no way she could get me in here. But even if I win, what's to stop her from attacking me again when I leave the Stadium?*

Granted, Braim felt a little bit more secure than he did before. Tashir had taught him a lot about sword-fighting, although it was mostly basic stuff that was pretty simple and easy to learn. Still, Braim was confident he could use a sword well now, which at least gave him a way to defend himself.

Once all of the godlings entered the entryway, the door closed behind them. Then a column of fire exploded from the floor before them and Grinf stepped out of it, sparks jumping off his cape and hair. He held the rulebook in his hands, which for some reason was not on fire, even though Grinf himself radiated enough heat that Braim could feel it from where he stood, and he stood in the back.

"Welcome, challengers, to the Skimif Sub-Bracket Challenge," said Grinf. He gestured at the doors behind him and the hallways on other side that seemed to stretch to other doors similar to the ones behind him. "This is the final sub-bracket challenge in the Tournament of the Gods. After this, we will move onto the actual bracket challenges, which will determine the winners of each bracket and thus who the new gods of Martir are going to be."

Braim nodded. He glanced at his fellow godlings, all of whom seemed to be thinking the same thing as him, namely, that this sub-bracket challenge was likely to be the most difficult one yet.

"The final sub-bracket challenge is simple in concept, but it will most assuredly require all of the intelligence and strength that each of you possesses in order to win," said Grinf. "In this challenge, two godlings must compete with one another to settle a dispute between two gods. The godling who can settle the dispute between the two gods assigned to them will be go onto the main bracket challenge later on."

Doesn't sound so difficult to me, Braim thought, though he didn't say that aloud because he was still listening to Grinf's explanation. *Then again, the gods can be very stubborn, so maybe it will be difficult after all.*

"All of the normal Tournament rules apply, so do not even think about breaking any of them," said Grinf. His expression suddenly became threatening and he pointed his gavel at them. "Any breaking of the rules is grounds for immediate disqualification from the Tournament. Am I clear?"

All ten of the godlings nodded to show that they did indeed understand. Not that any of them would ever think of breaking the rules, of course. After all, Grinf was far more frightening than Alira and would probably do worse to them than simply kick them out of the Tournament if he caught them cheating.

"Good," said Grinf. He drew a familiar pack of cards from his armor and said, "As usual, you will be paired up with whoever gets the card with the same color as yours. Once you find your competitor, you must then go and stand in front of your door and enter once I give you the order."

With that, Grinf threw the cards into the air. The deck of cards did not simply scatter all over the floor, but rather separated from each other and then flew toward the godlings. Dozens of hands shot up to grab the flying cards out of the air, with Braim being one of the first to get his. Lowering the card to look at it better, Braim saw that he had gotten a gray card, causing him to look up to see if he could spot who had gotten its twin.

That was when Braim saw Tamra, who had also received a gray card. She must have noticed him as well, because she walked over to him holding the gray card up for him to see.

"Well, this sucks, doesn't it?" said Tamra as she approached Braim. "I didn't want us to have to compete against each other in the sub-bracket challenge. I thought that we'd have to compete against other people."

"We'd probably have to compete against each other in the Tournament anyway, you know," said Braim. "So why don't we do our best and let the best godling win?"

Tamra smiled and nodded. "All right. I'm pretty good at conflict resolution, though, so don't complain if I solve the dispute between the gods faster than you."

"You sound way more confident than you did when I first met you," Braim said. "Feeling like you're in your natural environment now?"

"Yes," said Tamra. "Anyway, let's go find our doors to stand in front of. And quickly, before the others get all the good ones."

Braim nodded and looked at the nearest doors, but a couple of other godlings had already taken their place in front of those. So

Braim and Tamra walked down the hallway to the right, following its curve as they attempted to look for a set of doors that was not already taken by the others.

As they walked, Tamra looked at Braim. She seemed to be trying to look for something on his face, or so it seemed to him. It wasn't exactly annoying, but considering how Tamra wasn't saying anything to him, Braim decided to ask her outright what she was looking for so he wouldn't worry about it anymore.

"Why are you looking at me?" asked Braim. He rubbed his face. "Is there something on my face?"

Tamra shook her head. "No. I was just looking for any wounds on you. I heard about the assassin that attacked you and wanted to know if she hurt you."

"I'm fine," said Braim. "She didn't hurt me much. Didn't even scratch me. But thanks for asking about me anyway. I appreciate it."

"All right," said Tamra. "Do you even know who that woman was? Did she show her face or give you any clues about her identity?"

"Zero," said Braim as he and Tamra passed another couple of godlings standing in front of their own set of doors. "She was completely silent, but that didn't make her any less deadly. I don't even know why she wanted me dead, although it seems like everyone is out to kill me nowadays."

"Well, I hope that the assassin is caught," said Tamra. "I hate the idea that there is someone going around free who has already tried to kill one of us. She deserves only the harshest punishment for even attempting that, if you ask me."

Braim looked at Tamra in surprise. "Wow, Tamra, you sound

a lot more vicious than I thought you were. Do you really think that?"

Tamra shrugged. "I'm normally not this vicious, but I have no respect at all for assassins. In my opinion, they're the scum of the earth. Being paid to kill someone? What a terrible idea."

"I agree," said Braim. Then he noticed a couple of vacant doors up ahead and pointed. "Hey, looks like those doors are free. Let's grab 'em before someone else does."

Braim and Tamra took up their positions in front of the doors, but they also continued their conversation, as the doors were not yet opened and Braim could still hear the other godlings finding their doors to stand in front of.

"Anyway, I doubt it will take the Soldiers long to find her," said Braim, looking at Tamra as he slid his gray card into the pocket of his pants. "I was told that they have the best of the best searching for the assassin. It's only a matter of time before they find her, I'm sure."

"Do you know what her species was?" asked Tamra. "A katabans, perhaps?"

"Maybe, but she didn't strike me as a katabans," said Braim. "Something about the shape of her body and the way she moved made her seem a lot more human than katabans to me, although I don't know of any humans on World's End that would try to kill me like that."

"I hope it's not one of the other godlings," said Tamra with a shudder. "Wouldn't that just be awful if it was? It would mean that we couldn't trust any of them."

Braim was about to say that he already wasn't sure if he could trust them after Carmaz's betrayal, but before he could say that aloud, Grinf's voice rang out through the hallway. It sounded like Grinf was shouting right in Braim's ears, even though the god was nowhere to be seen.

"All right," said Grinf's voice, which sounded even more dramatic than it normally did. "Now that all of the challengers are set and ready to go, it is time for the Skimif Sub-Bracket Challenge to begin. Challengers, step inside your rooms as soon as the doors in front of you open."

Braim faced his door and glanced at Tamra to see that she was facing hers. Her hand was hovering near the pocket of her pants, rubbing against something thin and long against the outer layer of her clothes. Braim didn't know what it was, so he just assumed that it was a keepsake of hers, maybe a lucky charm or something.

Then the doors opened in front of them, revealing a wedge-shaped room on the other side. Braim gave Tamra one last look and nod before turning to face the open door and stepping inside again.

But just as Braim stepped inside, he suddenly realized what had been bothering him about his conversation with Tamra. Tamra had called the assassin a 'she' … even though Braim had not told her the gender of the assassin before she asked about the attack.

But Braim shook his head. *It means nothing. She's a woman. She probably just made that assumption because of her own gender. Or maybe she heard about it from someone else, as the knowledge of my near assassination seems to be pretty well-known among the other godlings already. Not worth worrying about.*

Anyway, the door closed behind Braim as soon as he entered

the room, so he couldn't go back out and ask Tamra where she had learned the assassin's gender even if he wanted to. So he instead focused on the room he had entered, which he was not alone in.

There were two other beings in the room with Braim, beings who radiated such intense power that there was no mistaking them for anything other than the gods they were. One was a tall and bulky being made entirely of ice and snow, radiating as much coldness as Grinf had radiated heat. The figure had an ice shield and spear, which made Braim feel uneasy because he had not been told that any of the gods would be armed. The temperature in the room was very cold due to this figure's presence, although it wasn't enough to freeze Braim.

Standing opposite the figure was a woman who appeared to be made out of rock and earth. She had long, onyx dreads and twin glowing green eyes. She was significantly shorter than the icy figure standing opposite her, but there was no question that she was as strong as her counterpart. She looked almost grandmotherly, but Braim knew from experience that appearances were almost always deceiving when it came to gods.

Nonetheless, Braim approached the two gods as confidently as he could. He doubted they would appreciate it if he came across to them as weak and indecisive, although he had to keep in mind that these two gods probably didn't like him anyway purely because he was a mortal who might one day rule over them both.

"Greetings, gods," said Braim as he stopped a few feet from them. He suppressed a shiver from the cold air radiating off the ice god. "I'm—"

"Braim Kotogs," said the ice god. His voice sounded like

cracking ice and tiny ice chips flew from his mouth when he spoke, along with a burst of cold air that made Braim shiver despite his best attempts to hide it. "The only mortal who returned from the dead."

"That's me," said Braim, brushing the ice chips off his shoulders. "And you two are—?"

"Xocion," said the ice god. "God of Ice and Mountains. I saw your resurrection because North Academy is located within the Great Berg, my domain, so I am already familiar with you and know that you are friends with one of my followers, Darek Takren."

"Right," said Braim, nodding. He looked at the earth goddess. "What's your name?"

"I am Mica," said the earth goddess. Her voice sounded like a rumbling earthquake, but it also reminded Braim of a kindly grandmother speaking to her grandchildren. "Goddess of Earth and Ink. It is a pleasure to meet you, Braim Kotogs."

"Thanks," said Braim, though he was somewhat taken aback by Mica's friendliness. "It's a pleasure to meet you, too."

"How exciting," said Mica. She leaned forward, causing the smell of dirt and ink to waft into Braim's nostrils. "I have always wanted to meet you, but Alira told us gods to stay away from the godlings. She seemed to think we'd manipulate you to change the outcome of the Tournament in our favor. What a silly thought."

Mica laughed, like it was a great joke, but Braim didn't think that that idea was entirely wrong. He still remembered how the Ghostly God had allied with Carmaz to kidnap him. He wouldn't put it past the gods to try to manipulate the godlings in order to win special favors, especially from the godlings in the Skimif

229

Bracket. Granted, he didn't know of any godlings who actually were being manipulated like that, but he found it unlikely that none of the gods were even trying to do that.

In any case, Braim said aloud, "Sure. Anyway, I'm here to resolve a dispute that has arisen between you two. Can you explain it to me? Start from the beginning and don't leave any facts out."

Mica and Xocion exchanged a look that quite clearly told Braim that, whatever their dispute was, it was very bad. Xocion looked like he wanted to stab Mica through the heart with his spear, while Mica looked like she wanted to smash Xocion into pieces with her boulder-like fists.

Then Mica looked away, causing Xocion to say to Braim, "Our dispute started about a week ago, on the Frozen Peaks."

"The Frozen Peaks?" said Braim. "Never heard of it. Is that located in the Great Berg?"

"No," said Xocion, shaking his head. "While the Frozen Peaks are located north of the rest of the Northern Isles, they are not as far north as the Great Berg. They are located on the island of Glathar, a harsh waste mostly uninhabitable to human life, although there are small towns and villages located on the shores where fish can be caught and rivers empty out into the sea."

"Ah," said Braim. "Okay. Go on, then."

"Glathar and the Frozen Peaks are largely inhabited by our followers," said Xocion, gesturing at himself and Mica. "There are others, too, of course, but Xocionians and Micans make up forty-five percent of the population each, with the followers of our other siblings making up the remaining ten percent. Glathar was discovered by Micans and Xocionians ages ago, shortly after

230

the Godly War, and is ruled by them, though the island's small population means that the other Northern Isles nations tend to ignore it."

Braim found Xocion's voice rather droning. In fact, he almost dozed off before he remembered that he needed to be awake, so he shook his head to regain his attention. "Uh, all right. Continue."

"The Xocionians and Micans have managed to work together over the centuries, despite their differences in worship, because the island's harsh terrain and weather make the sort of religious sectarian conflicts on other islands impractical for both sides," said Xocion. "But there has always been some tension between the two, which has only grown worse over the last year after Uron destroyed my temple in the Great Berg, which my followers blamed on Mica's followers—"

"Because your followers are fools," Mica muttered.

"—and which has resulted in more than a few clashes, including one where a Mican threatened to bury an entire Xocionian town underneath a rock slide if they did not stop attacking his fellow Micans," Xocion continued, without missing a beat. "But the worst is yet to come, for you see, our followers both wish to build a temple on one of the Peaks dedicated to one of us. My followers wish to build a temple for me, while Mica's followers wish to build a temple for her."

"Okay," said Braim. "What's the problem, then? Do you need me to speak with your followers and ask them to build their temples on different mountains or—?"

"The problem is that both Mica and I have given our blessing to our followers to build a temple dedicated to us on that same

231

spot," said Xocion. "And neither of us are willing to rescind our blessing and tell our followers to build our temple on another mountain."

Braim stroked his chin. "Oh. But if I may ask, why *can't* one of you just tell your followers to build a temple somewhere else?"

"Because that would make us look weak to our followers," Mica explained patiently, as if speaking to a dull child. "Our followers don't just see this as a conflict between themselves. They see it as a conflict between me and Xocion, with only one possible outcome: Either I win and get my temple built there or Xocion wins and gets his temple built there."

"You two don't seriously agree with them on that, do you?" said Braim.

Xocion and Mica exchanged that same murderous look from before, and then Xocion looked at Braim and said, "You do not understand. The place upon which they want to build their temples is considered holy space by both. Throw in the fact that Mica and I have not always gotten along and you see why we are at an impasse."

"Besides, wouldn't *you* make it personal if your younger brother—who really ought to learn to respect his older sister's wisdom—called *you* a 'cracked piece of granite useless for building anything useful'?" Mica asked. She glared at Xocion when she said that.

Xocion shrugged. "May I remind you, sister, that you are older than me by a few hours at most. In the beginning, the Powers created us all in roughly the same twenty-four hour period, so do not pretend that that makes you wiser or more knowledgeable than I."

"At least I'm not the one throwing around insults like a child," said Mica. "So if you don't want to be treated like a child, then I suggest that you stop acting like one."

Xocion simply shook his head. "I find that amusing coming from the woman who has continually refused to correct her followers after they named the Mican layer after you, even though our brother, Golar, God of Lava, has asked you to do so many times over the centuries."

"Golar has nothing to do with this," Mica said. Her tone rose to a sharp bite. "This conflict is between you and me. The other gods have nothing to do with it."

Xocion looked like he was going to disagree, prompting Braim to say, "Hey, hey, everyone, just calm down, okay? Let's take a moment to think this over like rational beings."

"Only if my younger brother decides to act like one," said Mica, folding her arms over her chest and looking away. "Not that I expect him to, of course, because his brain is frozen solid."

"I happen to agree with you, Braim, especially with the consequences that will happen if we do not come to an agreement quickly," said Xocion, although he threw Mica an annoyed look when he said that. "Mica and I fear that our followers will start an all-out war between each other if the two of us cannot come to a satisfactory agreement soon. Such a war would likely wipe out both parties and possibly even destroy Glathar entirely, seeing as it is already a fragile island and the pagomancers and geomancers on both sides are very powerful and more than willing to use their power to destroy the other side."

Braim bit his lower lip. "Well, that sounds very serious indeed. That's yet another reason not to act so mean toward each other. Don't you care about the lives of your followers?"

"Yes," said Mica, nodding. "Of course I do. Why wouldn't I? They love and adore me. It is Xocion's followers I don't much care for. They tend to be a very dim bunch, if you catch my drift."

"Actually, Micans are known to be far less intellectual than the vast majority of other followers," Xocion pointed out. "There has only been one major Mican writer on the subject of magic since the rise of magic as an academic discipline, and even then, she is only considered noteworthy because she writes in a rather obscure field of magic. Xocionians are disproportionately represented in the academic writings about magic, making up approximately twenty percent of the major magical writers in the last century alone despite making up only ten percent of mages."

Braim had no idea if that was true or not, but he decided not to wade into that subject because he didn't care too much about that. Xocion certainly spoke it with confidence and authority, even as Mica glared at him again, though Braim could not be sure if that was because the God of Ice was lying or if it was because he had offended her with the truth.

In any case, Braim said, "All right. So your followers both want to build a single temple on the same place on that mountain devoted to you guys, but they can't come to a reasonable agreement between themselves and neither can you."

"Exactly," said Xocion. "I'm glad you understand the problem. Now we need a solution to it, preferably right away."

Both of the gods looked at Braim expectantly, like they expected him to come up with a solution at that very moment. Braim would have been happy to oblige, but at that moment he was thinking hard about a possible solution to the problem. Braim had never worked as an arbiter before—at least from what he could remember, though neither Jenur nor Darek had ever mentioned that being in his personal history—but he supposed that now was as good a time to learn that skill as any.

Braim rubbed the back of his head. *Let's see ... how do I solve this problem in a way that will please them both? It sounds like their followers aren't exactly the most diplomatic types.*

After thinking it over for a couple of minutes, Braim said, "All right. Here's an idea: Have your followers build two temples right next to each other on the same spot."

Mica made a sound of disgust which sounded like rocks being crunched underneath a heavy weight. "No. My followers would never tolerate that. They can barely handle having his followers in the next town over."

"My followers likely would not stand for that, either," said Xocion, nodding. "Nor do I want any temple of mine built right next to Mica's, anyway. Such a compromise would only invite further conflict down the road. Besides, there isn't enough room on that spot for two temples of the sizes they are planning to build and I, for one, will not settle for a small temple."

"Neither will I," said Mica. She raised her hands to the ceiling. "I want a large temple dedicated to me. Beautiful and huge, a monument to my greatness. My followers are known for crafting beautiful stone buildings and artifacts, but they can't build a beautiful monument to me if they are forced to make room for Xocion's temple."

"Okay, okay, okay," said Braim, holding up his hands defensively. "So two slightly smaller temples side by side are out of the question, then. How's about one temple, one half made of stone and the other half made of ice, with the stone half dedicated to Mica and the ice half to Xocion?"

To Braim's relief, Mica and Xocion seemed to be seriously considering that idea. They looked at each other and then looked at Braim, making him hope that maybe they would agree to the idea after all.

But then Xocion said, in his usual flat and cold voice, "That is an interesting idea, but our followers already worship in separate temples and worship sites. They never worship together and are unlikely to do so even if we tell them to."

"I question the structural integrity of a temple made out of stone and ice," said Mica. "Even if they use magic, I think such a building would be rather fragile and thus a danger to both of our followers. Besides, we gods never share temples. It is simply not done."

"But why can't it be done?" asked Braim. "I know you gods prefer to be worshiped on your own, sure, but just because you've always done things a certain way doesn't mean that's necessarily the best way to do it."

Xocion and Mica exchanged surprised glances, as if they had never heard that idea before. That made Braim question just how smart the gods were, as this idea seemed fairly obvious to him.

"Well ..." Xocion tapped his chin in thought. "I suppose trying new things and new ways of doing things is not always bad. But I am not so sure that it would truly be the best solution to our problem."

"Of course it wouldn't," said Mica. "Give us a new solution. I'm not going to share worship space with my brother and neither will he share worship space with me."

Braim sighed heavily. He was now starting to wonder whether Skimif was lucky he didn't have to deal with these gods anymore, considering how stubborn they were. It made him wonder how Skimif ever got anything done, though now that he thought about it, he decided that Skimif probably never actually got anything done.

Nonetheless, Braim said, "All right. Give me a moment to think about another solution."

The two gods nodded to show that they understood, so Braim turned away and looked at the grass under his feet. He wasn't looking at anything in particular. He was just letting his mind wander a little so he could come up with a creative solution to the problem that Xocion and Mica gave him.

No temple dedicated to both, then, Braim thought. *And they seem pretty hostile to new ways of doing things, which limits my options quite a bit. But I'll just have to come up with something new anyway, whether the gods like it or not.*

Then Braim snapped his fingers and looked at the two gods again. "All right. Here's an idea: Have your followers build one temple dedicated to neither of you, but which can be used by both to worship you."

"That sounds similar to your other idea," Xocion said. "The one where you said they should build a temple half made of stone and half made of ice."

"But this is different," said Braim. "It is a generic temple not dedicated to any particular god, but which can be altered by the followers of a god. For example, Micans can change the temple's interior and exterior to fit their sensibilities when they worship in it, while the Xocionians can change it to fit their preferences

237

when they worship in it."

"How do you suggest that they decide who gets to worship there and who doesn't?" asked Mica.

"They take turns, of course," said Braim. "Both sides can negotiate to figure out an equitable way to allow followers of both of you to take an equal amount of turns in worship. Both are responsible for the care and upkeep of the temple, but neither one completely owns or controls it."

Xocion and Mica exchanged looks again, but this time, they didn't look angry or confused. They appeared to be giving his suggestion serious consideration, which gave Braim hope that they would accept it.

Then Xocion looked at Braim again and said, "That sounds … reasonable. What do you think, Mica?"

"I agree," said Mica. "It is not ideal, but it is reasonable and I think will work out for our followers. I'd much rather have the space all to myself, but this will work."

Braim sighed in relief. "Wonderful." Then he paused. "Wait, does that mean that I beat this challenge?"

"I believe so," said Xocion. He looked up at the ceiling. "I do not hear Grinf, which I find odd, unless you broke a rule that disqualified you that we are unaware of."

"But Grinf said that I only need to resolve your dispute in order to win," said Braim, folding his arms over his chest. "What else do I need to do? I haven't broken any rules that I know of."

"Maybe something came up that distracted our brother," Mica said. She leaned forward and whispered, "You may not know this, but Grinf has always been a very easily distracted god. He can be absolutely fearless when it comes to finding and punishing law-

238

breakers, but otherwise he finds it hard to concentrate. Don't tell him I told you that, though, because he hates it when I tell others about his weaknesses."

"Uh ..." Braim wasn't sure how to respond to that, but thankfully he didn't need to, because Xocion raised a hand suddenly and looked toward the wall on the right side of the room.

"Silence," said Xocion. "Did you hear that?"

Braim blinked. "Hear what?"

"Screams," said Xocion. He frowned. "Oh, I see. You wouldn't hear them because they are spiritual screams, which only we gods can hear. They appear to be coming from the room adjacent to ours."

"Spiritual screams?" Braim repeated. "What are those?"

"Contortions of the spirit," said Xocion. "That is, when a spirit is in pain, it often cries out for help. It is a rare occurrence for us gods to hear, mostly due to the fact that there aren't many things in Martir that can harm a spirit enough to cause it to scream."

"I heard them as well," said Mica. She rubbed her stone ears. "I thought it was a trick of my ears at first, but if you also heard them, then I suppose that means that they were real after all."

"But who is screaming?" said Braim, scratching the back of his head. "Is the Ghostly God torturing people or something?"

"They weren't mortal screams," said Xocion. "They were—"

Xocion did not get to finish his sentence, because in the next moment, the right wall, the one he was looking at, exploded. Chunks of rock and burning grass flew through the air toward them, but Xocion merely raised his hand and summoned a massively thick ice barrier that blocked most of the debris. But the debris struck hard, leaving thick cracks in the barrier's surface that distorted the view on the other side, although Braim saw flickering flames through the clear ice barrier nonetheless.

The loudness of the explosion faded quickly, but Braim's ears still rang. He rubbed them as Xocion lowered the ice barrier, allowing the three of them to see exactly what had caused that explosion.

At first, it was impossible to tell, because all Braim saw was high flames and burning rubble where the wall had been. The heat from the flames increased the temperature of the room quite a bit, though not to an unbearable height just yet. Nonetheless, Braim no longer felt like shivering, although he didn't feel very good about seeing those flames, either.

"What happened over there?" said Braim. He looked at the two gods. "Which two gods were on that side?"

"Kos, Goddess of Rain, and Henim, God of Dreams," said Xocion. "They had a conflict of their own that was supposed to be resolved by one of your fellow godlings. But I don't know which one. Do you?"

Braim thought about that. "Yes, I do. It's—"

A mad laugh came from the flames, cutting off Braim and making he and the two gods look in the direction that the laughter came from. It was a feminine laugh, familiar despite the fact that Braim had never heard it before. It sent shivers up Braim's spine despite the heat of the flames, shivers which had nothing to do with Xocion's cold aura.

And then, from out of the flames, stepped Tamra. Her clothes were burned away in some places, while her ponytail had come undone and her long black hair flowed about her like the hair of a mad woman. She carried a familiar thin piece of metal in her hands, which made Braim step back involuntarily.

"Who are you?" said Xocion. He held up his shield and aimed his spear at her. "Identify yourself, mortal."

Tamra chuckled, but it wasn't a kind chuckle. It was the chuckle of a woman who had long ago lost her sanity, a loss that she no longer tried to hide, but now embraced wholeheartedly. "Before today, I would have identified as Tamra, a silly girl from Itrija who loved magic but could not cast any spells herself. But that's not who I am anymore, so it would be dishonest of me to identify as that."

Braim noticed that Tamra's skin was glowing blue, which was definitely not a natural thing. Not only that, but though she stood among the flames, they didn't seem to hurt her at all.

"Instead, you can call me Tamra," said Tamra. Her eyes glittered with insanity. "The new Goddess of Martir ... and your doom."

Chapter Seventeen

PRINCESS, I APOLOGIZE for your disturbing your sleep, but you must wake up," said Keeper's voice, which Raya recognized even in her sleeping state. "There is something you need to see."

Although Raya heard and understood Keeper's voice just fine, she still didn't want to wake up. She just snuggled in deeper into his arms and muttered, "Five more minutes."

"Princess, I'm afraid five minutes is exactly the amount of time we *don't* have," said Keeper.

Raya still wanted to go to sleep, but there was a warning in Keeper's words that even she couldn't ignore. So Raya opened her eyes, yawning as she looked around at their environment. She saw the stars of the ethereal and the white road beneath them, as well as Alira—who was awake and who didn't look happy about it—lying in the crook of Keeper's arm opposite her, but Raya saw nothing out of the ordinary. She looked up at Keeper's face, which was staring at the side of the road.

Yawning again, Raya followed Keeper's eyes, but still didn't see anything unusual. "Keeper, what is the problem? Why are we still in the ethereal? I thought we'd be in World's End by now."

"Well, that is the thing I wished to tell you about," said Keeper. He nodded at the space beyond the ethereal road. "I cannot open an ethereal portal onto World's End."

Raya rubbed the sleep out of her eyes and then blinked several times. "Can't open an ethereal portal onto World's End? Why?"

"I don't know why," said Keeper, shaking his large metal head. "It's not a malfunction, because I can sense that my power core still works. It feels like someone cast a spell to make it impossible to leave or enter World's End through the ethereal."

Raya then looked at Alira. "Alira, do you—"

"I know nothing about this," said Alira with a shrug. "I have no idea who might have cast such a spell. I suspect one of the gods could have done it, but I am not sure."

"Do you think something bad happened on World's End that forced the gods to close off the ethereal?" asked Raya. She brushed her hair out of her eyes and looked around the ethereal worryingly. "Maybe the Void attacked again and they didn't want her to reach the ethereal."

"That is a possibility, but it seems unlikely to me," said Keeper. "World's End was not under attack when I was there. I think it is far more likely that the ethereal was closed by someone else."

Raya folded her arms across her chest and pouted. "Don't we have some other way of contacting the gods, at least to let them know that we're here and they can let us in?"

"Unfortunately, I don't know how to do that," said Keeper. He looked up and down the ethereal. "That might be why we have not run into any katabans on the way here. With World's End closed off, I imagine most of the katabans are stuck there."

"Or maybe I should try to open the ethereal," said Raya. "Maybe you really are malfunctioning and you just don't know it."

"Are you sure that you feel up to it, Princess?" said Keeper. "I know how much strain opening an ethereal portal puts on you. You don't have to do it."

"I'm fine," said Raya as she stretched her arms. "I got plenty of rest on the way here. Just let me down and let me try."

"If you insist," said Keeper.

Keeper knelt low enough for Raya to slip out of his arm and land on the ethereal. Raya's stomach suddenly growled, a reminder that she had not eaten in a long time, but Raya ignored it in order to focus on opening an ethereal portal. She told herself that she'd get a good meal as soon as she returned to World's End.

So Raya raised her bluish-white artificial hand and focused hard on opening an ethereal portal. She felt the energy drain from her body, but no portal opened. Instead, there was a rebound and Raya found herself staggering backwards, feeling like she had been socked in the mouth by a professional fighter. She staggered back into Keeper's leg, prompting the automaton guardian to say, "Princess! Are you all right?"

Panting, Raya looked down at her artificial hand. It looked cracked, as if it had absorbed the brunt of the rebound, though Raya didn't think it was going to shatter any time soon.

Looking up at Keeper and Alira, Raya said, "I'm fine. I just found out the hard way that you're right. Someone closed off the ethereal to World's End. The question is, who and why?"

"A better question is, what do we do now?" said Alira. She looked around Keeper's body. "I have a feeling that those Empty followers still want to kill us, even if they are afraid of Keeper. The longer we stay here in the ethereal, the more likely it becomes that they will come after us again, maybe with larger numbers so it will be harder for Keeper to fight back."

"Maybe we should search for another island and find a mage there," Keeper suggested. "Maybe we could even go to Carnag and ask the royal mages there to contact Grinf and ask him to send someone to get us."

Raya pushed off of Keeper's leg and focused on the spot where she had tried to open the portal again. "No. That would mean having to go somewhere else, which will take hours. I want to find out why we can't enter World's End through the ethereal again, even though we could do it before."

"I could tell you," said a voice above their heads.

Raya, Keeper, and Alira looked up in time to see a large, pale-armored being materialize above them. The figure lacked legs, instead having a wispy ghost-like tail, while his nose-less face was twisted in a crooked grin that made Raya stand closer to Keeper.

The figure floated down near them to a much closer level, his grin never leaving his face. Raya had never seen this figure before in her life, but she thought he seemed familiar.

Then Alira said, in a tone that made it quite clear she was holding back her anger, "The Ghostly God. What are you doing here?"

The deity put his hands together. "I was about to ask you the same question, Alira. Don't you have a Tournament to judge?"

"Wait," said Raya. She looked at the Ghostly God more closely. "You're the same Ghostly God who got Carmaz kicked out of the Tournament?"

The Ghostly God shrugged. "I didn't make Carmaz *do*

anything. He did it all of his own free will. But yes, I did work with him for a little while."

Raya shook her fist at him. "You bastard. If it weren't for you, Carmaz would still be in the Tournament."

"You must have wax in your ears, because I already said Carmaz broke the rules without any prompting from me," said the Ghostly God. "Not that I expect you to listen. Mortals tend to be bad listeners, but in all of my years, I've never known a royal mortal who even attempted to listen to us gods when we talk."

Raya took a step forward, even though there wasn't anything she could do against the Ghostly God, but then Alira said, "Carmaz wasn't the only one who received a punishment for breaking the rules. The other gods banished you from World's End for disrupting the Tournament and kidnapped Braim. So how did you get here?"

"This is the ethereal," said the Ghostly God, gesturing at their surroundings. "Not technically World's End. That means I am free to come and go from this place as much as I want. I am only exercising the freedoms I still have left."

The Ghostly God sounded quite pleased with himself, which just made Raya all the more angry at him. She was tempted to attack him, but didn't, knowing that his power infinitely dwarfed hers.

"But enough about me," said the Ghostly God. "What are you three doing locked out of World's End? I haven't been keeping up with recent events since my banishment."

"A lot of things have happened that you don't need to know about," said Alira. "Suffice to say, if we don't get to World's End quickly, Martir as we know it will be plunged into the bloodiest war you have ever seen, and many people will die."

"Even bloodier than the Godly War?" the Ghostly God said in surprise. "That is indeed bloody, then."

"Yes," said Alira, nodding. "Now, you said you could tell us why we cannot enter World's End via the ethereal."

"Oh, that," said the Ghostly God. "Yes, well, it appears that there is someone on World's End who doesn't want anyone leaving that island just yet."

"Just yet?" Alira repeated. "What does that mean?"

"It means that the person who is keeping us *out* of World's End will eventually allow us back in, but not yet," said the Ghostly God. "At least, that is my theory. I can't imagine anyone keeping the ethereal closed forever. Likely the individual who closed off the ethereal is simply trying to keep everyone in one place while keeping everyone off the island from interfering with their plan."

"And who is this individual and what might their plan be?" asked Alira. "Is it the Void? Is she trying to destroy World's End and everyone on it?"

"Unlikely," said the Ghostly God. "I mean, sure, it is possible, but I don't think the Void has personally stepped in to do this. She prefers to work through easily manipulated people like her followers. No, in all likelihood, she has someone on World's End who is probably trying to kill my brothers and sisters to make it easier for the Void to come in and take over."

"That still doesn't tell us who it is," Alira said. She yawned. "One of the katabans?"

"Possibly," said the Ghostly God. "But if you ask me, I think it is a mage. The katabans don't know how to cast these sorts of spells, but it is possible for a mortal mage to learn how to do it. And if it is it a mortal mage, then it is probably one of the godlings themselves, though who, I can't say."

"But why would one of the godlings work for the Void?" asked Alira. "That makes no sense. She has tried to kill the godlings several times already. No sane person would ever willingly work for her."

"That is true, but who says that all of the godlings are equally sane?" said the Ghostly God. "Granted, I know little about the godlings, but I know that mortals in general can easily lose their sanity if they aren't careful. I used to have a mortal servant who had lost her sanity, although I don't know if she ever had it to begin with."

"Well, regardless of who did it, we must find a way into World's End," said Alira. She gestured to the right, at the spot where Raya had attempted to open a portal. "Can you break the spell and let us all in?"

"I have tried, but sadly I cannot," said the Ghostly God. "My banishment from World's End has left me unable to use my own magical powers to affect it. I'm surprised, however, that you have not tried to break it, Alira, considering your own considerable strength."

"My powers were taken away from me and still have yet to return," said Alira. "Otherwise I would be using them right now to do exactly that."

"Who took them away from you?" said the Ghostly God. "Anyone I might know?"

"No," said Alira. "But if we don't get to World's End right away, then you and everyone else on Martir will know them soon

248

enough."

The Ghostly God tapped his chin, clearly thinking about Alira's warning. "Well, then there isn't much I can do about it, I'm afraid. Thus, it appears that we are at an impasse."

"But there has to be *something* you can do," said Raya. She rubbed her cracked artificial hand, even though she could not feel any pain from it. "Anything. I mean, you're a god. That means you are smarter and stronger than us."

"At least you have enough sense to admit that," said the Ghostly God. "Very few mortals do. But in any case, I cannot think of anything, because the spell used to lock the ethereal from World's End is as tight as any lock. Otherwise, I'd already be there."

Raya sighed in frustration and looked up at Keeper and Alira. "Do you two have any ideas about what we could do?"

Alira shook her head. "No. I'm not as knowledgeable about Martirian magic as I'd like to be, so I don't know if there is a counter-spell we could cast in order to break the lock."

"I, too, am rather ignorant on matters relating to magic," said Keeper. "One possible thing we could do is go to some other island and have the Ghostly God teleport us to World's End from that point."

Raya looked at the Ghostly God eagerly. "Is that possible, Ghostly God? Could you do that for us?"

Much to Raya's disappointment, the Ghostly God shook his head. "No. I cannot take you to World's End because I am banished from it."

"But you don't actually need to touch us to teleport us there, do you?" said Keeper. "Can't you teleport us there with a simple wave of your hand?"

"I can't even do that much," said the Ghostly God. "You mortals truly don't understand how complete a banishment from World's End is. I literally cannot enter it or use my powers on it unless the other gods agree to lift the banishment from me."

"And how do you get the gods to do that?" asked Raya.

"You don't," said the Ghostly God. "My brothers and sisters have to decide to do it on their own. Of course, I will be able to return to World's End after the Tournament is over, but I imagine it won't be over for quite some time and we really don't have the time to wait for that."

Raya threw up her hands in frustration. "So what, are we just stuck here in the ethereal while who-knows-what is happening on World's End? Is that it?"

"Right now, yes," said the Ghostly God, nodding. "I share your frustrations, mortal, but there's little either of us can do about this situation at the moment."

Raya lowered her hands and started grumbling under her breath about how unfair and dumb this situation was. It was the only thing she could think to do in this situation, because she was utterly powerless to do anything else (not that she would ever admit that to anyone else, of course, but she was willing to admit it to herself).

She looked up at Alira and Keeper again. Keeper's expression was as inscrutable as always, though Raya thought that he was probably puzzling over the situation just as much as her, while Alira was clearly giving this recent turn of events even more serious thought than he was. The Ghostly God appeared to be thinking it over as well, but Raya didn't trust the deity who got

Carmaz disqualified from the Tournament to come up with anything helpful.

That was when Raya felt something in the ethereal. It felt like someone was watching them, but when Raya looked around, she didn't see anyone else in the ethereal besides herself, Keeper, Alira, and the Ghostly God. Still, there was an ominous, dark feeling of someone dangerous watching them.

The feeling made Raya shiver and hug herself, even though the temperature in the ethereal had not changed. She looked at Alira and Keeper and said, "Is it me or does it feel like someone is watching us?"

To her relief, Alira nodded in agreement. "It isn't you. I feel it as well."

"Being an automaton, I feel nothing," said Keeper. "But if you believe we are being watched, then I will agree."

"Yes, I also have the odd feeling that we are not alone," said the Ghostly God. He looked around. "Someone else is in here with us, but who—"

Without warning, twin black tendrils shot from the ethereal road and wrapped around the Ghostly God's arms. The Ghostly God struggled against them, but the black tendrils clung to his arms like mud, severely limiting his movement and making it impossible for him to do anything.

At the same time, more tendrils rose from all sides, cutting off all possible avenues of escape. Raya drew closer to Keeper, though she wasn't sure if that made her any safer. It was an instinctive movement on her part, because she was starting to remember how it had felt to be surrounded by the Void's tendrils again.

And then, from within one of the tendrils, a figure walked out. The figure was at first pitch-black, with no distinguishing features at all, but then as it walked out of the Void, Raya recognized him and gasped.

"Saia?" said Raya. "Or ... Saia's body."

Saia—actually the Void, now that Raya thought about it— smiled when it saw Raya, revealing a set of jagged teeth that made it look like a monster. "Hello again, Princess Raya. It has been a while since we last spoke, but I hope that you have not forgotten about me. That would be rather disappointing, but either way, I will make sure to eliminate you and your friends completely this time, as is the way of the Void."

Chapter Eighteen

ARMAZ CROUCHED LOW in the undergrowth of the Swamp, near the gaping entrance to the cavern that led to the place beneath the surface where the golems were gathered, hidden from the sight of anyone on the bridge (although at the moment the bridge was empty). It had taken he and Herune a couple of hours to locate the place, as Carmaz had not been entirely certain of the cavern's relation to the sanctuary, but after locating it, the two had traveled there immediately.

At the moment, Herune was not with Carmaz, although he was in the general area. Herune had volunteered to search the surrounding area for any traps that might have been laid by the golems. It didn't seem likely that the golems would set such a trap, but Herune had insisted that he search just to be safe. Carmaz had allowed him to do so, even though he wanted to put their plan into action right away.

Wiping the sweat off his forehead, Carmaz looked around the area. It was completely silent. The golem that had been sent after him earlier was nowhere to be seen, but Carmaz did not know if that meant that the golem had been killed by Zeeree and Aorja or if it had returned at some point earlier and was back underground with its friends. Either way, the plan would work, but Carmaz hoped that Zeeree had already dealt with it, as that would mean there was one less golem in the world to cause trouble.

Speaking of Aorja and Zeeree, Carmaz kept glancing over his shoulder, thinking they would appear and attack him any minute now, even though neither of them knew where he was. Still, Aorja had seemed like the kind of person to hold a grudge against people who wronged her. Maybe she was still suffering from whatever spell Herune had cast on her that had paralyzed her or maybe the golem was giving she and Zeeree far more trouble than they had expected. In any case, Carmaz knew that he would sooner or later have to deal with Aorja and her half-god pet even if Herune and he successfully stopped the invasion.

That thought didn't make him feel comfortable, but he pushed it aside for now in order to focus on the present. Carmaz always believed that things should be done in order and right now stopping the golems' invasion of Martir was more urgent than dealing with Aorja and Zeeree.

Then Herune appeared next to him out of nowhere, causing Carmaz to start slightly. He bent down next to Carmaz and gave him the thumbs up. "No traps or anything. The area is secure."

"Good," said Carmaz. He was speaking in a whisper, even though there wasn't anyone else in the area who could hear them speaking. "Now let's put the plan into action."

Herune nodded. "Sounds good. But can we go over the plan one more time, just to be sure we don't gloss over anything?"

"All right," said Carmaz. "But we'll do it quickly."

Carmaz pointed at the entrance to the cave. "You will use your magic to bring down the cavern entrance. That will keep the golems from getting out."

Herune raised an eyebrow. "Forever?"

"I can't promise that," said Carmaz, shaking his head. "But I think it will at least delay the invasion, because they will need to dig themselves out first before they can do anything else."

"Seems pretty simple," said Herune. "What do we do after that?"

Carmaz stroked his chin in thought. "We can go back to your father and stay with him until the gods arrive and deal with the golems in a more permanent way. That's the best we can do at the moment, I'm afraid."

"All right," said Herune. He looked up at the trees above them. "I just wonder how Alira and Raya are doing. We haven't heard back from them at all since they left. Do you think they've reached World's End yet?"

"I don't know," said Carmaz. "It has been several hours since they left, but I bet that even traveling on the ethereal takes some time. We should just try to focus on what we need to do here and let Raya and Alira take care of themselves."

"I guess you're right," said Herune. "Still, if they ran into any problems on the ethereal, there's no way we can know about them and no way we can help them. That might mean that the gods won't be able to stop the invasion until it is well under way."

"Like I said, we just need to focus on what we can control, which is this problem that we are currently facing," said Carmaz, gesturing at the cave mouth again. "Anyway, now I think we both know what we need to do. Cast the spell now before something hits us out of the blue."

Herune nodded. "All right."

Herune raised and aimed his wand at the cavern's entrance. He then waved his wand once. Its tip glowed brown before fading away.

Then a chunk of the cavern's entrance fell. It crashed into the ground rather loudly despite not being a very large chunk, and then it was followed by the entire entrance collapsing on itself. The collapse was loud, causing Carmaz's to cover his ears to protect his hearing, but the collapse lasted only a minute and soon all was silent and still in the Swamp.

But then Herune waved his wand again and the collapsed entrance started to fold in on itself. Mud and water covered its surface, while the log bridge started to break apart with nothing to hold it together. In seconds, the cavern's entrance had turned into a sinkhole from which it was unlikely that any golem would ever emerge, at least any time soon.

Lowering his wand, Herune sighed and said, "Well, that was easy. I expected something to go wrong, like maybe the golems had somehow made the entrance immune to magic. I guess they must have just used normal mud and wood to make it."

Carmaz nodded. "Agreed, but I've found that it's never wise to complain about a plan that goes exactly the way it is supposed to. Otherwise you risk the gods deciding to mess with it."

"The gods don't even know about our plan," Herune said. "But I get your point. We should probably go back to my father now and inform him of the success of our plan."

"An excellent idea," said Carmaz. He stood up, but as he did so, he felt a rumble in the earth. He looked down at Herune. "Herune, did you feel that?"

"Feel what?" said Herune.

"A tremor in the earth," said Carmaz. He looked at the ground, but he saw nothing out of the ordinary. "Maybe I was just imagining it, but it certainly felt—"

Then something massive exploded out of the muddy sinkhole that had once been the entrance to the golems' cave. Chunks of mud and thick logs flew through the air, quite a few coming toward Carmaz and Herune. Carmaz was too surprised to react, but Herune stood up and waved his wand, causing a large glowing barrier to appear around them.

And just in the nick of time, too, because one of the massive logs would have landed on them both if the barrier had not been there to block it. As a result, the log bounced off the barrier and fell with a *splash* into the water before them, but it was the last log to come their way, so Herune lowered the barrier, allowing them to see exactly what had just burst out of the mud.

The structure that had burst out of the mud was unlike anything Carmaz had seen on Ruwa before. It looked like a massive spire, so huge that it even towered over many of the trees. Its massive spiked tip rose high into the sky, like a drill attempting to pierce the heavens. It was covered in mud, but underneath the mud was what appeared to be a thick, solid stone surface that could not be easily cracked except by the gods themselves.

"What the hell is that?" said Herune, looking at Carmaz in confusion. "Did the golems say anything about having a giant stone spire when you rescued Alira?"

Carmaz shook his head. "No. I—"

Carmaz was once again interrupted, this time by the front end of the spire opening up. Rather than swing open like a door, however, it fell down with a loud *splash*, sending more mud and water into the air, some of which got on Carmaz and Herune. The door now formed a bridge, like the old drawbridge in the ruins of Castle Ruwa, between the massive spire and the rest of the Swamp. The bridge was wide and thick and sank only a couple of inches into the mud, but not enough to sink it entirely. It occurred to Carmaz that the bridge was likely supported by the tree spikes that the golem from before had been implanting in the mud, which explained why it had not sunk very deeply.

Beyond the end of the bridge, Carmaz saw nothing except for darkness. He exchanged a bewildered look with Herune, who now looked even more confused than him.

"Should we go inside and check it out or …?" Carmaz's sentence trailed off.

Herune shrugged before looking at the bridge again and starting. "Uh oh."

Carmaz also looked at the spire again and felt his heart sink into the pit of his stomach.

From out of the darkness of the spire came two golems that looked similar to the first golem, except they had battle axes and hammers rather than swords and buzz saws. They were followed by another couple of golems, and another couple, and another, until there were at least two dozen massive golems marching from the interior of the spire across the bridge to the Swamp itself.

"Holy shit," said Herune. "The bastards are invading anyway. I bet they knew we were coming. They must have. It's the only reasonable explanation for how they could have reacted so quickly."

Carmaz shook his head. "It doesn't matter whether they planned for this or not. We still need to stop the invasion. Can you use your magic to break or sink the bridge?"

Herune shook his head as well and said, "No. I'm not much of a geomancer, but I can do this instead."

Herune jabbed his wand in the direction of the invading golems. Two massive hands made out of mud and swamp grass rose from the muddy waters upon which the stone bridge lay, hands which reminded Carmaz of the mud giant that the Hermit had summoned when Alira and he had arrived at the Hermit's home earlier. These two hands were at least as big as that mud giant, maybe even larger, and they immediately reached for the invading golems, which were moving at a rather slow pace for an invading army.

But before the hands could so much as touch the golems, they froze. Quite literally. As Carmaz watched, ice raced up the surface of the hands, completely covering them in less than a minute. Then one of the golems on the bridge hurled a large stone at them, which shattered the hands into a million pieces as easily as if they had been nothing more than clay dolls.

"What the hell?" said Carmaz. He looked at Herune. "What did you do?"

"I didn't do anything," said Herune, holding up his hands defensively. He then pointed at the spire. "*He*, however, did."

Carmaz looked at the spire again and saw a much smaller golem standing at the entrance. It was the golem who had called himself Stalac, his scorpion-like tail hovering above his head, chilled air emitting from the tip. He was looking directly at Carmaz and Herune now, a snarl on his face that made him look like a monster.

"Wait, so these golems can use magic, too?" said Carmaz. He groaned. "Damn it."

"Shouldn't be a problem for us, though," said Herune as he raised his wand. "That golem may think he's hot stuff, but he doesn't know the Swamp nearly as well as I do. Let's see how much he likes swimming."

Herune waved his wand at Stalac. Another mud hand leaped out of the water, wrapped around Stalac's waist, and dragged him into the muddy water before he could even cry out for help.

"There," said Herune. "His own weight ought to hold him down now."

Just as Herune said that, however, Stalac leaped out of the water with far too much agility and speed for a golem of his size and weight. He landed on the bridge and then shouted some words at a couple of the nearby golems in a language that Carmaz had never heard before. Nonetheless, he got the gist of what Stalac said when those golems stopped and looked in Herune and Carmaz's direction with their sightless eyes.

"Uh oh," said Carmaz. He stepped backwards. "Think they're going to get us?"

"No way," said Herune, shaking his head. "They'd need a bridge to get here."

As soon as Herune said that, Stalac shook his hands and the stone bridge suddenly split. Part of it went deeper into the Swamp, while the other half went all the way to where Herune and Carmaz stood.

Carmaz looked at Herune in annoyance. "Don't say another word."

Herune shrugged helplessly, as if to say, *Hey, don't blame me.*

Then two of the golems started walking across the new bridge toward Carmaz and Herune, prompting Carmaz to say, "We should run before they get here. If we move now—"

A loud crashing sound behind them made Carmaz look up in time to see a massive stone saw coming down toward Herune and him. Without thinking, Carmaz shoved Herune to the side and then jumped forward, landing on the end of the stone bridge with a roll. The stone saw slammed into the ground where they had stood, sending up cascades of mud and water that splattered all over Carmaz. Still, he managed to rise to his feet and look over his shoulder to see where that saw had come from.

Standing amidst the trees and mud of the Swamp was the first golem from before, except it was now much worse for the wear. Thick cracks ran all along its surface, while half of its face was missing, in addition to its sword, which was still snapped off and nowhere to be seen. Its head in particular looked so cracked that Carmaz was surprised it managed to hold together as well as it did.

Despite its damaged appearance, the golem didn't appear to be in any pain at all. It raised its mud-covered saw out of the Swamp and then took a step toward Carmaz. Though it walked slowly, that hardly comforted Carmaz, because he now realized that he was trapped between three golems: The one that had just tried to smash him underneath its saw and the two coming up behind him with their own hammers and saws.

"Herune?" said Carmaz, walking backwards away from the golem before him, even though he was aware that this was just leading him right into the other two golems behind him. "Help?"

Herune, having been knocked over by Carmaz, struggled to his feet. He was almost completely covered in mud and his clothes were soaked, but he still raised his hand to cast a spell at the first golem before he froze and said, "Uh oh. I lost my wand."

"You lost your wand?" Carmaz repeated, his eyes darting between Herune and the approaching golem as he attempted to keep both within his sights. "Can't you cast a spell anyway?"

"Not without my wand," said Herune, shaking his head. He bent over and started pushing aside bushes and branches in the water around him. "At least, if I did cast a spell, it would probably hurt both of us just as much as it would hurt the golems, if not more so, because I need my wand to control it."

Carmaz cursed, but he didn't say anything else. He just kept backing up until he reached the middle of the bridge, at which point he stopped and looked up and down the bridge. The golems may have been approaching him slowly, but it still would not take them long to reach him.

He considered simply jumping off the bridge and swimming through the water back to dry ground, but then he saw something large and reptilian slither just beneath the surface and decided against it.

By now, the golems from either end of the bridge were close enough now that there was little time to stand around and think about possible escape routes. And, although all three of them lacked facial expressions and emotions of any kind, Carmaz was aware of how absolutely merciless these creatures could be.

Run between their legs, Carmaz thought. *They're big enough that you can do that. Run to Herune and get out of here. There's nothing you can do against the golems.*

That seemed like a good idea to Carmaz, but then he considered it again. The gods did not seem to be coming. And if the golems were allowed to leave this area, they might well kill dozens if not hundreds of people on Ruwa. Right now, only he, Herune, and, to a lesser extent, the Hermit, were aware of this threat, and were also the only people who could deal with it.

Maybe if I can get Stalac, I can force him to call off his minions, Carmaz thought. *Even if he's stronger than me, I might be able to beat him with some luck and skill on my part.*

So Carmaz turned and ran down the bridge toward the two approaching golems coming from the spire. Neither of the two appeared surprised at his sudden movement. They just raised their massive weapons, ready to bring them down on Carmaz once he was within range, which only prompted Carmaz to run faster than ever. He then did a flying leap, jumping through the gap between the two golems. At the same time, the golems brought their hammers down on the bridge, creating a loud *boom* and *crack* that shook the bridge, almost knocking Carmaz down, but he recovered quickly enough and ran down the bridge to Stalac, who was watching him with a look of surprise on his rocky features.

"What a persistent little human you are," said Stalac. He shook his head. "Not that it matters. The invasion will proceed whether you want it to or not. I'll just have to take matters into my own hands, it appears."

Stalac fired a beam of ice from the tip of his tail. Carmaz dove, rolling underneath the ice beam, which struck the part of the bridge where he had been mere moments before. Rolling to his feet, Carmaz was now within feet of the golem general, who he rammed with his shoulder as hard as he could.

But slamming into Stalac was as effective as punching a boulder. The golem general didn't even budge under Carmaz's blow. Instead, he slammed his fist into Carmaz's gut, the blow enough to knock Carmaz to the ground. Carmaz tried to get up, but then Stalac kicked him in the chin. The blow sent Carmaz rolling backwards, his jaw aching and maybe even broken, his whole world spinning.

Nonetheless, he shook his head in time to see Stalac standing over him. Carmaz tried to get up, but Stalac unleashed another ice beam that struck Carmaz around the stomach, pinning him to the bridge. The ice was cold, far colder than anything Carmaz had felt in his life. He tried to cry out in pain, but his jaw was in so much pain that he couldn't even do that much.

"I am disappointed that Gol failed to kill you when I specifically sent him to kill you," said Stalac. He shook his head in disappointment. "Oh, well. You will still be the first casualty of the invasion, which is a great honor if you think about it. After all, how many humans can say that they have been killed by a golem? Not many, I should think."

Stalac raised one of his large feet above Carmaz's face, an evil pride in his eyes. "Too bad, of course, you won't get to see us raze your whole world to the ground."

Carmaz struggled to break the ice pinning him to the bridge, but it was too thick and solid. He just looked up at the underside of Stalac's foot, wondering what he would feel when it smashed his face in.

But before Stalac could bring his foot down on Carmaz's face, the bridge shook under their feet. It shook so badly that Stalac was almost knocked off balance, but he managed to retain his balance quickly enough to avoid falling over. He then looked around, a frown on his stony features, as he said, "What was that?"

As if in response to his question, a massive form rose from the Swamp water all around them. The form grew taller and taller, until soon it towered over even the spire. It took on a humanoid form, dripping mud off its massive frame, until soon Carmaz found himself staring at the Hermit's mud giant, except far, far bigger than it had been before.

And it wasn't alone. Another mud giant rose from the Swamp water on the other side of the bridge, and still another behind the spire, until soon four mud giants stood all around. The invading golems on the bridge actually looked up at the mud giants, raising their weapons as if they were fighting an opposing army.

"What is this?" said Stalac, looking around at the mud giants. "Where did these come from?"

The nearest mud giant lashed out, bringing its fist down on Stalac. The golem general jumped backwards, just barely avoiding its fist, which slammed into the bridge and sent mud flying everywhere, much of it covering Carmaz. But the impact of the mud also shattered the ice pinning Carmaz down, allowing him to scramble back to his feet and look around at the mud giants.

The other mud giants were now attacking the golems. They pulled the golems into the Swamp water, which the golems were too heavy to pull themselves out of, and hurled gobs of mud at those outside of their reach. A handful of golems tried fighting back, but their weapons did nothing against the mud giants, usually striking but leaving no lasting damage, or in some cases actually getting stuck in the giants' legs, which were the only parts of the mud giants' bodies that the golems could reach.

Carmaz looked over his shoulder. He saw the three golems

from before trying to attack the giants, but then they were also knocked into the Swamp water, where they got stuck in the mud. They struggled to free themselves, but it was clear that they weren't going anywhere anytime soon.

Carmaz also looked to see if Herune was responsible for this, but Herune was still apparently looking for his wand in the mud. He did, however, look up every now and then at the spectacle with shocked eyes, as if he couldn't believe what he was seeing.

Looking back at Stalac, Carmaz saw that the golem general was looking this way and that at the unexpected attack. His scorpion-like tail turned with him, but he didn't seem to know which giant to attack first.

"What kind of magic is this?" said Stalac. He sounded worried, the first time Carmaz had ever heard him sound that way. "Who summoned these creatures?"

"That would be I, golem," said a familiar elderly voice that seemed to come from everywhere at once.

Then the Hermit appeared next to Carmaz. He looked the same way he always did, with his long gray beard and his staff, but now there was anger in his eyes, a righteous anger that even made Carmaz step away out of fear that he might get harmed in the Hermit's rage.

"You?" said Stalac. "Who are you, old human?"

"Many things," said the Hermit. "I often go by the Hermit, but you may call me the King of the Swamp. Or your death, if you'd prefer. I really could not care less."

Stalac shook his head. "Well, if you are the one responsible for this, then prepare to die."

Stalac fired an ice beam at the Hermit. The Hermit, however, waved his wand and the nearest mud giant slammed its fist in between Stalac's ice beam and the Hermit and Carmaz. The ice beam struck the mud giant's fist, instantly freezing it, prompting Stalac to shout, "You think mud will protect you? What a foolish human."

The Hermit didn't respond. He just jerked his wand to the right and the mud giant raised its frozen fist. Carmaz wasn't sure how the mud giant's frozen fist was staying attached to its wrist, but he supposed it didn't matter, because the mud giant brought its fist above the head of Stalac. Stalac looked up, but before he could react, the mud giant slammed its frozen fist directly down on Stalac's head.

A loud shattering sound followed a small tremor in the bridge. Carmaz almost fell off the bridge, but the Hermit grabbed him before he could and pulled him to safety. Then Carmaz looked at where Stalac had stood.

The golem general now lay on the bridge, either unconscious or dead, amidst a large pile of frozen mud shards. As for the mud giant, it was missing its fist, but mud was already flowing from the other parts of its body to replace its shattered hand. It didn't look at all disturbed by losing its fist, although that may have had to do with the fact that it was merely a puppet and not an actual living being.

Carmaz looked at the Hermit, who seemed quite proud of his victory. "Why did you come? I thought you weren't going to help."

The Hermit nodded. "And I wouldn't have, under ordinary circumstances. But I wanted to help my son, as much as we may not get along. And after I was forced to abandon my home, well, I

267

decided that I had nothing better to do, so why not help?"

Carmaz rubbed some mud off his face and said, "Well, thank you anyway. I don't know what I would have done without you."

"Likely died," said the Hermit. "Anyway, it won't be long now before all of the golems are stuck in the mud like a bunch of boulders. It won't be a permanent solution, but it should give the gods some time to arrive and handle the situation for us in a more permanent fashion."

Then Carmaz heard someone running toward them and looked down the bridge to see Herune coming. He had his wand, but it seemed to Carmaz now that Herune wouldn't need it, seeing as the entire golem army was too disorganized to invade at the moment.

"Father?" said Herune as he approached. "What are you—"

"Save the questions for later," the Hermit interrupted. "Just know that these golems don't stand a chance against our might." He nodded at the spire. "Let's try to bury that thing again. This time, together."

Herune looked surprised at his father's insistence that they team up, but then he nodded and said, "Very well. Let's do this."

The Hermit and Herune stood side by side. Then they raised their wands and aimed them at the spire. Carmaz stood back, mostly because he wasn't sure what they were going to do and he didn't want to be in it.

But before they could cast any spells, another golem stepped out of the spire's entrance. This one was much smaller than the others and had wings sprouting from her back. She had diamond-colored skin and dangerous, glowing blue eyes.

"Who's that?" said Herune with a frown. "She looks different from the others."

"That's Lady Dia," said Carmaz. "She's the leader of the golems, I think. She's Stalac's boss."

"So she decided to come out and see us beating her army, huh?" said the Hermit. He smiled. "Well, I can't say I understand why any leader would want to see her best men get thrashed by the enemy, but that makes it so much easier to take her down. I bet if we kill her, her men will give up without another fight."

The Hermit waved his staff at the nearest mud giant. It then walked down toward the spire, where Lady Dia was standing, her hand on the entrance, watching the battle between the mud giants and her golems with surprise. She then looked up as the mud giant approached her, though without fear in her eyes for some reason. Not that it mattered, Carmaz supposed, because the mud giant was going to crush her whether or not she was afraid of it.

The mud giant raised both of its massive fists above its head. In fact, it didn't just raise its fists. It combined them both into one gigantic ball of mud, so huge that Carmaz was surprised that the mud giant had not yet fallen over due to the sheer weight of the ball it held. Again, Lady Dia still showed no fear, but Carmaz saw her look ready to run, even though there wasn't anywhere she could run except back into the spire.

Then Lady Dia's eyes squinted and she raised one hand. She then snapped her fingers.

Without warning, the mud giant froze. Not literally, of course, but it stopped increasing the size of its mud ball and had stopped moving entirely. The Hermit, frowning, waved his staff again, but the mud giant did not do anything.

Then, with a shudder, it collapsed. Chunks of mud fell into the

Timothy L. Cerepaka

Swamp water, splashing loudly, and when Carmaz looked around, he saw that the same was happening to the other three mud giants. They had also frozen and were collapsing under their own weight, bits and chunks of their bodies falling into the waters at their feet. They made no noise as they fell, except for the sound of their muddy bodies falling into the water.

"No," said the Hermit. He waved his staff again. "No, this can't be. Why?"

Herune was also waving his wand, but with the same success as his father. "I don't understand it, either, father. What is that female golem doing?"

"Destroying the mud giants, it looks like," Carmaz said. "That's not a good thing."

"Of course it isn't," the Hermit snapped. He shook his head. "Regardless, we can still kill her without those mud giants."

Just as he said that, Lady Dia looked in their direction. Then she suddenly ran and jumped into the air. She flew toward them and landed on the bridge next to the unconscious Stalac, who still hadn't recovered from being crushed by the mud giant from before. Some of the frozen mud shards covering him were starting to melt, but most were still frozen solid and looked quite heavy, meaning it was unlikely that he was going anywhere anytime soon.

"So you are the three humans who are trying to disrupt the invasion," said Lady Dia. She nodded at Carmaz. "I remember you. You were the one who rescued Alira earlier."

"Glad you remember," said Carmaz. He then gestured toward the sky. "But Alira isn't on Ruwa anymore. She's gone. She went to get the gods; once she does, your invasion will be ended before you even left the front door."

"I was about to ask where she was, but I guess you answered that for me," said Lady Dia. She sighed. "The gods' involvement will almost certainly complicate things, but I guess life does not always go the way you planned it. Not that that will make me retreat, of course."

Lady Dia then looked down at Stalac with disgust. "I do wish you hadn't taken out Stalac, but he was always overconfident and always over-promised. It means I must kill you three myself, which I can do, but I would rather not, as it is beneath my station as the Lady of the Golems."

"If you're as weak as Stalac, defeating you will take no time at all," said the Hermit. "Even if you destroyed our mud giants, that isn't the only trick we have up our sleeves. Take this!"

The Hermit and Herune jabbed their wands in her direction. Carmaz didn't know what kind of spell they were intending to cast on her, but he assumed it was probably going to hurt a lot.

But even though the Hermit and Herune were pointing their wands at her, Lady Dia didn't even flinch. She just looked around with a vague interest, as if she realized that something was supposed to happen but didn't. She even scratched her chin and yawned, as if bored.

"I don't see anything," said Lady Dia. She looked at the two mages. "Unless you think I am afraid of a couple of mortals pointing sticks at me, anyway."

Herune looked at his own wand like it was not functioning correctly, while the Hermit said, "Impossible. You should have been pulled into the Swamp waters by the plants underneath. Why didn't that work?"

"I see I forgot to tell you about all of my abilities," said Lady Dia. She smiled. "Magic doesn't work around me."

Just as those words left her mouth, Lady Dia dashed forward much faster than any of her golems could move. She reached the Hermit and Herune before they could react and punched them both in the face with her stone fists. Two sharp *cracks* echoed through the air as the Hermit fell backwards onto the bridge without a word, while Herune staggered off the bridge and fell into the Swamp water from which he did not emerge.

Alarmed, Carmaz stepped backwards again, but then he heard movement behind him and looked over his shoulder. The three golems from before had somehow managed to pull themselves out of the Swamp and back onto the bridge. They were advancing toward Carmaz again, their bodies covered in mud, except now they seemed angry to him, or maybe it was just Carmaz's imagination making him see things that weren't there.

In any case, Carmaz looked back toward Lady Dia, who looked quite pleased at this turn of events. There was blood on her fists from where she had punched the Hermit and Herune, but she didn't seem to notice or care.

"And then there was one," said Lady Dia. She slammed her right fist into her left. "And unlike those two, you don't even have magical powers. Not that that makes much of a difference. You'll die either way."

"Why?" said Carmaz. He didn't know why he was saying this, seeing as he had no idea how to stop her, but he wanted to say it anyway. "Why are you doing this? This invasion? What did we Martirians do to you golems to make you hate us?"

Lady Dia paused, as if seriously considering the question.

Then she scowled. "Nice try, but I'm not going to answer any of your questions. Today, you will die, and then the invasion will properly begin, starting with the complete and utter destruction of your precious island home. I hope you were faithful to whatever god you worship, human, because today you will meet your makers in the afterlife."

Chapter Nineteen

TAMRA LICKED HER lips, a mad gleam in her eyes. She stood all alone in the wreckage of the room she had been inside, her entire body glowing an eerie blue light. She looked almost like a goddess, even though she was just a normal mortal.

"The new Goddess of Martir?" Xocion repeated. He held his shield and spear in a defensive position. "What do you mean? The Tournament is not even over yet. How, then, can you claim that title? And what happened to Kos and Henim?"

Tamra chuckled, but Braim thought he heard two other voices mixed in with hers, two voices that he had never heard before. She raised one glowing hand and pointed at her chest. "They're right here, where they belong. You just can't see them."

"What does that even mean?" said Mica. "I only see you."

"I guess I wasn't clear enough about *where* they are," said Tamra. "What I meant was that their spirits are in my body. I have added their power to my own. And it is amazing."

Tamra held up her other hand. Immediately, it started raining heavily, putting out the flames behind her and completely soaking Braim to the bone, but then the rain vanished as quickly as it came. Still Tamra smiled, as if she had proven a point.

"Impossible," said Xocion, his body slightly shiny due to the rain drops that had fallen on him. "How can you have their spirits in your body? A god's spirit can never be taken away from them."

"So you think," said Tamra. She then held up something that was far too familiar to Braim: the Soul Collector. "But your brother, the Ghostly God, would like to disagree. Do you know what this is?"

"The Soul Collector," said Braim, causing Xocion and Mica to look at him in surprise. He didn't look at either of them, however, because his eyes were fixed on the Soul Collector in Tamra's hand. "But how—"

"You mean you still haven't put it together, Braim?" said Tamra. She curled her fingers around the Soul Collector again and lowered her hand to her side. "I stole it from you. Remember the female assassin who attacked you earlier? That was me. My main goal all along was to get the Soul Collector. I only tried to kill you because I wanted as little competition as possible in the Tournament, but I obviously did not succeed there."

The darkness in the back of Braim's head made him wince. He grabbed the back of his head as Xocion said, "But I don't understand. You are one of the godlings in the Tournament, yet you have stolen the souls of two of our siblings. Why?"

Tamra chuckled again. "Why? Because I want power, the kind of power that belongs to the gods and to the gods alone. And stealing the gods' souls and adding them to my own is a great way to do that, wouldn't you say?"

"But you seemed like such a nice girl," said Braim. "Let me guess, you're working for the Void, right?"

"The Void?" said Tamra. She shook her head in disgust. "Why would I ever work for the Void? She only wants the complete and utter destruction of Martir, while I wish to rule it. No, the Void isn't my friend or master. Once I attain the power I seek, then I will deal with her myself."

"Regardless of your affiliation to the Void, have you actually killed Kos and Henim?" said Xocion. His icy tone almost broke, like he was genuinely anguished by the possibility that two of his siblings were dead. "Even though mortals cannot kill gods?"

"I never said that I *killed* them," said Tamra. "Their bodies are still alive and functioning. They just lack their spirits to animate them." She put a hand over her heart. "I can feel them in my body, giving me their strength and power. It is thrilling, more intoxicating than even I thought it would be. I understand why you gods like your power so much."

"I didn't even know it was possible for a mortal to steal the soul of a god and put it in her body," said Xocion. "You should have died. No mortal body can handle the power of a god, no matter how powerful that mortal may be."

Tamra bit her lip, like she was trying to avoid screaming in pain, and then said, "I'm a godling. Our bodies are different from the bodies of other mortals. Because we have the potential to become gods, we can handle divine energy better than normal mortals. Of course, I still need some practice to gain full mastery over my new power, but my body is fully capable of handling it for the time being. Thanks for your concern, though. I appreciate it."

"How long have you been planning to do this?" said Xocion. He pointed his spear at her. "And why hasn't Grinf stopped you? Where is he?"

"Oh, I've been planning this thing ever since I was chosen to participate in the Tournament of the Gods," said Tamra. She gestured at herself. "It's been a long couple of months, but no one has suspected a thing. Yet it wasn't until recently that I was able to pull this plan off ... and it was all thanks to Braim."

Tamra nodded at Braim when she said that. Braim knew exactly what she was talking about, even though he wished that he didn't. Xocion and Mica looked at him, however, as if they didn't understand what she meant.

"In case you don't understand, it's because of the Soul Collector," said Tamra, holding up the device for them all to see. "When Braim brought it back with him from the Ghostly God's island, I saw exactly what I had been looking for. So I went to Braim's room and stole it. I tried to kill him, too, obviously, but that didn't work out, so I left after I got what I came for."

"You still have not explained why Grinf—and the other gods, for that matter—have not appeared yet to stop you," said Xocion, looking at Tamra with a cold anger that made Braim gulp.

"Oh, that's easy," said Tamra. She pointed at the ceiling. "I cast a spell to keep out the other gods. It was easy to do after I stole the souls of your siblings. The other gods cannot enter even if they wanted to. And they won't, not until I give them permission to, at least."

"I see," said Xocion. "So we are all on our own, then."

He looked at Mica. "Mica, are you ready to smite this mortal with me? Or are you still angry about the conflict between our followers?"

"I am still angry about it, but I am willing to put my anger aside for now to avenge our siblings and punish this mortal accordingly," said Mica. "I may not be the Goddess of Justice, but all gods have a duty to avenge their brethren if they are defeated by an enemy, as per the Treaty."

Xocion nodded and then looked at Tamra. He pointed his spear at her.

A second later, a massive blizzard materialized in the area where Tamra stood. The blizzard was loud, especially in the confined area of the room, and the snow within it was so thick that Braim couldn't see Tamra through it at all.

Then Mica jerked her hands forward and twin rock pillars shot out of the floor and stabbed the center of the blizzard, exactly where Tamra had been standing moments ago. The rock pillars crashed against each other, but it was still impossible to see whether they had hit Tamra or not. Still, Braim figured that they had to, seeing as there was no way Tamra could have dodged them in that concentrated blizzard. A quick glance around the room showed that Tamra was nowhere in sight.

Mica then lowered her hands and the floor cracked open underneath where Tamra had stood. Braim saw something fall out of the blizzard and into the wide-open crack, but then a second later Xocion's blizzard dumped a hundred tons of snow into the crack, at which point the crack closed shut with a massive *boom*. Then Xocion lowered his spear and the blizzard dissipated, revealing two frost-covered rock pillars where Tamra had been standing moments before. The godling herself was nowhere to be seen.

"There," said Mica. "She wasn't so difficult. It is amazing how arrogant mortals can be, though."

"Agreed," said Xocion, nodding. "Mortals always seem to think they can outwit us gods. And sometimes they can, but none can match us for raw power."

"What do we do now?" asked Braim. The room was a lot colder now due to the blizzard that Xocion had summoned, so cold that Braim could actually see his breath when he spoke.

"Easy," said Xocion. He gestured at the exit. "We leave the room and inform Grinf and the others about Tamra's betrayal. We may need to reschedule the Skimif Sub-Bracket Challenge, but better that than all of us dying at the hands of a mortal who had too much power."

"I guess so," said Braim. He hugged himself to stay warm. "Geez, though, this is cold."

"I had to make it that cold in order to kill her," said Xocion. "Most humans cannot stand temperatures below freezing for very long, at least without proper clothing. That blizzard I encased her in was about a thousand degrees below zero, so there is literally no way she could have survived—"

Xocion gasped in pain, cutting himself off in the process. It was a sharp, rattling gasp, causing Braim and Mica to look at him.

Standing behind Xocion, a foul scowl on her lips, was Tamra. Her hair looked even crazier now, with flicks of snow and ice on the edges, but she otherwise looked all right for a person who was buried underneath one hundred tons of snow and crushed between the earth. She was driving the Soul Collector into Xocion's back like a knife.

Braim could even see Xocion's power going into her. Whitish energy flowed from Xocion's back into the Soul Collector and then into Tamra's body. Xocion himself was completely frozen, like the Soul Collector had paralyzed his nerves (though Braim wasn't sure if a being made of ice even had nerves).

279

Then Tamra ripped the Soul Collector out of Xocion's back, sending bits of ice and snow flying, and then kicked him forward. The God of Ice fell face-first onto the floor, his whole body cracking on impact, but not shattering. Xocion did not move again.

Tamra staggered back. Now her skin was alternating between glowing blue and glowing white. She looked down at her hands, her scowl giving way to a bright smile that made Braim want to run. She then looked up at Mica and Braim.

"How did you survive all of that?" said Mica. There was fear in Mica's voice. Not much, but it was there and it made Braim fearful as well. "Xocion and I hit you with the kind of power that no mortal could ever hope to handle."

"I'm not a mere mortal, though," said Tamra. "I'm a godling with the souls of three gods now circulating through my veins. Did you really think that I would simply stand there and let you kill me? My, you gods truly are naïve, despite your immense ages."

Mica didn't even respond. She just stomped her foot on the floor and two gigantic stone hands tore through the floor. They slammed Tamra between them, but the crazed godling caught them both with her hands, keeping the hands from crushing her between them with what looked like no effort at all.

"Oh, so you really think that you could crush me so easily?" said Tamra. She didn't even sound like she was straining against the gigantic stone hands, even though Mica must have been putting all of her power into them. "*After* you just saw me take Xocion's soul? You're even thicker than I thought, though considering you're the Goddess of Earth that's not too surprising."

With a grunt, Tamra pushed the two hands back. They immediately shattered, but Mica didn't miss a beat. She stomped her foot again, this time causing the floor to shake. Braim fell on his behind, but so did Tamra, who looked like she had not expected that to happen.

Then stone bindings rose around Tamra and constricted around her like a snake. They soon covered her completely, obscuring her face and likely cutting off her air supply.

But as soon as the bindings covered Tamra, the earth around her froze and shattered. Tamra stood up, now with flecks of dirt in her hair, and shot an ice bolt at Mica, but the Goddess of Earth summoned a stone wall that blocked the ice bolt. She then caused the wall to fall over onto Tamra, but Tamra dodged it at the last second. And in retaliation, Tamra waved her hand, causing a giant, sharp icicle to materialize over Mica's head and fall onto her.

The goddess could not move in time to dodge it. The icicle crashed on her head, causing it to shatter and send chunks of ice flying everywhere. Braim ducked and covered his head to avoid getting hurt, but he still looked up at Mica anyway. She didn't seem hurt at all by the giant icicle that had fallen on her head, though she did look angry about it.

Then she looked down at Braim and snapped, "What are you standing around here looking like an idiot for? Get out of here and tell the other gods about this. I will hold off Tamra for as long as I can."

Braim didn't feel the need to argue against that. He nodded and turned and ran for the exit, but before he could even get halfway there, a thick layer of ice covered the door instantly.

Timothy L. Cerepaka

Skidding to a stop, Braim looked over at Tamra, who was pointing at the now-frozen door with a smug look on her face.

"Oh, no, Braim, you aren't going anywhere," said Tamra. "I want you to stay exactly where you are. I'll make sure to deal with you after I finish—"

Tamra did not get a chance to finish her sentence because a fist made of stone broke through the floor and slammed into her face. The blow sent her staggering backwards, but then another stone fist erupted from the earth and grabbed her around the waist. The hand then squeezed hard, probably with enough effort to turn her bones into dust, but Tamra broke it apart with a shrug of her shoulders. She landed on the ground, but as soon as she did, another stone fist rose from the earth underneath, which she dodged by jumping and landing on the floor again.

Braim looked at Mica, who seemed to have forgotten all about him now, because she was looking at Tamra intensely. The Goddess of Earth slammed her fists together, creating a shock wave that ripped through the floor, but as usual, Tamra avoided it.

Great, Braim thought, looking between the battle between Tamra and Mica and the frozen door. *Just my luck that I got caught in the middle of a battle between two beings who can probably sink whole islands by themselves if they want to. And there's nothing I can do about either of them except try to survive.*

Tamra jumped toward Mica. Mica responded by sending chunks of the floor flying at her, but Tamra vanished just as the debris flew at her. The chunks of floor struck the ceiling and fell back to the ground, leaving huge craters where they hit. Braim was starting to worry that Tamra's and Mica's fight might cause the entire Stadium to fall in on itself, which was seeming more

282

and more likely with each passing second.

Then Tamra reappeared behind Mica and tried to stab her with the Soul Collector. Mica, on the other hand, immediately collapsed into dust, causing the Soul Collector to pass harmlessly through her form. Then Mica's dust form flew into Tamra's open mouth, causing the godling to hack and cough in pain, but Mica kept filling her form with more and more dirt until soon every last dust particle of Mica had gone inside Tamra's body.

Tamra choked and fell to her hands and knees. She dropped the Soul Collector and grabbed her throat, hacking hard, but nothing came out. It was rather horrifying to watch, even though Braim hated Tamra right now. If she ended up dying this way, well, Braim could live with that.

And it certainly seemed like that was the way Tamra was going down, because after only a few more seconds of resistance, she stopped fighting and lay on the ground as still a stone. Her eyes were open, but there was no life in them.

Then Mica's dust form emptied from her mouth, slowing reforming Mica starting with her feet until soon the goddess's whole form had returned. Mica looked no worse for having forced herself inside Tamra's body, but then, Mica was a goddess, after all.

Nonetheless, Braim didn't walk over to either of them. He rubbed the back of his neck and said, "So … is she dead?"

Mica looked up at Braim suddenly, like she had forgotten that he was there. Then she nodded. "Yes. She is indeed dead."

Braim sighed in relief. "Whew. I seriously thought she was going to kill us there for a second."

"She was an arrogant mortal who believed that merely having

the power of my fellow gods was enough to make her stronger than me," said Mica, shaking her head. "What she failed to understand is that it takes more than raw power to be a god. You need experience and wisdom, something which she clearly lacked."

Mica did not sound sorrowful at all about Tamra's death. She was simply stating a fact, which Braim saw no need to argue with.

"How do we get the gods' souls out of her body, then?" said Braim, putting his hands on his hips and looking down at the dead Tamra. "Any ideas?"

"No," said Mica. "But it wouldn't surprise me if my siblings' souls returned to their bodies on their own, now that Tamra's body is—"

Without warning, Tamra jumped to her feet and stabbed Mica in the chest with the Soul Collector. Mica let out a gasp, but that was all she could do as the Soul Collector started to absorb her soul.

Alarmed, Braim tried to run over to help, but Tamra waved a hand in his direction and an ice wall materialized in his path. Braim slammed into the wall and staggered back, somewhat dazed by the impact, and shook his head. He then looked through the ice wall as the last of Mica's soul went into the Soul Collector, at which point Tamra pulled the Soul Collector away and kicked Mica over.

Like a stone statue, Mica fell without a word. She landed on the floor with a *clunk* and showed no more signs of life after that. She looked quite dead, more so than even Tamra had.

Tamra lowered the Soul Collector and looked at it with a satisfied smile on her face. Then she looked at the ice wall between her and Braim, which she waved at. The ice wall then melted, causing Braim to step backwards to avoid getting his shoes wet, even though that was the least of his problems at the moment.

Tamra turned to face Braim. She was still smiling, although there was dirt and sand in her teeth, which only added to her creepy appearance.

Now Braim wasn't much of a coward, but even he knew that he could not stand a chance against Tamra. Even so, he found it impossible to move. His legs were paralyzed, despite his mind telling his body to run away as fast as he could.

Despite his paralyzed legs, Braim's mouth still worked, so he said, "Are you going to kill me next?"

To his surprise, Tamra shook her head. She spat out dirt and wiped it off her lips. Then she put one hand over her mouth, which she opened wide.

Before Braim's startled eyes, dirt and sand flowed out of Tamra's open mouth. There was a lot more in her than Braim had thought, but she got rid of it soon enough and placed it all in a pile on the floor next to her. She coughed once or twice, but otherwise seemed okay despite having magically removed a pile of dirt and sand as tall as her ankles from her body.

"Ah," said Tamra. Her voice was rather scratchy, though her words were still clear. "That was a dirty trick on Mica's part, and no, I did not intend for that to be a pun. She really came very close to actually killing me. A little bit longer and I would have died for sure."

"But how did you survive?" asked Braim. He was still telling his legs to move, but they were ignoring his commands. "That looked pretty damn fatal to me."

"I'm very good at acting," said Tamra. "That, and the power of her siblings made me strong enough to survive. Still, I was worried for a while there that I actually would die, but I didn't, so I'm fine."

"Uh huh," said Braim. "So are you actually going to kill me or not?"

"No," said Tamra. "Of course I won't. I mean, sure, I tried to kill you before, but that was then and this is now. Instead, I think I'd rather have you join me. Together, you and I can rule the world. How does that sound?"

Braim blinked. "Why do you want me to rule the world with you? For that matter, why do you want to rule the world at all?"

Tamra sighed. "I was hoping you wouldn't ask that, but I can see that there's no avoiding the truth now. Braim, do you know what my job back on Kikasa was?"

Braim shook his head. "No. You never told me."

"That's because I didn't really have a 'job,' per se," said Tamra. She then raised her hand, upon which was a tattoo that looked like a phoenix. "On Kikasa, I was known as Princess Tamrarus, granddaughter of Nikar Aruga, the Head Councilman of Kikasa."

"You're royalty?" said Braim in surprise. "Like Raya?"

Tamra shook her head. "Not like Raya. Raya is vain, silly, and dumb. I'm glad she isn't here. I don't know where she is or who kidnapped her, but whether or not she is dead, I don't care. All I care about is getting the power I deserve."

"How come you kept that secret for so long?" asked Braim. "Are you ashamed of your heritage or something?"

"No, of course not," said Tamra. "But knowledge is power. I kept my heritage a secret from the other godlings in order to seem like everyone else. I didn't want unnecessary attention drawn to me, as that would have made it much harder to accomplish my goals."

"Oh," said Braim. He kept trying to move his legs, but still found no success. "Well, I guess that worked out for you, since not even I suspected that you were planning anything bad."

"Of course you didn't," said Tamra. She puffed out her chest in pride. "I am very good at keeping secrets. I'm a little surprised that I wasn't chosen to participate in the Hollech Bracket, but I guess that destiny must have seen that I would make a much better Goddess of Martir."

"Then why are you stealing the gods' souls?" asked Braim. He gestured at the lifeless bodies of Xocion and Mica. "I mean, why didn't you just try to win the Tournament fair and square?"

Tamra shook her head. "I hate leaving anything up to chance. Yes, I could, perhaps, try to win 'fair and square,' but in a fair Tournament like this, there is always a chance you can lose. After all, there is always someone better out there and there was a good chance that that someone better was competing against me in this Tournament."

"Are you talking about me or someone else?" asked Braim.

"No one in particular," said Tamra. "Every participant in our bracket is a threat to my destiny. Therefore, I decided that I would simply increase my odds and go straight for the kill."

Tamra held up the Soul Collector. "Of course, at first I didn't know for sure how I was going to do that until I heard the rumors of the Soul Collector. I originally planned to seduce you and have

287

you give it to me as a gift, but then I got impatient and just stole it outright, again because I couldn't be sure that I could make you give it to me."

"Well, you were right there," said Braim. "No way I'd ever give over something as important as the Soul Collector to anyone, even to the people I trust the most."

"See?" said Tamra. "I knew it. Had I tried to seduce you, I would have failed for sure."

"Well, even if your plan worked, that doesn't mean you need to keep doing it," said Braim. "You should return the souls back to the gods that you stole them from. Maybe if you do that, the gods won't punish you as harshly as they otherwise would have."

"Why?" said Tamra. She bit her lower lip again, but then resumed speaking as if nothing out of the ordinary had happened. "Do you even know what it feels like to have this kind of power inside you? It is glorious. And even if it didn't feel that way, there's no reason for me to avoid the quickest route to power just because you don't like it."

"You don't even know if absorbing the souls of the other gods will give you what you want," said Braim. "Even the Ghostly God said he didn't know what using the Soul Collector on a god would do."

Tamra flipped the Soul Collector between her fingers. "Well, I just used it four times and have discovered exactly what it does to a god. Maybe, when I steal the Ghostly God's soul, too, I will tell him what a success it was. As for not knowing if this will make me the Goddess of Martir … maybe it will, maybe it won't, but I do know that it will make me more powerful than all of the other gods, and isn't that what being the Goddess of Martir is all about anyway?"

"There's a lot more to that title than power," Braim pointed out. "I don't remember much about Skimif due to being dead for most of his reign, but I've heard he was a wise ruler who always looked out for the best interests of the gods and mortals. Can you say the same about yourself?"

"Of course I can," said Tamra, putting a hand on her chest. "As a Princess, I've had to learn how to rule over others. I know what's good for others even when they don't know what's good for themselves. I am the perfect candidate for the position of Goddess of Martir, so why should I have to compete with the likes you and your ilk for it?"

"If you think you're so great, then why do you want me to rule alongside you?" said Braim. The feeling in his legs was starting to return, but he didn't try to run just yet. "Why not just kill me like how you plan to kill the rest of them?"

"Because I'm ... fascinated by you, to put it lightly," said Tamra. "The only man in the world to come back to life would make the perfect companion for the new Goddess of Martir, wouldn't you say?"

"No, I wouldn't say that, mostly because I want nothing to do with you," said Braim. "But tell me, what will happen if I refuse to be your 'companion,' as you put it?"

Tamra played with the Soul Collector between her fingers. "Oh, nothing too horrible, I can assure you. If you won't be my companion, then I'll just have to put you in a cage somewhere and take care of you like a beloved pet. I'd rather not kill you, since you're so unique, but if you won't be my companion, then I won't let you be with anyone else."

"You're really good at wooing guys, you know that?" said Braim, his voice dripping with sarcasm. "You almost seduced me there with your 'like a beloved pet' talk. Real smooth."

"If I become the Goddess of Martir, then I'll have all the time in the world to seduce you," said Tamra. "And, eventually, I will, because no one can withstand the advances of the Goddess of Martir for long. Not even you."

"We'll see about that," said Braim. He could now move his legs again, but he stayed where he was because he didn't have anywhere to run to. The door was still frozen shut and there was no other exit. He considered possibly running into the room where Tamra had been, but that was assuming he could make it past her.

Tamra raised an eyebrow. "Is that an admission of defeat, then?"

"No," said Braim, shaking his head. "I just didn't want to hurt your feelings by shooting down your ridiculous idea, because I'm nice like that."

Anger flashed across Tamra's features, but then she simply smiled and shook her head. "Funny. I knew there was something I liked about you, aside from your … uniqueness, which I suppose is how I'd describe you. After all, there aren't too many men who can say they were dead and then they came back to life."

"Not too many at all," Braim said. He stepped back, even though he had no idea where he could or should go. "Now that we agree on something, what say you about having a reasonable discussion about your life choices? Like, maybe, just maybe, we can discuss how stealing the souls of the gods isn't the best life choice you could make."

"I know what you're trying to do," said Tamra. "And the answer is no. Discussions can't work if we aren't equal, anyway. I hold the power. You don't even have your magical powers anymore, much less the divine energy necessary to become my equal."

"Got me there," said Braim. He shivered in the cold air left over from Xocion's presence. "So I'd say we're at an impasse."

"Impasse?" said Tamra. She chuckled. "That would be true if —and only if—you and I could be thought of as equals. The fact is, while I may not be able to win you over right away, I can at least keep you where I want until I am able to make you see my way."

Braim shook his head. "Nah. I think I want to leave."

Braim darted off toward the other room, the one where Tamra had been earlier. He had no idea if Tamra had blocked off the door in there, but he thought it likely that maybe she hadn't. After all, there was no way she could have suspected that Braim would attempt to escape that way. If he was fast enough …

Tamra appeared in front of him. Braim skid to a stop, but before he could change course, she waved a hand in his direction. Immediately, a thick block of ice appeared around his legs, making him swing his arms to maintain his balance. The sheer cold of the ice block made him yelp in pain, but he couldn't get rid of it even when he slammed his fists against its surface.

Then Tamra walked up to him, still smiling, though it was an amused smile, like she wanted to see what other futile things Braim was going to try next. "Oh, Braim, you seem to think that you are so much smarter than me. Too bad you don't realize just how outsmarted and out-muscled you are."

Tamra stopped in front of Braim and then put one hand under his chin, forcing him to look at her. Despite having a thinner and smaller body than Braim, Tamra's grip was strong and Braim could not break it. He stared into her eyes, even though he didn't want to, and he saw a haughty look that was more befitting of a goddess than a mortal. He saw flashes of white and brown in her eyes, perhaps the spirits of Xocion and Mica, though he couldn't be sure about that.

"Now, Braim," said Tamra, her tone falsely sweet. "You can stay here, like a good boy. I'm going to steal the souls of as many gods as I can, probably starting with Grinf, who happens to be the god closest to me at the moment. I will be back, don't worry, although I can't say whether or not you'll still have the ability to walk by the time I return."

"Maybe I won't, but I'm not going to let you leave," said Braim. He stared her straight in the eyes, doing his best to keep her attention focused exclusively on him. "I'm going to stop you here and now."

Tamra smiled, though it was a slightly confused smile. "How do you intend to do that? Have you already forgotten about the vast power difference that separates you from me?"

"Nah," said Braim. "But you seem to have forgotten what happens when you try to steal the soul of a dead man walking."

With that, Braim grabbed Tamra's hand, the one holding the Soul Collector, and jammed the Soul Collector into his chest with Tamra still holding it. Tamra shouted in surprise, but that was all Braim heard before the pain in his body exploded as the Soul Collector attempted to take his spirit.

Now Braim had been expecting to feel this pain, because he

292

had already dealt with it before when the Ghostly God tried to steal his soul. Nonetheless, that did not make the pain hurt any easier to tolerate than normal. His entire body felt like it was being ripped apart from within, white hot flames devouring every inch of his soul. Breathing became impossible, rational thought was drowned in the insanity brought on by the sheer pain, and soon he knew nothing, nothing at all but the most awful pain imaginable.

And then, just like that, it was over. Braim's vision and rational thought returned to him and he realized that he wasn't holding Tamra's arm anymore. In fact, Tamra wasn't even standing in front of him. She was lying on the floor, screaming and grabbing her arm. It took Braim a moment to see it, but when he did, he wished he hadn't.

Tamra was missing her lower arm, which was now a bloody stump, revealing bone and tendon. The blood had splattered all over her clothes and even onto her face. If she hadn't been rolling all over the floor screaming in sheer and utter pain, then Braim might have assumed that she was dead.

Guess having the souls of four gods in her body doesn't change the fact that having your arm blown up really hurts, Braim thought, smiling despite the horrible event playing out before his eyes.

Much to his surprise, however, Tamra eventually stopped rolling around in pain and screaming. Biting her lip, she grabbed her bleeding arm and glared up at Braim. There was no more amusement in her eyes anymore, nothing but pure hatred and anger at him.

"This ... isn't ... over," Tamra said. Braim was surprised she could even say that much. "I'll … kill … you … later …"

With that, Tamra vanished, leaving only a puddle of fresh blood where she had been sitting mere moments before. The Soul Collector also lay a few feet away, perhaps sent flying by the explosion of her arm.

In any case, Braim didn't let his guard down. He looked around, expecting Tamra to show up again and finish him off anyway, but as the seconds ticked by and Tamra was still nowhere to be seen, Braim sighed and relaxed a little.

Damn, Braim thought. *How in the world did I survive* that*?*

At that moment, a pillar of fire rose from the ground several feet away and Grinf stepped out of it. He looked worried but pleased, as if happy that he had finally succeeded in getting here. He looked around the room for a moment before spotting Braim. His eyes also darted to the puddle of Tamra's blood and the Soul Collector, but he walked over to Braim first, his gavel at his side.

"Braim Kotogs?" said Grinf. "Are you hurt?"

Braim shook his head. He gestured at his frozen legs. "Thankfully, no. But maybe you could—"

Grinf didn't even let him finish. He snapped his fingers at the ice block and it immediately melted, though it resulted in Braim's pants and boots getting soaking wet. Still, Braim could tolerate it, if only because the alternative of losing the feeling in his legs was so much worse.

"What happened to my siblings?" said Grinf. "And where is Tamra?"

"Tamra stole their souls," said Braim. He pointed at the Soul Collector. "She used that. I managed to stop and wound her, but she got away. I don't know where she is now."

Grinf looked down at the Soul Collector. Then he looked over at Xocion and Mica's soul-less bodies. He looked shocked for a moment, but then he became angrier than Braim had ever seen Grinf or any other god become before.

With a loud roar, Grinf slammed his gavel onto the Soul Collector. As soon as he did, the entire floor shook, causing Braim to lose his balance and fall over. Grinf then raised his gavel off of the Soul Collector, allowing Braim to see that the Soul Collector had been broken into pieces, pieces that were as black as trees after a forest fire.

"How dare she," said Grinf. His hands shook. "That woman … I will kill her myself for daring to steal the souls of my siblings. It is unheard of. It is unjust."

Braim gulped. Grinf looked angry enough to do something very stupid, so Braim got back to his feet and said, "Hey, Grinf, I know you're angry and all, but maybe you should take a moment and think. We need to check on the rest of the godlings and their gods, just to make sure that Tamra hasn't gone after them, too. Not that I think she has, without the Soul Collector, but—"

Grinf looked at Braim. Just the god's stare was enough to make Braim's knees shake, but Braim didn't back down. He still saw absolute anger and madness in Grinf's burning eyes, the kind of anger that never led anywhere good.

But then Grinf shook his head. "I have already evacuated all of the godlings and my fellow gods from the Stadium. But I will still need to tell them what I have learned. And you will need to help, as you know more about Tamra and what she did than I do."

"Sure, sure," said Braim, nodding and feeling relieved that Grinf was now behaving in a rational manner. "I'll do whatever I

295

can to help."

"Good," said Grinf. "Without the Soul Collector, she is less of a threat than she could be, but that doesn't mean she is not still a threat. I will also have to speak with the Ghostly God about this, as he is the creator of the Soul Collector, is he not?"

Braim nodded. "Yeah. I got it from him originally."

"I suspected as much," said Grinf. "My brother has always had a fondness for dangerous, unpredictable inventions like this, but he has never made anything quite as dangerous as that. I believe it is long past time that my siblings and I confront him about this."

That sounded like a threat to Braim, a threat he wasn't sure that Grinf could back up, considering how he had no real authority over the Ghostly God. Nonetheless, Braim kept that thought to himself, mostly because he was afraid that Grinf was so angry that he might not think twice about 'punishing' Braim for any doubt he might express regarding the god's ability to carry out a threat.

So Braim simply nodded and said, "Sounds good. But what about the Tournament? About this sub-bracket challenge? Who won and who lost?"

Grinf humphed. "I will think about that later. For now, I am going to get you out of here and then going to make sure that the godlings are safe and that every god in Martir knows about Tamra. I can assure that there is not a single god—northern or southern—who will tolerate this sort of behavior from a mortal woman like her. I doubt she will live long enough to regret bringing down the collective wrath of the gods of Martir upon herself."

"If you can find her, anyway," said Braim. "She was badly wounded when she left, so she'll probably stay beneath the surface for a while."

"Oh, I will," said Grinf. "And if I won't, then my siblings will. The katabans will be recruited to find her as well. Maybe we will get some of our mortal servants to search for her, too."

Then Grinf grabbed Braim's arm and said, "Now, let us go. I want you to tell me and the rest of the gods every last thing you learned from Tamra, no matter how small or insignificant it may seem to you. Understood?"

The god's grip on his arm was so tight that Braim couldn't even move it. Nonetheless, he nodded and said, "Sure. I'll do whatever I can to help."

"All right," said Grinf. "Hold on, because my teleportation method is a bit different from what you're used to, so you may experience some nausea when we teleport to where we need to go."

Chapter Twenty

THE VOID?" SAID Raya in shock. She stepped closer to Keeper, even though she wasn't much safer with him than away from him. "I thought I had destroyed you when I banished you to the ethereal, when I cut you off from the rest of yourself."

Saia or the Void (Raya decided to think of her as Void Saia for simplicity's sake) shook her head. "I was merely weakened. Being cut off from the rest of my body traumatized me, turning me into a mere wisp of my original self. Nonetheless, I took the opportunity to keep low and recover."

Void Saia gestured at the tendrils surrounding them on all sides. "And as you can clearly see, I recovered well enough that I can put an end to you fools if I so wish."

"Then why haven't you?" asked Alira. She sat up in Keeper's arm, looking down on Void Saia with anger. "Why didn't you just kill us outright, instead of standing around talking?"

"A good question, Judge," said Void Saia. She smiled. "I prefer to destroy and devour, but I also like to destroy all hope in my enemies and make them despair first. What better way to instill such despair than to tell you just how your efforts to destroy me failed?"

"Well, it ... didn't work on ... me," said the Ghostly God,

298

who was straining against the tendrils grasping his arms. "I feel no despair. More like anger at you for attacking me."

Void Saia looked up at the Ghostly God with an unimpressed expression. "Oh? Maybe this will make you feel despair."

Void Saia gestured at the Ghostly God and one of the tendrils impaled the god through his chest. The Ghostly God let loose a roar of pain and gold blood leaked out from the wound. He fell down onto the ethereal with a crash and in a second he was covered by more of Void Saia's tendrils like a black blanket. He didn't even move. The Ghostly God just lay there like he was dead, although Raya thought that he was probably still alive.

"Of course, even that might not instill the despair within you that I want," said Void Saia. "But it's fine. If I had to choose between creating despair in my victims or killing them, I'd kill them every time."

Raya clung to Keeper's leg. Keeper aimed his finger guns at Void Saia, but Void Saia hardly seemed scared by them. She just looked up at the large automaton like he was nothing.

"Are you threatening me with simple bullets?" said Void Saia. "You do realize that those don't work on me, right?"

"I will protect Princess Raya and Judge Alira from you," said Keeper, his voice as fearless as always. "It is my duty as the Princess's bodyguard to protect her no matter the cost."

"As if I care," said Void Saia, shaking her head. "Either way, you will die, and when you do, there will be no one to defend your precious princess from anyone."

Void Saia snapped her fingers. Four tendrils flew through the air toward Keeper. Keeper turned to shoot them, but the tendrils moved faster than he, cutting through his metallic skin instantly.

His arms fell off his body and his body fell off his legs, leaving Keeper entirely without limbs. Alira had fallen out of his arm, but managed to land on the ethereal without trouble. She drew closer to Raya, however, due to the tendrils coming closer and closer around them every minute.

"Keeper," Raya said in shock. She took a step forward, but then another tendril impaled itself in Keeper's head and the lights in Keeper's eyes went out. "Keeper!"

"He's no longer with us," said Void Saia. "It's just you two and me now."

Raya turned to face Void Saia again. The entity looked quite content with the way things were turning out. Raya could sense Void Saia's power, but that didn't make Raya back down. She stepped forward, her hands balling into fists.

"You monster," said Raya. "You killed Keeper. How dare you."

"You think I care?" said Void Saia. She laughed. "What are you going to do? Yell at me? You cannot defeat the Void, for I am unstoppable."

Alira stepped up next to Raya. Even though she had less magical power than Raya at the moment, she looked even less frightened in the face of Void Saia. She adjusted her glasses and looked at Void Saia with the same stern look that she had once looked at Raya with when Raya had complained to her about the bracket she had been assigned to what seemed like ages ago now.

"Oh, you look so tough," said Void Saia. "What, did I break rule or something? Are you going to punish me for it?"

"No," said Alira, shaking her head. "There's not much I can do against you, frankly. But I'm not going to die cowering before you, either, or giving into despair. I know that that is exactly what you want and I will not give it to you."

"You mean you aren't going to try to survive?" said Void Saia. She sounded genuinely puzzled by that. "How odd. I thought all living beings held their own survival above all else. Yet you will not run or beg."

"I won't do either because I know that neither will save me," said Alira. "Or Raya, for that matter, but I can't speak for her and what she will do."

"I-I'm not running, either," said Raya. "I'm going to fight however I can, even if I can't beat you."

"You sound so brave, the both of you," said Void Saia. "But I wonder just how much of that bravery is real and how much is just bravado meant to intimidate me. Not that it *will* intimidate me, mind you, but I think I know how to find out."

Several tendrils reached down and wrapped around Alira and Raya's bodies. The two let out yelps of surprise as the tendrils carried them into the air. Raya struggled against her tendril as hard as she could, but the tendril held her so tightly that she could barely breathe, much less escape. She looked at Alira, who was struggling against Void Saia's tendrils at least as much as her, if not more so.

Then Raya felt it. It was like tiny teeth biting at her skin and clothing. It was not exactly painful, but it made Raya want to scream anyway, because it felt like something was eating her bit by bit. Yet she couldn't scream, because it was like she had lost the ability to scream entirely.

Below, Void Saia was looking up at them with a satisfied smile on her dark features. "Struggle all you like, but it won't do you any good. My power dwarfs yours by several magnitudes. You and your struggles are barely worth my notice. The only reason I haven't killed you outright is because I want revenge on the only mortal who has ever actually harmed me. But maybe I will skip the revenge and simply annihilate you both, as you deserve."

Raya didn't respond due to the sheer pain she was in. A part of her wanted to give in to Void Saia's power and let the Void's darkness consume her. It certainly would be easier than fighting a hopeless fight, after all.

But then Raya heard Alira shout, "Raya, don't give up! We have to keep fighting. We can do this!"

Raya, snapped out of her daze, looked over at Alira. The Judge's skin looked a lot grayer now for some reason, probably because of the Void. Yet Alira's determined expression had not changed and she continued to fight against Void Saia's tendrils with as much ferocity as ever, even though she had to be suffering from the same biting pain as Raya.

If Alira is not giving up, then what right do I have to give up? Raya thought. *I need to come up with a way to escape.*

Of course, that was easier said than done. Void Saia's tendrils were stronger than anything Raya had ever felt before. Their grip on her body was getting tighter and tighter with every passing second and Raya even felt her own soul leaving her, or so it seemed. It was probably just Void Saia's shadows making her think things that weren't so, but the pain still made thinking hard, especially whenever she remembered how Void Saia had killed Keeper.

Then Raya looked down at her bluish-white hand. It was still visible in the shadows of Void Saia, but Raya at first wasn't sure what, if anything, it could do to help her. But she was desperate enough to try anything at this point, no matter how unlikely its chances of success were.

So Raya focused on her artificial hand, trying to make it do something to help her. She still didn't quite know the full extent of its powers, but she figured that it had to have some sort of useful ability here.

Then the fingers of her artificial hand extended like knives. And they kept extending until they were as long as swords and then they cut through the base of the tendril holding Raya. The tendril immediately dissipated around Raya, causing her to fall to the ethereal, which she landed on rather ungracefully. It was not a very long fall, however, so Raya did not hurt herself and recovered quickly enough to get back to her feet and face Void Saia, who was staring at her in astonishment.

"How did you do that?" said Void Saia.

Raya didn't respond. She just slashed at Void Saia's chest with her long, sword-like fingers, slashing her chest. No blood or anything else came out, but the blow sent Void Saia staggering backwards, clutching the wound that Raya had made. The tendrils around them shuddered and became less solid, causing Alira to fall out of hers and land on the ethereal, though she also got to her feet and ran over to join Raya.

"Thanks for the save," said Alira. She was actually smiling at Raya, which Raya thought looked very strange on the normally stern face of the Judge. "I knew you could do it."

Raya nodded in response, but then looked back at Void Saia. Void Saia was standing on the edge of the ethereal now, grasping

303

her chest wound, which was hissing for some reason, even though Raya's long artificial fingers hadn't been on fire or even very hot when she attacked the Void with them.

"You managed to hurt me," said Void Saia through clenched teeth. "I see that this body of mine has a few kinks to work out."

Raya pointed the long blade-like fingers of her artificial hand at Void Saia. "Is that an admission of defeat? If so, then I accept."

"Admission of defeat?" Void Saia said. She chuckled, which was an awful sound. "You only scratched me. I would not be the Void if I was defeated so easily."

Void Saia waved her hand over her chest and the wound closed up. She then stood up straight, looking like she had not been attacked at all. "Neat trick on your part, but unfortunately for you, it will take more than neat tricks to get rid of me."

Void Saia raised her hands. The tendrils rose around them, becoming sharper and thicker in appearance than before. They blocked out the stars in the sky above, leaving absolutely no way for Raya or Alira to escape at all.

"Let us end this," said Void Saia, "end this the way I should have ended this much earlier, with your bodies devoured by my shado—"

An ethereal portal exploded open behind Void Saia, causing her to look over her shoulder in surprise. Then a massive flame shot out of the portal and struck Void Saia in the face.

Void Saia let out a roar of pain, but before she could do much else, someone jumped through the portal and smacked her in the face with a weapon. Void Saia staggered backwards, but the newcomer kept attacking her again and again, flames following every swing of his weapon.

304

That was when Raya recognized the being as Grinf. Even so, she was too shocked to do or say anything except watch Grinf as he beat on Void Saia mercilessly, not giving her even one chance to react to his relentless assault. Every blow of his gavel sent shadows flying everywhere, which were quickly regenerated by Void Saia, only to be destroyed just as quickly as they regenerated. Raya had never seen Grinf this angry before, although that wasn't saying much, considering how she had not seen him in person very often prior to this.

Then Grinf slammed his gavel into Void Saia's face so hard that she went flying. She crashed on the ethereal hard and lay there looking stunned from the attack. She tried to sit up, but Grinf unleashed a burst of flame onto Void Saia that completely consumed her form, causing her to shriek in sheer agony.

Along with her shriek, the tendrils and shadows around them started to retreat. The Ghostly God's form soon reemerged from the tendrils, and as soon as they were gone, he groaned in pain and pushed himself up with both hands. He shook his head and looked up, a confused expression on his face until he spotted Grinf continuing to bathe Void Saia in fire.

"Oh," said the Ghostly God. "Looks like my older brother decided to play the hero. He's good at that."

"We should leave now," said Alira. She grabbed Raya's hand, snapping Raya out of her shock and making her look at her. Alira pointed at the ethereal portal. "We should go through the portal now, which probably leads to World's End, before the Void can recover and retaliate."

"Uh, sure," said Raya, nodding.

"Are you going to join us, Ghostly God?" said Alira, looking

305

at the Ghostly God.

The southern god shook his head. "I cannot return to World's End, remember? Besides, I want to help my brother, because I'm not the kind of deity to forgive attempted murder on myself."

"All right," said Alira. She nodded at Raya. "Let's go!"

She then dashed toward the portal, pulling Raya along behind her. Raya did her best to keep up, her eyes focused entirely on the portal and whatever lay on the other side. She did, however, glance over her shoulder at Keeper's destroyed body parts and made a quick note to retrieve them later on or ask a katabans to do it for her at some point.

And then she and Alira passed through the portal. The sudden change in lighting and texture made Raya's head hurt, but when her eyes adjusted and she saw that she and Alira had emerged onto the streets of World's End, which were empty at the moment, she let out a sigh of relief. She still rubbed her head, however, because the headache was almost too much, though it was infinitely better than being in the ethereal in the Void's grasp.

"We did it," Alira said. She sounded incredulous, but happy. She turned to look at Raya. "Raya, we—Watch out!"

Alira pushed Raya to the street. Raya fell on her side, scraping her hands against the street's surface. It took her almost completely by surprise, but it also angered her, causing her to look up at Alira and shout, "What the hell was that for? Why did you—"

A single dark tendril—perhaps the Void's last one—shot through the open portal and stabbed Alira directly in the chest. Alira let out a gasp of pain, but did nothing else. She seemed too stunned by the pain to react, causing Raya to slash the tendril with her extended artificial fingers.

Raya's fingers cut through the tendril as easily as water, causing it to dissipate instantly. The ethereal portal also closed, cutting off the sounds of Void Saia's screams and Grinf's burning flames, but Raya paid no attention to that, because Alira collapsed onto the street and stopped moving.

"Alira!" Raya shouted. She crawled over to the fallen Judge, but before she could reach Alira, she heard the sounds of clanking armor and looked up.

A dozen Soldiers of the Gods were approaching her and Alira. Raya had no idea where they came from, but she didn't care. She just watched as half of them gathered around Alira and lifted her up to take her to who-knows-where, while the other half gathered around Raya.

"Princess Raya," said Captain Garvan. He bent down before her, worry and relief on his face in equal measure. "You're still alive. And with Judge Alira as well."

"Yes, yes, I am fine," said Raya, waving off Garvan's concern. She looked at the Soldiers who were carrying Alira away. "You should worry about Alira, not me. She's the one who got stabbed in the heart."

"My men are taking her to the nearest healer even as we speak," Garvan said. "We need to get you looked at as well, just to make sure you're all right."

"But I don't *need* to be looked at," Raya protested. "I'm perfectly ... perfectly fine ..."

Exhaustion was taking over Raya again, even though she had just rested for several hours in Keeper's arms, most likely because she hadn't had anything to eat and drink since breakfast. She immediately stopped protesting and simply sighed tiredly.

"See? You need help, whether you think you do or not," said Garvan. He stood up and gestured at his fellow Soldiers. "Men, take the godling to the nearest healer. Make sure she gets plenty of food and water as well, because she looks hungry and thirsty."

A chorus of "Yes sir!" followed and soon five pairs of hands grabbed Raya and lifted her up rather gently. Raya allowed them to do so, as she was in no mood to fight back. Still, as the Soldiers raised her, she looked in the direction that the other Soldiers had taken Alira, but she did not see either Alira or the Soldiers who had taken her anymore. She just hoped that Alira lived, because she was not sure what she would do if she did not.

Chapter Twenty-One

LADY DIA SWUNG her fists at Carmaz, forcing him to jump backwards to avoid getting hit. Her punches left her side wide open, so Carmaz kicked her, but his blow didn't even slow her down. She didn't even seem to feel it, because she just sent another fist flying toward his head, making Carmaz jump backwards again outside of her reach.

When Carmaz landed, he looked over his shoulder at the three golems still making their way back up the bridge toward him and Lady Dia. As usual, they did not move very fast or quick, but it would not be long before they arrived to protect their Lady. At which point, Carmaz knew he would die.

But Carmaz couldn't afford to worry about that at the moment. Lady Dia was advancing on him, slamming her stone fists together menacingly, forcing Carmaz to back up. The Hermit was still out cold and Herune was nowhere to be seen, but if Lady Dia was as magic-resistant as she made herself seem, then it didn't really matter whether they were helping him or not. Carmaz was on his own and therefore needed to come up with a plan on his own.

Of course, that was easier said than done. Carmaz had no weapons, nor did he have any magical powers he could use to defend himself. And with Lady Dia in front and the golems in the back, Carmaz had precious little time to figure out how to beat them both. The humidity and stickiness of the Swamp air also made it harder to think, but he had lived on Ruwa long enough to ignore that stuff when he needed to.

Carmaz looked around at his surroundings. He saw nothing he could use to get out of this situation alive. He looked at Lady Dia. She was the most pressing issue to deal with at the moment, so Carmaz put aside his other concerns to focus on her.

Lady Dia was certainly not in the mood to talk. She advanced on him silently, but she didn't need to say a word to look intimidating. Her strength was enough to intimidate him, but Carmaz ignored his fear. He dashed at her, making it look like he was going to attack her.

Lady Dia briefly looked surprised at his actions, but she didn't stay surprised long. She once again tried to punch him, but Carmaz saw that coming a mile away. He ducked and slammed into her as hard as he could. He actually succeeded in knocking her back a few feet, but he pushed himself away from her as she brought her fists down. Her fists smashed into the bridge, cracking its surface, as Carmaz stepped away from her as quickly as he could.

Then Lady Dia lifted her fists off the bridge. She looked at Carmaz in annoyance.

"You know you won't be able to keep this up forever," said Lady Dia. She gestured behind him, likely at the incoming golems, whose heavy footsteps Carmaz heard drawing closer and closer every second. "Sooner or later, you'll be crushed between us. Give up. The golems will conquer Martir. You are nothing more than a tiny bump on our road to conquest."

Carmaz shook his head, but didn't respond. He did, however, look over his shoulder and saw that the golems were nearly upon him now. He looked over Lady Dia's shoulder and saw the other golems still marching out of the spire and those that had been pulled into the swamp by the mud giants were crawling out to rejoin their brothers. Even Stalac was starting to stir, sitting up and shaking his head and looking around at the pile of mud he sat in like he wasn't sure what was going on. The Hermit still lay unconscious on the bridge behind Lady Dia, while Herune had not emerged from the Swamp yet and it seemed unlikely that he ever would.

"Even you can see it," said Lady Dia. "This was a valiant effort on your part, human, but in the end, it doesn't matter. The entire world will fall to our might. You might as well give up."

Despair clung to Carmaz's heart. It wasn't just the hopelessness of the current situation that got to him. There was also the knowledge that he had failed Saia and Ruwa. He had thought he could redeem himself after failing the Tournament, hoped that stopping this invasion would be enough to restore his reputation and maybe even convince the inhabitants of Conewood to let him back in.

But now ... now, even that was a farce. The golem army was moving unimpeded into the Swamp. There was still, perhaps, the possibility of Raya and Alira reaching World's End and telling the gods about what was happening, but there was still no sign of the gods anywhere. It was as if Carmaz was all on his own here.

Maybe it is pointless to keep fighting, Carmaz thought. His legs became weak as exhaustion started to take its toll. *Lady Dia is right. I can't beat her or her golems. I'm just a normal human being. I have no magical powers whatsoever.*

Dia must have sensed the despair in Carmaz's mind, because she smiled and said, "I take your silence as agreement. But I don't care if you agree with me or not. I will slay you here and now."

Dia was now right in front of Carmaz. She smelled of ancient dust and dirt. She raised her hands above her head, her fists thick enough to smash through his skull. Carmaz gulped, knowing that there was nothing he could do to stop her even if he wanted.

This is what I get for breaking the rules of the Tournament, for betraying Braim when I shouldn't have, Carmaz thought, looking up at Dia's fists, which shone in the light of the sun. *Death.*

Just as that thought crossed his mind, a loud roar ripped through the air. It was the loudest roar Carmaz had ever heard in his life. It was so loud that he had to cover his ears to protect them. It was so loud that even Dia froze. She was no longer looking at Carmaz. Instead, she was looking over his head, in the direction of the three golems, at something he couldn't see. Although it was risky, Carmaz looked over his shoulder once more to see whatever it was that Dia saw.

Through a gap in the three golems, Carmaz saw the trees of the Swamp being knocked down left and right. And then a massive humanoid figure burst through the trees, roaring loudly, carrying a fallen tree in both hands like a sword, and Carmaz realized that it was Zeeree.

The half-god looked the same as he had the last time Carmaz saw him, except with scars all across his chest, belly, and face, perhaps from his last fight with the golem. Uttering another ear-piercing roar, Zeeree dashed across the bridge, moving fast despite his injuries. The three golems turned to face him, but they were not fast enough to dodge or block Zeeree's tree, which knocked into all three of them and sent them falling into the mud on top of each other. One of the golems—the original one, the one that was already heavily damaged from its prior fight with Zeeree —struggled to get out of the mud, but a blow to the head from Zeeree's tree smashed its skull into pieces and it fell back on top of its brothers, although it was completely motionless now without its head.

Zeeree then jumped into the mud after the fallen golems and started whaling on them violently with his tree. Mud flew everywhere as Zeeree beat on the golems, each blow taking off huge chunks of each golem's skin. Between the mud, Zeeree's unrelenting beat down, and the corpse of their friend, the two remaining golems were completely unable to fight back.

"What?" said Lady Dia. "What is that thing and where did it come from?"

Carmaz whipped his head around to look at Dia again. She was staring at Zeeree's brutal attack on the golems. She seemed genuinely taken by surprise by Zeeree's attack and also seemed to have forgotten all about Carmaz.

So Carmaz, seeing an opportunity, wrapped his arms around Dia's body and shoved her hard to the left. Because Dia had not been expecting that, she was unable to dodge or resist his attack, and she went staggering over to the edge of the bridge. She swung her arms to regain her balance, but then Carmaz kicked her in the stomach, which sent her falling off the edge of the stone bridge into the mud with a shriek.

Without looking to make sure that she wasn't getting out

anytime soon, Carmaz dashed over to the Hermit. He bent over the elderly man and took a good look at his wounds. They were bloody and raw, but the Hermit *was* breathing, which meant he was still alive. Carmaz let out a sigh of relief, but then he heard footsteps down the bridge and looked up to see Stalac walking toward him.

The golem general looked beyond angry now. He walked with something of a limp and his head was cracked from where the mud giant's fist had come down, but that didn't change the fact that his tail appeared to be in working condition and he was easily ten times stronger than Carmaz.

"Foolish … mortal …" said Stalac, though it was more of a growl than a sentence. "How dare you assault my lady. For that, I —"

Stalac was interrupted by Herune bursting out of the mud. He landed on the bridge next to Stalac. The golem general turned to look at Herune, but before he could do anything, Herune jabbed his wand in Stalac's chest.

A burst of light followed from that and Stalac went flying and screaming. He flew too fast for Carmaz to follow, but Carmaz thought he caught a glimpse of a hole in Stalac's chest. Only for a moment, however, because Stalac crashed into the mud and sank rapidly out of sight.

Herune ran over to Carmaz. The mage was covered head to foot in mud, but otherwise looked unharmed and in good condition. He bent over his father with Carmaz, a look of genuine concern visible through his muddy face and beard.

"Herune?" said Carmaz in shock. "How did you—"

"Almost didn't," said Herune. He spat out some mud to the

side. "Fell unconscious, but woke up quickly enough. Used my magic to push me out of the mud. Looks like I was just in the nick of time. How's my father?"

"Injured and unconscious, but alive," said Carmaz. "I think we should get out of here while we can. Zeeree opened an escape route for us and both Dia and Stalac are out of commission for now."

"Sounds like a good idea," said Herune. "We should return to the sanctuary. We can heal my father there. We've done all we can to stop the golems. I hate to say it, but it's up to the gods now."

Carmaz nodded. "Let's carry your father between us, then."

Herune held up a hand in warning. "No. I'll carry him myself. You can lead the way."

"All right," said Carmaz. "But be quick, because I'm not sure how much time we have."

Herune didn't even nod. He just jammed his wand into his pocket and picked up his father, carrying the unconscious Hermit on his back. Even though Herune must have been in pretty bad shape himself, he nonetheless managed to stand without any difficulty and nodded at Carmaz to go.

Carmaz then turned and ran down the bridge back to the Swamp, with Herune following close behind. They didn't get far, however, before a familiar figure materialized on the bridge in front of them, an enraged scowl on her features. It was Aorja, who aimed her wand at them and forced them to stop before they got too close.

"Surprised to see me?" said Aorja. There was no humor in her voice at all, just anger. "You shouldn't be. Zeeree is over there beating on those weird golem things because that's what he does best. You should have known I would come after you again, especially after our last confrontation."

"Aorja, we have no time to play with you," said Carmaz. He gestured at Herune and the Hermit behind him. "We have an injured old man who—"

"Spare me the sob story," Aorja interrupted him. "I'm here to kill all three of you bastards regardless of who else has been beating on you recently."

"What?" said Carmaz. "Don't you realize that the golems are a far worse enemy than us?"

"Who cares about a bunch of dumb rock creatures?" said Aorja. "That's Zeeree's job to worry about, not mine. My job is to kill you idiots."

Aorja's wand glowed brilliantly, but then Herune drew his wand out of his pockets and pointed it at her. A large, thick chunk of mud flew out of the Swamp water on either side and struck Aorja directly in the chest. The blow sent her flying into the Swamp water, which she sank into without another word.

Panting, Carmaz didn't even wait to start running again. Herune followed as usual and soon the trio reached the end of bridge. They tore through the thick Swamp undergrowth as fast as they could, ignoring the sounds of Zeeree's roars and the golems vainly attempting to fight back. Carmaz had no idea if Zeeree would stop the invasion all by himself or not, but it didn't matter to him. What mattered was getting to a safe place where he, Herune, and the Hermit could rest and hide. That was all they could do for now.

Chapter Twenty-Two

BRAIM STOOD IN the Temple of the Gods, in the center of the Throne Room. He looked up at the hundreds of empty thrones all around him, including the massive gold and white one in which Skimif had sat before his death. None of the other gods had yet arrived to this meeting, even though Grinf had said he was going to call them all so they could hear Braim's story.

Braim had been under the impression that Grinf was going to gather the rest of the gods right away, yet he had been standing here for at least five minutes by himself and there was still no sign of the gods anywhere. Grinf had said that he was going to check on the ethereal first, after Braim explained that Tamra had closed it off, but Braim didn't know how long that would take or what the current status of Grinf's progress in that area was. He supposed that Grinf had probably figured out how to open it, though how, he didn't know.

Braim had been under the impression that Grinf was going to gather the rest of the gods right away, yet he had been standing here for at least five minutes by himself and there was still no sign of the gods anywhere. Grinf had said that he was going to check on the ethereal first, after Braim explained that Tamra had closed it off, but Braim didn't know how long that would take or

317

what the current status of Grinf's progress in that area was. He supposed that Grinf had probably figured out how to open it, though how, he didn't know.

So Braim decided that he could best take advantage of this brief period of stillness and silence to lie down in the sand and rest. He reasoned that none of the gods were here to see and judge him, so he wouldn't end up offending anyone or anything. Besides, he was tired after such a long and hard day that he felt he earned the right to a nap.

Just then, however, a surge of power flowed through the Temple. After that. the gods started to appear in their thrones dozens at a time. Braim looked up at all of the gods as they appeared from thin air, many of them talking among each other immediately. Most of them, however, looked down at Braim, who wasn't sure what to do or if he should start talking, though with more and more gods appearing, he decided to keep his mouth shut until all of the gods had gathered and were ready to listen.

That did not take too long, because in another couple of minutes, all of the thrones were full. Well, there were a handful that were not, such as the thrones that belonged to the gods that Uron had killed and the thrones belonging to the gods whose souls had been stolen by Tamra. And of course, the main throne where the God of Martir was supposed to sit was bare and not a single one of the gods looked like they were going to even try to sit there.

But even with all of the gods here, Braim wasn't sure how or where to begin addressing them. Then an ethereal portal opened up a few feet away and Grinf stepped out of it, followed— surprisingly enough—by the Ghostly God. The Ghostly God waved at Braim when he saw him, but Braim just stared at him in surprise and anger.

"The Ghostly God?" said Braim. He looked at Grinf in shock. "I thought he was banished from World's End. Why is he here?"

"Because we will need the aid of every god on Martir if we are going to survive what is to come," said Grinf. His skin was covered in cuts and he almost seemed to be limping, which made Braim wonder what he had been doing. "The banishment of another god from World's End can be temporarily lifted by any other god. I have decided to lift it long enough for the Ghostly God to join us here, as he is one of us."

"Don't worry, Braim, I won't try to steal you again," the Ghostly God said. Like Grinf, he, too, was covered in injuries, the most noticeable being the healed hole in his chest where he had apparently been stabbed. "While I still want to know how you came back to life, even I recognize that there are far more urgent issues to deal with at the moment."

Then the Ghostly God vanished. He reappeared on his throne among the other gods, but when he did, his nearest siblings leaned away from him in disgust. The only other god who didn't move was Diog, the God of the Grave, who Braim hadn't even noticed until now. The deity who resembled an animated corpse was glaring at Braim with such intense hatred that Braim was surprised Diog hadn't jumped off his own throne to come down and kill Braim already.

Maybe he thinks that there are more important things to worry about at the moment than killing me, Braim thought. *Sort of like the Ghostly God, except the Ghostly God at least tried to keep me alive.*

Grinf didn't seem to notice Braim's discomfort. He looked up at all of his fellow gods, who had gone silent now and watched him intently. Braim was glad that the gods' attention had diverted to Grinf, mostly because he felt nervous with the gaze of so many powerful beings upon him, especially knowing that a few of them didn't have his best interests at heart.

"My fellow gods," said Grinf. His voice was loud, likely enhanced by magic even though he was not the God of Sound. "I am pleased to see you have all answered my summons to discuss an urgent situation that has just come up."

"Where are Mica, Kos, Xocion, and Henim?" asked Tinkar. He was looking around the Throne Room as he said that. "We have heard rumors that they are dead, but none of us are sure."

"Not dead," said Braim. He didn't want to speak up, but he wanted to make sure that the gods did not misunderstand what happened to their siblings. "Tamra stole their souls. Their bodies still live, but they can't move on their own and have no power."

An uproar rose among the gods, but then Grinf raised his gavel above his head and unleashed a powerful blast of fire that made Braim jump in surprise. The loud fire caused the other gods to quiet down immediately, but there was still a lot of confusion and worry on the faces of the assembled deities.

"Tell us *exactly* what happened, Grinf," said Tinkar. He seemed to be the spokesman of the other gods, if the fact that none of them were speaking meant anything. "We have heard many rumors from the katabans and godlings already. Exactly what just happened in the Stadium?"

Grinf explained, with help from Braim, what happened. Actually, it was Braim who did most of the talking, because he had been there when Tamra had attacked and had listened to her every word. Braim was surprised at how much he recalled, but he supposed that the fact that it had happened so recently and had been so traumatic had burned the memories into his mind in a way that would make it impossible for him to forget them.

When he finished—which didn't take nearly as long as he thought it would—the gods looked among each other uneasily. Quite a few gods looked angry, but the general feeling among the gods, from what Braim could tell, was that they were having flashbacks to Uron, even though Tamra was nowhere near as powerful as Uron had been at his height.

"Does anyone know where Tamra is?" asked Tinkar. He looked around at the other gods as he spoke. "Anyone at all?"

None of the gods answered.

Grinf, however, said, "I believe she is cloaking her presence, likely with the power she attained by stealing the souls of our siblings. But that is why we must seek her out and destroy her before she can use her newly stolen power to harm us."

"Then what are we waiting for?" a short, green-skinned fat man who Braim recognized as the Loner God said. He was not kicking back, as he usually did when sitting in his throne, but was instead sitting upright and looking ready to go to war. "It's one thing for a mortal to mock us and refuse to worship us. It's another thing entirely for a mortal to strike against us so directly. I say we drop everything and make it our number one priority to utterly annihilate her before she can do anything else."

A lot of gods were nodding in agreement with the Loner God, but Grinf said, "Nay, my brother. I have learned a lot more besides Tamra's theft of the souls of our siblings."

321

"More?" said Tinkar. "Such as what?"

"Raya and Alira have returned to World's End," said Grinf. "They are both alive, though Alira was grievously injured upon her return and is currently being tended to by katabans healers."

"They are back?" said Tinkar. "When did they return? And where were they?"

"From what Princess Raya told me, their kidnappings brought them both to Ruwa, an obscure island in the Friana Archipelago," said Grinf. "Raya was kidnapped by Aorja Kitano, a Limitless mage, while Alira was kidnapped by an army of creatures calling themselves golems."

"Golems?" Tinkar repeated. "That sounds familiar. Where have I heard that term before?"

"The resting golems," Ranama, the God of Language, spoke up, causing the other gods to look at him. "Remember? We discovered them deep beneath Martir's surface some time ago. It sounds like these golems are the same as those."

"I agree, though I have not seen any of them myself," said Grinf. "Regardless, Raya and Alira returned via the ethereal. Raya told me that there is an army of those golems and that they are planning to invade Martir and destroy everything we know."

"Why do they want to destroy us?" asked Ranama. "What have we ever done to harm them? I don't think we have even touched them."

"Does it matter?" said the Loner God. He slammed his fists on the arms of his throne. "If these damn golems wants a war, war is what we'll give 'em. Where are they starting the invasion again?"

"Ruwa," said Grinf. "I have never visited the island myself, but I have heard of it. It is of little significance to the Northern

Isles, as I understand it, and its inhabitants are few and far between."

"There's your answer, then," said the Loner God. "I say we sink Ruwa into the sea. We've done that before, so why can't we do that again? If these golems are made of stone, then they'll sink to the bottom of the ocean like rocks."

"That seems hasty, brother," said Ranama. He adjusted his glasses and frowned. "If we are going to deal with the golems, I think we should do it without needlessly sacrificing an entire island of innocent human beings."

"We don't have time to fight off an invasion," the Loner God argued. He stood up on his throne, perhaps so the others could see him better. "Look at what we're dealing with. The Void is becoming stronger and stronger, a mortal woman has stolen the souls of four gods already, and we still don't have a new leader yet. Sacrificing a few human lives so we can focus on more *important* things seems like a reasonable sacrifice to me."

Braim didn't like the Loner God's idea at all. In fact, he was horrified by it. Ruwa may have been the home island of Carmaz, but despite his negative feelings toward the Ruwan, he agreed with Ranama that sinking the whole island just to end this invasion seemed like overkill.

Grinf obviously agreed, because he said, "I understand your point, brother, but I do not think we'd be well served by destroying that island just to deal with the golems. I think instead that we should send some of the gods to Ruwa to deal with the invasion there. From what Raya told me, it sounds like the invasion has yet to begin, so if we move fast, then we might be able to end it without needless bloodshed."

"Come on," said the Loner God. He looked around at the other gods. "Do any of you *really* believe that? Listen, I'm normally not one to care, but everything that's happened recently has put me on edge. I don't want to play games or anything. We should just get it done without any fuss."

"You'd have to convince the rest of us to agree with your plan," said Grinf. "And I, for one, know that most of us would never sink Ruwa for that reason. We should only do that if we have no other option before us."

The Loner God looked around at the other gods, but none of them, not even his fellow southern gods, seemed to want to come to his aid. Quite a few of the gods were avoiding his gaze entirely, as if they didn't want to anger him by showing their disagreement.

"So that's how it's going to be, then?" said the Loner God. He let out a bark-like laugh. "Fine, then. Waste time bickering and arguing about what to do. There's a reason my name translates to the *Loner* God in the human tongue. It is because I work on my own. So if you'll excuse me, I'm out of here to do what I actually need to do to save this world, whether you idiots agree or not."

With that, the Loner God vanished into thin air. The other gods exchanged surprised looks, like none of them had expected the Loner God to up and leave so abruptly like that. That was as ominous a sign to Braim as any about the current unity of the gods.

Grinf looked taken aback, but he then shook his head and said, "Let our brother do what he wants. He should have stayed long enough to listen to the other piece of news I have."

"And what, pray tell, would that be, brother?" said Tinkar. "Is it as bad as the other news you've shared so far?"

"Very," said Grinf. "The Void has invaded the ethereal. The Ghostly God and I fought and defeated her, but her essence is still there and growing."

Again, the gods exchanged worried looks with one another. That news also made Braim gulp, even though he never used the ethereal himself, though the news did explain why Grinf and the Ghostly God looked like they had been fighting in a war.

"If the Void is in the ethereal …" Ranama said.

"It is still possible to travel on it," Grinf said, though his expression and tone were as grim as ever. "But it is now very dangerous for anyone who isn't a god or goddess. I believe the Void has taken control of the ethereal in order to limit our movement and make it harder for us to fight against her."

"Then we won't use the ethereal," said Tinkar. "It is a simple solution, isn't it?"

"What about the katabans?" said Ranama. "They use the ethereal all the time to travel around Martir. Without it, most of them will be stuck here near the Void."

"Well, this just reconfirms how urgently we need to complete the Tournament, then," said Tinkar. He looked down at Grinf. "Brother, how is Alira doing? Is she doing well enough to preside over the Tournament again?"

"I cannot say," said Grinf. "Last I saw, she was in critical condition. She suffered a terrible chest wound from the Void, almost fatal. I am unsure whether or not our healers will be able to save her."

"Then send Atikos," said Tinkar. He looked around. "Where is she?"

"I'm here, brother," said a short, plump, and grandmotherly-

325

looking woman who Braim had not noticed before, but who he realized had to be Atikos, the Goddess of Healing and Steel. She had a steel chest plate. "Do I need to heal Alira?"

"Of course," said Tinkar. "Go and tend to her injuries. It may be impossible for mortal or katabans magic to heal her, but your divine magic might be just what she needs."

"Then I will do my best," said Atikos.

Like the Loner God before her, Atikos vanished into thin air, though with far less hostility than the Loner God had. While Braim did not think of Alira as a friend, he hoped that Atikos was successful in healing her anyway. Alira's death was the last thing they needed right now. In fact, Braim didn't even want to think about what would happen if Alira died. It might not be as bad as the death of a god, but if Alira died, it might mean that the Tournament would have to be canceled or at least heavily delayed.

"Let us pray to the Powers that Atikos succeeds in healing Alira," said Grinf. "For now, we must prepare a plan of attack against the golems, as well as decide who is going to track down Tamra."

"What about me?" asked Braim, pointing at himself. "How can I help?"

Grinf looked at Braim. "You don't need to help. You are not strong enough. Instead, I am going to send you back to your room at the inn."

"But—"

Grinf raised a hand, silencing Braim instantly. "Do not argue with me. There is nothing you can do against Tamra or the golems or the Void. As a participant in the Tournament, you may be destined to ascend to godhood, and thus we cannot risk your life needlessly by sending you after powerful beings who could kill you in an instant."

"We should speed up the Tournament's progress," said Tinkar, causing the other gods to look at him again. There was fear on his features. "We cannot go much longer with an incomplete pantheon, nor can Martir go for much longer without its god. As much as I hate to admit it, we need a leader if we are going to stop the Void and the other threats to Martir once and for all."

"I will speak with Alira about speeding up the progress of the Tournament," said Grinf, "after she has recovered, that is. But I agree, brother, that we must not put this off any longer. We no longer have the time or luxury to do that."

Grinf put a strong hand on Braim's shoulder. "Braim Kotogs, I suggest that you rest tonight. Tomorrow, we will have a better plan for dealing with these new threats to Martir. Until then, you and the rest of the godlings must focus on the Tournament and nothing else."

Braim wanted to argue against that, but he knew there was no way he could convince the gods to listen to him. He just nodded, albeit reluctantly, and said, "Well, if you can think of any way for me to help, I'll be happy to do it."

"Good," said Grinf.

With that, Braim found himself standing in his room at the inn with a single blink of his eyes. The shutters were closed and there was no sound from outside at all, like the streets were dead. The room was the same as it had been when Tamra had attempted to assassinate him, though now it felt like the city itself had changed, as if something truly vile had happened that had shaken

327

the city entirely.

Not if, Braim thought as he sat down on the bed, feeling exhausted. *Something truly vile did happen. And the future is looking even more uncertain than before.*

But such thoughts were too much for him right now. The exhaustion from earlier, which he had thought had left him, now returned in full force, prompting Braim to push those thoughts out of his mind, lie down on his bed, and go to sleep, though it was not an easy sleep, particularly with the darkness in the back of his head gnawing at him as it always did.

Concluded in:

Ascension of the Chosen

When an attempt to restore his magical powers goes wrong, Braim Kotogs must win the Tournament of the Gods in order to ascend to godhood and avoid certain death. But with time running out, and a sudden attack on the Tournament by an enemy that wishes to consume the whole world, Braim might not live long enough to win the Tournament.

Raya Mana also wishes to win the Tournament of the Gods, but to do so, she must not only complete the final challenge in her bracket, but also survive a sudden interruption in the Tournament from an enemy who desires to kill her. If she fails to win the final challenge in her bracket, then she will not only lose her one and only chance at godhood, but her own life as well.

With the golems rampaging across Ruwa, Carmaz Korva must work with a human-eating god to save his people and the world from the golems' invasion. But when it turns out that the golems have the support of an enemy even stronger than the gods, Carmaz and his divine ally must fight for their lives.

Now available wherever books are sold!

Glossary:

Aorja Kitano. A former student at North Academy who specialized in musical magic. Though she is good at pretending to be kind and intelligent, in truth she is insane and violent and is currently on the run from the authorities for her crimes against Martir. She has a 'pet' half-god called Zeeree who she managed to tame. She is also a mage known as a 'Limitless,' which means that she has access to unlimited magical energy (although that does not make her invincible).

Aquarians. A species of fish-like humanoids that live in the Undersea, which is the name for the part of Martir underneath the Crystal Sea. Like humans, aquarians worship the northern gods and can use magic, although they have different names for the gods and also do magic differently from their human counterparts. They have a variety of different appearances and races, much like humans, although their differences tend to be even more dramatic than the ones between humans.

Automatons. Mechanical beings created by the Mechanical Goddess to carry out her will, although the Carnagian Royal Family has been experimenting with making automatons of their own in recent years.

Darek Takren. The adopted son of Jenur Takren and a graduate of North Academy. He specializes in pagomancy, or ice magic, and is currently the leader of the Xocionian Monks. He was the protagonist in the Mages of Martir novels and is a good friend of Braim Kotogs.

Diog. The God of the Grave. Aquarian name: Hamafa.

Godling. Name for human beings who are destined to become gods.

Half-gods. The prototypes of the gods that the Powers abandoned in the Void after finishing Martir. Half-gods, while stronger than mortals, are not quite as strong as gods, although they can give the gods a good fight. They also tend to be more animalistic and lack some of the higher reasoning functions of the gods themselves due to their incompleteness, which makes it possible for beings who are weaker than them to control or manipulate them. The most well-known half-god is Zeeree, the Half-God of Poison, who serves Aorja Kitano.

Harnum. The world that existed before Martir. It was destroyed by Uron, one of its inhabitants, and everyone who lived there was killed off. The Powers arrived many years later and used Harnum's remains as the foundation for Martir, although some Harnumian buildings and objects can still be found deep beneath Martir's surface.

Jenur Takren. A native of Ruwa and current Magical Superior of North Academy and adoptive mother of Darek Takren. Like Malock, she was a major character in the Prince Malock World novels. In her youth, she was a member of the Dark Tigers Guild, an assassin's guild based in Ruwa, but eventually left it when she became disgusted with the Guild's mission. She adopted Darek Takren when he was only five years old after his birth mother was murdered by an enemy of hers.

Katabans. A species of intelligent beings who exist to serve the gods. 'Katabans' means 'minor spirit,' as katabans are spirits who often take on physical forms in order to follow the gods' commands. Their appearances range from human to beast, depending on their preferences, personality, and what they need to complete whatever mission given to them by the gods.

King Tojas Malock. The son of Queen Markinia and King Halock of Carnag. Current King of Carnag. He was the protagonist of the Prince Malock World novels and is married to Queen Hanarova. He is a fair and just ruler, although he spoils his daughter too much.

-Mancy. A suffix usually attached to Latin prefixes that denotes the name of a magical discipline. For example, hydromancy means 'water magic,' pyromancy means 'fire magic,' panamancy means 'healing magic,' and so on.

North Academy. The most prestigious and most difficult to get into magical school in the world. It is located in the northernmost reaches of the Great Berg and can only be reached with great difficulty. It is run by Jenur Takren, who is the current Magical Superior of the school.

Northern Isles. A region of the world located on the northern half of the Dividing Line that consists of thousands of island nations of various sizes. It is where almost all of Martir's human population is located, as well as many aquarians.

Northern Pantheon. The gods who rule the northern half of Martir. In contrast to their southern siblings, the northern gods are kinder and more respectful to mortals. They also tend to take mortal names (for example, Grinf), rather than titles translated from Godly Divina (for example, the Loner God).

Ooka. The God of Knives and Shadow. Aquarian name: Ooka.

Queen Hanarova. The katabans wife of King Malock and mother of Princess Raya Mana. Like Malock, she was a major character in the Prince Malock World novels. While not a bad person, she has a fierce rivalry with Jenur Takren that started in their youth and continues to this day.

Rock Isle. The most secure prison in the Northern Isles. Home to many of the most dangerous criminals in the Northern Isles.

Silver spoon. A slang term, common in the Northern Isles, usually applied to princesses, especially spoiled or bratty ones. The male equivalent is gold blood and the terms come from the folk song *Princess Silver Spoon and Prince Gold Blood.*

Skimif. The previous God of Martir. He was once an aquarian farmer who was chosen by the Powers to announce their return to Martir back in the Prince Malock World series. The Powers eventually made him into the God of Martir, but he was killed by Uron thirty years after his ascension.

Southern Pantheon. The gods who rule the southern half of Martir. In contrast to their northern siblings, they hate mortals and see them as no different than any other kind of animal. They tend to be more vicious and animalistic and don't understand humans as well as their northern siblings do.

The Almighty Ones. A group of four beings who live in the Spirit Lands and are responsible for judging and guiding the spirits of the dead. Originally consisted of the Dark Lady, the Arbiter, the Great Snake, and the Mysterious One before the Arbiter and the Great Snake were killed. They are far more powerful than the gods, but typically do not directly interfere with the physical realm, preferring to focus instead on the Spirit Lands where they rule.

The Dividing Line. The exact line that divides the northern and southern sides of Martir. This line can be crossed by any god or mortal, but if a southern god crosses it, then this god cannot kill any mortals on the northern side.

The gods of Martir. Super-powerful and immortal beings who each control a particular domain of Martir, such as the elements or even abstract concepts. The gods used to be one united force, but after the Godly War, they were separated into the Northern Pantheon and the Southern Pantheon and have remained that way ever since.

The Godly War. An ancient conflict that took place shortly after the creation of Martir eons ago. The War started over a disagreement between the gods over how to treat mortals. Half of them wished to use mortals for sport and food, while the other half wanted to have them as worshipers and followers. The two sides waged a war that killed many gods and countless mortals before the Powers stepped in, ended the conflict, and wrote up the Treaty to govern relations between the two sides.

The Ghostly God. The God of Ghosts and Mist. A southern god. Highly intelligent, but cruel and antisocial. Has an intense fascination with studying the dead and where ghosts go after their bodies die.

The Mechanical Goddess. The Goddess of Machines. A southern goddess. She is the creator of the automatons. Queen Hanarova served her in her youth.

The Mysterious One. One of the Almighty Ones. Originally pretended to be the mythical God of Mystery and Magic before revealing his true identity at the end of the Mages of Martir series. Strange and enigmatic, he nonetheless cares about Martir and does what he can to help protect it.

The Powers. A group of six powerful and ancient entities who created Martir, the gods, humanity, and everything else within Martir. Their exact nature is a mystery, but it is known that they are currently creating other worlds beyond the Void. They have only visited Martir once since creating the world but otherwise are not actively involved in the world's day-to-day functions, which are instead regulated by the gods themselves.

The Spirit Lands. A land where all spirits go when they die and where they are judged by the Mysterious One for their deeds in life. Those who are judged as righteous go beyond the Gates to rest eternally, while the ones judged wicked are banished to the Unknown to be tortured forever.

The Thief's Way. A magical discipline generally practiced by followers of the late Hollech, the former God of Deception, Thieves, and Horses. Practitioners of the Thief's Way can travel through shadow and also detach body parts and have them emerge from the shadows to attack someone or steal from them. Most practitioners of the Thief's Way are scorned by their fellow mages and generally treated as criminals even if they do not actually commit any crimes.

The Treaty. A document that governs relations between the Northern and Southern Pantheons, written by the Powers themselves.

The Void. A powerful and evil force that exists beyond the edge of Martir. Its sole purpose is to destroy and devour everything that exists. While the Void does not technically have a gender, it is usually referred to with female pronouns.

Tinkar. The God of Fate and Time. One of the oldest gods and a northern god. Aquarian name: Seyar.

Uron. A powerful being who existed in the world before Martir, where he was a bitter scientist who was hated by everyone. He allowed the Almighty One known as the Great Snake to possess him so he could get back at his people, but due to a series of unforeseen events, Uron and the Great Snake ended up banished to the physical realm without a body for centuries. After Uron got a body, he then attempted to destroy Martir, but was ultimately destroyed by Braim Kotogs and now no longer exists as a spiritual or physical being.

World's End. Also known as the Throne of the Gods. The final island in the southern seas and home to most of the katabans on Martir.

About the Author

Timothy L. Cerepaka writes fantasy as an indie author. He is the author of the Prince Malock World fantasy novels, the Mages of Martir fantasy novels, and the Two Worlds science-fantasy series. He lives in Texas.

Find out more at his at www.timothylcerepaka.com.

Other books by Timothy L. Cerepaka

Prince Malock World:

The Mad Voyage of Prince Malock

The Return of Prince Malock

The New Era of Prince Malock

The Coronation of Prince Malock

Mages of Martir:

The Mage's Grave

The Mage's Limits

The Mage's Sea

The Mage's Ghost

Two Worlds:

Reunification

Alliance

Allegiance

Retaliation

Desinence

Tournament of the Gods:

Gathering of the Chosen

Betrayal of the Chosen

Invasion of the Chosen

Ascension of the Chosen

Standalones:

The Last Legend: Glitch Apocalypse

www.ingramcontent.com/pod-product-compliance
Lightning Source LLC
Chambersburg PA
CBHW050546260626
47157CB00002B/456